ISAAC ASIMOV
Presents

THE GREAT SCIENCE FICTION STORIES

Volume 3, 1941

Edited by
Isaac Asimov and
Martin H. Greenberg

DAW BOOKS, INC.
Donald A. Wollheim, Publisher

1633 Broadway
New York, N.Y.   10019

FIRST PRINTING, MARCH 1980

1 2 3 4 5 6 7 8 9

 DAW TRADEMARK REGISTERED
U.S. PAT. OFF. MARCA
REGISTRADA. HECHO EN U.S.A.

PRINTED IN U.S.A.

GOLDEN TREASURES

1941 may have been a difficult year for the world historically but in the science fiction world it was another of the truly great years of the Golden Age. As in the previous selections by Dr. Asimov, again you will find a treasure trove of the memorable stories which built the foundations of the future yet to come.

The best way to find out what a gem this anthology is would be to turn to the contents and see for yourself. You will find a veritable Who's Who in the cosmos of the imagination—**a universe of giants!**

Anthologies from DAW

THE 1975 ANNUAL WORLD'S BEST SF
THE 1976 ANNUAL WORLD'S BEST SF
THE 1977 ANNUAL WORLD'S BEST SF
THE 1978 ANNUAL WORLD'S BEST SF
THE 1979 ANNUAL WORLD'S BEST SF

WOLLHEIM'S WORLD'S BEST SF: Vol. 1
WOLLHEIM'S WORLD'S BEST SF: Vol. 2
WOLLHEIM'S WORLD'S BEST SF: Vol. 3

THE DAW SCIENCE FICTION READER

THE YEAR'S BEST HORROR STORIES: 1
THE YEAR'S BEST HORROR STORIES: II
THE YEAR'S BEST HORROR STORIES: III
THE YEAR'S BEST HORROR STORIES: IV
THE YEAR'S BEST HORROR STORIES: V
THE YEAR'S BEST HORROR STORIES: VI
THE YEAR'S BEST HORROR STORIES: VII

THE YEAR'S BEST FANTASY STORIES: 1
THE YEAR'S BEST FANTASY STORIES: 2
THE YEAR'S BEST FANTASY STORIES: 3
THE YEAR'S BEST FANTASY STORIES: 4
THE YEAR'S BEST FANTASY STORIES: 5

THE BEST FROM THE REST OF THE WORLD

AMAZONS!

HEROIC FANTASY

ASIMOV PRESENTS THE GREAT SF STORIES: 1
ASIMOV PRESENTS THE GREAT SF STORIES: 2

ACKNOWLEDGMENTS

LIAR!—Copyright © 1941 by Street & Smith Publications; copyright renewed 1968 by Isaac Asimov. Reprinted by permission of the author.

NIGHTFALL—© Copyright 1941 by Street & Smith Publications; copyright renewed 1968 by Isaac Asimov. Reprinted by permission of the author.

ADAM AND NO EVE—© Copyright 1941 by Street & Smith Publications. Reprinted by permission of the author.

A GNOME THERE WAS—© Copyright 1941 by Street & Smith Publications, and © Copyright 1968 by Henry Kuttner. Reprinted by permission of the Harold Matson Company, agents for the author's estate.

MECHANICAL MICE—© Copyright 1941 by Street & Smith Publications. Reprinted by permission of the agents for the author's estate, the Scott Meredith Literary Agency, Inc., 845 Third Avenue, New York, NY 10022.

SHOTTLE BOP—© Copyright 1941 by Street & Smith Publications; copyright renewed © 1968 by Theodore Sturgeon. Reprinted by permission of the author and his agents, Kirby McCauley Ltd.

MICROCOSMIC GOD—© Copyright 1941 by Street & Smith Publications; copyright renewed © 1968 by Theodore Sturgeon. Reprinted by permission of the author and his agents, Kirby McCauley Ltd.

HEREAFTER, INC.—Copyright © 1941 by Street & Smith Publications. Reprinted by permission of the author and his agents, The Scott Meredith Literary Agency, Inc., 845 Third Avenue, New York, NY 10022.

SNULBUG—Copyright © 1941 by Street & Smith Publications. Reprinted by permission of Curtis Brown, Ltd., agents for the author's estate.

Table of Contents

Introduction

In the world outside reality, it was yet another very bad year. On February 9 Field Marshal Rommel led his troops from Italy to Africa, where they soon began to blunt the British offensive designed to protect the Suez Canal. German U-boat attacks increased in intensity all through the year. On April 13 the U.S.S.R. signed an agreement with Japan promising neutrality and tacitly allowing Japanese expansionism to continue. The House of Commons was destroyed in a German air raid on May 10, the same day that Rudolf Hess flew on his mysterious "peace" mission to England. On May 24 the German pocket battleship *Bismarck* sank *H.M.S. Hood* and was itself sunk three days later by the Royal Navy.

Not unexpectedly, except by the Russians, Germany invaded the Soviet Union on June 22 in one of the most fateful moves of the war; by the end of the month they had control of a large portion of European Russia and the Ukraine. On August 11, Churchill and Roosevelt signed the "Atlantic Charter" on a ship in the ocean of the same name. On September 8, Leningrad was surrounded and a long siege had begun—German armies were sixty miles from Moscow by October 16. The Russian counteroffensive began on November 29.

On December 7, "a day that will live in infamy," Japanese carrier-based aircraft attacked Pearl Harbor and surrounding military installations. The United States declared war on Japan one day later and on Germany and Italy on the 11th, one day after *H.M.S. Prince of Wales* and *Repulse* were sunk in the Indian Ocean. Hong Kong surrendered to the Japanese on Christmas Day.

During 1941 Edmund Wilson published his major study of utopian and socialist thought, *To The Finland Station*. The "Manhattan Project" leading to the atomic bomb was initiated at the end of the year. Léger painted "Divers Against a Yellow Background." Bruce Smith of the University of Minnesota won the Heisman Trophy as college football's outstanding player. Benjamin Britten composed his "Violin Concerto." *The Fall of Paris* by Ilya Ehrenburg was published. Brecht's *Mother Courage and Her Children* was produced. Minnesota repeated as National College Football Champion. The year's outstanding films included *Citizen Kane, How Green Was My Valley, The Big Store* (the Marx Brothers' last film) and *The First of The Few,* one of the last films of Leslie Howard, who was to die over the English Channel.

The population of the United States was 131,000,000; China's was estimated at 450,000,000. The record for the mile run was *still* the 4:06:4 set in 1937 by Sydney Wooderson of Great Britain. Nathaniel Micklem published *The Theology of Politics.* William Walton's "Scapino Overture" was performed. Bobby Riggs won the United States Tennis Association Championship. F. Scott Fitzgerald published *The Last Tycoon.* Noel Coward's *Blithe Spirit* was a hit. Whirlaway, with Eddie Arcaro on board, won the Kentucky Derby, while Wisconsin had the top basketball team. There were 38,800,-000 private cars in the United States. The Yankees won the series from the Dodgers, Ted Williams led the majors with 37 home runs and an incredible .406 average, but Joe DiMaggio won the Most Valuable Player Award in the American League. Franz Werfel's *The Song of Bernadette* was published. Gary Cooper (for *Sergeant York*) and Joan Fontaine (for *Suspicion*) won Academy Awards. Joe Louis was still the heavyweight champion, but he almost lost the title to Billy Conn, saving his crown with a late-round knockout.

Death took Henri Bergson, James Joyce, Sherwood Anderson, Virginia Woolf, Kaiser Whilhelm II, and Ignaz Paderewski.

Mel Brooks was still Melvin Kaminsky.

But in the real world, it was a super year.

In the real world the third World Science Fiction Convention (the Denvention) was held in Denver, Colorado, continuing (you should excuse the expression) its trek westward. The first "Boskone" was held in Boston. In the real world "Methuselah's Children" by Robert A. Heinlein and the long awaited "Second Stage Lensman" by "Doc" Smith appeared in *Astounding.*

More wondrous and sad things occurred in the real world: *Stirring Science Stories* and *Cosmic Stories* began their too brief lives, but *Comet Stories* died. *Unknown* changed its name to *Unknown Worlds* without damage or effect.

But as compensation, many more wonderful people made their maiden flights into reality: in January—Fredric Brown with "Not Yet The End"; in February—Cleve Cartmill with "Oscar," William Morrison with "Bad Medicine," and Damon Knight with "Resilience"; in May—Wilson Tucker (aka Bob) with "Interstellar Way-Station"; and in November—Ray Bradbury with the co-authored "Pendulum."

On August 1, while riding the subway to visit John Campbell, Isaac Asimov first thought about the fall and rise of intergalactic empires (with a little help from Gibbons) and the first hint of the Foundation rose mistily in his mind.

And distant wings were beating as Gregory Benford and Jane Gaskell were born.

Let us travel back to that honored year of 1941 and enjoy the best stories that the real world bequeathed to us.

EDITORIAL NOTE

The reader should note that selections by Robert A. Heinlein are missing because arrangements for their use could not be made. We regret their absence and direct the reader to *The Past Through Tomorrow* (New York: Putnam, 1967, paperback edition by Berkley), which contains all the stories.

MECHANICAL MICE

Astounding Science Fiction
January

by Maurice A. Hugi
(Eric Frank Russell, 1905-1978)

The late Eric Frank Russell is the most underappreciated of the major science fiction writers of the "second generation" (his first story was published in 1937). His 1939 Unknown *novel* Sinister Barrier *thrust him into prominence for a time, and he did win the Hugo Award in 1955 for his story "Allamagoosa," but he has been badly neglected by the academic community.*

This clever story caused some confusion because Maurice G. Hugi was a real person, but the story was Russell's.

(I never could understand the trick of using pseudonyms. I know that there are reasons for it, like not wanting the neighbors to know you are disgracing yourself by displaying an imagination, or not wanting the Dean to know you are making money on the side—but, my goodness, you lose credit. For instance, I enormously enjoyed "The Mechanical Mice" when I first read it and I always thought of it as a beautifully crafted story and I never knew E. F. Russell had written it until quite recently. Terrible—I admit I wrote the Lucky Starr stories under a Paul French pseudonym, but I had over-riding reasons for that, and I put them under my own name as soon as I could. But then, I am so self-appreciative; I would never consent to give up an atom of credit.—I. A.)

It's asking for trouble to fool around with the unknown. Burman did it! Now there are quite a lot of people who hate like the very devil anything that clicks, ticks, emits whirring sounds, or generally behaves like an asthmatic alarm clock. They've got mechanophobia. Dan Burman gave it to them.

Who hasn't heard of the Burman Bullfrog Battery? The same chap! He puzzled it out from first to last and topped it with his now world-famous slogan: "Power in Your Pocket." It was no mean feat to concoct a thing the size of a cigarette packet that would pour out a hundred times as much energy as its most efficient competitor. Burman differed from everyone else in thinking it a mean feat.

Burman looked me over very carefully, then said, "When that technical journal sent you around to see me twelve years ago, you listened sympathetically. You didn't treat me as if I were an idle dreamer or a congenital idiot. You gave me a decent write-up and started all the publicity that eventually made me much money."

"Not because I loved you," I assured him, "but because I was honestly convinced that your battery was good."

"Maybe." He studied me in a way that conveyed he was anxious to get something off his chest. "We've been pretty pally since that time. We've filled in some idle hours together, and I feel that you're the one of my few friends to whom I can make a seemingly silly confession."

"Go ahead," I encouraged. We had been pretty pally, as he'd said. It was merely that we liked each other, found each other congenial. He was a clever chap, Burman, but there was nothing of the pedantic professor about him. Fortyish, normal, neat, he might have been a fashionable dentist to judge by appearances.

"Bill," he said, very seriously, "I didn't invent that damn battery."

"No?"

"No!" he confirmed. "I pinched the idea. What makes it madder is that I wasn't quite sure of what I was stealing and, crazier still, I don't know from whence I stole it."

"Which is as plain as a pikestaff," I commented.

"That's nothing. After twelve years of careful, exacting work I've built something else. It must be the most complicated thing in creation." He banged a fist on his knee, and his voice rose complainingly. "And now that I've done it, I don't know what I've done."

"Surely when an inventor experiments he knows what he's doing?"

"Not me!" Burman was amusingly lugubrious. "I've invented only one thing in my life, and that was more by accident than by good judgment." He perked up. "But that one thing was the key to a million notions. It gave me the battery. It has nearly given me things of greater importance. On several occasions it has nearly, but not quite, placed within my inadequate hands and half-understanding mind plans that would alter this world far beyond your conception." Leaning forward to lend emphasis to his speech, he said, "Now it has given me a mystery that has cost me twelve years of work, and a nice sum of money. I finished it last night. I don't know what the devil it is."

"Perhaps if I had a look at it—"

"Just what I'd like you to do." He switched rapidly to mounting enthusiasm. "It's a beautiful job of work, even though I say so myself. Bet you that you can't say what it is, or what it's supposed to do."

"Assuming it can do something," I put in.

"Yes," he agreed. "But I'm positive it has a function of some sort." Getting up, he opened a door. "Come along."

It was a stunner. The thing was a metal box with a glossy, rhodium-plated surface. In general size and shape it bore a faint resemblance to an upended coffin, and had the same brooding, ominous air of a casket waiting for its owner to give up the ghost.

There were a couple of small glass windows in its front through which could be seen a multitude of wheels as beautifully finished as those in a first-class watch. Elsewhere, several tiny lenses stared with sphinx-like indifference. There were three small trapdoors in one side, two in the other, and a large one in the front. From the top, two knobbed rods of metal stuck up like goat's horns, adding a satanic touch to the thing's vague air of yearning for midnight burial.

"It's an automatic layer-outer," I suggested, regarding the contraption with frank dislike. I pointed to one of the trapdoors. "You shove the shroud in there, and the corpse comes out the other side reverently composed and ready wrapped."

"So you don't like its air, either," Burman commented. He lugged open a drawer in a nearby tier, hauled out a mass of drawings. "These are its innards. It has an electric circuit, valves, condensers, and something that I can't quite understand, but which I suspect to be a tiny, extremely efficient electric furnace. It has parts I recognize as cog-cutters and pinion-shapers. It embodies several small-scale multiple stampers, apparently for dealing with sheet metal. There are vague suggestions of an assembly line ending in that large compartment shielded by the door in front. Have a look at the drawings yourself. You can see it's an extremely complicated device for manufacturing something only little less complicated."

The drawings showed him to be right. But they didn't show everything. An efficient machine designer could correctly have deduced the gadget's function if given complete details. Burman admitted this, saying that some parts he had made "on the spur of the moment," while others he had been "impelled to draw." Short of pulling the machine to pieces, there was enough data to whet the curiosity, but not enough to satisfy it.

"Start the damn thing and see what it does."

"I've tried," said Burman. "It won't start. There's no starting handle, nothing to suggest how it can be started. I tried everything I could think of, without result. The electric circuit ends in those antennae at the top, and I even sent current through those, but nothing happened."

"Maybe it's a self-starter," I ventured. Staring at it, a thought struck me. "Timed," I added.

"Eh?"

"Set for an especial time. When the dread hour strikes, it'll go of its own accord, like a bomb."

"Don't be so melodramatic," said Burman, uneasily.

Bending down, he peered into one of the tiny lenses.

"Bz-z-z!" murmured the contraption in a faint undertone that was almost inaudible.

Burman jumped a foot. Then he backed away, eyed the thing warily, turned his glance at me.

"Did you hear that?"

"Sure!" Getting the drawings, I mauled them around. That little lens took some finding, but it was there all right. It has a selenium cell behind it. "An eye," I said. "It saw you, and reacted. So it isn't dead even if it does just stand there seeing no evil, hearing no evil, speaking no evil." I put a white handkerchief against the lens.

"Bz-z-z!" repeated the coffin, emphatically.

Taking the handkerchief, Burman put it against the other lenses. Nothing happened. Not a sound was heard, not a funeral note. Just nothing.

"It beats me," he confessed.

I'd got pretty fed up by this time. If the crazy article had performed, I'd have written it up and maybe I'd have started another financial snowball rolling for Burman's benefit. But you can't do anything with a box that buzzes whenever it feels temperamental. Firm treatment was required, I decided.

"You've been all nice and mysterious about how you got

hold of this brain wave," I said. "Why can't you go to the same source for information about what it's supposed to be?"

"I'll tell you—or, rather, I'll show you."

From his safe, Burman dragged out a box, and from the box he produced a gadget. This one was far simpler than the useless mass of works over by the wall. It looked just like one of those old-fashioned crystal sets, except that the crystal was very big, very shiny, and was set in a horizontal vacuum tube. There was the same single dial, the same cat's whisker. Attached to the lot by a length of flex was what might have been a pair of headphones, except in place of the phones were a pair of polished, smoothly rounded copper circles shaped to fit outside the ears and close against the skull.

"My one and only invention." said Burman, not without a justifiable touch of pride.

"What is it?"

"A time-traveling device."

"Ha, ha!" My laugh was very sour. I'd read about such things. In fact, I'd written about them. They were bunkum. Nobody could travel through time, either backward or forward. "Let me see you grow hazy and vanish into the future."

"I'll show you something very soon." Burman said it with assurance I didn't like. He said it with the positive air of a man who knows darned well that he can do something that everybody else knows darned well can't be done. He pointed to the crystal set. "It wasn't discovered at the first attempt. Thousands must have tried and failed. I was the lucky one. I must have picked a peculiarly individualistic crystal; I still don't know how it does what it does; I've never been able to repeat its performance even with a crystal apparently identical."

"And it enables you to travel in time?"

"Only forward. It won't take me backward, not even as much as one day. But it can carry me forward an immense distance, perhaps to the very crack of doom, perhaps everlastingly through infinity."

I had him now! I'd got him firmly entangled in his own absurdities. My loud chuckle was something I couldn't control.

"You can travel forward, but not backward, not even one day back. Then how the devil can you return to the present once you've gone into the future?"

"Because I never leave the present," he replied, evenly. "I don't partake of the future. I merely survey it from the vantage point of the present. All the same, it is time-traveling in the correct sense of the term." He seated himself. "Look here, Bill, what *are* you?"

"Who, me?"

"Yes, what are you." He went on to provide the answer. "Your name is Bill. You're a body and a mind. Which of them is Bill?"

"Both," I said, positively.

"True—but they're different parts of you. They're not the same even though they go around like Siamese twins." His voice grew serious. "Your body moves always in the present, the dividing line between the past and the future. But your mind is more free. It can think, and is in the present. It can remember, and at once is in the past. It can imagine, and at once is in the future, in its own choice of all the possible futures. *Your mind can travel through time!*"

He'd outwitted me. I could find points to pick upon and argue about, but I knew that fundamentally he was right. I'd not looked at it from this angle before, but he was correct in saying that anyone could travel through time within the limits of his own memory and imagination. At that very moment I could go back twelve years and see him in my mind's eyes as a younger man, paler, thinner, more excitable, not so cool and self-possessed. The picture was as perfect as my memory was excellent. For that brief spell I was twelve years back in all but the flesh.

"I call this thing a psychophone," Burman went on. "When you imagine what the future will be like, you make a characteristic choice of all the logical possibilities, you pick your favorite from a multitude of likely futures. The psychophone, somehow—the Lord alone knows how—tunes you into future *reality*. It makes you depict within your mind the future as it will be shaped in actuality, eliminating all the alternatives that will not occur."

"An imagination-stimulator, a dream-machine," I scoffed, not feeling as sure of myself as I sounded. "How do you know it's giving you the McCoy?"

"Consistency," he answered, gravely. "It repeats the same features and the same trends far too often for the phenomena to be explained as mere coincidence. Besides," he waved a persuasive hand, "I got the battery from the future. It works, doesn't it?"

"It does," I agreed, reluctantly. I pointed to his psychophone. "I, too, may travel in time. How about letting me have a try? Maybe I'll solve your mystery for you."

"You can try if you wish," he replied, quite willingly. He pulled a chair into position. "Sit here, and I'll let you peer into the future."

Clipping the headband over my cranium, and fitting the copper rings against my skull where it sprouted ears, Burman connected his psychophone to the mains, switched it on; or rather he did some twiddling that I assumed was a mode of switching on.

"All you have to do," he said, "is close your eyes, compose yourself, then try and permit your imagination to wander into the future."

He meddled with the cat's whisker. A couple of times he said, "Ah!" And each time he said it I got a peculiar dithery feeling around my unfortunate ears. After a few seconds of this, he drew it out to, "A-a-ah!" I played unfair, and peeped beneath lowered lids. The crystal was glowing like rats' eyes in a forgotten cellar. A furtive crimson.

Closing my own optics, I let my mind wander. Something was flowing between those copper electrodes, a queer, indescribable something that felt with stealthy fingers at some secret portion of my brain. I got the asinine notion that they were the dexterous digits of a yet-to-be-born magician who was going to shout, "Presto!" and pull my abused lump of think-meat out of a thirtieth-century hat—assuming they'd wear hats in the thirtieth century.

What was it like, or, rather, what would it be like in the thirtieth century? Would there be retrogression? Would humanity again be composed of scowling, fur-kilted creatures lurking in caves? Or had progress continued—perhaps even to the development of men like gods?

Then it happened! I swear it! I pictured, quite voluntarily, a savage, and then a huge-domed individual with glittering eyes—the latter being my version of the ugliness we hope to attain. Right in the middle of this erratic dreaming, those weird fingers warped my brain, dissolved my phantoms, and replaced them with a dictated picture which I witnessed with all the helplessness and clarity of a nightmare.

I saw a fat man spouting. He was quite an ordinary man as far as looks went. In fact, he was so normal that he looked henpecked. But he was attired in a Roman toga, and he wore a small, black box where his laurel wreath ought to have been. His audience was similarly dressed, and all were balancing their boxes like a convention of fish porters. What

Fatty was orating sounded gabble to me, but he said his piece as if he meant it.

The crowd was in the open air, with great, curved rows of seats visible in the background. Presumably an outside auditorium of some sort. Judging by the distance of the back rows, it must have been a devil of a size. Far behind its sweeping ridge a great edifice jutted into the sky, a cubical erection with walls of glossy squares, like an immense glasshouse.

"F'wot?" bellowed Fatty, with obvious heat. "Wuk, wuk, wuk, mor, noon'n'ni'! Bok onned, ord this, ord that." He stuck an indignant finger against the mysterious object on his cranium. "Bok onned, wuk, wuk, wuk. F'wot?" he glared around. "F'nix!" The crowd murmured approval somewhat timidly. But it was enough for Fatty. Making up his mind, he flourished a plump fist and shouted, "Th'ell wit'm!" Then he tore his box from his pate.

Nobody said anything, nobody moved. Dumb and wide-eyed, the crowd just stood and stared as if paralyzed by the sight of a human being sans box. Something with a long, slender streamlined body and broad wings soared gracefully upward in the distance, swooped over the auditorium, but still the crowd neither moved nor uttered a sound.

A smile of triumph upon his broad face, Fatty bawled, "Lem see'm make wuk now! Lem see'm—"

He got no further. With a rush of mistiness from its tail, but in perfect silence, the soaring thing hovered and sent down a spear of faint, silvery light. The light touched Fatty. He rotted where he stood, like a victim of ultra-rapid leprosy. He rotted, collapsed, crumbled within his sagging clothes, became dust as once he had been dust. It was horrible.

The watchers did not flee in utter panic; not one expression of fear, hatred or disgust came from their tightly closed lips. In perfect silence they stood there, staring, just staring, like a horde of wooden soldiers. The thing in the sky circled to survey its handiwork, then dived low over the mob, a stubby antenna in its prow sparking furiously. As one man, the crowd turned left. As one man it commenced to march, left, right, left, right.

Tearing off the headband, I told Burman what I'd seen, or what his contraption had persuaded me to think that I'd seen. "What the deuce did it mean?"

"Automatons," he murmured. "Glasshouses and reaction ships." He thumbed through a big diary filled with notations in his own hands. "Ah, yes, looks like you were very early in the thirtieth century. Unrest was persistent for twenty years prior to the Antibox Rebellion."

"What rebellion?"

"The Antibox—the revolt of the automatons against the thirty-first century Technocrats. Jackson-Dkj-99717, a successful and cunning schemer with a warped box, secretly warped hundreds of other boxes, and eventually led the rebels to victory in 3047. His great-grandson, a greedy, thick-headed individual, caused the rebellion of the Boxless Freemen against his own clique of Jacksocrats."

I gaped at this recital, then said, "The way you tell it makes it sound like history."

"Of course it's history," he asserted. "History that is yet to be." He was pensive for a while. "Studying the future will seem a weird process to you, but it appears quite a normal procedure to me. I've done it for years, and maybe familiarity has bred contempt. Trouble is though, that selectivity is poor. You can pick on some especial period twenty times in succession, but you'll never find yourself in the same month, or even the same year. In fact, you're fortunate if you strike twice in the same decade. Result is that my data is very erratic."

"I can imagine that," I told him. "A good guesser can guess the correct time to within a minute or two, but never to within ten or even fifty seconds."

"Quite!" he responded. "So the hell of it has been that mine was the privilege of watching the panorama of the future, but in a manner so sketchy that I could not grasp its prizes. Once I was lucky enough to watch a twenty-fifth century power pack assembled from first to last. I got every detail before I lost the scene which I've never managed to hit upon again. But I made that power pack—and you know the result."

"So that's how you concocted your famous battery!"

"It is! But mine, good as it may be, isn't as good as the one I saw. Some slight factor is missing." His voice was suddenly tight when he added, "I missed something because I had to miss it!"

"Why?" I asked, completely puzzled.

"Because history, past or future, permits no glaring paradox. Because, having snatched this battery from the twenty-fifth century, I am recorded in that age as the twentieth-century inventor of the thing. They've made a mild improvement to it in those five centuries, but that improvement was automatically withheld from me. Future history is as fixed and unalterable by those of the present time as is the history of the past."

"Then," I demanded, "explain to me that complicated contraption which does nothing but say *bz-z-z.*"

"Damn it" he said, with open ire, "that's just what's making me crazy! It can't be a paradox, it just can't." Then, more carefully, "So it must be a seeming paradox."

"O.K. You tell me how to market a seeming paradox, and the commercial uses thereof, and I'll give it a first-class write up."

Ignoring my sarcasm, he went on, "I tried to probe the future as far as human minds can probe. I saw nothing, nothing but the vastness of a sterile floor upon which sat a queer machine, gleaming there in silent, solitary majesty. Somehow, it seemed aware of my scrutiny across the gulf of countless ages. It held my attention with a power almost hypnotic. For more than a day, for a full thirty hours, I kept that vision without losing it—the longest time I have ever kept a future scene."

"Well?"

"I drew it. I made complete drawings of it, performing the task with all the easy confidence of a trained machine draughtsman. Its insides could not be seen, but somehow they came to me, somehow I knew them. I lost the scene at four o'clock in the morning, finding myself with masses of very complicated drawings, a thumping head, heavy-lidded eyes, and a half-scared feeling in my heart." He was silent for a short time. "A year later I plucked up courage and started to build the thing I had drawn. It cost me a hell of a lot of time and hell of a lot of money. But I did it—it's finished."

"And all it does is buzz," I remarked, with genuine sympathy.

"Yes," he sighed, doubtfully.

There was nothing more to be said. Burman gazed moodily at the wall, his mind far, far away. I fiddled aimlessly with the copper ear-pieces of the psychophone. My imagination, I reckoned, was as good as anyone's, but for the life of me I could neither imagine nor suggest a profitable market for a metal coffin filled with watchmaker's junk. No, not even if it did make odd noises.

A faint, smooth *whir* came from the coffin. It was a new sound that swung us round to face it pop-eyed. *Whir-r-r!* it went again. I saw finely machined wheels spin behind the window in its front.

"Good heavens!" said Burman.

Bz-z-z! Whir-r! Click! The whole affair suddenly slid side-wise on its hidden casters.

The devil you know isn't half so frightening as the devil you don't. I don't mean that this sudden demonstration of life and motion got us scared, but it certainly made us leery, and our hearts put in an extra dozen bumps a minute. This coffin-thing was, or might be, a devil we didn't know. So we stood there, side by side, gazing at it fascinatedly, feeling apprehensive of we knew not what.

Motion ceased after the thing had slid two feet. It stood there, silent, imperturbable, its front lenses eyeing us with glassy lack of expression. Then it slid another two feet. Another stop. More meaningless contemplation. After that, a swifter and farther slide that brought it right up to the laboratory table. At that point it ceased moving, began to emit varied but synchronized ticks like those of a couple of sympathetic grandfather clocks.

Burman said, quietly, "Something's going to happen!"

If the machine could have spoken it would have taken the words right out of his mouth. He'd hardly uttered the sentence when a trapdoor in the machine's side fell open, a jointed, metallic arm snaked cautiously through the opening and reached for a marine chronometer standing on the table.

With a surprised oath, Burman dashed forward to rescue the chronometer. He was too late. The arm grabbed it, whisked it into the machine, the trapdoor shut with a hard snap, like the vicious clash of a sprung bear trap. Simultaneously, another trapdoor in the front flipped open, another jointed arm shot out and in again, spearing with ultra-rapid motion too fast to follow. That trapdoor also snapped shut, leaving Burman gaping down at his torn clothing from which his expensive watch and equally expensive gold chain had been ripped away.

"Good heavens!" said Burman, backing from the machine.

We stood looking at it a while. It didn't move again, just posed there ticking steadily as if ruminating upon its welcome meal. Its lenses looked at us with all the tranquil lack of interest of a well-fed cow. I got the idiotic notion that it was happily digesting a mess of cogs, pinions and wheels.

Because its subtle air of menace seemed to have faded away, or maybe because we sensed its entire preoccupation with the task in hand, we made an effort to rescue Burman's valuable timepiece. Burman tugged mightily at the trapdoor through which his watch had gone, but failed to move it. I tugged with him, without result. The thing was sealed as solidly as if welded in. A large screwdriver failed to pry it open. A crowbar, or a good jimmy would have done the job, but at that point Burman decided that he didn't want to damage the machine which had cost him more than the watch.

Tick-tick-tick! went the coffin, stolidly. We were back where we'd started, playing with our fingers, and no wiser than before. There was nothing to be done, and I felt that the accursed contraption knew it. So it stood there, gaping through its lenses, and jeered *tick-tick-tick*. From its belly, or where its belly would have been if it'd had one, a slow warmth radiated. According to Burman's drawings, that was the location of the tiny electric furnace.

The thing was functioning; there could be no doubt about that! If Burman felt the same way as I did, he must have been pretty mad. There we stood, like a couple of prize boobs, not knowing what the machine was supposed to do, and all the time it was doing under our very eyes whatever it was designed to do.

From where was it drawing its power? Were those antennae sticking like horns from its head busily sucking current from the atmosphere? Or was it, perhaps, absorbing radio power? Or did it have internal energy of its own? All the evidence suggested that it was making something, giving birth to something, but giving birth to what?

Tick-tick-tick! was the only reply.

Our questions were still unanswered, our curiosity was still unsatisfied, and the machine was still ticking industriously at the hour of midnight. We surrendered the problem until next morning. Burman locked and double-locked his laboratory before we left.

Police officer Burke's job was a very simple one. All he had to do was walk around and around the block, keeping a wary eye on the stores in general and the big jewel depot in particular, phoning headquarters once per hour from the post at the corner.

Night work suited Burke's taciturn disposition. He could wander along, communing with himself, with nothing to bother him or divert him from his inward ruminations. In that particular section nothing ever happened at night, nothing.

Stopping outside the gem-bedecked window, he gazed through the glass and the heavy grille behind it to where a low-power bulb shed light over the massive safe. There was a rajah's ransom in there. The guard, the grille, the automatic alarms and sundry ingenious traps preserved it from the adventurous fingers of anyone who wanted to ransom a rajah. Nobody had made the brash attempt in twenty years. Nobody had even made a try for the contents of the grille-protected window.

He glanced upward at a faintly luminescent path of cloud behind which lay the hidden moon. Turning, he strolled on. A cat sneaked past him, treading cautiously, silently, and hugging the angle of the wall. His sharp eyes detected its slinking shape even in the nighttime gloom, but he ignored it and progressed to the corner.

Back of him, the cat came below the window through which he just had stared. It stopped, one forefoot half-raised, its ears cocked forward. Then it flattened belly-low against the concrete, its burning orbs wide, alert, intent. Its tail waved slowly from side to side.

Something small and bright came skittering toward it, moving with mouselike speed and agility close in the angle of the wall. The cat tensed as the object came nearer. Suddenly, the thing was within range, and the cat pounced with lithe eagerness. Hungry paws dug at a surface that was not soft and furry, but hard, bright, and slippery. The thing darted around like a clockwork toy as the cat vainly tried to hold it. Finally, with an angry snarl, the cat swiped it viciously, knocking it a couple of yards where it rolled onto its back and emitted softly protesting clicks and tiny, urgent impulses that its feline attacker could not sense.

Gaining the gutter with a single leap, the cat crouched again. Something else was coming. The cat muscled, its eyes glowed. Another object slightly similar to the curious thing it had just captured, but a little bit bigger, a fraction noisier, and much different in shape. It resembled a small, gold-plated cylinder with a conical front from which projected a slender blade, and it slid along swiftly on invisible wheels.

Again the cat leaped. Down on the corner, Burke heard its brief shriek and following gurgle. The sound didn't bother Burke—he'd heard cats and rats and other vermin make all sorts of queer noises in the night. Phlegmatically, he continued on his beat.

Three quarters of an hour later, Police Officer Burke had worked his way around to the fatal spot. Putting his flash on the body, he rolled the supine animal over with his foot. Its throat was cut. Its throat had been cut with an utter savage-

that had half-severed its head from its body. Burke scowled down at it. He was no lover of cats himself, but he found difficulty in imagining anyone hating like that!

"Somebody," he muttered, "wants flaying alive."

His big foot shoved the dead cat back into the gutter where street cleaners could cart it away in the morning. He turned his attention to the window, saw the light still glowing upon the untouched safe. His mind was still on the cat while his eyes looked in and said that something was wrong. Then he dragged his attention back to business, realized what was wrong, and sweated at every pore. It wasn't the safe, it was the window.

In front of the window the serried trays of valuable rings still gleamed undisturbed. To the right, the silverwares still shone untouched. But on the left had been a small display of delicate and extremely expensive watches. They were no longer here, not one of them. He remembered that right in front had rested a neat, beautiful calendar-chronometer priced at a year's salary. That, too, was gone.

The beam of his flash trembled as he tried the gate, found it fast, secure. The door behind it was firmly locked. The transom was closed, its heavy wire guard still securely fixed. He went over the window, eventually found a small, neat hole, about two inches in diameter, down in the corner on the side nearest the missing display.

Burke's curse was explosive as he turned and ran to the corner. His hand shook with indignation while it grabbed the telephone from its box. Getting headquarters, he recited his story. He thought he'd a good idea of what had happened, fancied he'd read once of a similar stunt being pulled elsewhere.

Looks like they cut a disk with a rotary diamond, lifted it out with a suction cup, then fished through the hole with a telescopic rod." He listened a moment, then said. "Yes, yes. That's just what gets me—the rings are worth ten times as much."

His still-startled eyes looked down the street while he paid attention to the voice at the other end of the line. The eyes wandered slowly, descended, found the gutter, remained fixed on the dim shape lying therein. Another dead cat! Still clinging to his phone, Burke moved out as far as the cord would allow, extended a boot, rolled the cat away from the curb. The flash settled on it. Just like the other—ear to ear!

"And listen," he shouted into the phone, "some maniac's ~~d~~ering around slaughtering cats."

Replacing the phone, he hurried back to the maltreated window, stood guard in front of it until the police car rolled up. Four men piled out.

The first said, "Cats! I'll say somebody's got it in for cats! We passed two a couple of blocks away. They were bang in the middle of the street, flat in the headlights, and had been damn near guillotined. Their bodies were still warm."

The second grunted, approached the window, stared at the small, neat hole, and said, "The mob that did this would be too cute to leave a print."

"They weren't too cute to leave the rings," growled Burke.

"Maybe you've got something there," conceded the other. "If they've left the one, they might have left the other. We'll test for prints, anyway."

A taxi swung into the dark street, pulled up behind the police car. An elegantly dressed, fussy, and very agitated individual got out, rushed up to the waiting group. Keys jangled in his pale, moist hand.

"Maley, the manager—you phoned me," he explained, breathlessly. "Gentlemen, this is terrible, terrible! The window show is worth thousands, thousands! What a loss, what a loss!"

"How about letting us in?" asked one of the policemen, calmly.

"Of course, of course."

Jerkily, he opened the gate, unlocked the door, using about six keys for the job. They walked inside. Maley switched on the lights, stuck his head between the plateglass shelves, surveyed the depleted window.

"My watches, my watches," he groaned.

"It's awful, it's awful!" said one of the policemen, speaking with beautiful solemnity. He favored his companions with a sly wink.

Maley leaned farther over, the better to inspect an empty corner. "All gone, all gone," he moaned, "all my show of the finest makes in—*Yeeouw!*" His yelp made them jump. Maley bucked as he tried to force himself through the obstructing shelves toward the grille and the window beyond it. "My watch! My own watch!"

The others tiptoed, stared over his shoulders, saw the gold buckle of a black velvet fob go through the hole in the window. Burke was the first outside, his ready flash searching the concrete. Then he spotted the watch. It was moving rapidly along, hugging the angle of the wall, but it stopped dead as his beam settled upon it. He fancied he saw something else,

equally bright and metalilc, scoot swiftly into the darkness
beyond the circle of his beam.

Picking up the watch, Burke stood and listened. The noises
of the others coming out prevented him from hearing clearly,
but he could have sworn he'd heard a tiny whirring noise,
and a swift, juicy ticking that was not coming from the instrument in his hand. Must have been only his worried fancy.
Frowning deeply, he returned to his companions.

"There was nobody," he asserted. "It must have dropped
out of your pocket and rolled."

Damn it, he thought, could a watch roll that far? What the
devil was happening this night? Far up the street, something
screeched, then it bubbled. Burke shuddered—he could make
a shrewd guess at that! He looked at the others, but apparently they hadn't heard the noise.

The papers gave it space in the morning. The total was
sixty watches and eight cats, also some oddments from the
small stock of a local scientific instrument maker. I read
about it on my way down to Burman's place. The details
were fairly lavish, but not complete. I got them completely at
a later time when we discovered the true significance of what
had occurred.

Burman was waiting for me when I arrived. He appeared
both annoyed and bothered. Over in the corner, the coffin
was ticking away steadily, its noise much louder than it had
been the previous day. The thing sounded a veritable hive of
industry.

"Well?" I asked.

"It's moved around a lot during the night," said Burman.
"It's smashed a couple of thermometers and taken the mercury out of them. I found some drawers and cupboards shut,
some open, but I've an uneasy feeling that it's made a thorough search through the lot. A packet of nickel foil has vanished, a coil of copper wire has gone with it." He pointed an
angry finger at the bottom of the door through which I'd just
entered. "And I blame it for gnawing ratholes in that. They
weren't there yesterday."

Sure enough, there were a couple of holes in the bottom of
that door. But no rat made those—they were neat and
smooth and round, almost as if a carpenter had cut them
with a keyhole saw.

"Where's the sense in it making those?" I questioned. "It
can't crawl through apertures that size."

"Where's the sense in the whole affair?" Burman countered. He glowered at the busy machine which stared back at him with its expressionless lenses and churned steadily on. *Tick-tick-tick!* persisted the confounded thing. Then, *whir-thump-click!*

I opened my mouth intending to voice a nice, sarcastic comment at the machine's expense when there came a very tiny, very subtle and extremely high-pitched whine. Something small, metallic, glittering shot through one of the rat holes, fled across the floor toward the churning monstrosity. A trapdoor opened and swallowed it with such swiftness that it had disappeared before I realized what I'd seen. The thing had been a cylindrical, polished object resembling the shuttle of a sewing machine, but about four times the size. And it had been dragging something also small and metallic.

Burman stared at me; I stared at Burman. Then he foraged around the laboratory, found a three-foot length of half-inch steel pipe. Dragging a chair to the door, he seated himself, gripped the pipe like a bludgeon, and watched the rat holes. Imperturbably, the machine watched him and continued to *tick-tick-tick*.

Ten minutes later, there came a sudden click and another tiny whine. Nothing darted inward through the holes, but the curious object we'd already seen—or another one exactly like it—dropped out of the trap, scooted to the door by which we were waiting. It caught Burman by surprise. He made a mad swipe with the steel as the thing skittered elusively past his feet and through a hole. It had gone even as the weapon walloped the floor.

"Damn!" said Burman, heartily. He held the pipe loosely in his grip while he glared at the industrious coffin. "I'd smash it to bits except that I'd like to catch one of these small gadgets first."

"Look out!" I yelled.

He was too late. He ripped his attention away from the coffin toward the holes, swinging up the heavy length of pipe, a startled look on his face. But his reaction was far too slow. Three of the little mysteries were through the holes and halfway across the floor before his weapon was ready to swing. The coffin swallowed them with the crash of a trapdoor.

The invading trio had rushed through in single file, and I'd got a better picture of them this time. The first two were golden shuttles, much like the one we'd already seen. The third was bigger, speedier, and gave me the notion that it could dodge around more dexterously. It had a long, sharp projection in front, a wicked, ominous thing like a surgeon's scalpel. Sheer speed deprived me of a good look at it, but I fancied that the tip of the scalpel had been tinged with red. My spine exuded perspiration.

Came an irritated scratching upon the outside of the door and a white-tipped paw poked tentatively through one of the holes. The cat backed to a safe distance when Burman opened the door, but looked lingeringly toward the laboratory. Its presence needed no explaining—the alert animal must have caught a glimpse of those infernal little whizzers. The same thought struck both of us; cats are quick on the pounce, very quick. Given a chance, maybe this one could make a catch for us.

We enticed it in with fair words and soothing noises. Its eagerness overcame its normal caution toward strangers, and it entered. We closed the door behind it; Burman got his length of pipe, sat by the door, tried to keep one eye on the holes and the other on the cat. He couldn't do both, but he tried. The cat sniffed and prowled around, mewed defeatedly. Its behavior suggested that it was seeking by sight rather than scent. There wasn't any scent.

With feline persistence, the animal searched the whole laboratory. It passed the buzzing coffin several times, but ignored it completely. In the end, the cat gave it up, sat on the corner of the laboratory table and started to wash its face.

Tick-tick-tick! went the big machine. Then *whir-thump!* A trap popped open, a shuttle fell out and raced for the door. A second one followed it. The first was too fast even for the cat, too fast for the surprised Burman as well. *Bang!* The length of the steel tube came down viciously as the leading shuttle bulleted triumphantly through a hole.

But the cat got the second one. With a mighty leap, paws extended, claws out, it caught its victim one foot from the door. It tried to handle the slippery thing, failed, lost it for an instant. The shuttle whisked around in a crazy loop. The cat got it again, lost it again, emitted an angry snarl, batted it against the skirting board. The shuttle lay there, upside down, four midget wheels in its underside spinning madly with a high, almost inaudible whine.

Eyes alight with excitement, Burman put down his weapon, went to pick up the shuttle. At the same time, the cat slunk toward it ready to play with it. The shuttle lay there, helplessly functioning upon its back. Before either could reach it the big machine across the room went *clunk!* opened a trap and ejected another gadget.

With astounding swiftness, the cat turned and pounced upon the newcomer. Then followed pandemonium. Its prey swerved agilely with a fitful gleam of gold; the cat swerved with it, cursed and spat. Black-and-white fur whirled around in a fighting haze in which gold occasionally glowed; the cat's hissings and spittings overlay a persistent whine that swelled and sank in the manner of accelerating or decelerating gears.

A peculiar gasp came from the cat, and blood spotted the floor. The animal clawed wildly, emitted another gasp followed by a gurgle. It shivered and flopped, a stream of crimson pouring from the great gash in its gullet.

We'd hardly time to appreciate the full significance of the ghastly scene when the victor made for Burman. He was standing by the skirting board, the still-buzzing shuttle in his hand. His eyes were sticking out with utter horror, but he retained enough presence of mind to make a frantic jump a second before the bulleting meance reached his feet.

He landed behind the thing, but it reversed in its own length and came for him again. I saw the mirrorlike sheen of its scalpel as it banked at terrific speed, and the sheen was drowned in sticky crimson two inches along the blade. Burman jumped over it again, reached the lab table, got up on that.

"Lord!" he breathed.

By this time I'd got the piece of pipe which he'd discarded. I hefted it, feeling its comforting weight, then did my best to bat the buzzing lump of wickedness through the window and over the roofs. It was too agile for me. It whirled, accelerated, dodged the very tip of the descending steel, and flashed twice around the table upon which Burman had taken refuge. It ignored me completely. Somehow, I felt that it was responding entirely to some mysterious call from the shuttle Burman had captured.

I swiped desperately, missed it again, though I swear I missed by no more than a millimeter. Something whipped through the holes in the door, fled past me into the big machine. Dimly, I heard traps opening and closing and beyond all other sounds that steady, persistent *tick-tick-tick*. Another furious blow that accomplished no more than to dent the floor and jar my arm to the shoulder.

Unexpectedly, unbelievably, the golden curse ceased its insane gyrations on the floor and around the table. With a hard click, and a whir much louder than before, it raced easily up one leg of the table and reached the top.

Burman left his sanctuary in one jump. He was still clinging to the shuttle. I'd never seen his face so white.

"The machine!" he said, hoarsely. "Bash it to hell!"

Thunk! went the machine. A trap gaped, released another
demon with a scalpel. *Tzz-z-z!* a third shot in through the
holes in the door. Four shuttles skimmed through behind it,
made for the machine, reached it safely. A fifth came
through more slowly. It was dragging an automobile valve
spring. I kicked the thing against the wall even as I struck a
vain blow at one with a scalpel.

With another jump, Burman cleared an attacker. A second
sheared off the toe of his right shoe as he landed. Again he
reached the table from which his first toe had departed. All
three things with scalpels made for the table with a reckless
vim that was frightening.

"Drop that damned shuttle," I yelled.

He didn't drop it. As the fighting trio whirred up the legs,
he flung the shuttle with all his might at the coffin that had
given it birth. It struck, dented the casing, fell to the floor.
Burman was off the table again. The thrown shuttle lay battered and noiseless, its small motive wheels stilled.

The armed contraptions scooting around the table seemed
to change their purpose coincidently with the captured
shuttle's smashing. Together, they dived off the table, sped
through the holes in the door. A fourth came out of the
machine, escorting two shuttles, and those too vanished beyond the door. A second or two later, a new thing different
from the rest, came in through one of the holes. It was long,
round-bodied, snub-nosed, about half the length of a policeman's nightstick, had six wheels beneath, and a double row of
peculiar serrations in front. It almost sauntered across the
room while we watched it fascinatedly. I saw the serrations
jerk and shift when it climbed the lowered trap into the
machine. They were midget caterpillar tracks!

Burman had had enough. He made up his mind. Finding
the steel pipe, he gripped it firmly, approached the coffin. Its
lenses seemed to leer at him as he stood before it. Twelve
years of intensive work to be destroyed at a blow. Endless
days and nights of effort to be undone at one stroke. But Burman was past caring. With a ferocious swing he demolished
the glass, with a fierce thrust he shattered the assembly of
wheels and cogs behind.

The coffin shuddered and slid beneath his increasingly angry blows. Trapdoors dropped open, spilled out lifeless
samples of the thing's metallic brood. Grindings and raspings

came from the accursed object while Burman battered it to pieces. Then it was silent, a shapeless, useless mass of twisted and broken parts.

I picked up the dented shape of the object that had sauntered in. It was heavy, astonishingly heavy, and even after partial destruction its workmanship looked wonderful. It had a tiny, almost unnoticeable eye in front, but the miniature lens was cracked. Had it returned for repairs and overhaul?

"That," said Burman, breathing audibly, "is that!"

I opened the door to see if the noise had attracted attention. It hadn't. There was a lifeless shuttle outside the door, a second a yard behind it. The first had a short length of brass chain attached to a tiny hook projecting from its rear. The nose cap of the second had opened fanwise, like an iris diaphragm, and a pair of jointed metal arms were folded inside, hugging a medium-sized diamond. It looked as if they'd been about to enter when Burman destroyed the big machine.

Picking them up, I brought them in. Their complete inactivity, though they were undamaged, suggested that they had been controlled by the big machine and had drawn their motive power from it. If so, then we'd solved our problem simply, and by destroying the one had destroyed the lot.

Burman got his breath back and began to talk.

He said, "The Robot Mother! That's what I made—a duplicate of the Robot Mother. I didn't realize it, but I was patiently building the most dangerous thing in creation, a thing that is a terrible menace because it shares with mankind the ability to propagate. Thank Heaven we stopped it in time!"

"So," I remarked, remembering that he claimed to have got it from the extreme future, "that's the eventual master, or mistress, of Earth. A dismal prospect for humanity, eh?"

"Not necessarily. I don't know just how far I got, but I've an idea it was so tremendously distant in the future that Earth had become sterile from humanity's viewpoint. Maybe we'd emigrated to somewhere else in the cosmos, leaving our semi-intelligent slave machines to fight for existence or die. They fought—and survived."

"And then wangle things to try to alter the past in their favor," I suggested.

"No, I don't think so." Burman had become much calmer by now. "I don't think it was a dastardy attempt so much as an interesting experiment. The whole affair was damned in advance because success would have meant an impossible paradox. There are no robots in the next century, nor any knowledge of them. Therefore the intruders in this time must have been wiped out and forgotten."

"Which means," I pointed out, "that you must not only have destroyed the machine, but also all your drawings, all your notes, as well as the psychophone, leaving nothing but a few strange events and a story for me to tell."

"Exactly—I shall destroy everything. I've been thinking over the whole affair, and it's not until now I've understood that the psychophone can never be of the slightest use to me. It permits me to discover or invent only those things that history has decreed I shall invent, and which, therefore, I shall find with or without the contraption. I can't play tricks with history, past or future."

"Humph!" I couldn't find any flaw in his reasoning. "Did you notice," I went on, "the touch of bee psychology in our antagonists? You built the hive, and from it emerged workers, warriors, and"—I indicated the dead saunterer—"one drone."

"Yes," he said, lugubriously. "And I'm thinking of the honey—eighty watches! Not to mention any other items the late papers may report, plus any claims for slaughtered cats. Good thing I'm wealthy."

"Nobody knows you've anything to do with those incidents. You can pay secretly if you wish."

"I shall," he declared.

"Well," I went on, cheerfully, "all's well that ends well. Thank goodness we've got rid of what we brought upon ourselves."

With a sigh of relief, I strolled toward the door. A high whine of midget motors drew my startled attention downward. While Burman and I stared aghast, a golden shuttle slid easily through one of the rat holes, sensed the death of the Robot Mother and scooted back through the other hole before I could stop it.

If Burman had been shaken before, he was doubly so now. He came over to the door, stared incredulously at the little exit just used by the shuttle, then at the couple of other undamaged but lifeless shuttles lying about the room.

"Bill," he mouthed, "your bee analogy was perfect. Don't you understand? There's another swarm! A queen got loose!"

There was another swarm all right. For the next forty-eight hours it played merry hell. Burman spent the whole time down at headquarters trying to convince them that his evidence wasn't just a fantastic story, but what helped him to persuade the police of his veracity was the equally fantastic reports that came rolling in.

To start with, old Gildersome heard a crash in his shop at midnight, thought of his valuable stock of cameras and miniature movie projectors, pulled on his pants and rushed downstairs. A razor-sharp instrument stabbed him through the right instep when halfway down, and he fell the rest of the way. He lay there, badly bruised and partly stunned, while things clicked, ticked and whirred in the darkness and the gloom. One by one, all the contents of his box of expensive lenses went through a hole in the door. A quantity of projector cogs and wheels went with them.

Ten people complained of being robbed in the night of watches and alarm clocks. Two were hysterical. One swore that the bandit was "a six-inch cockroach" which purred like a toy dynamo. Getting out of bed, he'd put his foot upon it and felt its cold hardness wriggle away from beneath him. Filled with revulsion, he'd whipped his foot back into bed "just as another cockroach scuttled toward him." Burman did not tell that agitated complainant how near he had come to losing his foot.

Thirty more reports rolled in next day. A score of houses had been entered and four shops robbed by things that had the agility and furtiveness of rats—except that they emitted tiny ticks and buzzing noises. One was seen racing along the road by a homing railway worker. He tried to pick it up, lost his forefinger and thumb, stood nursing the stumps until an ambulance rushed him away.

Rare metals and fine parts were the prey of these ticking marauders. I couldn't see how Burman or anyone else could wipe them out once and for all, but he did it. He did it by baiting them like rats. I went around with him, helping him on the job, while he consulted a map.

"Every report," said Burman, "leads to this street. An alarm clock that suddenly sounded was abandoned near here. Two automobiles were robbed of small parts near here. Shuttles have been seen going to or from this area. Five cats were dealt with practically on this spot. Every other incident has taken place within easy reach."

"Which means," I guessed, "that the queen is somewhere near this point?"

"Yes." He stared up and down the quiet empty street over which the crescent moon shed a sickly light. It was two o'clock in the morning. "We'll settle this matter pretty soon!"

He attached the end of a reel of firm cotton to a small

piece of silver chain, nailed the reel to the wall, dropped the chain on the concrete. I did the same with the movement of a broken watch. We distributed several small cogs, a few clock wheels, several camera fitments, some small, tangled bunches of copper wire, and other attractive oddments.

Three hours later, we returned accompanied by the police. They had mallets and hammers with them. All of us were wearing steel leg-and-foot shields knocked up at short notice by a handy sheet-metal worker.

The bait had been taken! Several cotton strands had broken after being unreeled a short distance, but others were intact. All of them either led to or pointed to a steel grating leading to a cellar below an abandoned warehouse. Looking down, we could see a few telltale strands running through the window frame beneath.

Burman said, "Now!" and we went in with a rush. Rusty locks snapped, rotten doors collapsed, we poured through the warehouse and into the cellar.

There was a small, coffin-shaped thing against one wall, a thing that ticked steadily away while its lenses stared at us with ghastly lack of emotion. It was very similar to the Robot Mother, but only a quarter of the size. In the light of a police torch, it was a brooding, ominous thing of dreadful significance. Around it, an active clan swarmed over the floor, buzzing and ticking in metallic fury.

Amid angry whirs and the crack of snapping scalpels on steel, we waded headlong through the lot. Burman reached the coffin first, crushing it with one mighty blow of his twelve-pound hammer, then bashing it to utter ruin with a rapid succession of blows. He finished exhausted. The daughter of the Robot Mother was no more, nor did her alien tribe move or stir.

Sitting down on a rickety wooden case, Burman mopped his brow and said, "Thank heavens that's done!"

Tick-tick-tick!

. . He shot up, snatched his hammer, a wild look in his eyes.

"Only my watch," apologized one of the policemen. "It's a cheap one, and it makes a hell of a noise." He pulled it out to show the worried Burman.

"Tick! tick!" said the watch, with mechanical aplomb.

AND HE BUILT
A CROOKED HOUSE

Astounding Science Fiction
February

by Robert A. Heinlein (1907-　　　)

Robert A. Heinlein continued his dominance of the science fiction world in 1941, which featured his novel Methuselah's Children, *which ran as a three-part serial in* Astounding. *His short fiction was every bit as good, and this volume contains four of his stories.*

"And He Built a Crooked House" represented another innovative contribution by Heinlein. The quality of a story is often a matter of perception, and of course point of view is an important ingredient in all fiction, but it was never supposed to be like this!

(I appreciated Bob's work from the very beginning, from his first story, but I must admit that I didn't actually decide he was the best science fiction writer who ever was—and not merely one of the best—till I read this one. It was so light-hearted and so clever that I couldn't get it out of my mind. Of course, what got me right in betwixt the short ribs was his beginning and the knowledge that he had worked his way down to the very address he was living at at the time.—I.A.)

SHOTTLE BOP

Unknown
February

by Theodore Sturgeon (1918-   )

By the end of 1941 Theodore Sturgeon had a spectacular string of stories to his credit. In less than three years he had established himself as a master of both science fiction and fantasy. Along with Heinlein, he ruled over the peak of the Golden Age.

Few writers could combine a feel for horror— "Bianca's Hands," "It"—with a talent for comedy. This story shows Sturgeon at his funniest.

(I suppose that every once in a while as a story recedes into the past but lives on in your memory, there is a chance that you may confuse the author. You may attribute a story of one man to another. Thus, I frequently notice that people attribute one of Arthur C. Clarke's stories to me, which pleases me, or one of my stories to him, which rouses my indignation. Here is one case in which I am guilty. I persist in thinking that "Shottle Bop" was written by John Collier. I'm wrong, of course, but Collier is a terrifically clever writer of the gently fantastic—and so is Ted.—I. A.)

I'd never seen the place before, and I lived just down the block and around the corner. I'll even give you the address, if you like. "The Shottle Bop," between Twentieth and Twenty-first Streets, on Tenth Avenue in New York City. You can find it if you go there looking for it. Might even be worth your while, too.

But you'd better not.

"The Shottle Bop." It got me. It was a small shop with a weather-beaten sign swung from a wrought crane, creaking dismally in the late fall wind. I walked past it, thinking of the engagement ring in my pocket and how it had just been handed back to me by Audrey, and my mind was far removed from such things as shottle bops. I was thinking that Audrey might have used a gentler term than "useless" in describing me: and her neatly turned remark about my being a "constitutional psychopathic incompetent" was as un-called-for as it was spectacular. She must have read it somewere, balanced as it was by "And I wouldn't marry you if you were the last man on earth!" which is a notably worn cliché.

"Shottle Bop!" I muttered, and then paused, wondering where I had picked up such oddly rhythmic syllables with which to express myself. I'd seen it on that sign, of course, and it had caught my eye. "And what," I asked myself, "might be a Shottle Bop?" Myself replied promptly, "Dunno. Toddle back and have a look." So toddle I did, back along the east side of Tenth, wondering what manner of man might be running such an establishment in pursuance of what kind of business. I was enlightened on the second point by a sign in the window, all but obscured by the dust and ashes of apparent centuries, which read:

WE SELL BOTTLES

There was another line of smaller print there. I rubbed at the crusted glass with my sleeve and finally was able to make out.

With things in them.

Just like that:

WE SELL BOTTLES
With things in them.

Well of course I went in. Sometimes very delightful things come in bottles, and the way I was feeling, I could stand a little delighting.

"Close it!" shrilled a voice, as I pushed through the door. The voice came from a shimmering egg adrift in the air behind the counter, low-down. Peering over, I saw that it was not an egg at all, but the bald pate of an old man who was clutching the edge of the counter, his scrawny body streaming away in the slight draft from the open door, as if he were made of bubbles. A mite startled, I kicked the door with my

heel. He immediately fell on his face, and then scrambled
smiling to his feet.

"Ah, it's so good to see you again," he rasped.

I think his vocal cords were dusty, too. Everything else
here was. As the door swung to, I felt as if I were inside a
great dusty brain that had just closed its eyes. Oh yes, there
was light enough. But it wasn't the lamp light and it wasn't
daylight. It was like—like light reflected from the cheeks of
pale people. Can't say I enjoyed it much.

"What do you mean, 'again'?" I asked irritably. "You
never saw me before."

"I saw you when you came in and I fell down and got up
and saw you again," he quibbled, and beamed. "What can I
foo for do?"

"Huh?" I huhed, and then translated it into "What can I
do for you?"

"Oh, I said. "Well, I saw your sign. What have you got in
a bottle that I might like?"

"What do you want?"

"What've you got?"

He broke into a piping chant—I remember it yet, word for
word.

> *"For half a buck, a vial of luck*
> *Or a bottle of nifty breaks*
> *Or a flask of joy, or Myrna Loy*
> *For luncheon with sirloin steaks*

> *"Pour out a mug from this old jug,*
> *And you'll never get wet in rains.*
> *I've bottles of grins and racetrack wins*
> *and lotions to ease your pains.*

> *"Here's bottles of imps and wet-pack shrimps*
> *From a sea unknown to man,*
> *And an elixir to banish fear,*
> *And the sap from the pipes of Pan.*

> *"With the powdered horn of a unicorn*
> *You can win yourself a mate;*
> *With the rich hobnob; or get a job—*
> *It's yours at a lowered rate."*

"Now wait right there!" I snapped. "You mean you actually sell dragon's blood and ink from the pen of Friar Bacon
and all such mumbo-jum?"

He nodded rapidly and smiled all over his improbable face.
I went on—"The genuine article?"
He kept on nodding.

I regarded him for a moment. "You mean to stand there
with your teeth in your mouth and your bare face hanging
out and tell me that in this day and age, in this city and in
broad daylight, you sell such trash and then expect me—me,
an enlightened intellectual—"

"You are very stupid and twice as bombastic," he said quietly.

I glowered at him and reached for the doorknob—and
there I froze. And I mean froze. For the old man whipped
out an ancient bulb-type atomizer and squeezed a couple of
whiffs at me as I turned away; and so help me, *I couldn't
move!* I could cuss, though, and boy, did I.

The proprietor hopped over the counter and ran over to
me. He must have been standing on a box back there, for
now I could see he was barely three feet tall. He grabbed my
coat tails, ran up my back and slid down my arm, which was
extended doorward. He sat down on my wrist and swung his
feet and laughed up at me. As far as I could feel, he weighed
absolutely nothing.

When I had run out of profanity—I pride myself on never
repeating a phrase of invective—he said, "Does that prove
anything to you, my cocky and unintelligent friend? That was
the essential oil from the hair of the Gorgon's head. And until I give you an antidote, you'll stand there from now till a
week from text Nuesday!"

"Get me out of this," I roared, "or I smack you so hard
you lose your brains through the pores in your feet!"

He giggled.

I tried to tear loose again and couldn't. It was as if all my
epidermis had turned to high-carbon steel. I began cussing
again, but quit in despair.

"You think altogether too much of yourself," said the proprietor of the Shottle Bop. "Look at you! Why, I wouldn't
hire you to wash my windows. You expect to marry a girl
who is accustomed to the least of animal comfort, and then
you get miffed because she turns you down. Why does she
turn you down? Because you won't get a job. You're a no-
good. You're a bum. He, he! And you have the nerve to walk
around pelling teople where to get off. Now if I were in your
position I would ask politely to be released, and then I would
see if anyone in this shop would be good enough to sell you a
bottle full of something that might help out."

Now I never apologize to anybody, and I never back down, and I never take any guff from mere tradesmen. But this was different. I'd never been petrified before, nor had my nose rubbed in so many galling truths. I relented. "O.K., O.K.; let me break away then. I'll buy something."

"Your tone is sullen," he said complacently, dropping lightly to the floor and holding his atomizer at the ready. "You'll have to say 'Please. Pretty please.' "

He went back of the counter and returned with a paper of powder which he had me sniff. In a couple of seconds I began to sweat, and my limbs lost their rigidity so quickly that it almost threw me. I'd have been flat on my back if the man hadn't caught me and solicitously led me to a chair. As strength dribbled back into my shocked tissues, it occurred to me that I might like to flatten this hobgoblin for pulling a trick like that. But a strange something stopped me—strange because I'd never had the experience before. It was simply the idea that once I got outside I'd agree with him for having such a low opinion of me.

He wasn't worrying. Rubbing his hands briskly, he turned to his shelves. "Now, let's see . . . what would be best for you, I wonder? Hm-m-m. Success is something you couldn't justify. Money? You don't know how to spend it. A good job? You're not fitted for one." He turned gentle eyes on me and shook his head. "A sad case. *Tsk, tsk.*" I crawled. "A perfect mate? Uh-huh. You're too stupid to recognize perfection, too conceited to appreciate it. I don't think that I can— Wait!"

He whipped four or five bottles and jars off the dozens of shelves behind him and disappeared somewhere in the dark recesses of the store. Immediately there came sounds of violent activity—clinkings and little crashes; stirrings and then the rapid susurrant grating of a mortar and pestle; then the slushy sound of liquid being added to a dry ingredient during stirring; and at length, after quite a silence, the glugging of a bottle being filled through a filtering funnel. The proprietor reappeared triumphantly bearing a four-ounce bottle without a label.

"This will do it!" he beamed.

"That will do what?"

"Why, cure you!"

"Cure—" My pompous attitude, as Audrey called it, had returned while he was mixing. "What do you mean cure? I haven't got anything!"

"My dear little boy," he said offensively, "you most certainly have. Are you happy? Have you ever been happy? No. Well, I'm going to fix all that up. That is, I'll give you the start you need. Like any other cure, it requires your cooperation.

"You're in a bad way, young fellow. You have what is known in the profession as retrogressive metempsychosis of the ego in its most malignant form. You are a constitutional unemployable; a downright sociophagus. I don't like you. Nobody likes you."

Feeling a little bit on the receiving end of a blitz, I stammered, "W-what do you aim to do?"

He extended the bottle. "Go home. Get into a room by yourself—the smaller the better. Drink this down, right out of the bottle. Stand by for developments. That's all."

"But—what will it do to me?"

"It will do nothing *to* you. It will do a great deal *for* you. It can do as much for you as you want it to. But mind me, now. As long as you use what it gives you for your self-improvement, you will thrive. Use it for self-glorification, as a basis for boasting, or for revenge, and you will suffer in the extreme. Remember that, now."

"But what is it? How—"

"I am selling you a talent. You have none now. When you discover what kind of a talent it is, it will be up to you to use it to your advantage. Now go away. I still don't like you."

"What do I owe you?" I muttered, completely snowed under by this time.

"The bottle carries its own price. You won't pay anything unless you fail to follow my directions. Now will you go, or must I uncork a bottle of jinn—and I don't mean London Dry?"

"I'll go," I said. I'd seen something swirling in the depths of a ten-gallon carboy at one end of the counter, and I didn't like it a bit. "Good-by."

"Bood-gy," he returned.

I went out and I headed down Tenth Avenue and I turned east up Twentieth Street and I never looked back. And for many reasons I wish now that I had, for there was, without doubt, something very strange about that Shottle Bop.

I didn't simmer down until I got home; but once I had a cup of black Italian coffee under my belt I felt better. I was skeptical about it at last. I was actually inclined to scoff. But somehow I didn't want to scoff too loudly. I looked at the bottle a little scornfully, and there was a certain something about the glass of it that seemed to be staring back at me. I sniffed and threw it up behind some old hats on top of the closet, and then sat down to unlax. I used to love to unlax. I'd put my feet on the doorknob and slide down in the upholstery until I was sitting on my shoulder blades, and as the old saying has it, "Sometimes I sets and thinks, and sometimes I just sets." The former is easy enough, and is what even an accomplished loafer has to go through before he reaches the latter and more blissful state. It takes years of practice to relax sufficiently to be able to "just set." I'd learned it years ago.

But just as I was about to slip into the vegetable status, I was annoyed by something. I tried to ignore it. I manifested a superhuman display of lack of curiosity, but the annoyance persisted. A light pressure on my elbow, where it draped over the arm of the chair. I was put in the unpleasant predicament of having to concentrate on what it was; and realizing that concentration on anything was the least desirable thing there could be. I gave up finally, and with a deep sigh, opened my eyes and had a look.

It was the bottle.

I screwed up my eyes and then looked again, but it was still there. The closet door was open as I had left it, and its shelf almost directly above me. Must have fallen out. Feeling that if the damn thing were on the floor it couldn't fall any farther, I shoved it off the arm of the chair with my elbow.

It bounced. It bounced with such astonishing accuracy that it wound up in exactly the same spot it had started from—on the arm of the easy-chair, by my elbow. Startled, I shoved it violently. This time I pushed it hard enough to send it against the wall, from which it rebounded to the shelf under my small table, and thence back to the chair arm—and this time it perched cozily against my shoulder. Jarred by the bouncing, the stopper hopped out of the bottle mouth and rolled into my lap; and there I sat, breathing the bittersweet fumes of its contents, feeling frightened and silly as hell.

I grabbed the bottle and sniffed. I'd smelled that somewhere before—where was it? Uh—oh, yes; that mascara the Chinese honkytonk girls use in Frisco. The liquid was dark —smoky black. I tasted it cautiously. It wasn't bad. If it wasn't alcoholic, then the old man in the shop had found a darn good substitute for alcohol. At the second sip, I liked it and at the third I really enjoyed it and there wasn't any fourth because by then the little bottle was a dead marine.

That was about the time I remembered the name of the black ingredient with the funny smell. Kohl. It is an herb the Orientals use to make it possible to see supernatural beings. Silly superstition!

And then the liquid I'd just put away, lying warm and comfortable in my stomach, began to fizz. Then I think it began to swell. I tried to get up and couldn't. The room seemed to come apart and throw itself at me piecemeal, and I passed out.

Don't you ever wake up the way I did. For your own sake be careful about things like that. Don't swim up out of a sodden sleep and look around you and see all those things fluttering and drifting and flying and creeping and crawling around you—puffy things dripping blood, and filmy, legless creatures, and little bits and snatches of pasty human anatomy. It was awful. There was a human hand afloat in the air an inch away from my nose; and at my startled gasp it drifted away from me, fingers fluttering in the disturbed air from my breath. Something veined and bulbous popped out from under my chair and rolled across the floor. I heard a faint clicking, and looked up into a gnashing set of jaws without any face attached. I think I broke down and cried a little. I know I passed out again.

The next time I awoke—must have been hours later, because it was broad daylight and my clock and watch had both stopped—things were a little better. Oh, yes, there were a few of the horrors around. But somehow they didn't bother me much now. I was practically convinced that I was nuts; now that I had the conviction, why worry about it? I dunno; it must have been one of the ingredients in the bottle that had calmed me down so. I was curious and excited, and that's about all. I looked around me and I was almost pleased.

The walls were green! The drab wallpaper had turned to something breathtakingly beautiful. They were covered with what seemed to be moss; but never moss like that grew for human eyes to see before. It was long and thick, and it had a slight perpetual movement—not that of a breeze, but of growth. Fascinated, I moved over and looked closely. Growing indeed, with all the quick magic of spore and cyst and root and growth again to spore; and the swift magic of it was only a part of the magical whole, for never was there such a green. I put out my hand to touch and stroke it, but I only felt the wallpaper. But when I closed my fingers, on it, I could feel that light touch of it in the palm of my hand, the weight of twenty sunbeams, the soft resilience of jet-darkness in a closed place. The sensation was a delicate ecstasy, and never have I been happier than I was at that moment.

Around the baseboards were little snowy toadstools, and the floor was grassy. Up the hinged side of the closet door climbed a mass of flowering vines, and their petals were hued in tones indescribable. I felt as if I had been blind until now, and deaf, too; for now I could hear the whispering of scarlet, gauzy insects among the leaves and the constant murmur of growth. All around me was a new and lovely world, so delicate that the wind of my movements tore petals from the flowers, so real and natural that it defied its own impossibility. Awestruck, I turned and turned, running from wall to wall, looking under my old furniture, into my old books; and everywhere I looked I found newer and more beautiful things to wonder at. It was while I was flat on my stomach looking up at the bed springs, where a colony of jewellike lizards had nested, that I first heard the sobbing.

It was young and plaintive, and had no right to be in my room where everything was so happy. I stood up and looked around, and there in the corner crouched the translucent figure of a little girl. She was leaning back against the wall. Her thin legs were crossed in front of her, and she held the leg of a tattered toy elephant dejectedly in one hand and cried into the other. Her hair was long and dark, and it poured and tumbled over her face and shoulders.

I said, "What's the matter, kiddo?" I hate to hear a child cry like that.

She cut herself off in the middle of a sob and shook the hair out of her eyes, looking up and past me, all fright and olive skin and big, filled violet eyes. "Oh!" she squeaked.

I repeated, "What's the matter? Why are you crying?"

She hugged the elephant to her breast defensively, and whimpered, "W-where are you?"

Surprised, I said, "Right here in front of you, child. Can't you see me?"

She shook her head. "I'm scared. Who are you?"

"I'm not going to hurt you. I heard you crying, and I wanted to see if I could help you. Can't you see me at all?"

"No," she whispered. "Are you an angel?"

I guffawed. "By no means!" I stepped closer and put my hand on her shoulder. The hand went right through her and she winced and shrank away, uttering a little wordless cry.

"I'm sorry," I said quickly. "I didn't mean . . . you can't see me at all? I can see you."

She shook her head again. "I think you're a ghost," she said.

"Do tell!" I said. "And what are you?"

"I'm Ginny," she said. "I have to stay here, and I have no one to play with." She blinked, and there was a suspicion of further tears.

"Where did you come from?" I asked.

"I came here with my mother," she said. "We lived in lots of other rooming houses. Mother cleaned floors in office buildings. But this is where I got so sick. I was sick a long time. Then one day I got off the bed and came over here, but then when I looked back I was still on the bed. It was awful funny. Some men came and put the 'me' that was on the bed onto a stretcher-thing and took it—me—out. After a while Mummy left, too. She cried for a long time before she left, and when I called to her she couldn't hear me. She never came back, and I just got to stay here."

"Why?"

"Oh, I got to. I—don't know why. I just—got to."

"What do you do here?"

"I just stay here and think about things. Once a lady lived here, had a little girl just like me. We used to play together until the lady watched us one day. She carried on somethin' awful. She said her little girl was possessed. The girl kept callin' me, 'Ginny! Ginny! Tell Mamma you're here!'; an' I tried, but the lady couldn't see me. Then the lady got scared an' picked up her little girl an' cried, an' so I was sorry. I ran over here an' hid, an' after a while the other little girl forgot about me, I guess. They moved," she finished with pathetic finality.

I was touched. "What will become of you, Ginny?"

"I dunno," she said, and her voice was troubled. "I guess I'll just stay here and wait for Mummy to come back. I been here a long time. I guess I deserve it, too."

"Why, child?"

She looked guiltily at her shoes. "I couldn' stand feelin' so awful bad when I was sick. I got up out of bed before it was time. I shoulda stayed where I was. This is what I get for quittin'. But Mummy'll be back; just you see."

"Sure she will," I muttered. My throat felt tight. "You take it easy, kid. Any time you want someone to talk to, you just pipe up, I'll talk to you any time I'm around."

She smiled, and it was a pretty thing to see. What a raw deal for a kid! I grabbed my hat and went out.

Outside things were the same as in the room to me. The hallways, the dusty stair carpets wore new garments of brilliant, nearly intangible foliage. They were no longer dark, for each leaf had its own pale and different light. Once in a while I saw things not quite so pretty. There was a giggling thing that scuttled back and forth on the third-floor landing. It was a little indistinct, but it looked a great deal like Barrelhead Brogan, a shanty-Irish bum who'd returned from a warehouse robbery a year or so ago, only to shoot himself accidentally with his own gun. I wasn't sorry.

Down on the first floor, on the bottom step, I saw two youngsters sitting. The girl had her head on the boy's shoulder, and he had his arms around her, and I could see the banister through them. I stopped to listen. There voices were faint, and seemed to come from a long way away.

He said, "There's one way out."

She said, "Don't talk that way, Tommy!"

"What else can we do? I've loved you for three years, and we still can't get married. No money, no hope—no nothing. Sue, if we did do it, I just *know* we'd always be together. Always and always—"

After a long time she said, "All right, Tommy. You get a gun, like you said." She suddenly pulled him even closer. "Oh, Tommy, are you sure we'll always be together just like this?"

"Always," he whispered, and kissed her. "Just like this."

Then there was a long silence, while neither moved. Suddenly they were as I had first seen them, and he said:

"There's only one way out."

And she said, "Don't talk that way, Tommy!"

And he said, "What else can we do? I've loved you for three years—" It went on like that, over and over and over.

I felt lousy. I went on out into the street.

It began to filter through to me what had happened. The man in the shop had called it a "talent." I couldn't be crazy, could I? I didn't *feel* crazy. The draught from the bottle had opened my eyes on a new world. What was this world?

It was a thing peopled by ghosts. There they were—storybook ghosts, and regular haunts, and poor damned souls—all the fixings of a storied supernatural, all the things we have heard about and loudly disbelieve and secretly wonder about. So what? What had it all to do with me?

As the days slid by, I wondered less about my new, strange surroundings, and gave more and more thought to that question. I had bought—or been given—a talent. I could see ghosts. I could see all parts of a ghostly world, even the vegetation that grew in it. That was perfectly reasonable—the trees and birds and fungi and flowers. A ghost world is a world as we know it, and a world as we know it must have vegetation. Yes, I could see them. But they couldn't see me!

O.K.; what could I get out of it? I couldn't talk about it or write about it because I wouldn't be believed; and besides, I had this thing exclusive, as far as I knew; why cut a lot of other people in on it?

On what, though?

No, unless I could get a steer from somewhere, there was no percentage in it for me that I could see. And then, about six days after I took that eye-opener, I remembered the one place where I might get that steer.

The Shottle Bop!

I was on Sixth Avenue at the time, trying to find something in a five-and-dimie that Ginny might like. She couldn't touch anything I brought her but she enjoyed things she could look at—picture books and such. By getting her a little book of photographs of trains since the "De Witt Clinton," and asking her which of them was like ones she had seen, I found out approximately how long it was she'd been there. Nearly eighteen years. Anyway, I got my bright idea and headed for Tenth Avenue and the Shottle Bop. I'd ask that old man—he'd tell me.

At the corner of Ninth Avenue I bumped into Happy Sam Healy and Fred Bellew. Fred was good people, but I never had much use for Happy Sam. He went for shaggy hats and lapelled vests, and he had patent-leather hair and too much collar-ad good looks. I was in a hurry and didn't want to talk to anyone, but Sam grabbed me by the arm.

"Slow down, mug, slow down! Long time no see. Where you bound in such a hurry?"

"Going over to Tenth to see a man about you."

Sam quit grinning and Fred walked over. "Why can't you guys quit knocking each other?" he asked quietly.

If it weren't for Fred, Sam and I would have crossed bows even more than we did, which was still altogether too much.

"I'll always speak civilly to a human being," I said. "Sam's different."

Sam said, "Don't set yourself up, chum. I'm cutting some ice with a certain party that froze you out."

"If you say exactly what you mean, I'll probably rap you for it," I flared.

Fred pushed hastily between us. "I'll see you later, Sam," he said. He pushed me with some difficulty away from the scene.

Sam stood staring after us for a minute and then put his hands in his pockets, shrugged, grinned, and went jauntily his own way.

"Aw, why do you always stand in front of that heel when I want to scrape him off the sidewalk?" I complained.

"Calm down, you big lug," Fred grinned. "That bantam wants trouble with you because of Audrey. If you mess him up, he'll go running to her about it, and you'll be really out."

"I am already, so what?"

He glanced at me. "That's up to you." Then, seeing my face, he said quickly, "O.K., don't tell me. It's none of my business. I know. How've you been?"

I was quiet for a while, walking along. Fred was a darn good egg. You could tell a guy like that practically anything. Finally, I said, "I'm looking for a job, Fred."

He nodded. "Thought you would. Doing what?" Anybody else, knowing me, would have hooted and howled.

"Well, I—" Oh, what the hell, I thought, I'll tell him. If he thinks I'm nuts, he won't say so to anyone but me. Old Fred didn't look like much, with his sandy hair and his rimless specs and those stooped shoulders that too much book reading gave him, but he had sense.

"I was walking down Tenth," I began—

By the time I had come to the part about the ghost of the kid in my room, we had reached Tenth Avenue in the late Twenties, and turned south. I wasn't paying much attention to where we were, to tell you the truth, and that's why what happened did happen.

Before I had a chance to wind up with the question that was bothering me—"I have it . . . what will I do with it?" Fred broke in with "Hey! Where is this place of yours?"

"Why—between Nineteenth and Twentieth," I said. "Holy smoke—we're at Eighteenth! We walked right past it!"

Fred grinned and swung around. We went back up the avenue with our eyes peeled, and not a sign of the Shottle Bop did we see. For the first time a doubtful look crept onto Fred's bland face. He said:

"You wouldn't kid me, would you, lug?"

"I tell you—" I began.

Then I saw a penny lying on the sidewalk. I bent to pick it up, and heard him say, "Hey! There it is! Come on."

"Ah! I knew it was on this block!" I said, and turned toward Fred. Or where Fred had been. Facing me was a blank wall. The whole side of the block was void of people. There was no sign of a shop or of Fred Bellew.

I stood there for a full two minutes not even daring to think. Then I walked downtown toward Twentieth, and then uptown to Twenty-first. Then I did it again. No shop. No Bellew.

I stood frothing on the uptown corner. What had that guy done; hopped a passing truck or sunk into the ground or vanished into the shop? Yeah; and no shop there! A wise guy after all. I trod the beat once more with the same results. Then I headed for home. I hadn't gone twenty feet when I heard the pound of someone running, and Fred came panting up and caught my shoulder. We both yelped at once—"Hey! Where've you been?"

I said, "What was the idea of ducking out like that? Man, you must've covered a hundred yards in about six seconds to get away from me while I picked up a penny off the sidewalk!"

"Duck out nothing!" said Bellow, angrier than I'd ever seen him. "I saw the store and went in. I thought you were right behind me. I look around and you're outside, staring at the shop like it was something you didn't believe. Then you walk off. Meanwhile the little guy in the store tries to sell me some of his goods. I stall him off, still looking for you. You walk past two or three times, looking in the window. I call you; you don't bat an eyelash. I tell the little guy: 'Hold on—I'll be back in a second with my friend there.' He rears back on his heels and laughs like a maniac and waves me out. Come on, dope. Let's go back. That old man really has something there. I'd say I was in the market for some of that stuff of his!"

"O.K., O.K.," I said. "But Fred—I'll swear I didn't see the place. Come on then; lead me to it. I must be going really screwball."

"Seems like," said Fred.

So we went back, and there was no shop at all. Not a sign of one. And then and there we had one pip of an argument. He said I'd lied about it in the first place, and I said, well, why did he give me that song-and-dance about his seeing it, and he said it was some kind of a joke I'd pulled on him; and then we both said, "Oh yeah?" a couple of times and began to throw punches. I broke his glasses for him. He had them in his pocket and fell down on them. I wound up minus a very good friend and without my question answered—what was I going to do with this "talent?"

I was talking to Ginny one afternoon about this and that when a human leg, from the knee down, complete and puffy, drifted between us. I recoiled in horror, but Ginny pushed it gently with one hand. It bent under the touch, and started toward the window, which was open a little at the bottom. The leg floated toward the crack and was sucked through like a cloud of cigarette smoke, reforming again on the other side. It bumbled against the pane for a moment and then balooned away.

"My gosh!" I breathed. "What *was* that?"

Ginny laughed. "Oh, just one of the Things that's all 'e time flying around. Did it scare you? I used to be scared, but I saw so many of them that I don't care any more, so's they don't light on me."

"But what in the name of all that's disgusting are they?"

"Parts." Ginny was all childish savoir-faire.

"Parts of what?"

"People, silly. It's some kind of a game, *I* think. You see, if someone gets hurt and loses something—a finger or an ear or something, why, the ear—the *inside* part of it, I mean, like me being the inside of the 'me' they carried out of here—it goes back to where the person who owned it lived last. Then it goes back to the place before that, and so on. It doesn't go very fast. Then when something happens to a whole person, the 'inside' part comes looking for the rest of itself. It picks up bit after bit—Look!" She put out a filmy forefinger and thumb and nipped a flake of gossamer out of the air.

I leaned over and looked closely; it was a small section of semitransparent human skin, ridged and whorled.

"Somebody must have cut his finger," said Ginny matter-of-factly, "while he was living in this room. When something happens to um—you see! He'll be back for it!"

"Good heavens!" I said. "Does this happen to everyone?"

"I dunno. Some people have to stay where they are—like me. But I guess if you haven't done nothing to deserve bein' kept in one place, you have to come all around pickin' up what you lost."

I'd thought of more pleasant things in my time.

For several days I'd noticed a gray ghost hovering up and down the block. He was always on the street, never inside.

He whimpered constantly. He was—or had been—a little inoffensive man of the bowler hat and starched collar type. He paid no attention to me—non of them did, for I was apparently invisible to them. But I saw him so often that pretty soon I realized that I'd miss him if he went away. I decided I'd chat with him the next time I saw him.

I left the house one morning and stood around for a few minutes in front of the brownstone steps. Sure enough, pressing through the flotsam of my new, weird coexistent world, came the slim figure of the wraith I had noticed, his rabbit face screwed up, his eyes deep and sad, and his swallowtail coat and striped waistcoat immaculate. I stepped up behind him and said, "Hi!"

He started violently and would have run away, I'm sure, if he'd known where my voice was coming from.

"Take it easy, pal," I said. "I won't hurt you."

"Who are you?"

"You wouldn't know if I told you," I said. "Now stop shivering and tell me about yourself."

He mopped his ghostly face with a ghostly handkerchief, and then began fumbling nervously with a gold toothpick. "My word," he said. "No one's talked to me for years. I'm not quite myself, you see."

"I see," I said. "Well, take it easy. I just happen to've noticed you wandering around here lately. I got curious. You looking for somebody?"

"Oh, no," he said. Now that he had a chance to talk about his troubles, he forgot to be afraid of this mysterious voice from nowhere that had accosted him. "I'm looking for my home."

"Hm-m-m," I said. "Been looking a long time?"

"Oh, yes." His nose twitched. "I left for work one morning a long time ago, and when I got off the ferry at Battery Place I stopped for a moment to watch the work on that new-fangled elevated railroad they were building down there. All of a sudden there was a loud noise—my goodness! It was terrible—and the next thing I knew I was standing back from the curb and looking at a man who looked just like me! A girder had fallen, and—my word!" He mopped his face again. "Since then I have been looking and looking. I can't seem to find anyone who knows where I might have lived, and I don't understand all the things I see floating around me, and I never thought I'd see the day when grass would grow on lower Broadway—oh, it's terrible." He began to cry.

I felt sorry for him. I could easily see what had happened. The shock was so great that even his ghost had amnesia! Poor little egg—until he was whole, he could find no rest. The thing interested me. Would a ghost react to the usual cures for amnesia? If so, then what would happen to him?

"You say you got off a ferryboat?"

"Yes."

"Then you must have lived on the Island . . . Staten Island, over there across the bay!"

"You really think so?" He stared through me, puzzled and hopeful.

"Why sure! Say, how'd you like me to take you over there? Maybe we could find your house."

"Oh, that would be splendid! But—oh, my, what will my wife say?"

I grinned. "She might want to know where you've been. Anyway, she'll be glad to have you back, I imagine. Come on; let's get going!"

I gave him a shove in the direction of the subway and strolled down behind him. Once in a while I got a stare from a passerby for walking with one hand out in front of me and talking into thin air. It didn't bother me very much. My companion, though, was very self-conscious about it, for the inhabitants of his world screeched and giggled when they saw him doing practically the same thing. Of all humans, only I was invisible to them, and the little ghost in the bowler hat blushed from embarrassment until I thought he'd burst.

We hopped a subway—it was a new experience for him, I gathered—and went down to South Ferry. The subway system in New York is a very unpleasant place to one gifted as I was. Everything that enjoys lurking in the dark hangs out there, and there is quite a crop of dismembered human remains. After this day I took the bus.

We got a ferry without waiting. The little gray ghost got a real kick out of the trip. He asked me about the ships in the harbor and their flags, and marveled at the dearth of sailing vessels. He *tsk, tsked* at the Statue of Liberty; the last time he had seen it, he said, was while it still had its original brassy gold color, before it got its patina. By this I placed him in the late '70s; he must have been looking for his home for over sixty years!

We landed at the Island, and from there I gave him his head. At the top of Fort Hill he suddenly said, "My name is John Quigg. I live at 45 Fourth Avenue!" I've never seen anyone quite so delighted as he was by the discovery. And from then on it was easy. He turned left, and then right, and then left again, straight down for two blocks and again right. I noticed—he didn't—that the street was marked "Winter Avenue." I remembered vaguely that the streets in this section had been numbered years ago.

He trotted briskly up the hill and then suddenly stopped and turned vaguely. "I say, are you still with me?"

"Still here," I said.

"I'm all right now. I can't tell you how much I appreciate this. Is there anything I could do for you?"

I considered. "Hardly. We're of different times, you know. Things change."

He looked, a little pathetically, at the new apartment house on the corner and nodded. "I think I know what happened to me," he said softly. "But I guess it's all right. . . . I made a will, and the kids were grown." He sighed. "But if it hadn't been for you I'd still be wandering around Manhattan. Let's see—ah; come with me!"

He suddenly broke into a run. I followed as quickly as I could. Almost at the top of the hill was a huge old shingled house, with a silly cupola and a complete lack of paint. It was dirty and it was tumble-down, and at the sight of it the little fellow's face twisted sadly. He gulped and turned through a gap in the hedge and down beside the house. Casting about in the long grass, he spotted a boulder sunk deep into the turf.

"This is it," he said. "Just you dig under that. There is no mention of it in my will, except a small fund to keep paying the box rent. Yes, a safety-deposit box, and the key and an authorization are under that stone. I hid it"—he giggled—"from my wife one night, and never did get a chance to tell her. You can have whatever's any good to you." He turned to the house, squared his shoulders, and marched in the side door, which banged open for him in a convenient gust of wind. I listened for a moment and then smiled at the tirade that burst forth. Old Quigg was catching real hell from his wife, who'd sat waiting for over sixty years for him! It was a bitter stream of invective, but—well, she must have loved him. She couldn't leave the place until she was complete, if Ginny's theory was correct, and she wasn't really complete until her husband came home! It tickled me. They'd be all right now!

I found an old pinchbar in the drive and attacked the

ground around the stone. It took quite a while and made my hands bleed, but after a while I pried the stone up and was able to scrabble around under it. Sure enough, there was an oiled silk pouch under there. I caught it up and carefully unwrapped the strings around it. Inside was a key and letter addressed to a New York bank, designating only "Bearer" and authorizing use of the key. I laughed aloud. Little old meek and mild John Quigg, I'd bet, had set aside some "mad money." With a layout like that, a man could take a powder without leaving a single sign. The son-of-a-gun! I would never know just what it was he had up his sleeve, but I'll bet there was a woman in the case. Even fixed it up with his will! Ah, well—I should kick!

It didn't take me long to get over to the bank. I had a little trouble getting into the vaults, because it took quite a while to look up the box in the old records. But I finally cleared the red tape, and found myself the proud possessor of just under eight thousand bucks in small bills—and not a yellowback among 'em!

Well, from then on I was pretty well set. What did I do? Well, first I bought clothes, and then I started out to cut ice for myself. I clubbed around a bit and got to know a lot of people, and the more I knew the more I realized what a lot of superstitious dopes they were. I couldn't blame anyone for skirting a ladder under which crouched a genuine basilisk, of course, but what the heck—not one in a thousand have beasts under them! Anyway, my question was answered. I dropped two grand on an elegant office with drapes and dim indirect lighting, and I got a phone installed and a little quiet sign on the door—Psychic Consultant. And, boy, I did all right.

My customers were mostly upper crust, because I came high. It was generally no trouble to get contact with people's dead relatives, which was usually what they wanted. Most ghosts are crazy to get in contact with this world anyway. That's one of the reasons that almost anyone can become a medium of sorts if he tries hard enough; Lord knows that it doesn't take much to contact the average ghost. Some, of course, were not available. If a man leads a pretty square life, and kicks off leaving no loose ends, he gets clear. I never did find out where these clear spirits went to. All I knew was that they weren't to be contacted. But the vast majority of people have to go back and tie up those loose ends after they die—righting a little wrong here, helping someone they've hindered, cleaning up a bit of dirty work. That's where luck itself comes from, I do believe. You don't get something for nothing.

If you get a nice break, it's been arranged that way by someone who did you dirt in the past, or someone who did wrong to your father or your grandfather or your great uncle Julius. Everything evens up in the long run, and until it does, some poor damned soul is wandering around the earth trying to do something about it. Half of humanity is walking around crabbing about its tough breaks. If you and you and you only knew what dozens of powers were begging for the chance to help you if you'll let them! And if you let them, you'll help clear up the mess they've made of their lives here, and free them to go wherever it is they go when they're cleaned up. Next time you're in a jam, go away somewhere by yourself and open your mind to these folks. They'll cut in and guide you all right, if you can drop your smugness and your mistaken confidence in your own judgment.

I had a couple of ghostly stooges to run errands for me. One of them, an ex-murderer by the name of One-eye Rachuba, was the fastest spook ever I saw, when it came to locating a wanted ancestor; and then there was Professor Grafe, a frog-faced teacher of social science who'd embezzled from a charity fund and fallen into the Hudson trying to make a getaway. He could trace the most devious genealogies in mere seconds, and deduce the most likely whereabouts of the ghost of a missing relative. The pair of them were all the office force I could use, and although every time they helped out one of my clients they came closer to freedom for themselves, they were both so entangled with their own sloppy lives that I was sure of their services for years.

But do you think I'd be satisfied to stay where I was, making money hand over fist without really working for it? Oh, no. Not me. No, I had to bigtime. I had to brood over the events of the last few months, and I had to get dramatic about that screwball Audrey, who really wasn't worth my trouble. I had to lie awake nights thinking about Happy Sam and his gibes. It wasn't enough that I'd proved Audrey wrong when she said I'd never amount to anything. I wasn't happy when I thought about Sam and the eighteen a week he pulled down driving a light delivery truck. Uh-huh. I had to show them up.

I even remembered what the little man in the Shottle Bop had said to me about using my "talent" for bragging or for revenge. That didn't make any difference to me. I figured I had the edge on everyone, everything. Cocky, I was. Why, I could send one of my ghostly stooges out any time and find out exactly what anyone had been doing three hours ago come Michaelmas. With the shade of the professor at my shoulder, I could back-track on any far-fetched statement and give immediate and logical reasons for back-tracking. No one had anything on me, and I could out-talk, out-maneuver, and out-smart anyone on earth. I was really quite a feller. I began to think, "What's the use of my doing as well as this when the gang on the West Side don't know anything about it?" and "Man, would that half-wit Happy Sam burn up if he saw me drifting down Broadway in my new eight-thousand-dollar roadster!" and "To think I used to waste my time and tears on a dope like Audrey!" In other words, I was tripping up on an inferiority complex. I acted like a veridam fool, which I was. I went over to the West Side.

It was a chilly, late winter night. I'd taken a lot of trouble to dress myself and my car so we'd be bright and shining and would knock some eyes out. Pity I couldn't brighten my brains up a little.

I drove up in front of Casey's pool room, being careful to do it too fast, and concentrating on shrieks from the tires and a shuddering twenty-four-cylinder roar from the engine before I cut the switch. I didn't hurry to get out of the car, either. Just leaned back and lit a fifty-cent cigar, and then tipped my hat over one ear and touched the horn button, causing it to play "Tuxedo Junction" for forty-eight seconds. Then I looked over toward the pool hall.

Well, for a minute I thought that I shouldn't have come, if that was the effect my return to the fold was going to have. And from then on I forgot about anything except how to get out of here.

There were two figures slouched in the glowing doorway of the pool room. It was up a small side street, so short that the city had depended on the place, and old institution, to supply the street lighting. Looking carefully, I made out one of the silhouetted figures as Happy Sam, and the other was Fred Bellew. They just looked out at me; they didn't move; they didn't say anything, and when I said, "Hiya, small fry— remember me?" I noticed that along the darkened walls flanking the bright doorway were ranked the whole crowd of them—the whole gang. It was a shock; it was a little too casually perfect. I didn't like it.

"Hi," said Fred quietly. I knew he wouldn't like the big-timing. I didn't expect any of them to like it, of course, but Fred's dislike sprang from distaste, and the others' from resentment, and for the first time I felt a little cheap. I climbed out over the door of the roadster and let them have a gander at my fine feathers.

Sam snorted and said, "Jellybean!" very clearly. Someone else giggled, and from the darkness beside the building came a high-pitched, "Woo-woo!"

I walked up to Sam and grinned at him. I didn't feel like grinning. "I ain't seen you in so long I almost forgot what a heel you were," I said. "How you making?"

"I'm doing all right," he said, and added offensively, "I'm still *working* for a living."

The murmur that ran through the crowd told me that the really smart thing to do was to get back into that shiny new automobile and hoot along out of there. I stayed.

"Wise, huh?" I said weakly.

They'd been drinking, I realized—all of them. I was suddenly in a spot. Sam put his hands in his pockets and looked at me down his nose. He was the only short man that ever could do that to me. After a thick silence he said:

"Better get back to yer crystal balls, phony. We like guys that sweat. We even like guys that have rackets, if they run them because they're smarter or tougher than the next one. But luck and gab ain't enough. Scram."

I looked around helplessly. I was getting what I'd begged for. What had I expected, anyway? Had I thought that these boys would crowd around and shake my hand off for acting this way? There was something missing somewhere, and when I realized what it was, it hit me. Fred Bellew—he was just standing there saying nothing. The old equalizer wasn't functioning any more. Fred wasn't aiming to stop any trouble between me and Sam. I was never so alone in my life!

They hardly moved, but they were all around me suddenly. If I couldn't think of something quickly, I was going to be mobbed. And when those mugs started mobbing a man, they did it up just fine. I drew a deep breath.

"I'm not asking for anything from you, Sam. Nothing; that means advice, see?"

"You're gettin' it!" he flared. "You and your seeanses. We heard about you. Hanging up widow-women for fifty bucks a throw to talk to their 'dear departed'! P-sykik investigator! With a line! Go on; beat it!"

I had a leg to stand on now. "A phony, huh? Why you

gabby Irishman, I'll bet I could put a haunt on you that would make that hair of yours stand up on end, if you have guts enough to go where I tell you to."

"You'll bet? That's a laugh. Listen at that, gang." He laughed, then turned to me and talked through one side of his mouth. "All right, you wanted it. Come on, rich guy; you're called. Fred'll hold the stakes. How about ten of your lousy bucks for every one of mine? Here, Fred—hold this sawbuck."

"I'll give you twenty to one," I said half hysterically. "And I'll take you to a place where you'll run up against the home-liest, plumb-meanest old haunt you ever heard of."

The crowd roared. Sam laughed with them, but didn't try to back out. With any of that gang, a bet was a bet. He'd taken me up, and he'd set odds, and he was bound. I just nodded and put two century notes into Fred Bellew's hand. Fred and Sam climbed into the car, and just as we started, Sam leaned out and waved.

"See you in hell, fellas," he said. "I'm goin' to raise me a ghost, and one of us is going to scare the other one to death!"

I honked my horn to drown out the whooping and hollering from the sidewalk and got out of there. I turned up the parkway and headed out of town.

"Where to?" Fred asked after a while.

"Stick around," I said, not knowing.

There must be some place not far from here where I could find an honest-to-God haunt, I thought, one that would make Sam back-track and set me up with the boys again. I opened the compartment in the dashboard and let Ikey out. Ikey was a little twisted imp who'd got his tail caught in between two sheets of steel when they were assembling the car, and had to stay there until it was junked.

"Hey, Ike," I whispered. He looked up, the gleam of the compartment light shining redly in his bright little eyes. "Whistle for the professor, will you? I don't want to yell for him because those mugs in the back seat will hear me. They can't hear you."

"O.K., boss," he said; and putting his fingers to his lips, he gave vent to a blood-curdling, howling scream.

That was the prof's call-letters, as it were. The old man flew ahead of the car, circled around and slid in beside me through the window, which I'd opened a crack for him.

"My goodness," he panted, "I wish you wouldn't summon me to a location which is traveling with this high degree of celerity. It was all I could do to catch up with you."

"Don't give me that, professor," I whispered. "You can catch a stratoliner if you want to. Say, I have a guy in the back who wants to get a real scare from a ghost. Know of any around here?"

The professor put on his ghostly pince-nez. "Why, yes. Remember my telling you about the Wolfmeyer place?"

"Golly—he's bad."

"He'll serve your purpose admirably. But don't ask me to go there with you, None of us ever associates with Wolfmeyer. And for Heaven's sake, be careful."

"I guess I can handle him. Where is it?"

He gave me explicit directions, bade me good night and left. I was a little surprised; the professor traveled around with me a great deal, and I'd never seen him refuse a chance to see some new scenery. I shrugged it off and went my way. I guess I just didn't know any better.

I headed out of town and into the country to a certain old farmhouse. Wolfmeyer, a Pennsylvania Dutchman, had hanged himself there. He had been, and was, a bad egg. Instead of being a nice guy about it all, he was the rebel type. He knew perfectly well that unless he did plenty of good to make up for the evil, he'd be stuck where he was for the rest of eternity. That didn't seem to bother him at all. He got surly and became a really bad spook. Eight people had died in that house since the old man rotted off his own rope. Three of them were tenants who had rented the place, and three were hobos, and two were psychic investigators. They'd all hanged themselves. That's the way Wolfmeyer worked. I think he really enjoyed haunting. He certainly was thorough about it anyway.

I didn't want to do any real harm to Happy Sam. I just wanted to teach him a lesson. And look what happened!

We reached the place just before midnight. No one had said much, except that I told Fred and Sam about Wolfmeyer, and pretty well what was to be expected from him. They did a good deal of laughing about it, so I just shut up and drove. The next item of conversation was Fred's, when he made the terms of the bet. To win, Sam was to stay in the house until dawn. He wasn't to call for help and he wasn't to leave. He had to bring in a coil of rope, tie a noose in one end and string the other up on "Wolfmeyer's Beam"—the great oaken beam on which the old man had hung himself, and eight others after him. This was as an added temptation to Wolfmeyer to work on Happy Sam, and

was my idea. I was to go in with Sam, to watch him in case
the thing became dangerous. Fred was to stay in the car a
hundred yards down the road and wait.

I parked the car at the agreed distance and Sam and I got
out. Sam had my tow rope over his shoulder, already noosed.
Fred had quieted down considerably, and his face was dead
serious.

"I don't think I like this," he said, looking up the road at
the house. It hunched back from the highway, and looked
like a malign being deep in thought.

I said, "Well, Sam? Want to pay up now and call it quits?"

He followed Fred's gaze. It sure was a dreary-looking
place, and his liquor had fizzed away. He thought a minute,
then shrugged and grinned. I had to admire the rat. "Hell, I'll
go through with it. Can't bluff me with scenery, phony."

Surprisingly, Fred piped up, "I don't think he's a phony,
Sam. He showed me something one day, over on Tenth Avenue. A little store. There was something funny about it. We
had a little scrap afterward, and I was sore for a long time,
but—I think he has something there."

The resistance made Sam stubborn, though I could see by
his face that he knew better. "Come on, phony," he said and
swung up the road.

We climbed into the house by way of a cellar door that
slanted up to a window on the first floor. I hauled out a flash-
light and lit the way to the beam. It was only one of many
that delighted in turning the sound of one's footsteps into
laughing whispers that ran round and round the rooms and
halls and would not die. Under the famous beam the dusty
floor was dark-stained.

I gave Sam a hand in fixing the rope, and then clicked
off the light. It must have been tough on him then. I didn't
mind, because I knew I could see anything before it got to
me, and even then, no ghost could see me. Not only that, for
me the walls and floors and ceilings were lit with the phos-
phorescent many-hued glow of the ever-present ghost plants.
For its eerie effect I wished Sam could see the ghost-molds
feeding greedily on the stain under the beam.

Sam was already breathing heavily, but I knew it would
take more than just darkness and silence to get his goat. He'd
have to be alone, and then he'd have to have a visitor or so.

"So long, kid," I said, slapping him on the shoulder; and I
turned and walked out of the room.

I let him hear me go out of the house and then I crept

silently back. It was without doubt the most deserted place I have ever seen. Even ghosts kept away from it, excepting, of course, Wolfmeyer's. There was just the luxurous vegetation, invisible to all but me, and the deep silence rippled by Sam's breath. After ten minutes or so I knew for certain that Happy Sam had more guts than I'd ever have credited him with. He had to be scared. He couldn't—or wouldn't—scare himself.

I crouched down against the wall of an adjoining room and made myself comfortable. I figured Wolfmeyer would be along pretty soon. I hoped earnestly that I could stop the thing before it got too far. No use in making this any more than a good lesson for a wiseacre. I was feeling pretty smug about it all, and I was totally unprepared for what happened.

I was looking toward the doorway opposite when I realized that for some minutes there had been the palest of pale glows there. It brightened as I watched; brightened and flickered gently. It was green, the green of things moldy and rotting away; and with it came a subtly harrowing stench. It was the smell of flesh so very dead that it had ceased to be really odorous. It was utterly horrible, and I was honestly scared out of my wits. It was some moments before the comforting thought of my invulnerability came back to me, and I shrank lower and closer to the wall and watched.

And Wolfmeyer came in.

His was the ghost of an old, old man. He wore a flowing, filthy robe, and his bare forearms thrust out in front of him were stringy and strong. His head, with its tangled hair and beard, quivered on a broken, ruined neck like the blade of a knife just thrown into soft wood. Each slow step as he crossed the room set his head to quivering again. His eyes were alight; red they were, with deep green flames buried in them. His canine teeth had lengthened into yellow, blunt tusks, and they were like pillars supporting his crooked grin. The putrescent green glow was a horrid halo about him. He was a bright and evil thing.

He passed me, completely unconscious of my presence, and paused at the door of the room where Sam waited by the rope. He stood just outside it, his claws extended, the quivering of his head slowly dying. He stared in at Sam, and suddenly opened his mouth and howled. It was a quiet, deadly sound, one that might have come from the throat of a distant dog, but, though I couldn't see into the other room, I knew that Sam had jerked his head around and was staring at the ghost. Wolfmeyer raised his arms a trifle, seemed to totter a bit, and then moved into the room.

I snapped myself out of the crawling terror that gripped me and scrambled to my feet. If I didn't move fast—

Tiptoeing swiftly to the door, I stopped just long enough to see Wolfmeyer beating his arms about erratically over his head, a movement that made his robe flutter and his whole figure pulsate in the green light; just long enough to see Sam on his feet, wide-eyed, staggering back and back toward the rope. He clutched his throat and opened his mouth and made no sound, and his head tilted, his neck bent, his twisted face gaped at the ceiling as he clumped backward away from the ghost and into the ready noose. And then I leaned over Wolfmeyer's shoulder, put my lips to his ear, and said: *"Boo!"*

I almost laughed. Wolfmeyer gave a little squeak, jumped about ten feet, and, without stopping to look around, high-tailed out of the room so fast that he was just a blur. That was one scared old spook!

At the same time Happy Sam straightened, his face relaxed and relieved, and sat down with a bump under the noose. That was as close a thing as ever I want to see. He sat there, his face soaking wet with cold sweat, his hands between his knees, staring limply at his feet.

"That'll show you!" I exulted, and walked over to him. "Pay up, scum, and may you starve for that week's pay!" He didn't move. I guess he was plenty shocked.

"Come on!" I said, "Pull yourself together, man! Haven't you seen enough? That old fellow will be back any second now. On your feet!"

He didn't move.

"Sam!"

He didn't move.

"Sam!" I clutched at his shoulder. He pitched over sideways and lay still.

He was quite dead.

I didn't do anything and for a while I didn't say anything. Then I said hopelessly, as I knelt there. "Aw, Sam. Sam—cut it out, fella."

After a minute I rose slowly and started for the door. I'd taken three steps when I stopped. Something was happening! I rubbed my hand over my eyes. Yes, it—it was getting dark! The vague luminescence of the vines and flowers of the ghost-world was getting dimmer, fading, fading—

But that had never happened before!

No difference. I told myself desperately, it's happening now, all right. *I got to get out of here!*

See? You see? It was the stuff—that damn stuff from the Shottle Bop. It was wearing off! When Sam died it . . . it stopped working on me! Was this what I had to pay for the bottle? Was this what was to happen if I used it for revenge?

The light was almost gone—and now it was gone. I couldn't see a thing in the room but one of the doors. Why could I see that doorway? What was that pale-green light that set off its dusty frame?

Wolfmeyer!

I got to get out of here!

I couldn't see ghosts any more. Ghosts could see me now. I ran. I darted across the dark room and smashed into the wall on the other side. I reeled back from it, blood spouting from between the fingers I slapped to my face. I ran again. Another wall clubbed me. Where was that other door? I ran again, and again struck a wall. I screamed and ran again. I tripped over Sam's body. My head went through the noose. It whipped down on my windpipe, and my neck broke with an agonizing crunch. I floundered there for half a minute, and then dangled.

Dead as hell, I was. Wolfmeyer, he laughed and laughed.

Fred found me and Sam in the morning. He took our bodies away in the car. Now I've got to stay here and haunt this damn old house. Me and Wolfmeyer.

THE ROCKET OF 1955

April

by C. M. Kornbluth (1923-1958)

*C. M. Kornbluth was a member of the legend-
ary Futurians, that group of New York kids who
were in at the beginning of fandom and from
whose ranks came many of the major writers and
editors in the field. Kornbluth's solo stories were often grim, reflecting his personality and generally
cynical attitude toward the world as he saw it. His
collaborations with Frederik Pohl have become
classics, but he was a very important individual
voice in science fiction, and he has never really
been replaced.*

*The short-short is one of the most difficult of
literary forms, but not for Cyril Kornbluth*

(I'm sure that Marty never met Cyril Kornbluth, who died
of a heart attack at a tragically young age, but I did. He was,
I believe, the youngest of the Futurians, three years younger
than myself so that he was only fifteen when the organization
was born with both him and myself as members. He was also
perhaps the most brilliant of us all—but erratically and
morosely brilliant. Of us all, he was closest to Fred Pohl. To
me, he was never close at all. As I look back at it, I think he
never liked me: because, I think, I was loud and cheerful and
so self-centered that I never noticed he never liked me. After
he died and I worked it out, I felt bad that I had made no effort to make him like me better, but, of course, it was too
late—I.A.)

The scheme was all Fein's, but the trimmings that made it
more than a pipe dream and its actual operation depended on
me. How long the plan had been in incubation I do not
know, but Fein, one spring day, broke it to me in crude

form. I pointed out some errors, corrected and amplified on the thing in general, and told him that I'd have no part of it—and changed my mind when he threatened to reveal certain indiscretions committed by me some years ago.

It was necessary that I spend some months in Europe, conducting research work incidental to the scheme. I returned with recorded statements, old newspapers, and photostatic copies of certain documents. There was a brief, quiet interview with that old, bushy-haired Viennese worshipped incontinently by the mob; he was convinced by the evidence I had compiled that it would be wise to assist us.

You all know what happened next—it was the professor's historic radio broadcast. Fein had drafted the thing, I had rewritten it, and told the astronomer to assume a German accent while reading. Some of the phrases were beautiful: "American dominion over the very planets! . . . veil at last ripped aside . . . man defies gravity . . . travel through limitless space . . . plant the red-white-and-blue banner in the soil of Mars!"

The requested contributions poured in. Newspapers and magazines ostentatiously donated yard-long checks of a few thousand dollars; the government gave a welcome half-million; heavy sugar came from the "Rocket Contribution Week" held in the nation's public schools; but independent contributions were the largest. We cleared seven million dollars, and then started to build the spaceship.

The virginium that took up most of the money was tin plate; the monoatomic fluorine that gave us our terrific speed was hydrogen. The takeoff was a party for the newsreels: the big, gleaming bullet extravagant with vanes and projections; speeches by the professor; Farley, who was to fly it to Mars, grinning into the cameras. He climbed an outside ladder to the nose of the thing, then dropped into the steering compartment. I screwed down the soundproof door, smiling as he hammered to be let out. To his surprise, there was no duplicate of the elaborate dummy controls he had been practicing on for the past few weeks.

I cautioned the pressmen to stand back under the shelter, and gave the professor the knife switch that would send the rocket on its way. He hesitated too long—Fein hissed into his ear: "Anna Pareloff of Cracow, Herr Professor . . ."

The triple blade clicked into the sockets. The vaned projectile roared a hundred yards into the air with a wobbling curve—then exploded.

A photographer, eager for an angle shot, was killed; so

were some kids. The steel roof protected the rest of us. Fein and I shook hands, while the pressmen screamed into the telephones which we had provided.

But the professor got drunk, and, disgusted with the part he had played in the affair, told all and poisoned himself. Fein and I left the cash behind and hopped a freight. We were picked off it by a vigilance committee (headed by a man who had lost fifty cents in our rocket). Fein was too frightened to talk or write so they hanged him first, and gave me a paper and pencil to tell the story as best I could.

Here they come, with an insulting thick rope.

THEY

Unknown
April

by Robert A. Heinlein

Robert Heinlein's popularity and skill as a science-fiction writer has obscured his real talent and feel for fantasy. "They" is a stunning accomplishment and one of his finest efforts. It is a story in the tradition of Robert Sheckley and Philip K. Dick before there was one.

(Do you know what "solipsism" is? Any person with a spark of introversion has gone through a period of solipsism and wondered what he (or she) was and how it had happened that he (or she) was *the* living thing for whom the whole illusion had been created. Generally, as one grows up and becomes involved with the world, one forgets, unless one is "paranoid" in the morbid sense. Well Bob Heinlein has here written the classical tale of solipsism. It can never be done again, and no one who has read this would even dream of trying.—I.A.)

EVOLUTION'S END

Thrilling Wonder Stories
April

by Robert Arthur (1909-1969)

Robert Arthur (born Robert A. Feder) became a well known Hollywood screenwriter, but he was also a talented (and sadly neglected) author of mystery, fantasy, and science fiction, whose "Murchison Morks" series in Argosy *had a devoted following. He was also a neglected editor who "ghosted" several of the books credited to Alfred Hitchcock and (under his own name) edited the excellent anthology* Davy Jones' Haunted Locker *(1965). Unfortunately, his best short fiction has never been collected.*

"Evolution's End" addresses several profound questions, including The Purpose of Man and The Future of Mankind. It also happens to be one of the very best stories of 1941.

(Such is science fiction these days that its stars, and even a number of its second-raters, have no trouble whatever in getting exposure. The world gets to know them and to make much of them.

Forty years ago, however, even the greatest writers were obscure. The conventions were few and small, and outside the immediate field of science fiction all was dark.

So it was that Robert Arthur labored without applause. I never met him and knew him only as a name attached to stories. My opinion of his abilities can be measured by this, however. In the first decade of television when I noted that some screenplays were written by Robert Alan Aurthur, I had the vague feeling that it was "my" Robert Arthur with his last name unaccountably misspelled. I.A.)

Aydem was pushing the humming vacuum duster along the endless stone corridors of the great underground Repository of Natural Knowledge when Ayveh, coming up quietly behind him, put her hands over his eyes.

He whirled, to see Ayveh's laughing face, mischief dancing on it.

"Ayveh!" he exclaimed eagerly. "But what are you doing here? It is forbidden any woman—"

"I know." Ayveh threw back her head, her long hair, richly golden, rippling down her shoulders to contrast with the pale apple-green of the shapeless linen robe she wore—a robe identical to Aydem's, the universal garb of the human slaves of the more-than-human Masters who ruled the world. It was an underground world. Generations since, the Masters, their great, thin-skulled heads and mighty brains proving uncomfortably vulnerable to the ordinary rays of the sun, had retreated underground.

"But Dmu Dran wishes to see you, Aydem," the girl Ayveh went on, "and he sent me to fetch you. There are visitors arriving, and you must convey them from the tube station to his demonstration chambers. They are very important visitors."

"But why did he not transmit the order to me by directed thinking?" Aydem asked, puzzled. "He knows that even out here, in the Exhibit Section, I would receive it."

"Perhaps he sent me because he knew I wished to see you." Ayveh suggested happily. "And because he knew you hungered for the sight of me. There are times, Aydem, when Dmu Dran actually seems to understand what feelings are."

"A Master understand feelings?" Aydem's tone was scornful. "The Masters are nothing but brains. Great machines for thought, which know nothing of joy or sorrow or hunger for another."

"Shh!" Frightened, Ayveh put her fingers to his lips. "You must not say such things. Generous as Dmu Dran is, he is still a Master, and if his mind should chance to be listening, he would have to punish you. It might even mean the fuel chambers."

Aydem kissed the fingers that had stopped his speech. Then, seeing the mingled fear and longing in her face, he drew her close and kissed her savagely, tasting the sweetness of her lips until a pulse was beating like a hammer in his throat.

Shaken, Ayveh freed herself and looked about, fearful that someone might have seen. There was no one. The corridors of the exhibit chambers of this tremendous museum of natural history of which their Master, Dmu Dran, was curator, wound endlessly away in darkness except for the tiny lighted area that enclosed them.

"There is no one to see," Ayden reassured her. "I alone tend the exhibit chambers, and only I am permitted to leave the Master's quarters without orders. And if any did see, who would tell?"

"Ekno," the girl whispered. "He would tell. He would like to see you sent into the fuel chambers, because he knows that we—that we—"

Her voice faltered and trailed off at the look of grimness in the man's face. Aydem stared down at her, at her loveliness, before he spoke. He himself stood nearly six feet tall, and his dark hair was a shaggy mane dropping almost to his shoulders. He was beardless, for all facial hair had been removed by an unguent when he was a youth—a whim of Dmu Dran's, though many Masters were less fastidious.

His body held the sturdiness of the trunk of an oak—which he had never seen. And though his duties were light in this mechanized, sub-surface world to which man's life on Mother Earth had retreated with the evolution of the Masters, muscles corded his body and were but lightly hidden by the green robe that swathed him.

And there was a tension in those muscles now, as if they would explode into action if only they had something to seize upon and rend and tear.

"Ayveh," he said, "I have seen the mating papers. I took them from the machine to the Master a period ago. Our request to be assigned as each other's mate has been denied. On the basis of the Selector Machine rating, I have been assigned to Teema, your assistant in overseeing the Master's household, and you to Ekno, who tends to minor repairs."

"That ugly hairy one?" Horror almost robbed Ayveh of her voice. "Who smells so bad and is always looking after me when I pass? No! I—I would rather kill myself first."

"I"—there was savagery in Ayden's words—"would rather kill the Masters!"

"Oh, no!" the girl whispered in terror. "You must not speak it. If you harmed Dmu Dran—if it became known even that you wished to—we should all be destroyed. Not in the fuel chambers. We should go to the example cells. And we would not die—for a long time."

"Better that," Aydem said stonily, "than to be slaves, to be mated to those we despise, to keep forever our silence and obey orders, to live and die like beasts!"

Then, at Ayveh's sudden gasp of terror, Aydem whirled.

His own features paled as he drew himself to attention. For Dmu Dran, their Master, had come silently up behind them as they spoke, the air-suspended chair which carried him making no sound.

And Dmu Dran, his great round face blank, his large popping eyes unreadable, stared at Aydem with an unusual intensity. Yet no thoughts were coming from the mind within the huge globular, thin-walled skull over which only a little wispy hair, like dried hay, was plastered.

Had Dmu Dran heard? Had he caught the emanations of violent emotion which must have been spreading all over the vicinity from Aydem? Was he now probing into their minds for the words they had just spoken? If he knew or guessed them, their fate would be a terrible one.

But when Dmu Dran spoke—for mental communication with the undeveloped slave mind was fatiguing for a Master—his voice was mild.

"I fear," he said, in a thin piping tone, "that my servants are not happy. Perhaps they are upset by the mating orders that have arrived?"

Aydem of course was supposed to know nothing of the contents of the orders, having in theory no ability to read. But since Dmu Dran evidently knew he *could* read—he had been taught in his boyhood by a wise old slave long dead— boldness seemed the only course.

"Master," he said, "the girl Ayveh and I hoped to be mates. It is true we are not happy, because we have been assigned to others."

"Happiness." Dmu Dran spoke the word reflectively. "Unhappiness. Mmm. Those are things not given us to feel. You are aware emotion is not a desirable characteristic in a slave?"

"Aye, Master," Aydem agreed submissively.

"The selector machine," Dmu Dran went on, "shows both you and the girl Ayveh to be capable of much emotion. It also indicates in both of you a brain capacity large for a slave. It is for these reasons you have been denied each other. It is desired that slaves should be strong and healthy, intelligent, but not too intelligent, and lacking in emotion so they will not become discontented. You understand these things, do you not?"

"Aye, Master," Aydem agreed in some astonishment. Ayveh pressed close to him, frightened by the strange conduct of Dmu Dran—for no Master ever spoke so familiarly with a slave.

Dmu Dran was silent, as if thinking. While he waited, Aydem reflected that Dmu Dran was not exactly as other Masters were. To an untrained eye, all Masters looked much alike—a great, globular head set upon a small neckless body, the neck having disappeared in the course of evolution of the great head, so that the weight might be better rested on the stronger back and shoulder muscles.

But Dmu Dran was perceptibly taller than other Masters Aydem had seen. Aydem had not seen many—there were only some thousand of them, and they lived in small groups in far-flung underground Centers, if not entirely alone, as did Dmu Dran. Dmu Dran's cranium was also slightly smaller in diameter.

Now an odd expression touched the flat countenance of the Master.

"Aydem," he said, "You have seen the contents of these halls many times. But Ayveh has not. So come with me now, both of you. We have a little time, and I wish to view some specimens. It is many years since I last examined them."

He turned his chair, and Aydem, exchanging a look of puzzlement with Ayveh, followed him down the corridor between the great, glass-enclosed, hermetically sealed exhibits.

As they went, light sprang on alongside them, activated by the heat of their bodies on thermo-couples, and died away behind them. The Master led them several hundred yards, and halted at last in a section devoted to ancient animals of the Earth's youth.

There were here many beasts, huge and ferocious in appearance, reproduced in their natural environment, seen, save by Aydam, not more than half a dozen times a year. Only six or eight Masters were born each year, just enough to keep the total of a thousand from dwindling. They visited the Repository of Natural Knowledge in the course of their educational studies.

In the glass cases that lined the miles of corridors were exhibits, many of them animated so cunningly that the artificial replicas of man and animal of the past seemed endowed with life, encompassing all the natural history of the world from the mists of the unknown, millions of years before, to the present day. But since the great brains of the Masters needed to be apprised of a fact but once to make it theirs forever, there was never really occasion for a Master to come here twice.

Now Dmu Dran, Aydem and Ayveh stood before a great, orange-colored beast with black stripes, a snarl frozen upon his features, huge fangs, many inches in length, protruding from his jaws. Even though he was but a model of a beast dead many millennia, Ayveh instinctively drew closer to Aydem, as if the creature were indeed about to leap, and as if they were part of that group of men and women, much like themselves, that faced it in desperation with long, pointed sticks in their hands.

"The saber-tooth tiger," Dmu Dran said. "When it reigned on this Earth uncounted years ago, it was Master of Aiden, the world above, a scourge feared and hated by all other animals. For many thousands of years it grew more and more powerful, its dominance contested by few. By its great teeth it was known—terrible weapons for rending and tearing its prey. But in the end it ceased to be. Why did a beast like that, which no natural enemy could oppose, die, think you?"

"It must indeed have been a fearful opponent that conquered it, Master," Ayveh ventured uncertainly.

What might have been a smile, had a Master known smiling, rippled over the pale moon-face.

"Nature killed it," Dmu Dran informed them. "Nature destroyed it by her very generosity. Those tusks you see that gave it its name—Nature continued to add to their length and strength. But, alas! In her enthusiasm, she made them so long in the course of time that their possessor could not close its mouth, could not eat, and so eventually starved to death. Aye, Nature evolved her great and dread child right out of existence."

"That was indeed strange." Aydem frowned. "I do not understand. Why did she do so?"

"Nature has curious ways." Dmu Dran shrugged. "And having an infinity of time, she can afford an infinity of experiments. What she is not satisfied with, though she has made it supreme, she destroys."

Dmu Dran shot his chair a few yards to the left.

"And here," he said, "is another great beast that was once master of the world when it was young."

The creature he now indicated stood far above a man's head, even a slave's. Three times, four times, five times higher than a slave did it tower.

"The great dinosaur of the Earth's infancy," Dmu Dran told them. "The hugest beast ever to shake the world with its tread. That one"—he pointed—"the largest land animal ever evolved. The enemies that could conquer it were few or none. Unmolested by the lesser denizens of the day and the night, it ruled the Earth by its very bulk. Yet it too passed. Why, think you?"

Aydem and Ayveh were silent, so Dmu Dran explained.

"Again Nature was overgenerous. To this creature whose bulk made it sovereign, it added still more bulk. Alack! In time she so increased the size of the beast that it could not get enough to eat, though it fed twenty-four hours of the day. It simply could not ingest fuel enough for its huge body. So in the end it too passed."

The man and the girl were still silent, their eyes wide with wonder. Dmu Dran abruptly shot his air car a hundred yards down the corridor and stopped again, the lights coming on automatically the moment he paused.

He was now before the section devoted to the evolution of man himself, beginning with a creature half man, half beast, and rising to a reproduction of the Masters who now ruled the world.

Uneducated though they were, Aydem and Ayveh saw and understood the procession of figures, each more erect, each less hairy, each larger-headed than the one before it.

Near the end of the line was an upright figure which caused Ayveh to gasp, it was so like Aydem.

"Man of the Early Machine Age"

Dmu Dran read the inscription on the imperishable metal plate at the foot of the figure. "Aye, your Aydem does look like him. For it was man of that period, balanced between ignorance and knowledge, that we Masters thought it best our slaves should resemble. But here is the exhibit that I have most pondered upon."

He moved a few feet, and they stood before the last half dozen figures.

"There"—and Dmu Dran, with one short arm, indicated a figure as tall as Aydem, but differing from the one just before it in that its head was half again as large—"there is the first of the Masters. A mutant, with a brain-weight double anything ever known in man before. John Master, his name was, and it was appropriate. For in the last ten thousand years, all humankind save slaves have been his descendants—not men now, but Masters. I have often speculated upon the chance that saw him born, and wondered if, had he never been conceived and brought to issue, the human species might not have turned in quite another direction."

Dmu Dran was silent, thinking, and the two slaves did not intrude upon his thoughts. Instead they studied the figures following this John Master of the large head. Each was larger-headed than the one before it, each smaller-bodied, shorter-necked, until the last figure might have been Dmu Dran himslf.

"It is an interesting point on which to wonder," Dmu Dran said after a time. "How would mankind have evolved had not my ancestor been born? The old records show that he was a cold and ruthless man, without sentiment. That by the power of his logical mind, and with the aid of his children, he seized the rule of the world and made his descendants supreme forever. Forever? Well—supreme ever since. So that now we Masters, the highest species of animal ever to evolve, are despotic rulers of the world, and if we wished, of the Solar System—even of the Universe.

"But we do not wish. The Solar System, save for this world, is lifeless, and it has never been worth our while to consider whether the stars beyond were worth reaching. We feel nothing, we enjoy nothing, for the capacity for those things has been bred out of us—evolved away in the course of yesterday's eons. We merely think, with our almost perfect brains, here in the bowels of the Earth, served by our slaves in a world almost effortless even for them.

"We are, so far as we know—and there is little we do not know—the Masters, nature's final product, evolution's end!"

Abruptly Dmu Dran's piping voice ceased, leaving tiny echoes rustling in the corridors. Aydem and Ayveh were alarmed and uneasy. Could Dmu Dran by chance be mad? Madness did sometimes afflict a Master, though rarely one of Dmu Dran's age. Usually they were much younger or much older, when the unexplainable insanity that was the only ailment the Masters had not conquered, took them.

"I sometimes think," Dmu Dran said after a moment, in a quieter tone now, "that though we consider ourselves the last step in evolution's chain, we may be wrong. Who knows what plans nature has for us? None of us. But we shall. I am going to put it to the test, the momentous test that may decide the whole future of the world, aye, of the Universe itself. For know, my servants, that my visitors today are the Masters of the Supreme Council, come at my invitation to examine a machine that I have made my life's work.

"It is a matter of electricity and rays that will stimulate the latent change that lies in all plants and animals. So that in one generation, an animal may progress from the form it was born with to the form its descendants a thousand generations away would have. Aye—in less than a generation, in a few periods!

"And I am going to propose to the Supreme Council that a chosen few of us Masters subject ourselves to the influence of this machine, that we may know what we are to become, in Nature's hidden scheme, in the persons of our grandchildren many times removed. I shall propose to them we raise ourselves now to the glories of the final form destined to the Masters, and I think they will agree.

"For we Masters, the favored children of nature, will hardly be loath to rise to the final position scarcely lower than gods that our philosophers have foreseen as ultimately ours!"

Excitement shone in Dmu Dran's popping eyes. But in a moment it died. He gestured.

"Return to your quarters, my servants. I shall meet my visitors myself, Aydem. Say nothing to anyone, and worry not for the moment concerning the mating assignments. Nothing will be done about such matters until I—know."

With that cryptic remark, he shot away down the corridor in his air-chair as Aydem and Ayveh stared at each other in perplexity and mounting hope.

In the periods of waiting that followed, there was tension in the slaves' quarters. All knew of the unprecedented visit of the Supreme Council, and somehow word got about that the mating assignments had come, but had not yet been announced by Dmu Dran.

Curiosity regarding these matters, however, was not as strong as it might have been had not slaves been for so many generations bred for docility and lack of emotion. Aydem and Ayveh's fellow servants exhibited only mild curiosity about any occurrence, and when not working, for the most part contented themselves with eating, sleeping, and playing simple games.

Only Ekno, the hairy one who coveted Ayveh, had a brain that busied itself with affairs outside its immediate concern. And Ekno, hatred in his face as he watched Aydem covertly, knew that something of great import was transpiring. He could scarcely contain himself to know what, and even took the great risk, unthinkable to the others, of snooping about Dmu Dran's private quarters under the pretense of making repairs, hoping to pick up some scrap of information.

In time, after many secret sessions in Dmu Dran's demonstration chambers, the Supreme Council left, each Master boarding his private air-car and being shot away through the great maze of tunnels that honeycombed the earth to his home center. With the President of the Council, the oldest living Master, went a large, heavy package which Aydem transported to his car with great care, little dreaming that the destiny of himself and Ayveh and countless millions of their unborn descendants lay within those careful wrappings.

After this, for some periods more, nothing happened. The other slaves almost forgot anything unusual had occurred. Only Ekno still watched Aydem's every move, eager for some evidence of wrong-doing he could present to Dmu Dran, or even to the Board of Slave Mating, supreme authority in regard to all slaves.

But with Dmu Dran's strange words ringing in his mind, Aydem made no move Ekno could seize upon. Save when outside the living quarters, to which Ekno by the nature of his duties was usually confined, Aydem and Ayveh did not even exchange words.

But Aydem's chief duty was to keep the interminable corridors of the exhibit section free from the natural rock dust that gathered, and only he was permitted to enter it. Ekno dared not follow him there, so it was there he and Ayveh met.

It was a great risk Ayveh took, for no woman was permitted to leave the living quarters at all. But Dmu Dran's words had given them courage. And it was possible for her, since she was chief of the women, to slip away from her duties for stolen moments from time to time.

On these occasions they exchanged few words. Their hearts spoke for them, and their tongues could be silent. Aydem eagerly showed the girl through the multitudinous exhibits that traced man's life on the planet.

Long years these had fascinated him. Countless periods he had spent studying them, and scanning the engraved metal placards that explained each detail of what he saw.

Though Ayveh could not read, he could interpret for her. And many of the exhibits spoke for themselves. Almost all were animated. A touch of a button set them in motion, and countless replicas of countless types of men who had walked the world and vanished, went through the acts of life again.

In engrossed silence, Aydem and Ayveh watched hairy men of the Earth's infancy defend themselves with fire and spear and arrow against the attacks of wild animals. They saw other men, higher in the scale of evolution, build simple dwellings, strike fire from flints or produce it from spun sticks, hunt, plant seed, weave cloth, cook, and do all the multitudinous acts that were necessary to existence.

Most of all, Aydem was fascinated not by the exhibits

showing the machine world just before the coming of the Masters, but by the reproductions of man in his younger days. Haltingly he tried to explain to Ayveh that he felt within himself a kinship to those long dead men who had made bows and arrows, planted and reaped their crops with their hands, had tamed wild horses and on their backs ridden down the wild boar and the wolf, had, with spear and arrow, defended themselves against their enemies.

He stretched his arms, and his mighty muscles coiled and knotted.

"Sometimes in my sleep," he told Ayveh, his eyes burning, "I am no longer within these underground dominions of the Masters, but am free upon Aiden, the Earth's surface. I know what it must be like, for I can see it all in my dreams. I can feel the warm touch of what they call the sun, and underfoot the roughness of the growing things called grass. Animals, not artificial like these, but alive, roam the land, and in my dreams I combat them."

"It must be a wonderful place," Ayveh whispered wistfully. "So strange and different from this."

"Sometimes I feel as if I were going to burst, forever locked away within these walls of rock where the Masters choose to live!" Aydem burst out. "I wish to work, to fight, to conquer—"

Somewhere nearby there was a scraping noise. Ayveh gasped with terror, and Aydem whirled instantly. The sound of running footsteps sprang up several corridors away. Aydem dashed in that direction, caught a glimpse of a man running toward the living quarters.

He put on a burst of speed, but the other outdistanced him and ducked through a door before Aydem could get close to identify the spying one.

"But it was Ekno," he said, his voice grim, as he hurried back to take the frightened Ayveh to her quarters. "It was Ekno, and he was spying on us. He overheard. He will report to Dmu Dran."

"But the Master," Ayveh faltered, "he did not mind before—"

Aydem took her hand.

"There is no telling what a Master will do," he growled. "He may have been amusing himself. We must be prepared. Do not sleep this period. Wait for me behind this door that leads from the quarters to the exhibits. Come if I call. Have food with you."

"But Aydem!" Ayveh exclaimed, wide-eyed. "You would not question the decree of a Master?"

"If Dmu Dran condemns me to the fuel chamber," Aydem answered, "I will kill him and we will try to escape. See!"

From beneath his tunic he withdrew a knife with a long gleaming blade and a heavy handle.

"I have had this long," he boasted. "It is part of an exhibit that became out of order. I fixed it under Dmu Dran's direction. And stole this unnoticed. I will kill Dmu Dran with it if I must. There are many tunnels that may have been abandoned leading out from this center. I have heard it whispered, by old Temu who taught me when I was young, that one leads to the world above. We will seek it. We will seek escape. If we must, we will die. But I will not go to the fuel chambers."

He looked at her white face.

"But I can go alone—" he began.

Ayveh flung herself into his arms.

"No, Aydem, no!" she whispered. "Where you go, I will go. If you live, I will live. If you die, I will die."

He kissed her then strongly, passionately. And as he kissed her, the command came. By directed thinking. To report at once to Dmu Dran.

With unfaltering stride Aydem entered Dmu Dran's personal quarters. As he went in, he passed Ekno, and there was a smirk of triumph on the hairy one's features. Aydem did not deign to glance at the other. He closed the door behind him, and was in the presence of Dmu Dran.

The flat, pop-eyed face of the Master was as blank as ever.

"Aydem, my servant," he piped, "a charge has been placed against you. A serious charge. You merit punishment. If I do not punish you, the charge may come to the attention of the Board of Slave Mating. It will wish to know why. It will send for you, and when you are placed beneath the instruments, it will know I have been guilty of a crime too. It will know that you are far above the allowed intelligence quotient for a slave, and that I have falsified your records since childhood, as I have falsified those of the servant Ayveh."

Aydem stared at him in speechless astonishment.

"You are startled, Servant Aydem," the Master said. "But it is true I, a Master, have violated one of the most rigid rules of the few that Masters must observe. I have deliberately preserved from destruction in the fuel chambers a man and a woman of as high a physical and mental level as the world has known since the days of the first Master.

"I have done this for reasons of my own. I think we shall soon know whether I have been right to—"

He did not finish, for behind him a section of the wall grew luminous, and a figure began to appear, seemingly within it.

Dmu Dran made a gesture. Aydem withdrew quickly to one side, beyond the seeing range of the communicator panel, and the Master turned. A voice, piping but stern, spoke from the wall:

"Dmu Dran! Nalu Tah, president of the Supreme Council, speaks."

"Dmu Dran listens."

"Dmu Dran! Of the ten subjects upon whom the Supreme Council has been testing the apparatus devised by you for the precipitating of evolutionary change, the last has just gone mad. The brain capacity of all increased by fifty per cent, and the skulls enlarged during their subjection to the rays of your apparatus. Each, however, after reaching an increase of approximately fifty per cent in brain size, was afflicted by the dread madness. All have been destroyed. Dmu Dran, you are ordered to report at once to Judicial Center to make explanation, and be judged."

"Dmu Dran hears."

The glow in the wall died. The great-headed figure of the president of the Supreme Council vanished. Dmu Dran let out a little sigh.

"Mad," he whispered. "All went mad. As some are going mad already, and as in a hundred thousand years all will, the entire race of Masters. So that they will be no more. In a hundred thousand years, the supreme creation of Nature, the mightiest thinking machine she has ever produced, will be destroyed. By the irresistible force of Nature herself, adding always to the gift she has given, until the weight of it crushes us out of existence. Yes, crushes us literally out of existence."

He turned, faced the wondering Aydem.

"Aydem, my servant," he said, "I have been right. I have feared a certain thing, and I have learned that my fears are well founded. I have concentrated the evolutionary development of a hundred thousand years in certain selected Masters, and all have gone mad. The reason I can easily guess. Their brains grew in size, until the very weight of the brain crushed many of its own cells. The very multiplicity of the cells piled layer upon top of layer destroyed the more delicate. The process can already be seen at work occasionally now. In time it will encompass all.

"The bulk of the dinosaur, which made it supreme, killed it. The teeth of the saber-tooth tiger destroyed it. And the brain of the Masters, which has made them supreme, is foredestined to destroy them just as utterly.

"Aydem, you are a man as men were before the sudden branching that produced the Masters. A branching that I now know was but another experiment on Nature's part, leading nowhere. Hark you—the ultimate evolution of man is yet to come. Yes, yet to come.

"Yet, if the Masters live out their existence, Nature may well be foiled, or at the least, set back a thousand million years in her plans. For in a hundred thousand years, when the Masters are gone, man may well be gone too.

"Yet, if the Masters were to vanish now, while you and Ayveh lived, from *your* loins might spring the line that will yet reach upward to the stars."

Dmu Dran's voice piped off into silence. But he was not finished speaking, for after a moment he shook himself and continued.

"What man will be like in the end I do not know. He will not be a great-headed thinking machine, I am sure. He will have a mind, yes, but soul too, and body, all balanced into a whole that will far surpass us, the Masters.

"What I am going to do is hard. Yet perhaps I am but a tool of Nature's too. Perhaps she designed me for this very purpose—to put evolution back upon its proper track.

"Aydem, you may never understand. That does not matter. These are my last orders. Take Ayveh. Go to the very end of the exhibit section. There, in a section where the rooms have been crushed by falling rock, you will find one stone perfectly round and seemingly too great for a thousand men to move. Upon one side is a red spot. Push at this spot. The rock will roll aside and you will see an entrance. Descend. A passageway will lead you upward and in time you will come out upon Aiden, the surface of the Earth above—a region into which we Masters have not chosen to venture save but fleetingly for a thousand years.

"You will have the half of one period in which to do this. Then I will press a button here beside me. The details you would not understand. But when I do, every inch of these vast tunnels that we Masters have created throughout the Earth's interior will collapse. Every Master will die at the same instant. And every slave—for there are none living save yourselves whose blood may go into the lifestream of the Man to come. It would take centuries for them to evolve again as a group to your level. So you two, Aydem and Ayveh, will be, to all historical appearance, the first man and woman. The gap between you and your ancestors will be broken when I press this button.

"You will not understand my reasons, I say. But you will survive above, for you have long studied the great exhibit chambers and know what you must do to wrest a living from Nature. In time you will forget that such things as Masters ever existed. And your kind will mount upward toward the stars, on a true course which has been sidetracked for only a little while."

Dmu Dran fell silent, as if musing, and his pale round face seemed sad. Aydem, in truth, understood but little. Yet he understood Dmu Dran's instructions, and his heart leaped within his breast.

Dmu Dran looked up.

"Go now," he ordered.

Aydem forced his way through the tangle of weeds and roots that choked the entrance of the cave, in which the long tunnel he and Ayveh had traversed for an interminable time ended. He stood upright, and drew Ayveh after him.

They had emerged upon the surface of the Earth at night. The moon, a thing of wondrous beauty to them, rode the heavens low in the east, a great orange ball. A summer night's wind breathed through the great masses of tangled vegetation that surrounded them, and the scent of flowers was carried by it.

The man and the woman breathed deep, speechless with wonder and joy. Somewhere near a nightbird was trilling, and from farther away came the cry of an unknown animal. Both sounds alike were music to their ears.

"Free!" Aydem whispered exultingly. "Ayveh, we are free! We are slaves no more!"

Bathed by the moonlight, caressed by the night breeze, they stood close together, his arm about her, and feasted their eyes and ears on the world.

"The knife I stole," Aydem said, "I will keep. With it we will make what we need, kill what we need. Ayveh, Ayveh—"

His words broke off. Of a sudden the very earth beneath them had begun to tremble. It seemed to shudder. One long-drawn puff of air, like a hollow death-gasp, seemed forced from the cavern before which they stood, and the ground under them shook, Ayveh was thrown into Aydem's arms, and he held her close until the violent tremor had passed.

"Dmu Dran has pressed the button," he said, understanding. "The Masters are no more. Ayveh, my mate, the Masters are no more! We are free, and there is no one to come after us. We will know struggle and conflict and labor, but we are free!"

He held her close and kissed her. Then at last, hand in hand, they set out together into the world Dmu Dran had given them. Aydem—the first man. And Ayveh—the first woman.

MICROCOSMIC GOD

Astounding Science Fiction
April

by Theodore Sturgeon

*There are many who feel that this is the finest
story to come from the typewriter of Theodore
Sturgeon. It was selected by the Science Fiction
Writers of America for their* Hall of Fame *short
story volume, and it has received critical acclaim
from numerous quarters.*

The theme of survival *has a long history in
science fiction, but no one ever surpassed the Sturgeon who wrote this inventive and convincing
story.*

(Finest story? Yes, I am among those that Marty refers to
as "many." However, truth is truth. I think this is the best of
his *science fiction* stories. I placed both "It" and "Bianca's
Hands" above it, but they are both fantasies. I must say that
what struck me most about the story, was pity and sorrow for
the small creatures and indignation at the "god" who, in my
mind, at the time I read the book was very much like the
"God" we were so busily taught to love and admire. Remember what 1941 was like!—I.A.)

Here is a story about a man who had too much power, and
a man who took too much, but don't worry; I'm not going
political on you. The man who had the power was named
James Kidder, and the other was his banker.

Kidder was quite a guy. He was a scientist and he lived on
a small island off the New England coast all by himself. He
wasn't the dwarfed little gnome of a mad scientist you read
about. His hobby wasn't personal profit, and he wasn't a meg-
alomaniac with a Russian name and no scruples. He wasn't
insidious, and he wasn't even particularly subversive. He kept
his hair cut and his nails clean and lived and thought like a
reasonable human being. He was slightly on the baby-faced

side; he was inclined to be a hermit; he was short and plump and—brilliant. His specialty was biochemistry, and he was always called *Mr.* Kidder. Not Dr." Not "Professor." Just Mr. Kidder.

He was an odd sort of apple and always had been. He had never graduated from any college or university because he found them too slow for him, and too rigid in their approach to education. He couldn't get used to the idea that perhaps his professors knew what they were talking about. That went for his texts, too. He was always asking questions, and didn't mind very much when they were embarrassing. He considered Gregor Mendel a bungling liar, Darwin an amusing philosopher, and Luther Burbank a sensationalist. He never opened his mouth without leaving his victim feeling breathless. If he was talking to someone who had knowledge, he went in there and got it. If he was talking to someone whose knowledge was already in his possession, he only asked repeatedly, "How do you know?" His most delectable pleasure was taken in cutting a fanatical eugenicist into conversational ribbons. So people left him alone and never, never asked him to tea. He was polite, but not politic.

He had a little money of his own, and with it he leased the island and built himself a laboratory. Now I've mentioned that he was a biochemist. But being what he was, he couldn't keep his nose in his own field. It wasn't too remarkable when he made an intellectual excursion wide enough to perfect a method of crystallizing Vitamin B_1 profitably by the ton—if anyone wanted it by the ton. He got a lot of money for it. He bought his island outright and put eight hundred men to work on an acre and a half of his ground, adding to his laboratory and building equipment. He got messing around with sisal fiber, found out how to fuse it, and boomed the banana industry by producing a practically unbreakable cord from the stuff.

You remember the popularizing demonstration he put on at Niagara, don't you? That business of running a line of the new cord from bank to bank over the rapids and suspending a ten-ton truck from the middle of it by razor edges resting on the cord? That's why ships now moor themselves with what looks like heaving line, no thicker than a lead pencil, that can be coiled on reels like garden hose. Kidder made cigarette money out of that, too. He went out and bought himself a cyclotron with part of it.

After that money wasn't money any more. It was large numbers in little books. Kidder used to use little amounts of it to have food and equipment sent out to him, but after a while that stopped, too. His bank dispatched a messenger by seaplane to find out if Kidder was still alive. The man returned two days later in a mused state, having been amazed something awesome at the things he'd seen out there. Kidder was alive, all right, and he was turning out a surplus of good food in an astonishingly simplified synthetic form. The bank wrote immediately and wanted to know if Mr. Kidder, in his own interest, was willing to release the secret of his dirtless farming. Kidder replied that he would be glad to, and enclosed the formulas. In a P. S. he said that he hadn't sent the information ashore because he hadn't realized anyone would be interested. That from a man who was responsible for the greatest sociological change in the second half of the twentieth century—factory farming. It made him richer; I mean it made his bank richer. He didn't give a rap.

But Kidder didn't really get started until about eight months after the bank messenger's visit. For a biochemist who couldn't even be called "Dr." he did pretty well. Here is a partial list of the things that he turned out:

A commercially feasible plan for making an aluminum alloy stronger than the best steel so that it could be used as a structural metal.

An exhibition gadget he called a light pump, which worked on the theory that light is a form of matter and therefore subject to physical and electromagnetic laws. Seal a room with a single light source, beam a cylindrical vibratory magnetic field to it from the pump, and the light will be led down it. Now pass the light through Kidder's "lens"—a ring which perpetuates an electric field along the lines of a high-speed iris-type camera shutter. Below this is the heart of the light pump—a ninety-eight-percent efficient light absorber, crystalline, which, in a sense, *loses* the light in its internal facets. The effect of darkening the room with this apparatus is slight but measurable. Pardon my layman's language, but that's the general idea.

Synthetic chlorophyll—by the barrel.

An airplane propeller efficient at eight times sonic speed.

A cheap goo you brush on over old paint, let harden, and then peel off like strips of cloth. The old paint comes with it. That one made friends fast.

A self-sustaining atomic disintegration of uranium's isotope 238, which is two hundred times as plentiful as the old standby, U-235.

That will do for the present. If I may repeat myself; for a

biochemist who couldn't even be called "Dr.," he did pretty well.

Kidder was apparently unconscious of the fact that he held power enough on his little island to become master of the world. His mind simply didn't run to things like that. As long as he was left alone with his experiments, he was well content to leave the rest of the world to its own clumsy and primitive devices. He couldn't be reached except by a radiophone of his own design, and its only counterpart was locked in a vault of his Boston bank. Only one man could operate it—the bank president. The extraordinarily sensitive transmitter would respond only to President Conant's own body vibrations. Kidder had instructed Conant that he was not to be disturbed except by messages of the greatest moment. His ideas and patents, when Conant could pry one out of him, were released under pseudonyms known only to Conant—Kidder didn't care.

The result, of course, was in infiltration of the most astonishing advancements since the dawn of civilization. The nation profited—the world profited. But most of all, the bank profited. It began to get a little oversize. It began getting its fingers into other pies. It grew more fingers and had to bake more figurative pies. Before many years had passed, it was so big that, using Kidder's many weapons, it almost matched Kidder in power.

Almost.

Now stand by while I squelch those fellows in the lower left-hand corner who've been saying all this while that Kidder's slightly improbable; that no man could ever perfect himself in so many ways in so many sciences.

Well, you're right. Kidder was a genius—granted. But his genius was not creative. He was, to the core, a student. He applied what he knew, what he saw, and what he was taught. When first he began working in his new laboratory on his island he reasoned something like this:

"Everything I know is what I have been taught by the sayings and writings of people who have studied the sayings and writings of people who have—and so on. Once in a while someone stumbles on something new and he or someone cleverer used the idea and disseminates it. But for each one that finds something really new, a couple of million gather and pass on information that is already current. I'd know more if I could get the jump on evolutionary trends. It takes too long to wait for the accidents that increase man's knowledge—my knowledge. If I had ambition enough now to figure out how to travel ahead in time, I could skim the surface of the future and just dip down when I saw something interesting. But time isn't that way. It can't be left behind or tossed ahead. What else is left?

"Well, there's the proposition of speeding intellectual evolution so that I can observe what it cooks up. That seems a bit inefficient. It would involve more labor to discipline human minds to that extent than it would to simply apply myself along those lines. But I can't apply myself that way. No one man can.

"I'm licked. I can't speed myself up, and I can't speed other men's minds up. Isn't there an alternative? There must be—somewhere, somehow, there's got to be an answer."

So it was to this, and not to eugenics, or light pumps, or botany, or atomic physics, that James Kidder applied himself. For a practical man, the problem was slightly on the metaphysical side, but he attacked it with typical thoroughness, using his own peculiar brand of logic. Day after day he wandered over the island, throwing shells impotently at sea gulls and swearing richly. Then came a time when he sat indoors and brooded. And only then did he get feverishly to work.

He worked in his own field, biochemistry, and concentrated mainly on two things—genetics and animal metabolism. He learned, and filed away in his insatiable mind, many things having nothing to do with the problem in hand, and very little of what he wanted. But he piled that little on what little he knew or guessed, and in time had quite a collection of known factors to work with. His approach was characteristically unorthodox. He did things on the order of multiplying by pears, and balancing equations by adding $\log \sqrt{-1}$ to one side and ∞ to the other. He made mistakes, but only one of a kind, and later, only one of a species. He spent so many hours at his microscope that he had to quit work for two days to get rid of a hallucination that his heart was pumping his own blood through the mike. He did nothing by trial and error because he disapproved of the method as sloppy.

And he got results. He was lucky to begin with, and even luckier when he formularized the law of probability and reduced it to such low terms that he knew almost to the item what experiments not to try. When the cloudy, viscous semifluid on the watch glass began to move of itself he knew he was on the right track. When it began to seek food on its own he began to be excited. When it divided and, in a few hours, redivided, and each part grew and divided again, he was triumphant, for he had created life.

He nursed his brain children and sweated and strained over them, and he designed baths of various vibrations for them, and inoculated and dosed and sprayed them. Each move he made taught him the next. And out of his tanks and tubes and incubators came amoebalike creatures, and then ciliated animalcules, and more and more rapidly he produced animals with eye spots, nerve cysts, and then—victory of victories—a real blastopod, possessed of many cells instead of one. More slowly he developed a gastropod, but once he had it, it was not too difficult for him to give it organs, each with a specified function, each inheritable.

Then came cultured mollusklike things, and creatures with more and more perfected gills. The day that a nondescript thing wriggled up an inclined board out of a tank, threw flaps over its gills and feebly breathed air, Kidder quit work and went to the other end of the island and got disgustingly drunk. Hangover and all, he was soon back in the lab, forgetting to eat, forgetting to sleep, tearing into his problem.

He turned into a scientific byway and ran down his other great triumph—accelerated metabolism. He extracted and refined the stimulating factors in alcohol, cocoa, heroin, and Mother Nature's prize dope runner, *cannabis indica*. Like the scientist who, in analyzing the various clotting agents for blood treatments, found that oxalic acid and oxalic acid alone was the active factor, Kidder isolated the accelerators and decelerators, the stimulants and soporifics, in every substance that ever undermined a man's morality and/or caused a "noble experiment." In the process he found one thing he needed badly—a colorless elixir that made sleep the unnecessary and avoidable waster of time it should be. Then and there he went on a twenty-four-hour shift.

He artifically synthesized the substances he had isolated, and in doing so sloughed away a great many useless components. He pursued the subject along the lines of radiations and vibrations. He discovered something in the longer reds which, when projected through a vessel full of air vibrating in the supersonics, and then polarized, speeded up the heartbeat of small animals twenty to one. They ate twenty times as much, grew twenty times as fast, and—died twenty times sooner than they should have.

Kidder built a huge hermetically sealed room. Above it was another room, the same length and breadth but not quite so high. This was his control chamber. The large room was

divided into four sealed sections, each with its individual heat
and atmosphere controls. Over each section were miniature
cranes and derricks—handling machinery of all kinds. There
were also trapdoors fitted with air locks leading from the upper to the lower room.

By this time the other laboratory had produced a warm-
blooded, snake-skinned quadruped with an astonishingly rapid
life cycle—a generation every eight days, a life span of about
fifteen. Like the echidna, it was oviparous and mammalian.
Its period of gestation was six hours; the eggs hatched in
three; the young reached sexual maturity in another four
days. Each female laid four eggs and lived just long enough
to care for the young after they hatched. The males generally
died two or three hours after mating. The creatures were
highly adaptable. They were small—not more than three
inches long, two inches to the shoulder from the ground.
Their forepaws had three digits and a triple-jointed, opposed
thumb. They were attuned to life in an atmosphere with a
large ammonia content. Kidder bred four of the creatures
and put one group in each section of the sealed room.

Then he was ready. With his controlled atmospheres he
varied temperatures, oxygen content, humidity. He killed
them off like flies with excesses of, for instance, carbon diox-
ide, and the survivors bred their physical resistance into the
next generation. Periodically he would switch the eggs from
one sealed section to another to keep the strains varied. And
rapidly, under these controlled conditions, the creatures began
to evolve.

This, then, was the answer to his problem. He couldn't
speed up mankind's intellectual advancement enough to have
it teach him the things his incredible mind yearned for. He
couldn't speed himself up. So he created a new race—a race
which would develop and evolve so fast that it would surpass
the civilization of man; and from them he would learn.

They were completely in Kidder's power. Earth's normal
atmosphere would poison them, as he took care to demonstrate to every fourth generation. They would make no attempt to escape from him. They would live their lives and
progress and make their little trial-and-error experiments
hundreds of times faster than man did. They had the edge on
man, for they had Kidder to guide them. It took man six
thousand years to really discover science, three hundred to
really put it to work. It took Kidder's creatures two hundred
days to equal man's mental attainments. And from then

on—Kidder's spasmodic output made the late, great Tom Edison look like a home handicrafter.

He called them Neoterics, and he teased them into working for him. Kidder was inventive in an ideological way; that is, he could dream up impossible propositions providing he didn't have to work them out. For example, he wanted the Neoterics to figure out for themselves how to build shelters out of porous material. He created the need for such shelters by subjecting one of the sections to a high-pressure rainstorm which flattened the inhabitants. The Neoterics promptly devised waterproof shelters out of the thin waterproof material he piled in one corner. Kidder immediately blew down the flimsy structures with a blast of cold air. They built them up again so that they resisted both wind and rain. Kidder lowered the temperature so abruptly that they could not adjust their bodies to it. They heated their shelters with tiny braziers. Kidder promply turned up the heat until they began to roast to death. After a few deaths, one of their bright boys figured out how to build a strong insulant house by using three-ply rubberoid, with the middle layer perforated thousands of times to create tiny air pockets.

Using such tactics, Kidder forced them to develop a highly advanced little culture. He caused a drought in one section and a liquid surplus in another, and then opened the partition between them. Quite a spectacular war was fought, and Kidder's notebooks filled with information about military tactics and weapons. Then there was the vaccine they developed against the common cold—the reason why that affliction has been absolutely stamped out in the world today, for it was one of the things that Conant, the bank president, got hold of. He spoke to Kidder over the radiophone one winter afternoon with a voice so hoarse from laryngitis that Kidder sent him a vial of the vaccine and told him briskly not ever to call him again in such a disgustingly inaudible state. Conant had it analyzed and again Kidder's accounts—and the bank's —swelled.

At first Kidder merely supplied them with the materials he thought the Neoterics might need, but when they developed an intelligence equal to the task of fabricating their own from the elements at hand, he gave each section a stock of raw materials. The process for really strong aluminum was developed when he built in a huge plunger in one of the sections, which reached from wall to wall and was designed to descend at the rate of four inches a day until it crushed whatever was at the bottom. The Neoterics, in self-defense, used what strong material they had in hand to stop the inexorable death that threatened them. But Kidder had seen to it that they had nothing but aluminum oxide and a scattering of other elements, plus plenty of electric power. At first they ran up dozens of aluminum pillars; when these were crushed and twisted they tried shaping them so that the soft metal would take more weight. When that failed they quickly built stronger ones; and when the plunger was halted, Kidder removed one of the pillars and analyzed it. It was hardened aluminum, stronger and tougher than molybd steel.

Experience taught Kidder that he had to make certain changes to increase his power over his Neoterics before they got too ingenious. There were things that could be done with atomic power that he was curious about; but he was not willing to trust his little superscientists with a thing like that unless they could be trusted to use it strictly according to Hoyle. So he instituted a rule of fear. The most trivial departure from what he chose to consider the right way of doing things resulted in instant death of half a tribe. If he was trying to develop a Diesel-type power plant, for instance, that would operate without a flywheel starter, and a bright young Neoteric used any of the materials for architectural purposes, half the tribe immediately died. Of course, they had developed a written language; it was Kidder's own. The teletype in a glass-enclosed area in a corner of each section was a shrine. Any directions that were given on it were obeyed, or else—. After this innovation, Kidder's work was much simpler. There was no need for any more indirection. Anything he wanted done was done. No matter how impossible his commands, three or four generations of Neoterics could find a way to carry them out.

This quotation is from a paper that one of Kidder's high-speed telescopic cameras discovered being circulated among the younger Neoterics. It is translated from the highly simplified script of the Neoterics.

"These edicts shall be followed by each Neoteric upon pain of death, which punishment will be inflicted by the tribe upon the individual to protect the tribe against him.

"Priority of interest and tribal and individual effort is to be given the commands that appear on the word machine.

"Any misdirection of material or power, or use thereof for any other purpose than the carrying out of the machine's commands, unless no command appears, shall be punishable by death.

"Any information regarding the problem at hand, or ideas

or experiments which might conceivably bear upon it, are to become the property of the tribe.

"Any individual failing to cooperate in the tribal effort, or who can be termed guilty of not expending his full efforts in the work; or the suspicion thereof, shall be subject to the death penalty."

Such are the results of complete domination. This paper impressed Kidder as much as it did because it was completely spontaneous. It was the Neoterics' own creed, developed by them for their own greatest good.

And so at last Kidder had his fulfillment. Crouched in the upper room, going from telescope to telescope, running off slowed-down films from his high-speed cameras, he found himself possessed of a tractable, dynamic source of information. Housed in the great square building with its four half-acre sections was a new world, to which he was god.

President Conant's mind was similar to Kidder's in that its approach to any problem was along the shortest distance between any two points, regardless of whether that approach was along the line of most or least resistance. His rise to the bank presidency was a history of ruthless moves whose only justification was that they got him what he wanted. Like an overefficient general, he would never vanquish an enemy through sheer force of numbers alone. He would also skillfully flank his enemy, not on one side, but on both. Innocent bystanders were creatures deserving no consideration.

The time he took over a certain thousand-acre property, for instance, from a man named Grady, he was not satisfied with only the title to the land. Grady was an airport owner—had been all his life, and his father before him. Conant exerted every kind of pressure on the man and found him unshakable. Finally judicious persuasion led the city officials to dig a sewer right across the middle of the field, quite efficiently wrecking Grady's business. Knowing that this would supply Grady, who was a wealthy man, with motive for revenge, Conant took over Grady's bank at half again its value and caused it to fold up. Grady lost every cent he had and ended his life in an asylum. Conant was very proud of his tactics.

Like many another who has had Mammon by the tail, Conant did not know when to let go. His vast organization yielded him more money and power than any other concern in history, and yet he was not satisfied. Conant and money were like Kidder and knowledge. Conant's pyramided enterprises were to him what the Neoterics were to Kidder. Each had made his private world; each used it for his instruction and profit. Kidder, though, disturbed nobody but his Neoterics. Even so, Conant was not wholly villainous. He was a shrewd man, and had discovered early the value of pleasing people. No man can rob successfully over a period of years without pleasing the people he robs. The technique for doing this is highly involved, but master it and you can start your own mint.

Conant's one great fear was that Kidder would some day take an interest in world events and begin to become opinionated. Good heavens—the potential power he had! A little matter like swinging an election could be managed by a man like Kidder as easily as turning over in bed. The only thing he could do was to call him periodically and see if there was anything that Kidder needed to keep himself busy. Kidder appreciated this. Conant, once in a while, would suggest something to Kidder that intrigued him, something that would keep him deep in his hermitage for a few weeks. The light pump was one of the results of Conant's imagination. Conant bet him it couldn't be done. Kidder did it.

One afternoon Kidder answered the squeal of the radiophone's signal. Swearing mildly, he shut off the film he was watching and crossed the compound to the old laboratory. He went to the radiophone, threw a switch. The squealing stopped.

"Well?"

"Hello, Kidder," said Conant. "Busy?"

"Not very," said Kidder. He was delighted with the pictures his camera had caught, showing the skillful work of a gang of Neoterics synthesizing rubber out of pure sulphur. He would rather have liked to tell Conant about it, but somehow he had never got around to telling Conant about the Neoterics, and he didn't see why he should start now.

Conant said, "Er . . . Kidder, I was down at the club the other day and a bunch of us were filling up an evening with loose talk. Something came up which might interest you."

"What?"

"Couple of the utilities boys there. You know the power setup in this country, don't you? Thirty percent atomic, the rest hydroelectric, diesel and steam?"

"I hadn't known," said Kidder, who was as innocent as a babe of current events.

"Well, we were arguing about what chances a new power source would have. One of the men there said it would be smarter to produce a new power and then talk about it. Another one waived that; said he couldn't name that new power, but he could describe it. Said it would have to have everything that present power sources have, plus one or two more things. It could be cheaper, for instance. It could be more efficient. It might supersede the others by being easier to carry from the power plant to the consumer. See what I mean? Any one of these factors might prove a new source of power competitive to the others. What I'd like to see is a new power with *all* of these factors. What do you think of it?"

"Not impossible."

"Think not?"

"I'll try it."

"Keep me posted." Conant's transmitter clicked off. The switch was a little piece of false front that Kidder had built into the set, which was something that Conant didn't know. The set switched itself off when Conant moved from it. After the switch's sharp crack, Kidder heard the banker mutter, "If he does it, I'm all set. If he doesn't, at least the crazy fool will keep himself busy on the isl—"

Kidder eyed the radiophone for an instant with raised eyebrows, and then shrugged them down again with his shoulders. It was quite evident that Conant had something up his sleeve, but Kidder wasn't worried. Who on earth would want to disturb him? He wasn't bothering anybody. He went back to the Neoterics' building, full of the new power idea.

Eleven days later Kidder called Conant and gave specific instructions on how to equip his receiver with a facsimile set which would enable Kidder to send written matter over the air. As soon as this was done and Kidder informed, the biochemist for once in his life spoke at some length.

"Conant—you implied that a new power source that would be cheaper, more efficient and more easily transmitted than any now in use did not exist. You might be interested in the little generator I have just set up.

"It has power, Conant—unbelievable power. Broadcast. A beautiful little tight beam. Here—catch this on the facsimile recorder." Kidder slipped a sheet of paper under the clips on his transmitter and it appeared on Conant's set. "Here's the wiring diagram for a power receiver. Now listen. The beam is so tight, so highly directional, that not three thousandths of one percent of the power would be lost in a two-thousand-mile transmission. The power system is closed. That is, any drain on the beam returns a signal along it to the transmitter, which automatically steps up to increase the power output. It

has a limit, but it's way up. And something else. This little
gadget of mine can send out eight different beams with a total horsepower output of around eight thousand per minute
per beam. From each beam you can draw enough power to
turn the page of a book or fly a superstratosphere plane.
Hold on—I haven't finished yet. Each beam, as I told you before, returns a signal from receiver to transmitter. This not
only controls the power output of the beam, but directs it.
Once contact is made, the beam will never let go. It will follow the receiver anywhere. You can power land, air or water
vehicles with it, as well as any stationary plant. Like it?"

Conant, who was a banker and not a scientist, wiped his
shining pate with the back of his hand and said, "I've never
known you to steer me wrong yet, Kidder. How about the
cost of this thing?"

"High," said Kidder promptly. "As high as an atomic
plant. But there are no high-tension lines, no wires, no
pipelines, no nothing. The receivers are little more complicated than a radio set. The transmitter is—well, that's quite a
job."

"Didn't take you long," said Conant.

"No," said Kidder, "it didn't, did it?" It was the lifework
of nearly twelve hundred highly cultured people, but Kidder
wasn't going into that. "Of course, the one I have here's just
a model."

Conant's voice was strained. "A—model? And it de-
livers—"

"Over sixty-thousand horsepower," said Kidder gleefully.

"Good heavens! In a full-sized machine—why, one transmitter would be enough to—" The possibilities of the thing
choked Conant for a moment. "How is it fueled?"

"It isn't," said Kidder. "I won't begin to explain it. I've
tapped a source of power of unimaginable force. It's—well,
big. So big that it can't be misused."

"What?" snapped Conant. "What do you mean by that?"

Kidder cocked an eyebrow. Conant *had* something up his
sleeve, then. At this second indication of it, Kidder, the least
suspicious of men, began to put himself on guard. "I mean
just what I say," he said evenly. "Don't try too hard to understand me—I barely savvy it myself. But the source of this
power is a monstrous resultant caused by the unbalance of
two previously equalized forces. Those equalized forces are
cosmic in quantity. Acutally, the forces are those which make
suns, crush atoms the way they crushed those that compose
the companion of Sirius. It's not anything you can fool with."

"I don't—" said Conant, and his voice ended puzzledly.

"I'll give you a parallel of it," said Kidder. "Suppose you take two rods, one in each hand. Place their tips together and push. As long as your pressure is directly along their long axes, the pressure is equalized; right and left hands cancel each other out. Now I come along; I put out one finger and touch the rods ever so lightly where they come together. They snap out of line violently; you break a couple of knuckles. The resultant force is at right angles to the original force you exerted. My power transmitter is on the same principle. It takes an infinitesimal amount of energy to throw those forces out of line. Easy enough when you know how to do it. The important question is whether or not you can control the resultant when you get it. I can."

"I—see." Conant indulged in a four-second gloat. "Heaven help the utility companies. I don't intend to. Kidder—I want a full-size transmitter."

Kidder clucked into the microphone. "Ambitious, aren't you? I haven't a staff out here, Conant—you know that. And I can't be expected to build four or five thousand tons of apparatus myself."

"I'll have five hundred engineers and laborers out there in forty-eight hours."

"You will not. Why bother me with it? I'm quite happy here, Conant, and one of the reasons is that I've no one to get in my hair."

"Oh, now, Kidder—don't be like that. I'll pay you—"

"You haven't got that much money," said Kidder briskly. He flipped the switch on his set. *His* switch worked.

Conant was furious. He shouted into the phone several times, then began to lean on the signal button. On his island, Kidder let the thing squeal and went back to his projection room. He was sorry he had sent the diagram of the receiver to Conant. It would have been interesting to power a plane or a car with the model transmitter he had taken from the Neoterics. But if Conant was going to be that way about it—well, anyway, the receiver would be no good without the transmitter. Any radio engineer would understand the diagram, but not the beam which activated it. And Conant wouldn't get his beam.

Pity he didn't know Conant well enough.

Kidder's days were endless sorties into learning. He never slept, nor did his Neoterics. He ate regularly every five hours, exercised for half an hour in every twelve. He did not keep track of time, for it meant nothing to him. Had he wanted to know the date, or the year, even, he knew he could get it from Conant. He didn't care, that's all. The time that was not spent in observation was used in developing new problems for the Neoterics. His thoughts just now ran to defense. The idea was born in his conversation with Conant; now the idea was primary, its motivation something of no importance. The Neoterics were working on a vibration field of quasi-electrical nature. Kidder could see little practical value in such a thing—an invisible wall which would kill any living thing which touched it. But still—the idea was intriguing.

He stretched and moved away from the telescope in the upper room through which he had been watching his creations at work. He was profoundly happy here in the large control room. Leaving it to go to the old laboratory for a bite to eat was a thing he hated to do. He felt like bidding it good-bye each time he walked across the compound, and saying a glad hello when he returned. A little amused at himself, he went out.

There was a black blob—a distant power boat—a few miles off the island, toward the mainland. Kidder stopped and stared distastefully at it. A white petal of spray was affixed to each side of the black body—it was coming toward him. He snorted, thinking of the time a yacht load of silly fools had landed out of curiosity one afternoon, spewed themselves over his beloved island, peppered him with lamebrained questions, and thrown his nervous equilibrium out for days. Lord, how he hated *people!*

The thought of unpleasantness bred two more thoughts that played half-consciously with his mind as he crossed the compound and entered the old laboratory. One was that perhaps it might be wise to surround his buildings with a field of force of some kind and post warnings for trespassers. The other thought was of Conant and the vague uneasiness the man had been sending to him through the radiophone these last weeks. His suggestion, two days ago, that a power plant be built on the island—horrible idea!

Conant rose from his seat on a laboratory bench as Kidder walked in.

They looked at each other wordlessly for a long moment. Kidder hadn't seen the bank president in years. The man's presence, he found, made his scalp crawl.

"Hello," said Conant genially. "You're looking fit."

Kidder grunted. Conant eased his unwieldy body back onto

the bench and said, "Just to save you the energy of asking questions, Mr. Kidder, I arrived two hours ago on a small boat. Rotten way to travel. I wanted to be a surprise to you; my two men rowed me the last couple of miles. You're not very well equipped here for defense, are you? Why, anyone could slip up on you the way I did."

"Who'd want to?" growled Kidder. The man's voice edged annoyingly into his brain. He spoke too loudly for such a small room; at least, Kidder's hermit's ears felt that way. Kidder shrugged and went about preparing a light meal for himself.

"Well," drawled the banker, "I might want to." He drew out a Dow-metal cigar case. "Mind if I smoke?"

"I do," said Kidder sharply.

Conant laughed easily and put the cigars away. "I might," he said, "want to urge you to let me build that power station on this island."

"Radiophone work?"

"Oh, yes. But now that I'm here you can't switch me off. Now—how about it?"

"I haven't changed my mind."

"Oh, but you should, Kidder, you should. Think of it— think of the good it would do for the masses of people that are now paying exorbitant power bills!"

"I hate the masses! Why do you have to build here?"

"Oh, that. It's an ideal location. You own the island; work could begin here without causing any comment whatsoever. The plant would spring full-fledged on the power markets of the country, having been built in secret. The island can be made impregnable."

"I don't want to be bothered."

"We wouldn't bother you. We'd build on the north end of the island—a mile and a quarter from you and your work. Ah—by the way—where's the model of the power transmitter?"

Kidder, with his mouth full of synthesized food, waved a hand at a small table on which stood the model, a four-foot, amazing intricate device of plastic and steel and tiny coils.

Conant rose and went over to look at it. "Actually works, eh?" He sighed deeply and said, "Kidder, I really hate to do this, but I want to build that plant rather badly. Corson! Robbins!"

Two bull-necked individuals stepped out from their hiding places in the corners of the room. One idly dangled a revolver by its trigger guard. Kidder looked blankly from one to the other of them.

"These gentlemen will follow my orders implicitly, Kidder. In half an hour a party will land here—engineers, contractors. They will start surveying the north end of the island for the construction of the power plant. These boys here feel about the same way I do as far as you are concerned. Do we proceed with your cooperation or without it? It's immaterial to me whether or not you are left alive to continue your work. My engineers can duplicate your model."

Kidder said nothing. He had stopped chewing when he saw the gunmen, and only now remembered to swallow. He sat crouched over his plate without moving or speaking.

Conant broke the silence by walking to the door. "Robbins—can you carry that model there?" The big man put his gun away, lifted the model gently, and nodded. "Take it down to the beach and meet the other boat. Tell Mr. Johansen, the engineer, that this is the model he is to work from." Robbins went out. Conant turned to Kidder. "There's no need for us to anger ourselves," he said oilily. "I think you are stubborn, but I don't hold it against you. I know how you feel. You'll be left alone; you have my promise. But I mean to go ahead on this job, and a small thing like your life can't stand in my way."

Kidder said, "Get out of here." There were two swollen veins throbbing at his temples. His voice was low, and it shook.

"Very well. Good day, Mr. Kidder. Oh—by the way— you're a clever devil." No one had ever referred to the scholastic Mr. Kidder that way before. "I realize the possibility of your blasting us off this island. I wouldn't do it if I were you. I'm willing to give you what you want—privacy. I want the same thing in return. If anything happens to me while I'm here, the island will be bombed by someone who is working for me. I'll admit they might fail. If they do, the United States government will take a hand. You wouldn't want that, would you? That's rather a big thing for one man to fight. The same thing goes if the plant is sabotaged in any way after I go back to the mainland. You might be killed. You will most certainly be bothered interminably. Thanks for your . . . er . . . cooperation." The banker smirked and walked out. followed by his taciturn gorilla.

Kidder sat there for a long time without moving. Then he shook his head, rested it in his palms. He was badly frightened; not so much because his life was in danger, but because his privacy and his work—his world—were threatened. He was hurt and bewildered. He wasn't a businessman. He couldn't handle men. All his life he had run away from humans and what they represented to him. He was like a frightened child when men closed in on him.

Cooling a little, he wondered vaguely what would happen when the power plant opened. Certainly the government would be interested. Unless—unless by then Conant was the government. That plant was an unimaginable source of power, and not only the kind of power that turned wheels. He rose and went back to the world that was home to him, a world where his motives were understood, and where there were those who could help him. Back at the Neoterics' building, he escaped yet again from the world of men into his work.

Kidder called Conant the following week, much to the banker's surprise. His two days on the island had gotten the work well under way, and he had left with the arrival of a shipload of laborers and material. He kept in close touch by radio with Johansen, the engineer in charge. It had been a blind job for Johansen and all the rest of the crew on the island. Only the bank's infinite resources could have hired such a man, or the picked gang with him.

Johansen's first reaction when he saw the model had been ecstatic. He wanted to tell his friends about this marvel; but the only radio set available was beamed to Conant's private office in the bank, and Conant's armed guards, one to every two workers, had strict orders to destroy any other radio transmitter on sight. About that time he realized that he was a prisoner on the island. His instant anger subsided when he reflected that being a prisoner at fifty thousand dollars a week wasn't too bad. Two of the laborers and an engineer thought differently, and got disgruntled a couple of days after they arrived. They disappeared one night—the same night that five shots were fired down on the beach. No questions were asked, and there was no more trouble.

Conant covered his surprise at Kidder's call and was as offensively jovial as ever. "Well, now! Anything I can do for you?"

"Yes," said Kidder. His voice was low, completely without expression. "I want you to issue a warning to your men not to pass the white line I have drawn five hundred yards north of my buildings, right across the island."

"Warning? Why, my dear fellow, they have orders that you are not to be disturbed on any account."

"You've ordered them. All right. Now warn them. I have an electric field surrounding my laboratories that will kill anything living which penetrates it. I don't want to have murder on my conscience. There will be no deaths unless there are trespassers. You'll inform your workers?"

"Oh, now, Kidder," the banker expostulated. "That was totally unnecessary. You won't be bothered. Why—" But he found he was talking into a dead mike. He knew better than to call back. He called Johansen instead and told him about it. Johansen didn't like the sound of it, but he repeated the message and signed off. Conant liked that man. He was, for a moment, a little sorry that Johansen would never reach the mainland alive.

But that Kidder—he was beginning to be a problem. As long as his weapons were strictly defensive he was no real menace. But he would have to be taken care of when the plant was operating. Conant couldn't afford to have genius around him unless it was unquestionably on his side. The power transmitter and Conant's highly ambitious plans would be safe as long as Kidder was left to himself. Kidder knew that he could, for the time being, expect more sympathetic treatment from Conant than he could from a horde of government investigators.

Kidder only left his own enclosure once after the work began on the north end of the island, and it took all of his unskilled diplomacy to do it. Knowing the source of the plant's power, knowing what could happen if it were misused, he asked Conant's permission to inspect the great transmitter when it was nearly finished. Insuring his own life by refusing to report back to Conant until he was safe within his own laboratory again, he turned off his shield and walked up to the north end.

He saw an awe-inspiring sight. The four-foot model was duplicated nearly a hundred times as large. Inside a massive three-hundred-foot tower a space was packed nearly solid with the same bewildering maze of coils and bars that the Neoterics had built so delicately into their machine. At the top was a globe of polished golden alloy, the transmitting antenna. From it would stream thousands of tight beams of force, which could be tapped to any degree by corresponding thousands of receivers placed anywhere at any distance. Kidder learned that the receivers had already been built, but his informant, Johansen, knew little about that end of it and was saying less. Kidder checked over every detail of the structure, and when he was through he shook Johansen's hand admiringly.

"I didn't want this thing here," he said shyly, "and I don't. But I will say that it's a pleasure to see this kind of work."

"It's a pleasure to meet the man that invented it."

Kidder beamed. "I didn't invent it," he said. "Maybe some day I'll show you who did. I—well, good-bye." He turned before he had a chance to say too much and marched off down the path.

"Shall I?" said a voice at Johansen's side. One of Conant's guards had his gun out.

Johansen knocked the man's arm down. "No." He scratched his head. "So that's the mysterious menace from the other end of the island. Eh! Why, he's a hell of a nice little feller!"

Built on the ruins of Denver, which was destroyed in the great Battle of the Rockies during the Western War, stands the most beautiful city in the world—our nation's capital, New Washington. In a circular room deep in the heart of the White House, the president, three army men, and a civilian sat. Under the president's desk a dictaphone unostentatiously recorded every word that was said. Two thousand and more miles away, Conant hung over a radio receiver, tuned to receive the signals of the tiny transmitter in the civilian's side pocket.

One of the officers spoke.

"Mr. President, the 'impossible claims' made for this gentleman's product are absolutely true. He has proved beyond doubt each item on his prospectus."

The president glanced at the civilian, back at the officer. "I won't wait for your report," he said. "Tell me—what happened?"

Another of the army men mopped his face with a khaki bandanna. "I can't ask you to believe us, Mr. President, but it's true all the same. Mr. Wright here has in his suitcase three or four dozen small . . . er . . . bombs—"

"They're not bombs," said Wright casually.

"All right. They're not bombs. Mr. Wright smashed two of them on an anvil with a sledge hammer. There was no result. He put two more in an electric furnace. They burned away like so much tin and cardboard. We dropped one down the barrel of a field piece and fired it. Still nothing." He paused and looked at the third officer, who picked up the account.

"We really got started then. We flew to the proving

grounds, dropped one of the objects and flew to thirty thousand feet. From there, with a small hand detonator no bigger than your fist, Mr. Wright set the thing off. I've never seen anything like it. Forty acres of land came straight up at us, breaking up as it came. The concussion was terrific—you must have felt it here, four hundred miles away."

The president nodded. "I did. Seismographs on the other side of the Earth picked it up."

"The crater it left was a quarter of a mile deep at the center. Why, one plane load of those things could demolish any city! There isn't even any necessity for accuracy!"

"You haven't heard anything yet," another officer broke in. "Mr. Wright's automobile is powered by a small plant similar to the others. He demonstrated it to us. We could find no fuel tank of any kind, or any other driving mechanism. But with a power plant no bigger than six cubic inches, that car, carrying enough weight to give it traction, outpulled an army tank!"

"And the other test!" said the third excitedly. "He put one of the objects into a replica of a treasury vault. The walls were twelve feet thick, super-reinforced concrete. He controlled it from over a hundred yards away. He . . . he burst that vault! It wasn't an explosion—it was as if some incredibly powerful expansive force inside filled it and flattened the walls from inside. They cracked and split and powdered, and the steel girders and rods came twisting and shearing out like . . . like—*whew!* After that he insisted on seeing you. We knew it wasn't usual, but he said he has more to say and would say it only in your presence."

The president said gravely, "What is it, Mr. Wright?"

Wright rose, picked up his suitcase, opened it and took out a small cube, about eight inches on a side, made of some light-absorbent red material. Four men edged nervously away from it.

"These gentlemen," he began, "have seen only part of the things this device can do. I'm going to demonstrate to you the delicacy of control that is possible with it." He made an adjustment with a tiny knob on the side of the cube, set it on the edge of the president's desk.

"You have asked me more than once if this is my invention or if I am representing someone. The latter is true. It might also interest you to know that the man who controls this cube is right now several thousand miles from here. He, and he alone, can prevent it from detonating now that I"—he pulled his detonator out of the suitcase and pressed a button—"have done this. It will explode the way the one we dropped from the plane did, completely destroying this city and everything in it, in just four hours. It will also explode"—he stepped back and threw a tiny switch on his detonator—"if any moving object comes within three feet of it or if anyone leaves this room but me—it can be compensated for that. If, after I leave, I am molested, it will detonate as soon as a hand is laid on me. No bullets can kill me fast enough to prevent me from setting it off."

The three army men were silent. One of them swiped nervously at the beads of cold sweat on his forehead. The others did not move. The president said evenly,

"What's your proposition?"

"A very reasonable one. My employer does not work in the open, for obvious reasons. All he wants is your agreement to carry out his orders; to appoint the cabinet members he chooses, to throw your influence in any way he dictates. The public—Congress—anyone else—need never know anything about it. I might add that if you agree to this proposal, this 'bomb,' as you call it, will not go off. But you can be sure that thousands of them are planted all over the country. You will never know when you are near one. If you disobey, it means instant annihilation for you and everyone else within three or four square miles.

"In three hours and fifty minutes—that will be at precisely seven o'clock—there is a commercial radio program on station RPRS. You will cause the announcer, after his station identification, to say 'Agreed.' It will pass unnoticed by all but my employer. There is no use in having me followed; my work is done. I shall never see or contact my employer again. That is all. Good afternoon, gentlemen!"

Wright closed his suitcase with a businesslike snap, bowed, and left the room. Four men sat frozen, staring at the little red cube.

"Do you think he can do all he says?" asked the president.

The three nodded mutely. The president reached for his phone.

There was an eavesdropper to all of the foregoing. Conant, squatting behind his great desk in the vault, where he had his sanctum sanctorum, knew nothing of it. But beside him was the compact bulk of Kidder's radiophone. His presence switched it on, and Kidder, on his island, blessed the day he had thought of that device. He had been meaning to call Conant all morning, but was very hesitant. His meeting with the young engineer Johansen had impressed him strongly. The man was such a thorough scientist, possessed of such complete delight in the work he did, that for the first time in his life Kidder found himself actually wanting to see someone again. But he feared for Johansen's life if he brought him to the laboratory, for Johansen's work was done on the island, and Conant would most certainly have the engineer killed if he heard of his visit, fearing that Kidder would influence him to sabotage the great transmitter. And if Kidder went to the power plant he would probably be shot on sight.

All one day Kidder wrangled with himself, and finally determined to call Conant. Fortunately he gave no signal, but turned up the volume on the receiver when the little red light told him that Conant's transmitter was functioning. Curious, he heard everything that occurred in the president's chamber three thousand miles away. Horrified, he realized what Conant's engineers had done. Built into tiny containers were tens of thousands of power receivers. They had no power of their own, but, by remote control, could draw on any or all of the billions of horsepower the huge plant on the island was broadcasting.

Kidder stood in front of his receiver, speechless. There was nothing he could do. If he devised some means of destroying the power plant, the government would certainly step in and take over the island, and then—what would happen to him and his precious Neoterics?

Another sound grated out of the receiver—a commercial radio program. A few bars of music, a man's voice advertising stratoline fares on the installment plan, a short silence, then:

"Station RPRS, voice of the nation's Capital, District of South Colorado."

The three-second pause was interminable.

"The time is exactly . . . er . . . *agreed*. The time is exactly seven p. m., Mountain Standard Time."

Then came a half-insane chuckle. Kidder had difficulty believing it was Conant. A phone clicked. The banker's voice:

"Bill? All set. Get out there with your squadron and bomb up the island. Keep away from the plant, but cut the rest of it to ribbons. Do it quick and get out of there."

Almost hysterical with fear, Kidder rushed about the room and then shot out the door and across the compound. There were five hundred innocent workmen in barracks a quarter mile from the plant. Conant didn't need them now, and he didn't need Kidder. The only safety for anyone was in the plant itself, and Kidder wouldn't leave his Neoterics to be bombed. He flung himself up the stairs and to the nearest teletype. He banged out, "Get me a defense. I want an impenetrable shield. Urgent!"

The words rippled out from under his fingers in the functional script of the Neoterics. Kidder didn't think of what he wrote, didn't really visualize the thing he ordered. But he had done what he could. He'd have to leave them now, get to the barracks; warn those men. He ran up the path toward the plant, flung himself over the white line that marked death to those who crossed it.

A squadron of nine clip-winged, mosquito-nosed planes rose out of a cove on the mainland. There was no sound from the engines, for there were no engines. Each plane was powered with a tiny receiver and drew its unmarked, light-absorbent wings through the air with power from the island. In a matter of minutes they raised the island. The squadron leader spoke briskly into a microphone.

"Take the barracks first. Clean 'em up. Then work south."

Johansen was alone on a small hill near the center of the island. He carried a camera, and though he knew pretty well that his chances of ever getting ashore again were practically nonexistent, he liked angle shots of his tower, and took innumerable pictures. The first he knew of the planes was when he heard their whining dive over the barracks. He stood transfixed, saw a shower of bombs hurtled down and turn the barracks into a smashed ruin of broken wood, metal and bodies. The picture of Kidder's earnest face flashed into his mind. Poor little guy—if they ever bombed his end of the island he would—But his tower! Were they going to bomb the plant?

He watched, utterly appalled, as the planes flew out to sea, cut back and dove again. They seemed to be working south. At the third dive he was sure of it. Not knowing what he could do, he nevertheless turned and ran toward Kidder's place. He rounded a turn in the trail and collided violently with the little biochemist. Kidder's face was scarlet with exertion, and he was the most terrified-looking object Johansen had ever seen.

Kidder waved a hand northward. "Conant!" he screamed over the uproar. "It's Conant! He's going to kill us all!"

"The plant?" said Johansen, turning pale.

"It's safe. He won't touch *that!* But . . . my place . . what about all those men?"

"Too late!" shouted Johansen.

"Maybe I can—Come on!" called Kidder, and was off down the trail, heading south.

Johansen pounded after him. Kidder's little short legs became a blur as the squadron swooped overhead, laying its eggs in the spot where they had met.

As they burst out of the woods, Johansen put on a spurt, caught up with the scientist and knocked him sprawling not six feet from the white line.

"Wh . . . wh—"

"Don't go any farther, you fool! Your own damned force field—it'll kill you!"

"Force field? But—I came through it on the way up— Here. Wait. If I can—" Kidder began hunting furiously about in the grass. In a few seconds he ran up to the line, clutching a large grasshopper in his hand. He tossed it over. It lay still.

"See?" said Johansen. "It—"

"Look! It jumped! Come on! I don't know what went wrong, unless the Neoterics shut it off. They generated that field—I didn't."

"Neo—huh?"

"Never mind," snapped the biochemist, and ran.

They pounded gasping up the steps and into the Neoterics' control room. Kidder clapped his eyes to a telescope and shrieked in glee. "They've done it! They've done it!"

"Who's—"

"My little people! The Neoterics! They've made the impenetrable shield! Don't you see—it cut through the lines of force that start up that field out there! Their generator is still throwing it up, but the vibrations can't get out! They're safe! They're safe!" And the overwrought hermit began to cry. Johansen looked at him pityingly and shook his head.

"Sure—your little men are all right. But we aren't," he added as the floor shook at the detonation of a bomb.

Johansen closed his eyes, got a grip on himself and let his curiosity overcome his fear. He stepped to the binocular telescope, gazed down it. There was nothing there but a curved sheet of gray material. He had never seen a gray quite like that. It was absolutely neutral. It didn't seem soft and it didn't seem hard, and to look at it made his brain reel. He looked up.

Kidder was pounding the keys on a teletype, watching the blank yellow tape anxiously.

"I'm not getting through to them," he whimpered. "I don't know what's the mat—Oh, Of *course!*"

"What?"

"The shield is absolutely impenetrable! The teletype impulses can't get through or I could get them to extend the screen over the building—over the whole island! There's nothing those people can't do!"

"He's crazy," Johansen said under his breath. "Poor little—"

The teletype began clicking sharply. Kidder dove at it, practically embraced it. He read off the tape as it came out. Johansen saw the characters, but they meant nothing to him.

"Almighty," Kidder read falteringly, "pray have mercy on us and be forebearing until we have said our say. Without orders we have lowered the screen you ordered us to raise. We are lost, O great one. Our screen is truly impenetrable, and so cut off your words on the word machine. We have never, in memory of any Neoteric, been without your word before. Forgive us our action. We will eagerly await your answer."

Kidder's fingers danced over the keys. "You can look now," he gasped. "Go on—the telescope!"

Johansen, trying to ignore the whine of sure death from above, looked.

He saw what looked like land—fantastic fields under cultivation, a settlement of some sort, factories, and—beings. Everything moved with incredible rapidity. He couldn't see one of the inhabitants except as darting pinky-white streaks. Fascinated, he stared for a long minute. A sound behind him made him whirl. It was Kidder, rubbing his hands together briskly. There was a broad smile on his face.

"They did it," he said happily. "You see?"

Johansen didn't see until he began to realize that there was a dead silence outside. He ran to a window. It was night outside—the blackest night—when it should have been dusk. "What happened?"

"The Neoterics," said Kidder, and laughed like a child. "My friends downstairs there. They threw up the impenetrable shield over the whole island. We can't be touched now!"

And at Johansen's amazed questions, he launched into a description of the race of beings below them.

Outside the shell, things happened. Nine airplanes suddenly went dead-stick. Nine pilots glided downward, powerless, and some fell into the sea, and some struck the miraculous gray shell that loomed in place of an island; slid off and sank.

And ashore, a man named Wright sat in a car, half dead with fear, while government men surrounded him, approached cautiously, daring instant death from a now-dead source.

In a room deep in the White House, a high-ranking army officer shrieked, "I can't stand it any more! I can't!" and leaped up, snatched a red cube off the president's desk, ground it to ineffectual litter under his shining boots.

And in a few days they took a broken old man away from the bank and put him in an asylum, where he died within a week.

The shield, you see, was truly impenetrable. The power plant was untouched and sent out its beams; but the beams could not get out, and anything powered from the plant went dead. The story never became public, although for some years there was heightened naval activity off the New England coast. The navy, so the story went, had a new target range out there—a great hemi-ovoid of gray material. They bombed it and shelled it and rayed it and blasted all around it, but never even dented its smooth surface.

Kidder and Johansen let it stay there. They were happy enough with their researches and their Neoterics. They did not hear or feel the shelling, for the shield was truly impenetrable. They synthesized their food and their light and air from the materials at hand, and they simply didn't care. They were the only survivors of the bombing, with the exception of three poor maimed devils that died soon afterward.

All this happened many years ago, and Kidder and Johansen may be alive today, and they may be dead. But that doesn't matter too much. The important thing is that the great gray shell will bear watching. Men die, but races live. Someday the Neoterics, after innumerable generations of inconceivable advancement, will take down their shield and come forth. When I think of that I feel frightened.

JAY SCORE

Astounding Science Fiction
May

by Eric Frank Russell

*"Jay Score" was somewhat overshadowed when it
first appeared because the May, 1941 Astounding
happened to contain two important Heinlein stories, "Universe" (too long for inclusion here), and
"Solution Unsatisfactory" (in his "Anson MacDonald" persona). In addition, there was "Liar!" by
one of your editors, and as a bonus, Heinlein provided a guide and outline to his still-in-process Future History. Sorry, Isaac, but they don't make sf
magazines like this any more.*

*Russell's contribution is a fine story and was the
first of a series of four, finally collected as* Men,
Martians and Machines *in 1955.*

(No, they don't, Marty. And I'm the first to agree. To this
day, people speak of the 1927 Yankees as the greatest ball
team of all time, and I agree. And my feeling is that the
1939-1941 *Astoundings* were the greatest science fiction magazines of all time, including my own, and that the May, 1941
issue and September, 1941 issue may be the greatest individual issues of all time. I'm surprised, looking back on it, that
John Campbell published *two* robot stories in the May issue,
but "Jay Score" was *so* good. In fact, from my own self-centered viewpoint it was the best robot story not written by myself since "Helen O'Loy" by Lester del Rey—I.A.)

There are very good reasons for everything they do. To the
uninitiated some of their little tricks and some of their regula-
tions seem mighty peculiar—but rocketing through the cosmos isn't quite like paddling a bathtub across a farm pond,
no, sir!

For instance, this stunt of using mixed crews is pretty sensible when you look into it. On the outward runs toward

Mars, the Asteroids, or beyond, they have white Terrestrials
to tend the engines because they're the ones who perfected
modern propulsion units, know most about them and can
nurse them like nobody else. All ships' surgeons are black
Terrestrials because for some reason none can explain no Negro gets gravity-bends or space nausea. Every outside repair
gang is composed of Martians, who use very little air, are tip-
top metal workers, and fairly immune to cosmic-ray burn.

As for the inward trips to Venus, they mix them similarly
except that the emergency pilot is always a big clunker like
Jay Score. There's a motive behind that; he's the one who
provided it. I'm never likely to forget him. He sort of sticks
in the mind, for keeps. What a character!

Destiny placed me at the top of the gangway the first time
he appeared. Our ship was the *Upskadaska City,* a brand new
freighter with limited passenger accommodation, registered in
the Venusian spaceport from which she took her name.
Needless to say she was known among hardened spacemen as
the *Upsydaisy.*

We were lying in the Colorado Rocket Basin, north of
Denver, with a fair load aboard, mostly watchmaking
machinery, agricultural equipment, aeronautical jigs, and
tools for Upskadaska, as well as a case of radium needles for
the Venusian Cancer Research Institute. There were eight
passengers, all emigrating agriculturalists planning on making
hay thirty million miles nearer the sun. We had ramped the
vessel and were waiting for the blow-brothers-blow siren, due
in forty minutes, when Jay Score arrived.

He was six feet nine, weighed at least three hundred
pounds yet toted this bulk with the easy grace of a ballet
dancer. A big guy like that, moving like that, was something
worth watching. He came up the duralumin gangway with all
the nonchalance of a tripper boarding the bus for Jackson's
Creek. From his hamlike right fist dangled a rawhide case not
quite big enough to contain his bed and maybe a wardrobe or
two.

Reaching the top, he paused while he took in the crossed
swords on my cap, said, "Morning, Sarge. I'm the new
emergency pilot. I have to report to Captain McNulty."

I knew we were due for another pilot now that Jew Durkin
had been promoted to the snooty Martial scent bottle *Prome-
theus.* So this was his successor. He was a Terrestrial all
right, but neither black nor white. His expressionless but capable face looked as if covered with old, well-seasoned
leather. His eyes held fires resembling phosphorescence.

There was an air about him that marked him an exceptional individual the like of which I'd never met before.

"Welcome, Tiny," I offered, getting a crick in the neck as I stared up at him. I did not offer my hand because I wanted it for use later on. "Open your satchel and leave it in the sterilizing chamber. You'll find the skipper in the bow."

"Thanks," he responded without the glimmer of a smile. He stepped into the airlock, hauling the rawhide haybarn with him.

"We blast in forty minutes," I warned.

Didn't see anything more of Jay Score until we were two hundred thousand out, with Earth a greenish moon at the end of our vapor-trail. Then I heard him in the passage asking someone where he could find the sergeant-at-arms. He was directed through my door.

"Sarge," he said, handing over his official requisition, "I've come to collect the trimmings." Then he leaned on the barrier, the whole framework creaked and the top tube sagged in the middle.

"Hey!" I shouted.

"Sorry!" He unleaned. The barrier stood much better when he kept his mass to himself.

Stamping his requisition, I went into the armory, dug out his needle-ray projector and a box of capsules for same. The biggest Venusian mud-skis I could find were about eleven sizes too small and a yard too short for him, but they'd have to do. I gave him a can of thin, multipurpose oil, a jar of graphite, a Lepanto power-pack for his microwave radiophone and, finally, a bunch of nutweed pellicules marked: "Compliments of the Bridal Planet Aromatic Herb Corporation."

Shoving back the spicy lumps, he said, "You can have 'em—they give me the staggers." The rest of the stuff he forced into his side-pack without so much as twitching an eyebrow. Long time since I'd seen anyone so poker-faced.

All the same, the way he eyed the spacesuits seemed strangely wistful. There were thirty bifurcated ones for the Terrestrials, all hanging on the wall like sloughed skins. Also there were six head-and-shoulder helmets for the Martians, since they needed no more than three pounds of air. There wasn't a suit for him. I couldn't have fitted him with one if my life had depended upon it. It'd have been like trying to can an elephant.

Well, he lumbered out lightly, if you get what I mean. The

casual, loose-limbed way he transported his tonnage made me think I'd like to be some place else if ever he got on the rampage. Not that I thought him likely to run amok; he was amiable enough though sphinxlike. But I was fascinated by his air of calm assurance and by his motion, which was fast, silent, and, eerie. Maybe the latter was due to his habit of wearing an inch of sponge rubber under his big dogs.

I kept an interested eye on Jay Score while the *Upsydaisy* made good time on her crawl through the void. Yes, I was more than curious about him because his type was a new one on me despite that I've met plenty in my time. He remained uncommunicative but kind of quietly cordial. His work was smoothly efficient and in every way satisfactory. McNulty took a great fancy to him, though he'd never been one to greet a newcomer with love and kisses.

Three days out, Jay made a major hit with the Martians. As everyone knows, those goggle-eyed, tententacled, half-breathing kibitzers have stuck harder than glue to the Solar System Chess Championship for more than two centuries. Nobody outside of Mars will ever pry them loose. They are nuts about the game and many's the time I've seen a bunch of them go through all the colors of the spectrum in sheer excitement when at last somebody has moved a pawn after thirty minutes of profound cogitation.

One rest-time Jay spent his entire eight hours under three pounds pressure in the starboard airlock. Through the lock's phones came long silences punctuated by wild and shrill twitterings as if he and the Martians were turning the place into a madhouse. At the end of the time we found our tentacled outside crew exhausted. It turned out that Jay had consented to play Kli Yang and had forced him to a stalemate. Kli had been sixth runner-up in the last Solar melee, had been beaten only ten times—each time by a brother Martian, of course.

The red-planet gang had a finger on him after that, or I should say a tentacle-tip. Every rest-time they waylaid him and dragged him into the airlock. When we were eleven days out he played the six of them simultaneously, lost two games, stalemated three, won one. They thought he was a veritable whizzbang—for a mere Terrestrial. Knowing their peculiar abilities in this respect, I thought so, too. So did McNulty. He went so far as to enter the sporting data in the log.

You may remember the stunt that the audiopress of 2270 boosted as "McNulty's Miracle Move"? It's practically a legend of the spaceways. Afterward, when we'd got safely home, McNulty disclaimed the credit and put it where it rightfully belonged. The audiopress had a good excuse, as usual. They said he was the captain, wasn't he? And his name made the headline alliterative, didn't it? Seems that there must be a sect of audio-journalists who have to be alliterative to gain salvation.

What precipitated that crazy stunt and whitened my hair was a chunk of cosmic flotsam. Said object took the form of a gob of meteoric nickel-iron ambling along at the characteristic speed of *pssst!* Its orbit lay on the planetary plane and it approached at right angles to our sunward course.

It gave us the business. I'd never have believed anything so small could have made such a slam. To the present day I can hear the dreadful whistle of air as it made a mad break for freedom through that jagged hole.

We lost quite a bit of political juice before the auto-doors sealed the damaged section. Pressure already had dropped to nine pounds when the compensators held it and slowly began to build it up again. The fall didn't worry the Martians; to them nine pounds was like inhaling pig-wash.

There was one engineer in that sealed section. Another escaped the closing doors by the skin of his left ear. But the first, we thought, had drawn his fateful number and eventually would be floated out like so many spacemen who've come to the end of their duty.

The guy who got clear was leaning against a bulwark, white-faced from the narrowness of his squeak. Jay Score came pounding along. His jaw was working, his eyes were like lamps, but his voice was cool and easy.

He said, "Get out. Seal this room. I'll try to make a snatch. Open up and let me out fast when I knock."

With that he shoved us from the room, which we sealed by closing its autodoor. We couldn't see what the big hunk was doing but the telltale showed he'd released and opened the door to the damaged section. Couple of seconds later the light went out, showing the door had been closed again. Then came a hard, urgent knock. We opened. Jay plunged through hell-for-leather with the engineer's limp body cuddled in his huge arms. He bore it as if it were no bigger and heavier than a kitten and the way he took it down the passage threatened to carry him clear through the end of the ship.

Meanwhile we found we were in a first-class mess. The rockets weren't functioning any more. The venturi tubes were okay and the combustion chambers undamaged. The injectors worked without a hitch—providing that they were pumped by hand. We had lost none of our precious fuel and the shell was intact save for that one jagged hole. What made us useless was the wrecking of our coordinated feeding and firing controls. They had been located where the big bullet went through and now they were so much scrap.

This was more than serious. General opinion called it certain death though nobody said so openly. I'm pretty certain that McNulty shared the morbid notion even if his official report did under-describe it as "an embarrassing predicament." That is just like McNulty. It's a wonder he didn't define our feelings by recording that we were somewhat nonplussed.

Anyway, the Martial squad poured out, some honest work being required of them for the first time in six trips. Pressure had crawled back to fourteen pounds and they had to come into it to be fitted with their head-and-shoulder contraptions.

Kli Yang sniffed offensively, waved a disgusted tentacle and chirruped, "I could swim!" He eased up when we got his dingbat fixed and exhausted it to his customary three pounds. That is the Martian idea of sarcasm: whenever the atmosphere is thicker than they like they make sinuous backstrokes and claim, "I could swim!"

To give them their due, they were good. A Martian can cling to polished ice and work continuously for twelve hours on a ration of oxygen that wouldn't satisfy a Terrestrial for more than ninety minutes. I watched them beat it through the airlock, eyes goggling through inverted fishbowls, their tentacles clutching power lines, sealing plates and quasi-arc welders. Blue lights made little auroras outside the ports as they began to cut, shape and close up that ragged hole.

All the time we continued to bullet sunward. But for this accursed misfortune we'd have swung a curve into the orbit of Venus in four hours' time. Then we'd have let her catch us up while we decelerated to a safe landing.

But when that peewee planetoid picked on us we were still heading for the biggest and brightest furnace hereabouts. That was the way we continued to go, our original velocity being steadily increased by the pull of our fiery destination.

I wanted to be cremated—but not yet!

Up in the bow navigation room Jay Score remained in constant conference with Captain McNulty and the two astro-computator operators. Outside, the Martians continued to crawl around, fizzing and spitting with flashes of ghastly blue light. The engineers, of course, weren't waiting for them to finish their job. Four in spacesuits entered the wrecked section and started the task of creating order out of chaos.

I envied all those busy guys and so did many others. There's a lot of consolation in being able to do something even in an apparently hopeless situation. There's a lot of misery in being compelled to play with one's fingers while others are active.

Two Martians came back through the lock, grabbed some more sealing-plates and crawled out again. One of them thought it might be a bright idea to take his pocket chess set as well, but I didn't let him. There are times and places for that sort of thing and knight to king's fourh on the skin of a busted boat isn't one of them. Then I went along to see Sam Hignett, our Negro surgeon.

Sam had managed to drag the engineer back from the rim of the grave. He'd done it with oxygen, adrenalin and heart-massage. Only his long, dexterous fingers could have achieved it. It was a feat of surgery that has been brought off before, but not often.

Seemed that Sam didn't know what had happened and didn't much care, either. He was like that when he had a patient on his hands. Deftly he closed the chest incision with silver clips, painted the pinched flesh with iodized plastic, cooled the stuff to immediate hardness with a spray of ether.

"Sam," I told him. "You're a marvel."

"Jay gave me a fair chance," he said. "He got him here in time."

"Why put the blame on him?" I joked, unfunnily.

"Sergeant," he answered, very serious, "I'm the ship's doctor. I do the best I can. I couldn't have saved this man if Jay hadn't brought him when he did."

"All right, all right," I agreed. "Have it your own way."

A good fellow, Sam. But he was like all doctors—you know, ethical. I left him with his feebly breathing patient.

McNulty came strutting along the catwalk as I went back. He checked the fuel tanks. He was doing it personally, and that meant something. He looked worried, and that meant a devil of a lot. It meant that I need not bother to write my last will and testament because it would never be read by anything living.

His portly form disappeared into the bow navigation room and I heard him say, "Jay, I guess you—" before the closing door cut off his voice.

He appeared to have a lot of faith in Jay Score. Well, that

individual certainly looked capable enough. The skipper and
the new emergency pilot continued to act like cronies even
while heading for the final frizzle.

One of the emigrating agriculturalists came out of his
cabin and caught me before I regained the armory. Studying
me wide-eyed, he said, "Sergeant, there's a half-moon
showing through my port."

He continued to pop them at me while I popped mine at
him. Venus showing half her pan meant that we were now
crossing her orbit. He knew it too—I could tell by the way he
bugged them.

"Well," he persisted, with ill-concealed nervousness, "how
long is this mishap likely to delay us?"

"No knowing." I scratched my head, trying to look stupid
and confident at one and the same time. "Captain McNulty
will do his utmost. Put your trust in him—Poppa knows
best."

"You don't think we are . . . er . . . in any danger?"

"Oh, not at all."

"You're a liar," he said.

"I resent having to admit it," said I.

That unhorsed him. He returned to his cabin, dissatisfied,
apprehensive. In short time he'd see Venus in three-quarter
phase and would tell the others. Then the fat would be in the
fire.

Our fat in the solar fire.

The last vestiges of hope had drained away just about the
time when a terrific roar and violent trembling told that the
long-dead rockets were back in action. The noise didn't last
more than a few seconds. They shut off quickly, the brief
burst serving to show that repairs were effective and satisfactory.

The noise brought out the agriculturalist at full gallop. He
knew the worst by now and so did the others. It had been impossible to conceal the truth for the three days since he'd
seen Venus as a half-moon. She was far behind us now. We
were cutting the orbit of Mercury. But still the passengers
clung to desperate hope that someone would perform an
unheard-of-miracle.

Charging into the armory, he yipped, "The rockets are
working again. Does that mean?"

"Nothing," I gave back, seeing no point in building false
hopes.

"But can't we turn round and go back?" He mopped perspiration trickling down his jowls. Maybe a little of it was forced out by fear, but most of it was due to the unpleasant fact that interior conditions had become anything but arctic.

"Sir," I said, feeling my shirt sticking to my back, "we've got more pull than any bunch of spacemen ever enjoyed before. And we're moving so goddam fast that there's nothing left to do but hold a lily."

"My ranch," he growled, bitterly. "I've been allotted five thousand acres of the best Venusian tobacco-growing territory, not to mention a range of uplands for beef."

"Sorry, but I think you'll be lucky ever to see it."

Crrrump! went the rockets again. The burst bent me backward and made him bow forward like he had a bad bellyache. Up in the bow, McNulty or Jay Score or someone was blowing them whenever he felt the whim. I couldn't see any sense in it.

"What's that for?" demanded the complainant, regaining the perpendicular.

"Boys will be boys," I said.

Snorting his disgust, he went to his cabin. A typical Terrestrial emigrant, big, healthy and tough, he was slow to crack and temporarily too peeved to be really worried in any genuinely soul-shaking way.

Half an hour later the general call sounded on buzzers all over the boat. It was a ground signal, never used in space. It meant that the entire crew and all other occupants of the vessel were summoned to the central cabin. Imagine guys being called from their posts in full flight!

Something unique in the history of space navigation must have been behind that call, probably a compose-yourselves-for-the-inevitable-end speech by McNulty.

Expecting the skipper to preside over the last rites, I wasn't surprised to find him standing on the tiny dais as we assembled. A faint scowl lay over his plump features but it changed to a ghost of a smile when the Martians mooched in and one of them did some imitation shark-dodging.

Erect beside McNulty, expressionless as usual, Jay Score looked at that swimming Martian as if he were a pane of glass. Then his strangely lit orbs shifted their aim as if they'd seen nothing more boring. The swim-joke was getting stale, anyway.

"Men and vedras," began McNulty—the latter being the Martian word for "adults" and, by implication, another piece of Martian sarcasm—"I have no need to enlarge upon the awkwardness of our position." That man certainly could pick his words—awkward! "Already we are nearer the sun than any vessel has been in the whole history of cosmic navigation."

"Comic navigation," murmured Kli Yang, with tactless wit.

"We'll need your humor to entertain us later," observed Jay Score in a voice so flat that Kli Yang subsided.

"We are moving toward the luminary," went on McNulty, his scowl reappearing, "faster than any ship moved before. Bluntly, there is not more than one chance in ten thousand of us getting out of this alive." He favored Kli Yang with a challenging stare but that tentacled individual was now subdued. "However, there *is* that one chance—and we are going to take it."

We gaped at him, wondering what the devil he meant. Every one of us knew our terrific velocity made it impossible to describe a U-turn and get back without touching the sun. Neither could we fight our way in the reverse direction with all that mighty drag upon us. There was nothing to do but go onward, onward, until the final searing blast scattered our disrupted molecules.

"What we intend is to try a cometary," continued McNulty. "Jay and myself and the astro-computators think it's remotely possible that we might achieve it and pull through."

That was plain enough. The stunt was a purely theoretical one frequently debated by mathematicians and astro-navigators but never tried out in grim reality. The idea is to build up all the velocity that can be got and at the same time to angle into the path of an elongated, elliptical orbit resembling that of a comet. In theory, the vessel might then skim close to the sun so supremely fast that it would swing pendulumlike far out to the opposite side of the orbit whence it came. A sweet trick—but could we make it?

"Calculations show our present condition fair enough to permit a small chance of success," said McNulty. "We have power enough and fuel enough to build up the necessary velocity with the aid of the sun-pull, to strike the necessary angle and to maintain it for the necessary time. The only point about which we have serious doubts is that of whether we can survive at our nearest to the sun." He wiped perspiration, unconsciously emphasizing the shape of things to come. "I won't mince words, men. It's going to be a choice sample of hell!"

"We'll see it through, Skipper," said someone. A low murmur of support sounded through the cabin.

Kli Yang stood up, simultaneously waggled four jointless arms for attention, and twittered, "It is an idea. It is excellent. I, Kli Yang, endorse it on behalf of my fellow vedras. We shall cram ourselves into the refrigerator and suffer the Terrestrial stink while the sun goes past."

Ignoring that crack about human odor, McNulty nodded and said, "Everybody will be packed into the cold room and endure it as best they can."

"Exactly," said Kli. "Quite," he added with bland disregard of superfluity. Wiggling a tentacle-tip at McNulty, he carried on, "But we cannot control the ship while squatting in the icebox like three and a half dozen strawberry sundaes. There will have to be a pilot in the bow. One individual can hold her on course—until he gets fried. So somebody has to be the fryee."

He gave the tip another sinuous wiggle, being under the delusion that it was fascinating his listeners into complete attention. "And since it cannot be denied that we Martians are far less susceptible to extremes of heat, I suggest that—"

"Nuts!" snapped McNulty. His gruffness deceived nobody. The Martians were nuisances—but grand guys.

"All right." Kli's chirrup rose to a shrill, protesting yelp. "Who else is entitled to become a crisp?"

"Me," said Jay Score. It was queer the way he voiced it. Just as if he were a candidate so obvious that only the stone-blind couldn't see him.

He was right, at that! Jay was the very one for the job. If anyone could take what was going to come through the fore observations ports it was Jay Score. He was big and tough, built for just such a task as this. He had a lot of stuff that none of us had got and, after all, he was a fully qualified emergency pilot. And most definitely this was an emergency, the greatest ever.

But it was funny the way I felt about him. I could imagine him up in front, all alone, nobody there, our lives depending on how much hell he could take, while the tremendous sun extended its searing fingers—

"You!" ejaculated Kli Yang, breaking my train of thought. His goggle eyes bulged irefully at the big, laconic figure on the dais. "You would! I am ready to mate in four moves, as you are miserably aware, and promptly you scheme to lock yourself away."

"Six moves," contradicted Jay, airily. "You cannot do it in less than six."

"Four!" Kli Yang fairly howled. "And right at this point you—"

It was too much for the listening McNulty. He looked as if on the verge of a stroke. His purple face turned to the semaphoring Kli.

"To hell with your blasted chess!" he roared. "Return to your stations, all of you. Make ready for maximum boost. I will sound the general call immediately it becomes necessary to take cover and then you will all go to the cold room." He stared around, the purple gradually fading as his blood pressure went down.

"That is, everyone except Jay."

More like old times with the rockets going full belt. They thundered smoothly and steadily. Inside the vessel the atmosphere became hotter and hotter until moisture trickled continually down our backs and a steaminess lay over the gloss of the walls. What it was like in the bow navigation-room I didn't know and didn't care to discover. The Martians were not inconvenienced yet; for once their whacky composition was much to be envied.

I did not keep check on the time but I'd had two spells of duty with one intervening sleep period before the buzzers gave the general call. By then things had become bad. I was no longer sweating: I was slowly melting into my boots.

Sam, of course, endured it most easily of all the Terrestrials and had persisted long enough to drag his patient completely out of original danger. That engineer was lucky, if it's luck to be saved for a bonfire. We put him in the cold room right away, with Sam in attendance.

The rest of us followed when the buzzer went. Our sanctuary was more than a mere refrigerator; it was the strongest and coolest section of the vessel, a heavily armored, triple-shielded compartment holding the instrument lockers, two sick bays and a large lounge for the benefit of space-nauseated passengers. It held all of us comfortably.

All but the Martians. It held them, but not comfortably. They are never comfortable at fourteen pounds pressure, which they regard as not only thick but also smelly—something like breathing molasses impregnated with aged goat.

Under our very eyes Kli Yang produced a bottle of *hooloo* scent, handed it to his half-parent, Kli Morg. The latter took it, stared at us distastefully, then sniffed the bottle in an ostentatious manner that was positively insulting. But nobody said anything.

All were present excepting McNulty and Jay Score. The skipper appeared two hours later. Things must have been raw up front, for he looked terrible. His haggard face was beaded and glossy, his once-plump cheeks sunken and blistered. His usually spruce, well-fitting uniform hung upon him sloppily. It needed only one glance to tell that he'd had a darned good roasting, as much as he could stand.

Walking unsteadily, he crossed the floor, went into the first-aid cubby, stripped himself with slow, painful movements. Sam rubbed him with tannic jelly. We could hear the tormented skipper grunting hoarsely as Sam put plenty of pep into the job.

The heat was now on us with a vengeance. It pervaded the walls, the floor, the air and created a multitude of fierce stinging sensations in every muscle of my body. Several of the engineers took off their boots and jerkins. In short time the passengers followed suit, discarding most of their outer clothing. My agriculturalist sat a miserable figure in tropical silks, moody over what might have been.

Emerging from the cubby, McNulty flopped onto a bunk and said, "If we're all okay in four hours' time, we're through the worst part."

At that moment the rockets faltered. We knew at once what was wrong. A fuel tank had emptied and a relay had failed to cut in. An engineer should have been standing by to switch the conduits. In the heat and excitement, someone had blundered.

The fact barely had time to register before Kli Yang was out through the door. He'd been lolling nearest to it and was gone while we were trying to collect our overheated wits. Twenty seconds later the rockets renewed their steady thrum.

An intercom bell clanged right in my ear. Switching its mike, I croaked a throaty, "Well?" and heard Jay's voice coming back to me from the bow.

"Who did it?"

"Kli Yang," I told him. "He's still outside."

"Probably gone for their domes," guessed Jay. "Tell him I said thanks."

"What's it like around where you live?" I asked.

"Fierce. It isn't so good . . . for vision." Silence a moment, then, "Guess I can stick it . . . somehow. Strap down or hold on ready for the next time I sound the . . . bell."

"Why?" I half yelled, half rasped.

"Going to rotate her. Try . . . distribute . . . the heat."

A faint squeak told that he'd switched off. I told the others to strap down. The Martians didn't have to bother about that because they owned enough saucer-sized suckers to weld them to a sunfishing meteor.

Kli came back, showed Jay's guess to be correct; he was dragging the squad's head-and-shoulder pieces. The load was as much as he could pull now that temperature had climbed to the point where even he began to wilt.

The Martian moochers gladly donned their gadgets, sealing the seams and evacuating them down to three pounds pressure. It made them considerably happier. Remembering that we Terrestrials use spacesuits to keep air inside, it seemed queer to watch those guys using theirs to keep it outside.

They had just finished making themselves comfortable and had laid out a chessboard in readiness for a minor journey when the bell sounded again. We braced ourselves. The Martians clamped down their suckers.

Slowly and steadily the *Upsydaisy* began to turn upon her longitudinal axis. The chessboard and pieces tried to stay put, failed, crawled along the floor, up the wall and across the ceiling. Solar pull was making them stick to the sunward side.

I saw Kli Morg's strained, heat-ridden features glooming at a black bishop while it skittered around, and I suppose that inside his goldfish bowl were resounding some potent samples of Martian invective.

"Three hours and a half," gasped McNulty.

That four hours estimate could only mean two hours of approach to the absolute deadline and two hours of retreat from it. So the moment when we had two hours to go would be the moment when we were at our nearest to the solar furnace, the moment of greatest peril.

I wasn't aware of that critical time, since I passed out twenty minutes before it arrived. No use enlarging upon the horror of that time. I think I went slightly nuts. I was a hog in an oven, being roasted alive. It's the only time I've ever thought of the sun as a great big shining bastard that ought to be extinguished for keeps. Soon afterward I became incapable of any thought at all.

I recovered consciousness and painfully moved in my straps ninety minutes after passing the midway point. My dazed mind had difficulty in realizing that we had now only half an hour to go to reach theoretical safety.

What had happened in the interim was left to my imagination and I didn't care to try to picture it just then. The sun blazing with a ferocity multi-million times greater than that of a tiger's eye, and a hundred thousand times as hungry for our blood and bones. The flaming corona licking out toward this shipload of half-dead entities, imprisoned in a steel bottle.

And up in front of the vessel, behind its totally inadequate quartz observation-ports, Jay Score sitting alone, facing the mounting inferno, staring, staring, staring—

Getting to my feet, I teetered uncertainly, went down like a bundle of rags. The ship wasn't rotating any longer and we appeared to be bulleting along in normal fashion. What dropped me was sheer weakness. I felt lousy.

The Martians already had recovered. I knew they'd be the first. One of them lugged me upright and held me steady while I regained a percentage of my former control. I noticed that another had sprawled right across the unconscious McNulty and three of the passengers. Yes, he'd shielded them from some of the heat and they were the next ones to come to life.

Struggling to the intercom, I switched it but got no response from the front. For three full minutes I hung by it dazedly before I tried again. Nothing doing. Jay wouldn't or couldn't answer.

I was stubborn about it, made several more attempts with no better result. The effort cost me a dizzy spell and down I flopped once more. The heat was still terrific. I felt more dehydrated than a mummy dug out of sand a million years old.

Kli Yang opened the door, crept out with dragging, pain-stricken motion. His air-helmet was secure on his shoulders. Five minutes later he came back, spoke through the helmet's diaphragm.

"Couldn't get near the bow navigation room. At the midway catwalk the autodoors are closed, the atmosphere sealed off, and it's like being inside a furnace." He stared around, met my gaze, answered the question in my eyes. "There's no air in the bow."

No air meant the observation ports had gone *phut*. Nothing else could have emptied the navigation room. Well, we carried spares for that job and could make good the damage once we got into the clear. Meanwhile here we were roaring along, maybe on correct course and maybe not, with an empty, airless navigation room and with an intercom system that gave nothing but ghastly silence.

Sitting around, we picked up strength. The last to come out of his coma was the sick engineer. Sam brought him through again. It was about then that McNulty wiped sweat, showed sudden excitement.

"Four hours, men," he said, with grim satisfaction. "We've done it!"

We raised a hollow cheer. By Jupiter, the super-heated atmosphere seemed to grow ten degrees cooler with the news. Strange how relief from tension can breed strength; in one minute we had conquered former weakness and were ready to go. But it was yet another four hours before a quartet of spacesuited engineers penetrated the forward hell and bore their burden from the airless navigation room.

They carried him into Sam's cubbyhole, a long, heavy, silent figure with face burned black.

Stupidly I hung around him saying, "Jay, Jay, how're you making out?"

He must have heard, for he moved the fingers of his right hand and emitted a chesty, grinding noise. Two of the engineers went to his cabin, brought back his huge rawhide case. They shut the door, staying in with Sam and leaving me and the Martians fidgeting outside. Kli Yang wandered up and down the passage as if he didn't know what to do with his tentacles.

Sam came out after more than an hour. We jumped him on the spot.

"How's Jay?"

"Blind as a statue." He shook his woolly head. "And his voice isn't there any more. He's taken an awful beating."

"So that's why he didn't answer the intercom." I looked him straight in the eyes. "Can you . . . can you do anything for him, Sam?"

"I only wish I could." His sepia face showed his feelings. "You know how much I'd like to put him right. But I can't." He made a gesture of futility. "He is completely beyond my modest skill. Nobody less than Johannsen can help him. Maybe when we get back to Earth—" His voice petered out and he went back inside.

Kli Yang said, miserably, "I am saddened."

A scene I'll never forget to my dying day was that evening we spent as guests of the Astro Club in New York. That club was then—as it is today—the most exclusive group of human beings ever gathered together. To qualify for membership one had to perform in dire emergency a feat of astro-navigation tantamount to a miracle. There were nine members in those days and there are only twelve now.

Mace Waldron, the famous pilot who saved that Martian liner in 2263, was the chairman. Classy in his soup and fish, he stood at the top of the table with Jay Score sitting at his side. At the opposite end of the table was McNulty, a broad smirk of satisfaction upon his plump pan. Beside the skipper was old, white-haired Knud Johannsen, the genius who designed the J-series and a scientific figure known to every spaceman.

Along the sides, manifestly self-conscious, sat the entire crew of the *Upsydaisy*, including the Martians, plus three of our passengers who'd postponed their trips for this occasion. There were also a couple of audio-journalists with scanners and mikes.

"Gentlemen and vedras," said Mace Waldron, "this is an event without precedent in the history of humanity, an event never thought of, never imagined by this club. Because of that I feel it doubly an honor and a privilege to propose that Jay Score, Emergency Pilot, be accepted as a fully qualified and worthy member of the Astro Club."

"Seconded!" shouted three members simultaneously.

"Thank you, gentlemen." He cocked an inquiring eyebrow. Eight hands went up in unison. "Carried," he said. "Unanimously." Glancing down at the taciturn and unmoved Jay Score, he launched into a eulogy. It went on and on and on, full of praise and superlatives, while Jay squatted beside him with a listless air.

Down at the other end I saw McNulty's gratified smirk grow stronger and stronger. Next to him, old Knud was gazing at Jay with a fatherly fondness that verged on the fatuous. The crew likewise gave full attention to the blank-faced subject of the talk, and the scanners were fixed upon him too.

I returned my attention to where all the others were looking, and the victim sat there, his restored eyes bright and glittering, but his face completely immobile despite the talk, the publicity, the beam of paternal pride from Johannsen.

But after ten minutes of this I saw J.20 begin to fidget with obvious embarrassment.

Don't let anyone tell you that a robot can't have feelings!

UNIVERSE

Astounding Science Fiction
May

by Robert A. Heinlein

Another SFWA HALL OF FAME story, "Universe" is justly famous, both as a story and as the prototype (if not the actual first) treatment of a self-contained, confined world, in this case an enormous spaceship whose inhabitants have forgotten who they were, what they were doing, and even the nature of their existence.

It is truly one of the most influential and important stories in science fiction.

(There was no one like Bob Heinlein for getting there first. The self-contained world is now not only a staple of science fiction, but a recognized part of science itself. I have written frequently of "star-ships" as representing the serious future of humanity in my non-fiction, and I tell you quite unabashedly that the idea came to me from "Universe." I can't say that Gerard O'Neill got the notion of his "space settlements" from "Universe," but if it turned out he had, I would be pleased, but not surprised. Ah, that golden year of 1941.—I.A.)

LIAR!

Astounding Science Fiction
May

by Isaac Asimov

(I was very fortunate to have squeezed a story into the
May, 1941, *Astounding,* if only that I found myself in company with giants, though I must admit it was frightening to
feel that I was in competition with them.

"Liar!" was only the fourth story I had sold to Campbell
and the second positronic robot story I had placed with him.
The first was "Reason." "Liar!" was also the first that John
had taken without requesting revision of any sort.

I wish he had, though. There were parts that were embar-
rassingly amateurish, and that I carefully revised nine years
later when I prepared the story for inclusion in *I, Robot.*
Here, however, because of the necessity of playing fair with
the reader and with the historical imperative, the story appears as it had appeared in the magazine. If you snicker at
my clumsiness here and there, please remember that I wrote
it when I was only 20.—I.A.)

Alfred Lanning lit his cigar carefully, but the tips of his
fingers were trembling slightly. His gray eyebrows hunched
low as he spoke between puffs.

"It reads minds all right—damn little doubt about that!
But why?" He looked at mathematician Peter Bogert. "Well?"

Bogert flattened his black hair down with both hands,
"That was the thirty-fourth RB model we've turned out, Lanning. All the others were strictly orthodox."

The third man at the table frowned. Milton Ashe was the
youngest officer of U. S. Robot & Mechanical Men, Inc., and
proud of his post.

"Listen, Bogert. There wasn't a hitch in the assembly from
start to finish. I guarantee that."

Bogert's thick lips spread in a patronizing smile, "Do you?
If you can answer for the entire assembly line, I recommend
your promotion. By exact count, there are seventy-five thou-

sand, two hundred and thirty-four operations necessary for the manufacture of a single positronic brain, each separate operation depending for successful completion upon any number of factors, from five to a hundred and five. If any one of them goes seriously wrong, the 'brain' is ruined. I quote our own information folder, Ashe."

Milton Ashe flushed, but a fourth voice cut off his reply.

"If we're going to start by trying to fix the blame on one another, I'm leaving." Susan Calvin's hands were folded tightly in her lap, and the little lines about her thin, pale lips deepened. "We've got a mind-reading robot on our hands and it strikes me as rather important that we find out just why it reads minds. We're not going to do that by saying, 'Your fault! My fault!' "

Her cold gray eyes fastened upon Ashe, and he grinned.

Lanning grinned too, and, as always at such times, his long white hair and shrewd little eyes made him the picture of a biblical patriarch, "True for you, Dr. Calvin."

His voice became suddenly crisp, "Here's everything in pill-concentrate form. We've produced a positronic brain of supposedly ordinary vintage that's got the remarkable property of being able to tune in on thought waves. It would mark the most important advance in robotics in decades if we knew how it happened. We don't, and we have to find out. Is that clear?"

"May I make a suggestion?" asked Bogert.

"Go ahead!"

"I'd say that until we do figure out the mess—and as a mathematician I expect it to be a very devil of a mess—we keep the existence of RB-34 a secret. I mean even from the other members of the staff. As heads of the departments, we ought not to find it an insoluble problem, and the fewer know about it—"

"Bogert is right," said Dr. Calvin. "Ever since the Interplanetary Code was modified to allow robot models to be tested in the plants before being shipped out to space, anti-robot propaganda has increased. If any word leaks out about a robot being able to read minds before we can announce complete control of the phenomenon, pretty effective capital could be made out of it."

Lanning sucked at his cigar and nodded gravely. He turned to Ashe, "I think you said you were alone when you first stumbled on this thought-reading business."

"I'll say I was alone—I got the scare of my life. RB-34 had just been taken off the assembly table and they sent him down to me. Obermann was off somewheres, so I took him down to the testing room myself—at least I started to take him down." Ashe paused, and a tiny smile tugged at his lips, "Say, did any of you ever carry on a thought conversation without knowing it?"

No one bothered to answer, and he continued, "You don't realize it at first, you know. He just spoke to me—as logically and sensibly as you can imagine—and it was only when I was most of the way down to the testing rooms that I realized that I hadn't said anything. Sure, I thought lots, but that isn't the same thing, is it? I locked that thing up and ran for Lanning. Having it walking beside me, calmly peering into my thoughts and picking and choosing among them gave me the willies."

"I imagine it would," said Susan Calvin thoughtfully. Her eyes fixed themselves upon Ashe in an oddly intent manner. "We are so accustomed to considering our own thoughts private."

Lanning broke in impatiently, "Then only the four of us know. All right! We've got to go about this systematically. Ashe, I want you to check over the assembly line from beginning to end—everything. You're to eliminate all operations in which there was no possible chance of an error, and list all those where there were, together with its nature and possible magnitude."

"Tall order," grunted Ashe.

"Naturally! Of course, you're to put the men under you to work on this—every single one if you have to, and I don't care if we go behind schedule, either. But they're not to know why, you understand."

"Hm-m-m, yes!" The young technician grinned wryly. "It's still a lulu of a job."

Lanning swiveled about in his chair and faced Calvin, "You'll have to tackle the job from the other direction. You're the robopsychologist of the plant, so you're to study the robot itself and work backward. Try to find out how he ticks. See what else is tied up with his telepathic powers, how far they extend, how they warp his outlook, and just exactly what harm it has done to his ordinary RB properties. You've got that?"

Lanning didn't wait for Dr. Calvin to answer.

"I'll coordinate the work and interpret the findings mathematically." He puffed violently at his cigar and mumbled the rest through the smoke, "Bogert will help me there, of course."

Bogert polished the nails of one pudgy hand with the other and said blandly, "I dare say. I know a little in the line."

"Well! I'll get started." Ashe shoved his chair back and rose. His pleasantly youthful face crinkled in a grin, "I've got the darnedest job of any of us, so I'm getting out of here and to work."

He left with a slurred, "B' seein' ye!"

Susan Calvin answered with a barely perceptible nod, but her eyes followed him out of sight and she did not answer when Lanning grunted and said, "Do you want to go up and see RB-34 now, Dr. Calvin?"

RB-34's photoelectric eyes lifted from the book at the muffled sound of hinges turning and he was upon his feet when Susan Calvin entered.

She paused to readjust the huge "No Entrance" sign upon the door and then approached the robot.

"I've brought you the texts upon hyperatomic motors, Herbie—a few anyway. Would you care to look at them?"

RB-34—otherwise known as Herbie—lifted the three heavy books from her arms and opened to the title page of one:

"Hm-m-m! 'Theory of Hyperatomics.' " He mumbled inarticulately to himself as he flipped the pages and then spoke with an abstracted air, "Sit down, Dr. Calvin! This will take me a few minutes."

The psychologist seated herself and watched Herbie narrowly as he took a chair at the other side of the table and went through the three books systematically.

At the end of half an hour, he put them down, "Of course, I know why you brought these."

The corner of Dr. Calvin's lip twitched, "I was afraid you would. It's difficult to work with you, Herbie. You're always a step ahead of me."

"It's the same with these books, you know, as with the others. They just don't interest me. There's nothing to your textbooks. Your science is just a mass of collected data plastered together by makeshift theory—and all so incredibly simple, that it's scarcely worth bothering about.

"It's your fiction that interests me. Your studies of the interplay of human motives and emotions." His mighty hand gestured vaguely as he sought the proper words.

Dr. Calvin whispered, "I think I understand."

"I see into minds, you see," the robot continued, "and you have no idea how complicated they are. I can't begin to understand everything because my own mind has so little in common with them—but I try, and your novels help."

"Yes, but I'm afraid that after going through some of the harrowing emotional experiences of our present-day sentimental novel"—there was a tinge of bitterness in her voice—"you find real minds like ours are dull and colorless."

"But I don't!"

The sudden energy in the response brought the other to her feet. She felt herself reddening, and thought wildly, "He must know!"

Herbie subsided suddenly, and muttered in a low voice from which the metallic timbre departed almost entirely. "But, of course, I know about it, Dr. Calvin. You think of it always, so how can I help but know?"

Her face was hard. "Have you—told anyone?"

"Of course not!" This, with genuine surprise. "No one has asked me."

"Well, then," she flung out, "I suppose you think I am a fool."

"No! It is a normal emotion."

"Perhaps that is why it is so foolish." The wistfulness in her voice drowned out everything else. Some of the woman peered through the layer of doctorhood. "I am not what you would call—attractive."

"If you are referring to mere physical attraction, I couldn't judge. But I know, in any case, that there are other types of attraction."

"Nor young." Dr. Calvin had scarcely heard the robot.

"You are not yet forty." An anxious insistence had crept into Herbie's voice.

"Thirty-eight as you count the years; a shriveled sixty as far as my emotional outlook on life is concerned. Am I a psychologist for nothing?"

She drove on with bitter breathlessness, "And he's barely thirty-five and looks and acts younger. Do you suppose he ever sees me as anything but . . . but what I am?"

"You are wrong!" Herbie's steel fist struck the plastic-topped table with a strident clang. "Listen to me—"

But Susan Calvin whirled on him now and the hunted pain in her eyes became a blaze, "Why should I? What do you know about it all, anyway, you . . . you machine. I'm just a specimen to you; an interesting bug with a peculiar mind spread-eagled for inspection. It's a wonderful example of frustration, isn't it? Almost as good as your books." Her voice, emerging in dry sobs, choked into silence.

The robot cowered at the outburst. He shook his head pleadingly. "Won't you listen to me, please? I could help you if you would let me."

"How?" Her lips curled. "By giving me good advice?"

"No, not that. It's just that I know what other people think—Milton Ashe, for instance."

There was a long silence, and Susan Calvin's eyes dropped. "I don't want to know what he thinks," she gasped. "Keep quiet."

"I think you would want to know what he thinks."

Her head remained bent, but her breath came more quickly. "You are talking nonsense," she whispered.

"Why should I? I am trying to help. Milton Ashe's thoughts of you—" he paused.

And then the psychologist raised her head, "Well?"

The robot said quietly, "He loves you."

For a full minute, Dr. Calvin did not speak. She merely stared. Then, "You are mistaken! You must be. Why should he?"

"But he does. A thing like that cannot be hidden, not from me."

"But I am so . . . so—" she stammered to a halt.

"He looks deeper than the skin, and admires intellect in others. Milton Ashe is not the type to marry a head of hair and a pair of eyes."

Susan Calvin found herself blinking rapidly and waited before speaking. Even then her voice trembled, "Yet he certainly never in any way indicated—"

"Have you ever given him a chance?"

"How could I? I never thought that—"

"Exactly!"

The psychologist paused in thought and then looked up suddenly. "A girl visited him here at the plant half a year ago. She was pretty, I suppose—blond and slim. And, of course, could scarcely add two and two. He spent all day puffing out his chest, trying to explain how a robot was put together." The hardness had returned, "Not that she understood! Who was she?"

Herbie answered without hesitation, "I know the person you are referring to. She is his first cousin, and there is no romantic interest there, I assure you."

Susan Calvin rose to her feet with a vivacity almost girlish. "Now isn't that strange? That's exactly what I used to pretend to myself sometimes, though I never really thought so. Then it all must be true."

She ran to Herbie and seized his cold, heavy hand in both hers. "Thank you, Herbie." Her voice was an urgent, husky whisper. "Don't tell anyone about this. Let it be our secret— and thank you again." With that, and a convulsive squeeze of Herbie's unresponsive metal fingers, she left.

Herbie turned slowly to his neglected novel, but there was no one to read *his* thoughts.

Milton Ashe stretched slowly and magnificently, to the tune of cracking joints and chorus of grunts, and then glared at Peter Bogert, Ph.D.

"Say," he said, "I've been at this for a week now with just about no sleep. How long do I have to keep it up? I thought you said the positronic bombardment in Vac Chamber D was the solution."

Bogert yawned delicately and regarded his white hands with interest. "It is. I'm on the track."

"I know what *that* means when a mathematician says it. How near the end are you?"

"It all depends."

"On what?" Ashe dropped into a chair and stretched his long legs out before him.

"On Lanning. The old fellow disagrees with me." He sighed, "A bit behind the times, that's the trouble with him. He clings to matrix mechanics as the all in all, and this problem calls for more powerful mathematical tools. He's so stubborn."

Ashe muttered sleepily, "Why not ask Herbie and settle the whole affair?"

"Ask the robot?" Bogert's eyebrows climbed.

"Why not? Didn't the old girl tell you?"

"You mean Calvin?"

"Yeah! Susie herself. That robot's a mathematical wiz. He knows all about everything plus a bit on the side. He does triple integrals in his head and eats up tensor analysis for dessert."

The mathematician stared skeptically, "Are you serious?"

"So help me! The catch is that the dope doesn't like math. He would rather read slushy novels. Honest! You should see the tripe Susie keeps feeding him: 'Purple Passion' and 'Love in Space.'"

"Dr. Calvin hasn't said a word of this to us."

"Well, she hasn't finished studying him. You know how she is. She likes to have everything just so before letting out the big secret."

"She told *you*."

"We sort of got to talking. I have been seeing a lot of her lately." He opened his eyes wide and frowned, "Say, Bogie, have you been noticing anything queer about the lady lately?"

Bogert relaxed into an undignified grin, "She's using lipstick, if that's what you mean."

"Hell, I know that. Rouge, powder and eye shadow, too. She's a sight. But it's not that. I can't put my finger on it. It's the way she talks—as if she were happy about something." He thought a little, and then shrugged.

The other allowed himself a leer, which, for a scientist past fifty, was not a bad job, "Maybe she's in love."

Ashe allowed his eyes to close again, "You're nuts, Bogie. You go speak to Herbie; I want to stay here and go to sleep."

"Right! Not that I particularly like having a robot tell me my job, nor that I think he can do it!"

A soft snore was his only answer.

Herbie listened carefully as Peter Bogert, hands in pockets, spoke with elaborate indifference.

"So there you are. I've been told you understand these things, and I am asking you more in curiosity than anything else. My line of reasoning, as I have outlined it, involves a few doubtful steps, I admit, which Dr. Lanning refuses to accept, and the picture is still rather incomplete."

The robot didn't answer, and Bogert said, "Well?"

"I see no mistake." Herbie studied the scribbled figures.

"I don't suppose you can go any further than that?"

"I daren't try. You are a better mathematician than I, and—well, I'd hate to commit myself."

There was a shade of complacency in Bogert's smile, "I rather thought that would be the case. It is deep. We'll forget it." He crumpled the sheets, tossed them down the waste shaft, turned to leave, and then thought better of it.

"By the way—"

The robot waited.

Bogert seemed to have difficulty. "There is something—that is, perhaps you can—" He stopped.

Herbie spoke quietly. "Your thoughts are confused, but there is no doubt at all that they concern Dr. Lanning. It is silly to hesitate, for as soon as you compose yourself, I'll know what it is you want to ask."

The mathematician's hand went to his sleek hair in the familiar smoothing gesture. "Lanning is nudging seventy," he said, as if that explained everything.

"I know that."

"And he's been director of the plant for almost thirty years." Herbie nodded.

"Well, now," Bogert's voice became ingratiating, "you would know whether . . . whether he's thinking of resigning. Health, perhaps, or some other—"

"Quite," said Herbie, and that was all.

"Well, do you know?"

"Certainly."

"Then—uh—could you tell me?"

"Since you ask, yes." The robot was quite matter-of-fact about it. "He has already resigned!"

"What!" The exclamation was an explosive, almost inarticulate, sound. The scientist's large head hunched forward, "Say that again!"

"He has already resigned," came the quiet repetition, "but it has not yet taken effect. He is waiting, you see, to solve the problem of—er—myself. That finished, he is quite ready to turn the office of director over to his successor."

Bogert expelled his breath sharply, "And this successor? Who is he?" He was quite close to Herbie now, eyes fixed fascinated on those unreadable dull-red photoelectric cells that were the robot's eyes.

Words came slowly, "You are the next director."

And Bogert relaxed into a tight smile. "This is good to know. I've been hoping and waiting for this. Thanks, Herbie."

Peter Bogert was at his desk until five that morning and he was back at nine. The shelf just over the desk emptied of its row of reference books and tables, as he referred to one after the other. The pages of calculations before him increased microscopically and the crumpled sheets at his feet mounted into a hill of scribbled paper.

At precisely noon, he stared at the final page, rubbed a blood-shot eye, yawned, and shrugged. "This is getting worse each minute. Damn!"

He turned at the sound of the opening door and nodded at Lanning, who entered, cracking the knuckles of one gnarled hand with the other.

The director took in the disorder of the room and his eyebrows furrowed together.

"New lead?" he asked.

"No," came the defiant answer. "What's wrong with the old one?"

Lanning did not trouble to answer, nor to do more than

bestow a single cursory glance at the top sheet upon Bogert's desk. He spoke through the flare of a match as he lit a cigar.

"Has Calvin told you about the robot? It's a mathematical genius. Really remarkable."

The other snorted loudly, "So I've heard. But Calvin had better stick to robopsychology. I've checked Herbie on math, and he can scarcely struggle through calculus."

"Calvin didn't find it so."

"She's crazy."

"And I don't find it so." The director's eyes narrowed dangerously.

"You!" Bogert's voice hardened. "What are you talking about?"

"I've been putting Herbie through his paces all morning, and he can do tricks you never heard of."

"Is that so?"

"You sound skeptical!" Lanning flipped a sheet of paper out of his vest pocket and unfolded it. "That's not my handwriting, is it?"

Bogert studied the large angular notation covering the sheet, "Herbie did this?"

"Right! And if you'll notice, he's been working on your time integration of Equation 22. It comes"—Lanning tapped a yellow fingernail upon the last step—"to the identical conclusion I did, and in a quarter the time. You had no right to neglect the Linger Effect in positronic bombardment."

"I didn't neglect it. For Heaven's sake, Lanning, get it through your head that it would cancel out—"

"Oh, sure, you explained that. You used the Mitchell Translation Equation, didn't you? Well—it doesn't apply."

"Why not?"

"Because you've been using hyper-imaginaries, for one thing."

"What's that to do with?"

"Mitchell's Equation won't hold when—"

"Are you crazy? If you'll reread Mitchell's original paper in the *Transactions of the Far*—"

"I don't have to. I told you in the beginning that I didn't like his reasoning, and Herbie backs me in that."

"Well, then," Bogert shouted, "let that clockwork contraption solve the entire problem for you. Why bother with nonessentials?"

"That's exactly the point. Herbie can't solve the problem. And if he can't, we can't—alone. I'm submitting the entire question to the National Board. It's gotten beyond us."

Bogert's chair went over backward as he jumped up a-snarl, face crimson. "You're doing nothing of the sort."

Lanning flushed in his turn, "Are you telling me what I can't do?"

"Exactly," was the gritted response. "I've got the problem beaten and you're not to take it out of my hands, understand? Don't think I don't see through you, you desiccated fossil. You'd cut your own nose off before you'd let me get the credit for solving robotic telepathy."

"You're a damned idiot, Bogert, and in one second I'll have you suspended for insubordination"—Lanning's lower lip trembled with passion.

"Which is one thing you won't do, Lanning. You haven't any secrets with a mind-reading robot around, so don't forget that I know all about your resignation."

The ash on Lanning's cigar trembled and fell, and the cigar itself followed, "What . . . what—"

Bogert chuckled nastily, "And I'm the new director, be it understood. I'm very aware of that; don't think I'm not. Damn your eyes, Lanning, I'm going to give the orders about here or there will be the sweetest mess that you've ever been in."

Lanning found his voice and let it out with a roar. "You're suspended, d'ye hear? You're relieved of all duties. You're broken, do you understand?"

The smile on the other's face broadened, "Now, what's the use of that? You're getting nowhere. I'm holding the trumps. I know you've resigned. Herbie told me, and he got it straight from you."

Lanning forced himself to speak quietly. He looked an old, old man, with tired eyes peering from a face in which the red had disappeared, leaving the pasty yellow of age behind, "I want to speak to Herbie. He can't have told you anything of the sort. You're playing a deep game, Bogert, but I'm calling your bluff. Come with me."

Bogert shrugged, "To see Herbie? Good! Damned good!"

It was also precisely at noon that Milton Ashe looked up from his clumsy sketch and said, "You get the idea? I'm not too good at getting this down, but that's about how it looks. It's a honey of a house, and I can get it for next to nothing."

Susan Calvin gazed across at him with melting eyes. "It's really beautiful," she sighed. "I've often thought that I'd like to—" Her voice trailed away.

"Of course," Ashe continued briskly, putting away his pencil, "I've got to wait for my vacation. It's only two weeks off, but this Herbie business has everything up in the air." His eyes dropped to his fingernails. "Besides, there's another point—but it's a secret."

"Then don't tell me."

"Oh, I'd just as soon, I'm just busting to tell someone—and you're just about the best—er—confidante I could find here." He grinned sheepishly.

Susan Calvin's heart bounded, but she did not trust herself to speak.

"Frankly," Ashe scraped his chair closer and lowered his voice into a confidential whisper, "the house isn't to be only for myself. I'm getting married!"

And then he jumped out of his seat, "What's the matter?"

"Nothing!" The horrible spinning sensation had vanished, but it was hard to get words out. "Married? You mean—"

"Why, sure! About time, isn't it? You remember that girl who was here last summer. That's she! But you *are* sick. You—"

"Headache!" Susan Calvin motioned him away weakly. "I've . . . I've been subject to them lately. I want to . . . to congratulate you, of course. I'm very glad—" The inexpertly applied rouge made a pair of nasty red splotches upon her chalk-white face. Things had begun spinning again. "Pardon me—please—"

The words were a mumble, as she stumbled blindly out the door. It had happened with the sudden catastrophe of a dream—and with all the unreal horror of a dream.

But how could it be? Herbie had said—

And Herbie knew! He could see into minds!

She found herself leaning breathlessly against the door jamb, staring into Herbie's metal face. She must have climbed the two flights of stairs, but she had no memory of it. The distance had been covered in an instant, as in a dream.

As in a dream!

And still Herbie's unblinking eyes stared into hers and their dull red seemed to expand into dimly shining nightmarish globes.

He was speaking, and she felt the cold glass pressing against her lips. She swallowed and shuddered into a certain awareness of her surroundings.

Still Herbie spoke, and there was agitation in his voice—as if he were hurt and frightened and pleading.

The words were beginning to make sense. "This is a dream," he was saying, "and you mustn't believe in it. You'll wake into the real world soon and laugh at yourself. He loves you, I tell you. He does, he does! But not here! Not now! This is an illusion."

Susan Calvin nodded, her voice a whisper, "Yes! Yes!" She was clutching Herbie's arm, clinging to it, repeating over and over, "It isn't true, is it? It isn't, is it?"

Just how she came to her senses, she never knew—but it was like passing from a world of misty unreality to one of harsh sunlight. She pushed him away from her, pushed hard against that steely arm, and her eyes were wide.

"What are you trying to do?" Her voice rose to a harsh scream. "What are you trying to do?"

Herbie backed away, "I want to help."

The psychologist stared, "Help? By telling me this is a dream? By trying to push me into schizophrenia?" An hysterical tenseness seized her, "This is no dream! I wish it were!"

She drew her breath sharply, "Wait! Why . . . why, I understand. Merciful Heavens, it's so obvious."

There was horror in the robot's voice, "I had to!"

"And I believed you! I never thought—"

Loud voices outside the door brought her to a halt. She turned away, fists clenching spasmodically, and when Bogert and Lanning entered, she was at the far window. Neither of the men paid her the slightest attention.

They approached Herbie simultaneously; Lanning angry and impatient, Bogert, coolly sardonic. The director spoke first.

"Here now, Herbie. Listen to me!"

The robot brought his eyes sharply down upon the aged director, "Yes, Dr. Lanning."

"Have you discussed me with Dr. Bogert?"

"No, sir." The answer came slowly, and the smile on Bogert's face flashed off.

"What's that?" Bogert shoved in ahead of his superior and straddled the ground before the robot. "Repeat what you told me yesterday."

"I said that—" Herbie fell silent. Deep within him his metallic diaphragm vibrated in soft discords.

"Didn't you say he had resigned?" roared Bogert. "Answer me!"

Bogert raised his arm frantically, but Lanning pushed him aside, "Are you trying to bully him into lying?"

"You heard him, Lanning. He began to say 'Yes' and

stopped. Get out of my way! I want the truth out of him, understand!"

"I'll ask him!" Lanning turned to the robot. "All right, Herbie, take it easy. Have I resigned?"

Herbie stared, and Lanning repeated anxiously, "Have I resigned?" There was the faintest trace of a negative shake of the robot's head. A long wait produced nothing further.

The two men looked at each other and the hostility in their eyes was all but tangible.

"What the devil," blurted Bogert, "has the robot gone mute? Can't you speak, you monstrosity?"

"I can speak," came the ready answer.

"Then answer the question. Didn't you tell me Lanning had resigned? Hasn't he resigned?"

And again there was nothing but dull silence, until from the end of the room, Susan Calvin's laugh rang out suddenly, high-pitched and semi-hysterical.

The two mathematicians jumped, and Bogert's eyes narrowed, "You here? What's so funny?"

"Nothing's funny." Her voice was not quite natural. "It's just that I'm not the only one that's been caught. There's irony in three of the greatest experts in robotics in the world falling into the same elementary trap, isn't there?" Her voice faded, and she put a pale hand to her forehead. "But it isn't funny!"

This time the look that passed between the two men was one of raised eyebrows. "What trap are you talking about?" asked Lanning stiffly. "Is something wrong with Herbie?"

"No." She approached them slowly. "Nothing is wrong with him—only with us." She whirled suddenly and shrieked at the robot, "Get away from me! Go to the other end of the room and don't let me look at you."

Herbie cringed before the fury of her eyes and stumbled away in a clattering trot.

Lanning's voice was hostile, "What is all this, Dr. Calvin?"

She faced them and spoke sarcastically, "Surely you know the fundamental First Law of Robotics."

The other two nodded together. "Certainly," said Bogert, irritably, "a robot may not injure a human being, or through inaction, allow him to come to harm."

"How nicely put," sneered Calvin. "But what kind of harm?"

"Why—any kind."

"Exactly! Any kind! But what about hurt feelings? What

about deflation of one's ego? What about the blasting of one's hopes? Is that injury?"

Lanning frowned, "What would a robot know about—" And then he caught himself with a gasp.

"You've caught on, have you? *This* robot reads minds. Do you suppose it doesn't know everything about mental injury? Do you suppose that if asked a question, it wouldn't give exactly that answer that one wants to hear? Wouldn't any other answer hurt us, and wouldn't Herbie know that?"

"Good Heavens!" muttered Bogert.

The psychologist cast a sardonic glance at him, "I take it you asked him whether Lanning had resigned. You wanted to hear that he had resigned and so that's what Herbie told you."

"And I suppose that is why," said Lanning, tonelessly, "it would not answer a little while ago. It couldn't answer either way without hurting one of us."

There was a short pause in which the men looked thoughtfully across the room at the robot, crouching in the chair by the bookcase, head resting in one hand.

Susan Calvin stared steadfastly at the floor, "He knew of all this. That . . . that devil knows everything—including what went wrong in his assembly." Her eyes were dark and brooding.

Lanning looked up, "You're wrong there, Dr. Calvin. He doesn't know what went wrong. I asked him."

"What does that mean?" cried Calvin. "Only that you didn't want him to give you the solution. It would puncture your ego to have a machine do what you couldn't. Did you ask him?" she shot at Bogert.

"In a way." Bogert coughed and reddened. "He told me he knew very little about mathematics."

Lanning laughed, not very loudly, and the psychologist smiled caustically. She said, "I'll ask him! A solution by him won't hurt my ego." She raised her voice into a cold, imperative, "Come here!"

Herbie rose and approached with hesitant steps.

"You know, I suppose," she continued, "just exactly at what point in the assembly an extraneous factor was introduced or an essential one left out."

"Yes," said Herbie, in tones barely heard.

"Hold on," broke in Bogert angrily. "That's not necessarily true. You want to hear that, that's all."

"Don't be a fool," replied Calvin. "He certainly knows as

much math as you and Lanning together, since he can read minds. Give him his chance."

The mathematician subsided, and Calvin continued, "All right, then, Herbie, give! We're waiting." And in an aside, "Get pencils and paper, gentlemen."

But Herbie remained silent, and there was triumph in the psychologist's voice, "Why don't you answer, Herbie?"

The robot blurted out suddenly, "I cannot. You know I cannot! Dr. Bogert and Dr. Lanning don't want me to."

"They want the solution."

"But not from me."

Lanning broke in, speaking slowly and distinctly, "Don't be foolish, Herbie. We do want you to tell us."

Bogert nodded curtly.

Herbie's voice rose to wild heights, "What's the use of saying that? Don't you suppose that I can see past the superficial skin of your mind? Down below, you don't want me to. I'm a machine, given the imitation of life only by virtue of the positronic interplay in my brain—which is man's device. You can't lose face to me without being hurt. That is deep in your mind and won't be erased. I can't give the solution."

"We'll leave," said Dr. Lanning. "Tell Calvin."

"That would make no difference," cried Herbie, "since you would know anyway that it was I that was supplying the answer."

Calvin resumed, "But you understand, Herbie, that despite that, Drs. Lanning and Bogert want that solution."

"By their own efforts!" insisted Herbie.

"But they want it, and the fact that you have it and won't give it hurts them. You see that, don't you?"

"Yes! Yes!"

"And if you tell them that will hurt them, too."

"Yes! Yes!" Herbie was retreating slowly, and step by step Susan Calvin advanced. The two men watched in frozen bewilderment.

"You can't tell them," droned the psychologist slowly, "because that would hurt and you mustn't hurt. But if you don't tell them, you hurt, so you must tell them. And if you do, you will hurt and you mustn't, so you can't tell them; but if you don't, you hurt, so you must; but if you do, you hurt, so you mustn't; but if you don't, you hurt, so you must; but if you do, you—"

Herbie was up against the wall, and here he dropped to his knees. "Stop!" he shrieked. "Close your mind! It is full of pain and frustration and hate! I didn't mean it, I tell you! I tried to help! I told you what you wanted to hear. I had to!"

The psychologist paid no attention. "You must tell them, but if you do, you hurt, so you mustn't; but if you don't, you hurt, so you must; but—"

And Herbie screamed!

It was like the whistling of a piccolo many times magnified—shrill and shriller till it keened with the terror of a lost soul and filled the room with the piercingness of itself.

And when it died into nothingness, Herbie collapsed into a huddled heap of motionless metal.

Bogert's face was bloodless, "He's dead!"

"No!" Susan Calvin burst into body-racking gusts of wild laughter. "Not dead—merely insane. I confronted him with the insoluble dilemma, and he broke down. You can scrap him now—because he'll never speak again."

Lanning was on his knees beside the thing that had been Herbie. His fingers touched the cold, unresponsive metal face and he shuddered. "You did that on purpose." He rose and faced her, face contorted.

"What if I did? You can't help it now." And in a sudden access of bitterness, "He deserved it."

The director seized the paralysed, motionless Bogert by the wrist, "What's the difference. Come, Peter." He sighed, "A thinking robot of this type is worthless anyway." His eyes were old and tired, and he repeated, "Come, Peter!"

It was minutes after the two scientists left that Dr. Susan Calvin regained part of her mental equilibrium. Slowly, her eyes turned to the living-dead Herbie and the tightness returned to her face. Long she stared while the triumph faded and the helpless frustration returned—and of all her turbulent thoughts only one infinitely bitter word passed her lips.

"Liar!"

That finished it for then, naturally. I knew I couldn't get any more out of her after that. She just sat there behind her desk, her white face cold and—remembering.

I said, "Thank you, Dr. Calvin!" but she didn't answer. It was two days before I could get to see her again.

SOLUTION UNSATISFACTORY

Astounding Science Fiction
May

by Robert A. Heinlein

*What an issue. Writing as "Anson MacDonald"
Robert Heinlein contributed this fine novelette of a
war of the future. It is a powerful story of man's
creation out of control, and it helped to establish
science fiction's popular reputation for "accurate"
prediction.*

*In this case, one that we hope never happens
again.*

(I don't know how many times I have used "Solution Unsatisfactory" in my talks about science fiction prophecy. In a
sense, Bob predicted the Manhattan Project before anyone
else dreamed of it. Predicting an actual nuclear weapon
wasn't difficult and Bob at least avoided the too-obvious
bomb and went straight to fallout. The real tickler, though,
was predicting the nuclear stalemate in perfect detail. As far
as I am concerned this story is the all-time record for an un-
clouded crystal ball.—I.A.)

TIME WANTS A SKELETON

Astounding Science Fiction
June

by Ross Rocklynne (1913-   )

*Ross Rocklynne contributed two stories to Vol-
ume 2 of this series "(Into the Darkness," June
Astonishing Stories and Quietus, from the September issue of Astounding), exceptional stories that
point up the relative neglect suffered during the
"Golden Age" by this talented and innovative
writer, who labored in the shadow of Heinlein,
Sturgeon, van Vogt, and others. Two relatively recent collections that feature the best of his early
work are The Sun Destroyers and The Men and the
Mirror (both 1973). His fiction continues to appear, but only infrequently.*

*This powerful story was one of four that consti-
tuted his "Darkness" series, published over an
eleven year period: "Daughter of Darkness" in the
November, 1941 Astounding; "Abyss of
Darkness" in the December, 1942, Astounding;
and after a long hiatus, "Revolt of the Devil Star"
in the February, 1951, Imagination.*

(Sometimes one does think that a certain weariness gets
into one's bones with age; that the good old days weren't
good at all, but that you were merely young then. In fact, I
go around saying this all the time. Every once in a while,
however, I am shaken.

I do read science fiction these days with not quite the eager
avidity of youth. Sometimes I would almost say I was jaded.
When I reread "Time Wants a Skeleton," however, I suddenly felt all the old excitement. I tried for a long time to put
my feelings into a phrase that wasn't a cliche and then gave
up. The cliche it had to be.

I said, "They don't write stories like that any more."
—I.A.)

Asteroid No. 1007 came spinning relentlessly up.

Lieutenant Tony Crow's eyes bulged. He released the choked U-bar frantically, and pounded on the auxiliary underjet controls. Up went the nose of the ship, and stars, weirdly splashed across the heavens, showed briefly.

Then the ship fell, hurling itself against the base of the mountain. Tony was thrown from the control chair. He smacked against the wall, grinning twistedly. He pushed against it with a heavily shod foot as the ship teetered over, rolled a bit, and then was still—still, save for the hiss of escaping air.

He dived for a locker, broke out a pressure suit, perspiration pearling his forehead. He was into the suit, buckling the helmet down, before the last of the air escaped. He stood there, pained dismay in his eyes. His roving glance rested on the wall calendar.

"Happy December!" he snarled.

Then he remembered. Johnny Braker was out there, with his two fellow outlaws. By now, they'd be running this way. All the more reason why Tony should capture them now. He'd need their ship.

He acted quickly, buckling on his helmet, working over the air lock. He expelled his breath in relief as it opened. Nerves humming, he went through, came to his feet, enclosed by the bleak soundlessness of a twenty-mile planetoid more than a hundred million miles removed from Earth.

To his left the mountain rose sharply. Good. Tony had wanted to put the ship down there anyway. He took one reluctant look at the ship. His face fell mournfully. The stern section was caved in and twisted so much it looked ridiculous. Well, that was *that*.

He quickly drew his Hampton and moved soundlessly around the mountain's shoulder. He fell into a crouch as he saw the gleam of the outlaw ship, three hundred yards distant across a plain, hovering in the shadow thrown by an overhanging ledge.

Then he saw the three figures leaping toward him across the plain. His Hampton came viciously up. There was a puff of rock to the front left of the little group. They froze.

Tony left his place of concealment, snapping his headset on.

"Stay where you are!" he bawled.

The reaction was unexpected. Braker's voice came blasting back.

"The hell you say!"

A tiny crater came miraculously into being to Tony's left. He swore, jumped behind his protection, came out a second later to send another projectile winging its way. One of the figures pitched forward, to move no more, the balloon rotundity of its suit suddenly lost. The other two turned tail, only to halt and hole up behind a boulder gracing the middle of the plain. They proceeded to pepper Tony's retreat.

Tony shrank back against the mountainside, exasperated beyond measure. His glance, roving around, came to rest on a cave, a fault in the mountain that tapered out a hundred feet up.

He stared at the floor of the cave unbelievingly.

"I'll be double-damned," he muttered.

What he saw was a human skeleton.

He paled. His stomach suddenly heaved. Outrageous, haunting thoughts flicked through his consciousness. The skeleton was—horror!

And it had existed in the dim, unutterably distant past, before the asteroids, before the human race had come into existence!

The thoughts were gone, abruptly. Consciousness shuddered back. For a while, his face pasty white, his fingers trembling, he thought he was going to be sick. But he wasn't. He stood there, staring. Memories! If he knew where they came from— His very mind revolted suddenly from probing deeper into a mystery that tore at the very roots of his sanity!

"It existed before the human race," he whispered. "Then where did the skeleton come from?"

His lips curled. Illusion! Conquering his maddening revulsion, he approached the skeleton, knelt near it. It lay inside the cave. Colorless starlight did not allow him to see it as well as he might. Yet, he saw the gleam of gold on the long, tapering finger. Old yellow gold, untarnished by atmosphere; and inset with an emerald, with a flaw, a distinctive, ovular air bubble, showing through its murky transparency.

He moved backward, away from it, face set stubbornly. "Illusion," he repeated.

Chips of rock, flaked off the mountainside by the exploding bullets of a Hampton, completed the transformation. He risked stepping out, fired.

The shot struck the boulder, split it down the middle. The two halves parted. The outlaws ran, firing back to cover their hasty retreat. Tony waited until the fire lessened, then stepped out and sent a shot over their heads.

Sudden dismay showed in his eyes. The ledge overhanging the outlaw ship cracked—where the bullet had struck it.

"What the hell—" came Braker's gasp. The two outlaws stopped stock-still.

The ledge came down, its ponderousness doubled by the absence of sound. Tony stumbled panting across the plain as the scene turned into a churning hell. The ship crumbled like clay. Another section of the ledge descended to bury the ship inextricably under a small mountain.

Tony Crow swore blisteringly. But ship or no ship, he still had a job to do. When the outlaws finally turned, they were looking into the menacing barrel of his Hampton.

"Get 'em up," he said impassively.

With studied insolence, Harry Jawbone Yates, the smaller of the two, raised his hands. A contemptuous sneer merely played over Braker's unshaved face and went upward to his smoky eyes.

"Why should I put my hands up? We're all pals, now—theoretically." His natural hate for any form of the law showed in his eyes. "You sure pulled a prize play, copper. Chase us clear across space, and end up getting us in a jam it's a hundred-to-one shot we'll get out of."

Tony held them transfixed with the Hampton, knowing what Braker meant. No ship would have reason to stop off on the twenty-mile mote in the sky that was Asteroid 1007.

He sighed, made a gesture. "Hamptons over here, boys. And be careful." The weapons arced groundward. "Sorry. I was intending to use your ship to take us back. I won't make another error like that one, though. Giving up this early in the game, for instance. Come here, Jawbone."

Yates shrugged. He was blond, had pale, wide-set eyes. By nature, he was conscienceless. A broken jawbone, protruding at a sharp angle from his jawline, gave him his nickname.

He held out his wrists. "Put 'em on." His voice was an effortless affair which did not go as low as it could; rather womanish, therefore. Braker was different. Strength, nerve, and audacity showed in every line of his heavy, compact body. If there was one thing that characterized him it was his violent desire to live. These were men with elastic codes of ethics. A few of their more unscrupulous activities had caught up with them.

Tony put cuffs over Yates' wrist.

"Now you, Braker."

"Damned if I do," said Braker.

"Damned if you don't," said Tony. He waggled the Hampton, his normally genial eyes hardening slightly. "I mean it, Braker," he said slowly.

Braker sneered and tossed his head. Then, as if resistance was below his present mood, he submitted.

He watched the cuffs click silently. "There isn't a hundred-to-one chance, anyway," he growled.

Tony jerked slightly, his eyes turned skyward. He chuckled.

"Well, what's so funny?" Braker demanded.

"What you just said." Tony pointed. "The hundred-to-one shot—there she is!"

Braker turned.

"Yeah," he said. "Yeah. Damnation!"

A ship, glowing faintly in the starlight, hung above an escarpment that dropped to the valley floor. It had no visible support, and, indeed, there was no trace of the usual jets.

"Well, that's an item!" Yates muttered.

"It is at that," Tony agreed.

The ship moved. Rather, it simply disappeared, and next showed up a hundred feet away on the valley floor. A valve in the side of the cylindrical affair opened and a figure dropped out, stood looking at them.

A metallic voice said, "Are you the inhabitants or just people?"

The voice was agreeably flippant, and more agreeably feminine. Tony's senses quickened.

"We're people," he explained. "See?" He flapped his arms like wings. He grinned. "However, before you showed up, we had made up our minds to be—inhabitants."

"Oh. Stranded." The voice was slightly chilly. "Well, that's too bad. Come on inside. We'll talk the whole thing over. Say, are those handcuffs?"

"Right."

"Hm-m-m. Two outlaws—and a copper. Well, come on inside and meet the rest of us."

An hour later, Tony, agreeably relaxed in a small lounge, was smoking his third cigarette, pressure suit off. Across the room was Braker and Yates. The girl, whose name, it developed, was Laurette, leaned against the door jamb, clad in jodhpurs and white silk blouse. She was blond and had clear, deep-blue eyes. Her lips were pursed a little and she looked angry. Tony couldn't keep his eyes off her.

Another man stood beside her. He was dark in complexion

and looked as if he had a short temper. He was snapping the fingernails of two hands in a manner that showed characteristic impatience and nervousness. His name was Erle Masters.

An older man came into the room, fitting glasses over his eyes. He took a quick look around the room. Tony came to his feet.

Laurette said tonelessly, "Lieutenant, this is my father. Daddy, Lieutenant Tony Crow of the IPF. Those two are the outlaws I was telling you about."

"Outlaws, eh?" said Professor Overland. His voice seemed deep enough to count the separate vibrations. He rubbed at a stubbled jaw. "Well, that's too bad. Just when we had the De-Tosque strata 1007 fitting onto 70. And there were ample signs to show a definite dovetailing of apex 1007 into Morrell's fourth crater on Ceres, which would have put 1007 near the surface, if not on it. If we could have followed those up without an interruption—"

"Don't let this interrupt you," Masters broke in. His nails clicked. "We'll let these three sleep in the lounge. We can finish up the set of indications we're working on now, and then get rid of them."

Overland shook his graying head doubtfully. "It would be unthinkable to subject those two to cuffs for a full month."

Masters said irritably, "We'll give them a parole. Give them their temporary freedom if they agree to submit to handcuffs again when we land on Mars."

Tony laughed softly. "Sorry. You can't trust those two for five minutes, let alone a month." He paused. "Under the circumstances, professor, I guess you realize I've got full power to enforce my request that you take us back to Mars. The primary concern of the government in a case like this would be placing these two in custody. I suggest if we get under way now, you can devote more time to your project."

Overland said helplessly, "Of course. But it cuts off my chances of getting to the Christmas banquet at the university." Disappointment showed in his weak eyes. "There's a good chance they'll give me Amos, I guess, but it's already December third. Well, anyway, we'll miss the snow."

Laurette Overland said bitterly, "I wish we hadn't landed on 1007. You'd have got along without us then, all right."

Tony held her eyes gravely. "Perfectly, Miss Overland. Except that we would have been inhabitants. And, shortly, very, very dead ones."

"So?" She glared.

Erle Masters grabbed the girl's arm with a muttered word and led her out of the room.

Overland grasped Tony's arm in a friendly squeeze, eyes twinkling. "Don't mind them, son. If you or your charges need anything, you can use my cabin. But we'll make Mars in forty-eight hours, seven or eight of it skimming through the Belt."

Tony shook his head dazedly. "Forty-eight hours?"

Overland grinned. His teeth were slightly tobacco-stained. "That's it. This is one of the new ships—the H-H drive. They zip along."

"Oh! The Fitz-Gerald Contraction?"

Overland nodded absently and left. Tony stared after him. He was remembering something now—the skeleton.

Braker said indulgently, "What a laugh."

Tony turned.

"What," he asked patiently, "is a laugh?"

Braker thrust out long, heavy legs. He was playing idly with a gold ring on the third finger of his right hand.

"Oh," he said carelessly, "a theory goes the rounds the asteroids used to be a planet. They're not sure the theory is right, so they send a few bearded long faces out to trace down faults and strata and striations on one asteroid and link them up with others. The girl's old man was just about to nail down 1007 and 70 and Ceres. Good for him. But what the hell! They prove the theory and the asteroids still play ring around the rosy and what have they got for their money?"

He absently played with his ring.

Tony as absently watched him turning it round and round on his finger. Something peculiar about— He jumped. His eyes bulged.

That ring! He leaped to his feet, away from it.

Braker and Yates looked at him strangely.

Braker came to his feet, brows contracting. "Say, copper, what ails you? You gone crazy? You look like a ghost."

Tony's heart began a fast, insistent pounding. Blood drummed against his temples. So he looked like a ghost? He laughed hoarsely. Was it imagination that suddenly stripped the flesh from Braker's head and left nothing but—a skull?

"I'm not a ghost." He chattered senselessly, still staring at the ring.

He closed his eyes tight, clenched his fists.

"He's gone bats!" said Yates, incredulously.

"Bats! Absolutely bats!"

Tony opened his eyes, looked carefully at Braker, at Yates, at the tapestried walls of the lounge. Slowly, the tensity left him. Now, no matter what developed he would have to keep a hold on himself.

"I'm all right, Braker. Let me see that ring." His voice was low, controlled, ominous.

"You take a fit?" Braker snapped suspiciously.

"I'm all right." Tony deliberately took Braker's cuffed hands into his own, looked at the gold band inset with the flawed emerald. Revulsion crawled in his stomach, yet he kept his eyes on the ring.

"Where'd you get the ring, Braker?" He kept his glance down.

"Why—'29, I think it was; or '28." Braker's tone was suddenly angry, resentful. He drew away. "What is this, anyway? I got it legal, and so what?"

"What I really wanted to know," said Tony, "was if there was another ring like this one—ever. I hope not . . . I don't know if I do. Damn it!"

"And I don't know what you're talking about," snarled Braker. "I still think you're bats. Hell, flawed emeralds are like fingerprints, never two alike. You know that yourself."

Tony slowly nodded and stepped back. Then he lighted a cigarette, and let the smoke inclose him.

"You fellows stay here," he said, and backed out and bolted the door behind him. He went heavily down the corridor, down a short flight of stairs, then down another short corridor.

He chose one of two doors, jerked it open. A half dozen packages slid from the shelves of what was evidently a closet. Then the other door opened. Tony staggered backward, losing his balance under the flood of packages. He bumped into Laurette Overland. She gasped and started to fall. Tony managed to twist around in time to grab her. They both fell anyway. Tony drew her to him on impulse and kissed her.

She twisted away from him, her face scarlet. Her palm came around, smashed into his face with all her considerable strength. She jumped to her feet, then the fury in her eyes died. Tony came erect, smarting under the blow.

"Sportsmanlike," he snapped angrily.

"You've got a lot of nerve," she said unsteadily. Her eyes went past him. "You clumsy fool. Help me get these packages back on the shelves before daddy or Erle come along. They're Christmas presents, and if you broke any of the wrappings— Come on, can't you help?"

Tony slowly hoisted a large carton labeled with a "Do Not Open Before Christmas" sticker, and shoved it onto the lower rickety shelf, where it stuck out, practically ready to fall again. She put the smaller packages on top to balance it.

She turned, seeming to meet his eyes with difficulty.

Finally she got out, "I'm sorry I hit you like that, lieutenant. I guess it was natural—your kissing me I mean." She smiled faintly at Tony, who was ruefully rubbing his cheek. Then her composure abruptly returned. She straightened.

"If you're looking for the door to the control room, that's it."

"I wanted to see your father," Tony explained.

"You can't see him now. He's plotting our course. In fifteen minutes—" She let the sentence dangle. "Erle Masters can help you in a few minutes. He's edging the ship out of the way of a polyhedron."

"Polyhedron?"

"Many-sided asteroid. That's the way we designate them." She was being patronizing now.

"Well, of course. But I stick to plain triangles and spheres and cubes. A polyhedron is a sphere to me. I didn't know we were on the way. Since when? I didn't feel the acceleration."

"Since ten minutes ago. And naturally there wouldn't be any acceleration with an H-H drive. Well, if you want anything, you can talk to Erle." She edged past him, went swinging up the corridor. Tony caught up with her.

"You can help me," he said, voice edged. "Will you answer a few questions?"

She stopped, her penciled brows drawn together. She shrugged. "Fire away, lieutenant."

She leaned against the wall, tapping it patiently with one manicured fingernail.

Tony said, "All I know about the Hoderay-Hammond drive, Miss Overland, is that it reverses the Fitz-Gerald Contraction principle. It makes use of a new type of mechanical advantage. A moving object contracts in the direction of motion. Therefore a stationary object, such as a ship, can be made to move if you contract it in the direction you want it to move. How that's accomplished, though, I don't know."

"By gravitons—Where have you been all your life?"

"Learning," said Tony, "good manners."

She flushed. Her fingers stopped drumming. "If you realized you were interrupting important work, you'd know why I forget my manners. We were trying to finish this up so daddy could get back to his farewell dinner at the university.

I guess the professors guessed right when they sent his—
Well, why should I explain that to you?"

"I'm sure," said Tony, "I don't know."

"Well, go on," she said coldly.

Tony lighted a cigarette, offered her one with an apology.
She shook her head impatiently.

Tony eyed her through the haze of smoke. "Back there on
1007 I saw a skeleton with a ring on its finger."

She seemed nonplused. "Well. Was it a pretty ring?"

Tony said grimly, "The point is, Braker never got near that
skeleton after I saw it, but that same ring is now on his finger."

Startlement showed in her eyes. "That doesn't sound very
plausible, lieutenant!"

"No, of course it doesn't. Because then the same ring is in
two different places at the same time."

"And of course," she nodded, "that would be impossible.
Go on. I don't know what you're getting at, but it certainly is
interesting."

"Impossible?" said Tony. "Except that it happens to be the
truth. I'm not explaining it away, Miss Overland, if that's
your idea. Here's something else. The skeleton is a human
skeleton, but it existed before the human race existed."

She shoved herself away from her indolent position. "You
must be crazy."

Tony said nothing.

"How did you know?" she said sharply.

"I *know*. Now *you* explain the H-H drive, if you will."

"I will!" She said: "Gravitons are the ultimate particle of
matter. There are 1846 in a proton, one in an electron, which
is the reason why a proton is 1846 times as heavy as an electron.

"Now you can give me a cigarette, lieutenant. I'm curious
about this thing, and if I can't get to the bottom of it, my father certainly will."

After a while, she blew out smoke nervously.

She continued, speaking rapidly: "A Wittenberg disrupter
tears atoms apart. The free electrons are shunted off into ac-
cumulators, where we get power for lighting, cooking, heating
and so forth. The protons go into the proton analyzer, where
the gravitons are ripped out of them and stored in a special
type of spherical field. When we want to move the ship, the
gravitons are released. They spread through the ship and everything in the ship.

"The natural place for a graviton is in a proton. The gravitons rush for the protons—which are already saturated with 1846 gravitons. Gravitons are unable to remain free in three-dimensional space. They escape along the time line, into the past. The reaction contracts the atoms of the ship and everything in the ship, and shoves it forward along the opposite space-time line—forward into the future and forward in space. In the apparent space of a second, therefore, the ship can travel thousands of miles, with no acceleration effects.

"Now, there you have it, lieutenant. Do what you can with it."

Tony said, "What would happen if the gravitons were forced into the future rather than the past?"

"Lieutenant, I would have been surprised if you hadn't said that! Theoretically, it's an impossibility. Anybody who knows gravitons would say so. But if Braker is wearing a ring that a skeleton older than the human race is also wearing—*Ugh!*"

She put her hands to her temples in genuine distaste. "We'll have to see my father," she said wearily. "He'll be the one to find out whether or not you make this up as you go along."

Erle Masters looked from Tony to Laurette.

"You believe this bilge he's been handing you?"

"I'm not interested in what you think, Erle. But I am in what you do, Daddy."

Overland looked uneasy, his stubbled jaws barely moving over a wad of rough-cut.

"It does sound like . . . er . . . bilge," he muttered. "If you weren't an IPF man, I'd think you were slightly off-center. But—one thing, young man. How did you know the skeleton was older than the human race?"

"I said it existed *before* the human race."

"Is there any difference?"

"I think there is—somehow."

"Well," said Overland patiently, "how do you know it?"

Tony hesitated. "I don't really know. I was standing at the mouth of the cave, and something—or someone—told me."

"*Someone!*" Masters blasted the word out incredulously.

"I don't know!" said Tony. "All I know is what I'm telling you. It couldn't have been supernatural—could it?"

Overland said quickly, "Don't let it upset you, son. Of course it wasn't supernatural. There's a rational explanation somewhere, I guess. But it's going to be hard to come by."

He nodded his head abstractedly, and kept on nodding it like a marionette. Then he smiled peculiarly.

"I'm old now, son—you know? And I've seen a lot. I don't disbelieve anything. There's only one logical step for a scientist to take now, and that's to go back and take a look at that skeleton."

Masters' breath sounded. "You can't do that!"

"But we're going to. And remember that I employ *you*, because Laurette asked me to. Now turn this ship back to 1007. This might be more important than patching up a torn-up world at that." He chuckled.

Laurette shook her blond head. "You know," she said musingly, "this might be the very thing we *shouldn't* do, going back like this. On the other hand, if we went on our way, *that* might be the thing we shouldn't do."

Masters muttered, "You're talking nonsense, Laurette."

He ostentatiously grabbed her bare arm, and led her from the room after her father, throwing Tony a significant glance as he passed.

Tony expelled a long breath. Then, smiling twistedly, he went back to the lounge, to wait—for what? His stomach contracted again with revulsion—or was it a premonition?

Braker came sharply to his feet. "What's up, Crow?"

"Let me see that ring again," Tony said. After a minute he raised his eyes absently. "It's the same ring," he muttered.

"I wish to hell," Braker exploded, "I knew what you were talking about!"

Tony looked at him obliquely, and said under his breath, "Maybe it's better you don't."

He sat down and lighted a cigarette. Braker swore, and finally wandered to the window. Tony knew what he was thinking: of Earth; of the cities that teemed; of the vast stretches of open space between the planets. Such would be his thoughts. Braker, who loved life and freedom.

Braker, who wore a ring—

Then the constellations showing through the port abruptly changed pattern.

Braker leaped back, eyes bulging. "What the—"

Yates, sitting sullenly in the corner, came alertly to his feet. Braker mutely pointed at the stars.

"I could have sworn," he said thickly.

Tony came to his feet. He had seen the change. But his thoughts flowed evenly, coldly, a smile frozen on his lips.

"You saw right, Braker," he said coldly, then managed to grab the guide rail as the ship bucked. Braker and Yates sailed across the room, faces ludicrous with surprise. The ship turned the other way. The heavens spun, the stars blurring. Something else Tony saw besides blurred stars: a dull-gray, monstrous landscape, a horizon cut with mountains, a bright, small sun fringing tumbled clouds with reddish, ominous silver. Then stars again, rushing past the port, simmering through an atmosphere—

Blackness crushed its way through Tony Crow's consciousness, occluding it until, finally, his last coherent thought had gone. Yet he seemed to know what had happened. There was a skeleton in a cave on an asteroid—millions of years from now. And the ship had struck.

Tony moved, opened his eyes. The lights were out, but a pale shaft of radiance was streaming through the still-intact port. Sounds insinuated themselves into his consciousness. The wet drip of rain, the low murmur of a spasmodic wind, a guttural *kutakikchkut* that drifted eerily, insistently, down the wind.

Tony slowly levered himself to his feet. He was lying atop Braker. The man was breathing heavily, a shallow gash on his forehead. Involuntarily, Tony's eyes dropped to the ring. It gleamed—a wicked eye staring up at him. He wrenched his eyes away.

Yates was stirring, mumbling to himself. His eyes snapped open, stared at Tony.

"What happened?" he said thickly. He reeled to his feet. *"Phew!"*

Tony smiled through the gloom. "Take care of Braker." he said, and turned to the door, which was warped off its hinges. He loped down the corridor to the control room, slowing down on the lightless lower deck ramp. He felt his way into the control room. He stumbled around until his foot touched a body. He stooped, felt a soft, bare arm. In sudden, stifling panic, he scooped Laurette's feebly breathing body into his arms. She might have been lead, as his feet seemed made of lead. He forced himself up to the upper corridor, kicked open the door of her father's room, placed her gently on the bed. There was light here, probably that of a moon. He scanned her pale face anxiously, rubbing her arms toward the heart. Blood came to her cheeks. She gasped, rolled over. Her eyes opened.

"Lieutenant," she muttered.

"You all right?"

Tony helped her to her feet.

"Thanks, lieutenant. I'll do." She tensed. "What about my father?"

"I'll bring him up," said Tony.

Five minutes later, Overland was stretched on the bed, pain in his open eyes. Three ribs were broken. Erle Masters hovered at the foot of the bed, dabbing at one side of his face with a reddened handkerchief, a dazed, scared look in his eyes. Tony knew what he was scared of, but even Tony wasn't playing with that thought now.

He found a large roll of adhesive in the ship's medicine closet. He taped Overland's chest. The breaks were simple fractures. In time, they would do a fair job of knitting. But Overland would have to stay on his back.

Masters met Tony's eyes reluctantly.

"We'll have to get pressure suits and take a look outside."

Tony shrugged. "We won't need pressure suits. We're already breathing outside air, and living under this planet's atmospheric pressure. The bulkheads must be stowed in some place."

Overland's deep voice sounded, slowly. "I think we've got an idea where we are, Erle. You can feel the drag of this planet—a full-size planet, too. Maybe one and a half gravities. I can feel it pulling on my ribs." A bleak expression settled on his stubbled face. He looked at Tony humorlessly. "Maybe I'm that skeleton, son."

Tony caught his breath. "Nonsense. Johnny Braker's wearing the ring. If anybody's that skeleton, he is. *Not* that I wish him any bad luck, of course." He nodded once, significantly, then turned toward the door with a gesture at Masters. Masters, plainly resenting the soundless command, hesitated, until Laurette made an impatient motion at him.

They prowled through the gloomy corridor toward the small engine room, pushed the door open. The overpowering odor of ozone and burning rubber flung itself at them.

Masters uttered an expressive curse as Tony played a beam over what was left of the reversed Fitz-Gerald Contraction machinery. His nails clicked startlingly loud in the heavy silence.

"Well, that's that," he muttered.

"What d'you mean—that's that?" Tony's eyes bored at him through the darkness.

"I mean that we're stuck here, millions of years ago." He laughed harshly, unsteadily.

Tony said without emotion, "Cut it out. Hasn't this ship got auxiliary rocket blasts?"

"Naturally. But this is a one and a half gravity planet. Anyway, the auxiliary jets won't be in such good condition after a fifty-foot drop."

"Then we'll fix 'em," said Tony sharply. He added, "What makes you so sure it's millions of years ago, Masters?"

Masters leaned back against the door jamb, face as cold and hard as stone.

"Don't make me bow to you any more than I have to, lieutenant," he said ominously. "I didn't believe your story before, but I do now. You predicted this crack-up—it had to happen. So I'm ready to concede it's millions of years ago; mainly because there wasn't any one and a half gravity planet within hundreds of millions of miles of the asteroid belt. But there *used* to be one."

Tony said, lips barely moving, "Yes?"

"There used to be one—*before the asteroids.*"

Tony smiled twistedly. "I'm glad you realize that."

He turned and went for the air lock, but, since the entire system of electric transmission had gone wrong somewhere, he abandoned it and followed a draft of wet air. He jerked open the door of a small storage bin, and crawled through. There was a hole here, that had thrust boxes of canned goods haphazardly to one side. Beyond was the open night.

Tony crawled out, stood in the lee of the ship, occasional stinging drops of rain lashing at their faces. Wind soughed across a rocky plain. A low roar heralded a nearby, swollen stream. A low *kutakikchkut* monotonously beat against the night, night-brooding bird, Tony guessed, nested in the heavy growth flanking a cliff that cut a triangular section from a heavily clouded sky. Light from a probable moon broke dimly through clouds on the leftward horizon.

Masters' teeth chattered in the cold.

Tony edged his way around the ship, looking the damage over. He was gratified to discover that although the auxiliary rocket jets were twisted and broken, the only hole was in the storage bin bulkheads. That could be repaired, and so, in time, could the jets.

They started to enter the ship when Masters grasped his arm. He pointed up into the sky, where a rift in the clouds showed.

Tony nodded slowly. Offsetting murkily twinkling stars, there was another celestial body, visible as a tiny crescent.

"A planet?" muttered Tony.

"Must be." Masters' voice was low.

They stared at it for a moment, caught up in the ominous, baleful glow. Then Tony shook himself out of it, went for the storage bin.

Walking down the corridor with Masters, Tony came upon Braker and Yates.

Braker grinned at him, but his eyes were ominous.

"What's this I hear about a skeleton?"

Tony bit his lip. "Where'd you hear it?"

"From the girl and her old man. We stopped outside their room a bit. Well, it didn't make sense, the things they were saying. Something about an emerald ring and a skeleton and a cave." He took one step forward, an ugly light in his smoky eyes. "Come clean, Crow. How does this ring I've got on my finger tie up with a skeleton?"

Tony said coldly, "You're out of your head. Get back to the lounge."

Braker sneered. "Why? You can't make us stay there with the door broken down."

Masters made an impatient sound. "Oh, let them go, lieutenant. We can't bother ourselves about something as unimportant as this. Anyway, we're going to need these men for fixing up the ship."

Tony said to Yates, "You know anything about electricity? Seems to me you had an E.E. once."

Yates' thin face lighted, before he remembered his sullen pose. "O. K., you're right," he muttered. He looked at Braker interrogatively.

Braker said: "Sorry. We're not obligated to work for you. As prisoners, you're responsible for us and our welfare. We'll help you or whoever's bossing the job *if* we're not prisoners."

Tony nodded. "Fair enough. But tonight, you stay prisoners. Tomorrow, maybe not," and he herded them back into the lounge. He cuffed them to the guide rail, and so left them, frowning a little. Braker had been too acquiescent.

The reason for that struck Tony hard. Walking back along the corridor, he saw something gleaming on the floor. He froze. Revulsion gripping him, he slowly picked up the ring.

Masters turned, said sharply, "What's up?"

Tony smiled lopsidedly, threw the ring into the air twice, speculatively, catching it in his palm. He extended it to Masters.

"Want a ring?"

Masters' face went white as death. He jumped back.

"Damn you!" he said violently. "Take that thing away!"

"Braker slipped it off his finger," said Tony, his voice edging into the aching silence. Then he turned on his heel, and walked back to the lounge. He caught Braker's attention.

He held the ring out.

"You must have dropped it," he said.

Braker's lips opened in a mirthful, raucous laugh.

"You can have it, copper," he gasped. "*I* don't want to be any damned skeleton!"

Tony slipped the ring into his pocket and walked back down the corridor with a reckless swing to his body.

He knocked on the door to Overland's room, opened it when Laurette's voice sounded.

Masters and Laurette looked at him strangely.

Overland looked up from the bed.

"Lieutenant," he said, an almost ashamed look on his face, "sometimes I wonder about the human mind. Masters seems to think that now *you've* got the ring, *you're* going to be the skeleton."

Masters' nails clicked. "It's true, isn't it? The outlaws know about the ring. We know about it. But Crow *has* the ring, and it's certain none of us is going to take it."

Overland made an exasperated clicking sound.

"It's infantile," he snapped. "Masters, you're acting like a child, not like a scientist. There's only one certainty, that one of us is going to be the skeleton. But there's no certainty which one. And there's even a possibility that all of us will die." His face clouded angrily. "And the most infantile viewpoint possible seems to be shared by all of you. You've grown superstitious about the ring. Now it's—a ring of death! Death to him who wears the ring! *Pah!*"

He stretched forth an imperative hand.

"Give it to me, lieutenant! I'll tell you right now that no subterfuge in the universe will change the fact of my being a skeleton if I *am* the skeleton; and vice versa."

Tony shook his head. "I'll be keeping it—for a while. And you might as well know that no scientific argument will convince anybody the ring is not a ring of death. For, you see, it is."

Overland sank back, lips pursed. "What are you going to do with it?" he charged. When Tony didn't answer, he said pettishly, "Oh, what's the use! On the face of it, the whole situation's impossible." Then his face lighted. "What did you find out?"

Tony briefly sketched his conclusions. It would be two or

three weeks before they could repair the rocket jets, get the electric transmission system working properly.

Overland nodded absently. "Strange, isn't it!" he mused. "All that work DeTosque, Bodley, Morrell, Haley, the Farr brothers and myself have done goes for nothing. Our being here proves the theory they were working on."

Laurette smiled lopsidedly at Tony.

"Lieutenant," she said, "maybe the skeleton was a woman."

"A woman!" Masters' head snapped around, horror on his face. "Not you, Laurette!"

"Why not? Women have skeletons, too—or didn't you know?" She kept her eyes on Tony. "Well, lieutenant? I put a question up to you."

Tony kept his face impassive. "The skeleton," he said, without a tremor, "was that of a man."

"Then," said Laurette Overland, stretching out her palm, cup-shaped, "give me the ring."

Tony froze, staring. That his lie should have this repercussion was unbelievable. Out of the corner of his eye he saw Overland's slowly blanching face. On Masters, Laurette's statement had the most effect.

"Damn you, Crow!" he said thickly. "This is just a scheme of yours to get rid of the ring!" He lunged forward.

The action was unexpected. Tony fell backward under the impact of the man's fist. He sprawled on his back. Masters threw himself at him.

"Erle, you utter fool!" That was Laurette's wail.

Disgust settled on Tony's face. He heaved, by sheer muscular effort, and threw Masters over on his back. His fist came down with a brief but pungent *crack*. Masters slumped, abruptly lifeless.

Tony drew himself to his feet, panting. Laurette was on her knees beside Masters, but her dismayed eyes were turned upward to Tony.

"I'm sorry, lieutenant!" she blurted.

"What have you got to be sorry about?" he snapped. "Except for being in love with a fool like that one."

He was sorry for it the second he said it. He didn't try to read Laurette's expression, but turned sullen eyes to Overland.

"It's night," he said abruptly, "and it's raining. Tomorrow, when the sun comes up, it'll probably be different. We can figure out the situation then, and start our plans for—" He let the sentence dangle. Plans for what? He concluded, "I suggest we all get some sleep," and left.

He arranged some blankets on the floor of the control room, and instantly went to sleep, though there were times when he stirred violently. The skeleton was in his dreams—

There were five of them at the breakfast table. Laurette serving; Masters beside her, keeping his eyes sullenly on the food; Braker, eating as heartily as his cuffed hands would allow; Yates, picking at his food with disinterest.

Tony finished his second cup of coffee, and scraped his chair back.

"I'll be taking a look around," he told Laurette in explanation. He turned to the door.

Braker leaned back in his chair until it was balanced on two legs, and grinned widely.

"Where you going, Mr. Skeleton?"

Tony froze.

"After a while, Braker," he said, eyes frigid, "the ring will be taken care of."

Yates' fork came down. "If you mean you're going to try to get rid of it, you know you can't do it. It'll come back." His eyes were challenging.

Masters looked up, a strange, milling series of thoughts in his sullen eyes. Then he returned to his food.

Tony, wondering what that expression had meant, shrugged and left the room; and shortly, the ship, by way of the cavity in the storage bin.

He wandered away from the ship, walking slowly, abstractedly, allowing impressions to slip into his mind without conscious resistance. There was a haunting familiarity in this tumbled plain, though life had no place in the remembrance. There was some animal life, creatures stirring in the dank humus, in long, thick grass, in gnarled tree tops. This was mountain country and off there was a tumbling mountain stream.

He impelled himself toward it, the tiny, yet phenomenally bright sun throwing a shadow that was only a few inches long. It was high "noon."

He stood on the brink of the rocky gorge, spray prismatically alive with color, dashing up into his face. His eyes followed the stream up to the mountain fault where water poured downward to crush at the rocks with the steady, pummeling blow of a giant. He stood there, lost in abstraction, other sounds drowned out.

All except the grate of a shoe behind him. He tried to whirl; too late! Hands pushed against his back—in the next second, he had tumbled off the brink of the chasm, clutching wildly, vainly, at thick spray. Then, an awful moment of freezing cold, and the waters had enclosed him. He was borne away, choking for air, frantically flailing with his arms.

He was swept to the surface, caught a chaotic glimpse of sun and clouded sky and rock, and then went under again, with a half lungful of air. He tensed, striving to sweep away engulfing panic. A measure of reason came back. Hands and feet began to work in purposeful unison. The surface broke around him. He stayed on top. But that was only because the stream was flowing darkly, swiftly, evenly. He was powerless to force himself against this current.

He twisted, savagely looking for some sign of release. A scaly, oily tree limb came at him with a rush. One wild grab, and the limb was bending downstream, straining against the pressure his body was exerting. He dashed hair from his eyes with one trembling hand, winced as he saw the needle-bed of rapids a hundred feet downstream. If that limb hadn't been there— His mind shuddered away from the thought.

Weakly, he drew himself hand over hand upward, until the tree trunk was solidly below him. He dropped to the ground, and lay there, panting. Then he remembered the hands on his back. With a vicious motion, he jerked out his key ring. That was the answer—the key to the cuffs was gone, taken during the night, of course! Erle Masters, then, had pulled this prize play, or perhaps one of the outlaws, after Masters released him.

After a while, he came to his feet, took stock of his surroundings. Off to his left, a cliff side, and scarcely a half-mile distant, the pathetically awry hulk of the ship, on the top of the slope that stretched away.

The cliff side came into his vision again. A fault in the escarpment touched a hidden spot in his memory. He involuntarily started toward it. But he slowed up before he got to the fault—which was really a cave that tapered out to nothingness as its sides rose.

The cave!

And this sloping plain, these mountains, composed the surface of Asteroid 1007, millions of years from now.

Tony dropped emotionlessly to his knees at the mouth of the cave. Not so long ago, he had done the same thing. Then there had been a complete, undisjointed skeleton lying there.

Somehow, then, he had known the skeleton existed before the human race—as if it were someone—the skeleton?—that had spoken to him across the unutterable years. The skeleton? That could not be! Yet, whence had come the memory?

He took the ring from his pocket and put it on his finger. It gleamed.

He knelt there for minutes, like a man who worships at his own grave, and he was not dead. Not dead! He took the ring from his finger, then, a cold, bleak smile growing on his face.

He came to his feet, a rising wind whipping at his hair. He took a half dozen running steps toward the river, brought his arm over his shoulder in a throwing gesture.

Somehow the ring slipped from his fingers and fell.

He stooped, picked it up. This time, he made it leave his hand. It spun away, twinkling in the faint sunlight. But the gravity had hold of it, and it fell on the brink of the river, plainly visible.

A dry, all-gone feeling rose in Tony's throat. Grimly, he went forward, picked it up again. Keeping his eyes on it, he advanced to the brink of the river gorge. He held the ring over the darkly swirling waters, slowly released it.

It struck the river like a plummet. The waters enclosed it and it was gone. He looked at the spot where it had disappeared, half expecting it to spring back up into his hand. But it was gone. Gone for good!

He started dazedly back to the ship, moving in an unreal dream. Paradoxical that he had been able to get rid of it. It had dropped from his hand once, fallen short of the river once. The third time it had given up trying!

When he came up to the ship, Masters was standing at the stern, looking at the broken rocket jets. He turned, and saw Tony, water still dripping from his uniform. He fell back a step, face turned pallid.

Tony's lips curled. "Who did it?"

"D-did what?"

"You know what I mean," Tony bit out. He took three quick steps forward.

Masters saw that, and went reckless. Tony side-stepped him, brought his left arm around in a short arc. Masters went down cursing. Tony knelt, holding Masters down by the throat. He felt through his pockets, unearthed the key to the cuffs. Then he hauled Masters to his feet and shook him. Masters' teeth clicked.

"Murderer!" Tony snapped, white with rage.

Masters broke loose. "I'd do it again," he said wildly, and

swung. He missed. Tony lashed out with the full power of his open palm, caught Masters on the side of the head. Masters went reeling back, slammed against the side of the ship. Tony glared at him, and then turned on his heel.

He met Laurette Overland coming down the stairs to the upper corridor.

"Lieutenant!" Her eyes danced with excitement. "I've been looking for you. Where in the world have you been?"

"Ask Masters." He urged himself down the corridor, jaw set. She fell into step beside him, running to keep up with his long strides.

"You're all wet!" she exclaimed. "Can't you tell me what happened? Did you go swimming?"

"Involuntarily." He kept on walking.

She grabbed his arm, and slowed him to a stop. An ominous glint replaced her excitement.

"What," she said, "did you mean when you said I should ask Erle about it? Did he push you in? If he did, I'll—" She was unable to speak.

Tony laughed humorlessly. "He admitted it. He stole my key to the handcuffs with the idea that it would be easier to free Braker and Yates that way after I was . . . uh . . . properly prepared to be a skeleton."

Her head moved back and forth. "That's horrible," she said lowly. "Horrible."

He held her eyes. "Perhaps I shouldn't have told you about it," he said, voice faintly acid. "He's your fiancé, isn't he?"

She nodded, imperceptibly, studying him through the half gloom. "Yes. But maybe I'll change my mind, lieutenant. Maybe I will. But in the meantime, come along with me. Daddy's discovered something wonderful."

Professor Overland's head was propped up. He had a pencil and paper on his pyramided legs.

"Oh. Lieutenant! Come in." His face lighted. "Look here! Gravitons *can* thrust their way through to the future, giving the ship a thrust into the past. But only if it happened to enter the spherical type of etheric vacuum. This vacuum would be minus everything—electrons, photons, cosmic rays and so forth, except under unusual circumstances. At some one time, in either the past or future, there might be a stream of photons bridging the vacuum. Now, when gravitons are ejected into the past, they grab hold of light photons, and become ordinary negative electrons. Now say the photons are farther away in the past than they are in the future. The gravitons therefore follow the line of least resistance and hook up with photons of the future. The photons in this case were perhaps hundreds of millions of years away in the vacuum. In traveling that time-distance, the gravitons kicked the ship back for a proportionate number of years, burned up our machinery, and wrecked us on this suddenly appearing before-the-asteroid world."

Laurette said brightly, "But that isn't the important part, daddy."

"I can find another of those etheric vacuums," Overland went on, preoccupiedly, pointing out a series of equations. "Same type, same structure. But we have to go to the planet Earth in order to rebuild the reversed contraction machinery. We'll find the materials we need there." He glanced up. "But we have to get off this world before it cracks up, lieutenant."

Tony started. "Before this world cracks up?"

"Certainly. Naturally. You can—" His heavy brows came down abruptly. "You didn't know about that, did you? Hm-m-m." He stroked his jaw, frowning. "You recall the crescent planet you and Masters saw? Well, he took some readings on that. It's wonderful, son!" His eyes lighted. "It's an ill wind that blows nobody good. Not only do we know now that the asteroid evolved from a broken-up planet, but we also know the manner in which that planet broke up. Collision with a heavy, smaller body."

Tony paled. "You mean—" he said huskily. "Good heavens!" Sweat stood out on his forehead. "How soon will that happen?" he said ominously.

"Well, Erle has the figures. Something over eighteen or nineteen days. It'll be a crack-up that'll shake the sun. And we'll be here to witness it." He smiled wryly. "I'm more scientist than man, I guess. I never stop to think we might die in the crack-up, and furnish six skeletons instead of one."

"There'll be no skeletons," Tony said, eyes narrowed. "For one thing, we can repair the ship, though we'll have to work like mad. For another—I threw the ring into the river. It's gone."

Laurette seemed to pale. "I . . . I don't see how that could be done," she stammered. "You couldn't get rid of it, not really—could you?"

"It's gone," Tony said stubbornly. "For good. And don't forget it. There'll be no skeleton. And you might try to impress that on Masters, so he doesn't try to produce one," he added significantly.

He left the room with a nod, a few seconds later stepped

into the lounge. Braker and Yates turned around. Both were cuffed.

Tony took the key from his pocket and the cuffs fell away. In brief, pungent tones, then, he explained the situation, the main theme being that the ship had to be well away from the planet before the crack-up. Yates would go over the wiring system. Braker, Masters and Tony would work with oxyacetylene torches and hammers over the hole in the hull and the rocket jets.

Then he explained about the ring.

Yates ran a thin hand through his yellow hair.

"You don't do it that easy," he said in his soft, effortless voice. "There's a skeleton up there, and it's got Braker's ring on its finger. It's got to be accounted for, don't it? It's either me or you or Braker or the girl or her old man or Masters. There ain't any use trying to avoid it, either." His voice turned sullen. He looked at Braker, then at Tony. "Anyway, I'm keeping my back turned the right way so there won't be any dirty work."

Braker's breath sounded. "Why, you dirty rat," he stated. He took a step toward Yates. "You would think of that. And probably you'd try it on somebody else, too. Well, don't go pulling it on me, understand." He scowled. "And you better watch him, too, Crow. He's pure poison—in case you got the idea we were friends."

"Oh, cut it out," Tony said wearily. He added, "If we get the ship in working order, there's no reason why all six of us shouldn't get off—alive." He turned to the door, waved Braker and Yates after him. Yet he was sickeningly aware that *his* back was turned to men who admittedly had no conscience to speak of.

A week passed. The plain rang with sledgehammer strokes directed against the twisted tubes. Three were irreplaceable.

Tony, haggard, tired, unbelievably grimed from his last trip up the twisted, hopeless-looking main blast tube, was suddenly shocked into alertness by sounds of men's voices raised in fury outside the ship. He ran for the open air lock, and urged himself toward the ship's stern. Braker and Yates were tangling it.

"I'll kill him!" Braker raged. He had a rock the size of his fist in his hand. He was attempting, apparently, to knock Jawbone Yates' brains out. Erle Masters stood near, chewing nervously at his upper lip.

With an oath, Tony wrenched the rock from Braker's

hand, and hauled the man to his feet. Yates scrambled erect, whimpering, mouth bleeding.

Braker surged wildly toward him. "The dirty—!" he snarled. "Comes up behind me with an oxy torch!"

Yates shrilled, backing up, "That's a lie!" He pointed a trembling hand at Braker. "It was *him* that was going to use the torch on *me!*"

"Shut up!" Tony bawled. He whirled on Masters. "You've got a nerve to stand there," he snarled. "But then you *want* a skeleton! Damned if you're going to get one! Which one did it?"

Masters stammered, "I didn't see it! I . . . I was just—"

"The hell you say!" Tony whirled on the other two, transfixing them with cold eyes.

"Cut it out," he said, lips barely moving. "Either you're letting your nerves override you, or either one or both of you is blaming the other for a move he made himself. You might as well know the skeleton I saw was intact. What do you think a blow torch would do to a skeleton?" His lips curled.

Braker slowly picked up his torch with a poisonous glance at Yates. Yates as slowly picked his sledgehammer. He turned on Tony.

"You said the skeleton was intact?" Eagerness, not evident from his carefully sullen voice, was alive in his eyes.

Tony's glance passed over the man's broken, protruding jaw.

"The head," he replied, "was in shadow."

He winced. The passing of hope was a hard thing to watch, even in a man like Jawbone Yates.

He turned, releasing his breath in a long, tired sigh. What a man-sized job this was. Outwitting fate—negating what *had* happened!

Tony worked longer than he expected that day, tracing down the web of asbestos-covered rocket fuel conduits, marking breaks down on the chart. The sun sank slowly. Darkness swept over the plain, along with a rising wind. He turned on the lights, worked steadily on, haggard, nerves worn. Too much work to allow a slowing up. The invading planet rose each night a degree or more larger. Increasing tidal winds and rainstorms attested to a growing gravitational attraction.

He put an x-mark on the check—and then froze. A scream had gone blasting through the night.

Tony dropped pencil and chart, went flying up the ramp to the upper corridor. He received the full impact of Masters' second scream. Masters had left his room, was running up the corridor, clad in pajamas. There was a knife sticking out of his shoulder.

Tony, gripped with horror, impelled himself after the man, caught up with him as he plunged face downward. He dropped to one knee, staring at a heavy meat knife that had been plunged clear through the neck muscles on Masters' left shoulder, clearly a bid for a heart stroke.

Masters turned on his side. He babbled, face alive with horror. Tony rose, went with the full power of his legs toward the lounge.

A figure showed, running ahead of him. He caught up with its, whipped his arm around the man's neck.

"You!"

Yates squirmed tigerishly. He turned, broke loose, face alive with fury. Tony's open palm lashed out, caught Yates full on the face. Yates staggered and fell. He raised himself to one elbow.

"Why'd you do it?" Tony rasped, standing over him.

Yates' face was livid. "Because I'd rather live than anything else I can think of!" His booted foot lashed out. Tony leaped back. Yates rose. Tony brought his bunched fist up from his knees with all the ferocity he felt. Yates literally rose an inch off the floor, sagged, and sopped to the floor.

Tony picked him up in one arm, and flung him bodily into the lounge.

Braker rose from his sleeping position on a cushioned bench, blinking.

Tony said cuttingly, "Your pal ran a knife through Masters' shoulder."

"Huh?" Braker was on his feet. "Kill him?" In the half-light his eyes glowed.

"You'd be glad if he did!"

Braker looked at Yates. Then, slowly, "Listen, copper. Don't make the mistake of putting me in the same class with a rat like Yates. I don't knife people in the back. But if Masters was dead, I'd be glad of it. It might solve a problem that's bothering the rest of us. What you going to do with him?"

"I already did it. But tell Yates he better watch out for Masters, now."

Braker grunted scornfully. "Huh. Masters'll crack up and down his yellow back."

Tony left.

Laurette and Overland were taking care of Masters in his room. The wound was clean, hardly bleeding.

Overland, somewhat pale, was hanging onto the door. "It's not serious, honey," he said, as her fingers nimbly wound bandages.

"Not serious?" She turned stricken eyes up to Tony. "Look at him. And Daddy says it's not serious!"

Tony winced. Masters lay face down on the bed, babbling hysterically to himself, his eyes preternaturally wide. His skin was a pasty white, and horror had etched flabby lines around his lips.

"Knifed me," he gasped. "Knifed me. I was sleeping, that was the trouble. But I heard him—" He heaved convulsively, and buried his face in his pillow.

Laurette finished her job, face pale.

"I'll stay here the rest of the night," Tony told her.

Overland gnawed painfully at his lower lip.

"Who did it?"

Tony told him.

"Can't we do something about it?"

"What?" Tony laughed scornfully. "Masters had the same trick pulled on him that he pulled on me. He isn't any angel himself."

Overland nodded wearily. His daughter helped him out of the room.

During the night, Masters tossed and babbled. Finally he fell into a deep sleep. Tony leaned back in a chair, moodily listening to the sough of the wind, later on watching the sun come up, staining the massed clouds with running, changing streaks of color.

Masters awoke. He rolled over. He saw Tony, and went rigid. He came to his feet, and huddled back against the wall.

"Get out," he gasped, making a violent motion with his hand.

"You're out of your head," said Tony angrily. "It was Yates."

Masters panted, "I know it was. What difference does it make? You're all in the same class. I'm going to watch myself after this. I'm going to keep my back turned the right way. I'm going to be sure that none of you—"

Tony put his hands on his hips, eyes narrowed.

"If you've got any sense, you'll try to forget this and act like a human being. Better to be dead than the kind of man you'll turn into."

"Get out. Get out!" Masters waved his hand again, shuddering.

Tony left, shaking his head slowly.

Tony stood outside the ship, smoking a cigarette. It was night. He heard a footstep behind him. He fell back a step, whirling.

"Nerves getting you, too?" Laurette Overland laughed shakily, a wool scarf blowing back in the heavy, unnatural wind.

Tony relaxed. "After two weeks of watching everybody watching everybody else, I guess so."

She shivered. He sensed it was not from the bite of the wind. "I suppose you mean Erle."

"Partly. Your father's up and around today, isn't he? He shouldn't have gotten up that night."

"He can get around all right."

"Maybe he better lock himself in his room." He smiled with little amusement. "The others are certain the ring will come back."

She was silent. Through the ominous gloom, lit now by a crescent planet that was visible as a small moon, and growing steadily larger, he saw a rueful, lopsided smile form on her face. Then it was gone.

She said, "Erle was telling me the jets are in bad condition. A trial blast blew out three more."

"That's what happened."

She went on: "He also told me there was a definite maximum weight the jets could lift in order to get us free of the gravity. We'll have to throw out everything we don't need. Books, rugs, clothing, beds." She drew a deep breath. "And in the end, maybe a human being."

Tony's smile was frozen. "Then the prophecy would come true."

"Yes. It is a prophecy, isn't it?" She seemed childishly puzzled. She added, "And it looks like it has to come true. Because— Excuse me, lieutenant," she said hurriedly, and vanished toward the air lock.

Tony stared after her, his mind crawling with unpleasant thoughts. It was unbelievable, fantastic. So you couldn't outwit fate. The ship would have to be lightened. Guesswork might easily turn into conviction. There might be one human being too many—

Professor Overland came slowly from the air lock, wincing from the cold after his two weeks of confinement. His haggard eyes turned on Tony. He came forward, looking up at the growing planet of destruction.

"Erle has calculated three days, eight hours and a few minutes. But it's ample time, isn't it, lieutenant?"

"One jet will straighten out with some man-size labor. Then we can start unloading extra tonnage. Lots of it."

"Yes. Yes. I know." He cleared his throat. His eyes turned on Tony, filled with a peculiar kind of desperation. "Lieutenant," he said huskily, "there's something I have to tell you. The ring came back."

Tony's head jerked. "It came back?" he blurted.

"In a fish."

"Fish?"

Overland ran a trembling hand across his brow. "Yesterday a week ago, Laurette served fried fish. She used an old dress for a net. I found the ring in what she brought to my room. Well, I'm not superstitious about the ring. One of us *is* the skeleton—up there. We can't avoid it. I put the ring on—more bravado than anything else. But this morning"—his voice sank to a whisper—"the ring was gone. Now I'm becoming superstitious, unscientifically so. Laurette is the only one who could—or would—have taken it. The others would have been glad it was on my finger rather than theirs. Even Erle."

Tony stared through him. He was remembering Laurette's peculiar smile. Abruptly, he strode toward the ship, calling back hurriedly:

"Better go inside, sir."

In the ship, he knocked sharply on Laurette's door.

She answered nervously, "Yes."

"May I come in?"

"No. No. Do you have to?"

He thought a moment, then opened the door and stepped inside. She was standing near her bed, her eyes haunted.

Tony extended a hand imperatively. "Give me the ring."

She said, her voice low, controlled, "Lieutenant, I'll keep the ring. You tell that to the others. Then there won't be any of this nervous tension and this murder plotting."

He said ominously, "You may wind up a skeleton."

"You said the skeleton was not a woman."

"I was lying."

"You mean," she said, "it *was* a woman?"

Tony said patiently, "I mean that I don't know. I couldn't tell. Do I get the ring, or don't I?"

She drew a deep breath. "Not in the slightest can it decide who will eventually die."

Tony advanced a step. "Even your father doesn't believe that now," he grated.

She winced. "I'll keep the ring and stay in my room except when I cook. You can keep everybody out of the ship. Then there won't be anybody to harm me."

Footsteps sounded in the corridor. Masters entered the room. Tension had drawn hollow circles under eyes that refused to stay still.

"You," he said to Tony, his voice thin, wavering. He stood with his back to the wall. He wet his lips. "I was talking with your father."

"All right, all right," she said irritably. "I've got the ring, and I'm keeping it."

"No, you can't, Laurette. We're going to get rid of it, this time. The six of us are going to watch."

"You can't get rid of it!" Then, abruptly, she snatched it off her finger. "Here!"

Imperceptibly, he shrank back against the wall.

"There's no use transferring it now. You've got it, you might as well carry it." His eyes swiveled, lighted with a sudden burst of inspiration. "Better yet, let Crow carry it. He represents the law. That would make it proper."

She seemed speechless.

"Can you imagine it? Can you imagine a sniveling creature like him— I'll keep the ring. First my father gets weak in the knees, and then—" She cast a disdainful look at Masters. "I wish you'd both leave me alone, please."

Tony shrugged, left the room, Masters edging out after him.

Tony stopped him.

"How much time have we got left?"

Masters said jerkily, "We've been here fourteen days. It happens on the twenty-fifth. That's eleven days from now, a few hours either way."

"How reliable are your figures?"

Masters muttered, "Reliable enough. We'll have to throw out practically everything. Doors, furniture, clothes. And then—"

"Yes?"

"I don't know," Masters muttered, and slunk away.

It was the twenty-fourth of December.

Tidal winds increased in savagery in direct proportion to

the growing angular diameter of the invading planet. Heavy, dully colored birds fought their way overhead. On the flanks of abruptly rising cliff edges, gnarled trees lashed. Rain fell spasmodically. Clouds moved in thoroughly indiscriminate directions. Tentacular leaves whirlpooled. Spray, under the wind's impact, cleared the river gorge. The waterfall was muted.

Rushing voluminous air columns caught at the growing pile emerging from the ship's interior, whisked away clothing, magazines, once a mattress. It did not matter. Two worlds were to crash in that momentous, before-history forming of the asteroids. There was but one certainty. This plain, these mountains—and a cave—were to stay intact through the millions of years.

Inside the air lock, Masters stood beside a heavy weight scale. Light bulbs, dishes, silverware, crashed into baskets indiscriminately, the results weighed, noted, discarded. Doors were torn off their hinges, floors ripped up. Food they would keep, and water, for though they eventually reached Earth, they could not know whether it yet supported life.

The ship, devoid of furnishings, had been a standard eleven tons for an H-H drive. Furnishing, food, et cetera, brought her to over thirteen tons. Under a one and a half gravity, it was twenty tons. Masters' figures, using the firing area the ship now had, with more than half the jets beyond use, were exact enough. The maximum lift the jets would or could afford was plus or minus a hundred pounds of ten and three quarter tons.

Masters looked up from his last notation, eyes red-rimmed, lips twitching. Braker and Yates and Tony were standing in the air lock, watching him.

Fear flurried in Masters' eyes. "What are you looking at me like that for?" he snarled. Involuntarily, he fell back a step.

Yates giggled.

"You sure do take the fits. We was just waiting to see how near we was to the mark. There ain't anything else to bring out."

"Oh, there isn't?" Masters glared. "We're still eight hundred pounds on the plus side. How about the contraction machinery?"

Tony said: "It's our only hope of getting back to the present. Overland needs it to rebuild the drive."

"Pressure suits!"

"We're keeping six of them, in case the ship leaks."

"Doors!" said Masters wildly. "Rugs!"

"All," said Tony, "gone."

Masters' nails clicked. "Eight hundred pounds more," he said hoarsely. He looked at his watch, said, "Eleven hours plus or minus," took off his watch and threw it out. He made a notation on his pad, grinning crookedly. "Another ounce gone."

"I'll get Overland," Tony decided.

"Wait!" Masters thrust up a pointing finger. "Don't leave me alone with those two wolves. They're waiting to pounce on us. Four times one hundred and fifty is six hundred."

"You're bats," said Braker coldly.

"Besides," said Yates, "where would we get the other two hundred pounds?"

Masters panted at Tony, "You hear that? He wants to know where they'd get the other two hundred pounds!"

"I was joking," said Yates.

"Joking! *Joking!* When he tried to knife me once!"

"Because," concluded Yates, "the cards call for only one skeleton. *I'll* get him."

He came back shortly with Laurette and her father.

Overland fitted his glasses over his weak eyes while he listened, glancing from face to face.

"It would be suicidal to get rid of the machinery, what's left of it. I have another suggestion. We'll take out all the direct-vision ports. They might add up to eight hundred pounds."

"Not a bad idea," said Braker slowly. "We can wear pressure suits. The ship might leak anyway."

Masters waved a hand. "Then get at it! Laurette, come here. You've got the ring. *You* don't want to be the skeleton, do you? Put your back to this wall with me."

"Oh, Erle," she said in disgust, and followed her father out.

Tony brought three hack saws from the pile of discarded tools. Working individual rooms, the three of them went through the ship, sawing the ports off at the hinges, pulling out the port packing material. The ship was now a truly denuded spectacle, the floors a mere grating of steel.

The ports and packing were placed on the scale.

"Five hundred—five twenty-five—five sixty-one. That's all!" Masters sounded as if he were going to pieces.

Tony shoved him aside. "Five sixty-one it is. There may be

a margin of error, though," he added casually. "Braker, Yates—out with this scale."

The two stooped, heaved. The scale, its computed weight already noted, went out—

Tony said, "Come on, Masters."

Masters trotted behind, doglike, as if he had lost the power of thought. Tony got the six pressure suits out of the corner of the control room, and gestured toward them. Everybody got into the suits.

Tony buckled his helmet down. "Now give her the gun."

Masters stood at the auxiliary rocket control board, face pale, eyes unnaturally wide.

He made numerous minor adjustments. He slowly depressed a plunger. A heavy, vibrating roar split the night. The ship leaped. There was a sensation of teetering motion. In the vision plates, the plain moved one step nearer, as if a new slide had been inserted in a projector. The roar swept against them voluminously. The picture remained the same.

Masters wrenched up the plunger, whirled.

"You see?" he panted. "I could have told you!"

Professor Overland silenced him with a wave of the hand, pain showing in his eyes.

"I make this admission almost at the expense of my sanity," he said slowly. "Events have shaped themselves—incredibly. Backward. In the future, far away, in a time none of us may ever see again, lies a skeleton with a ring on its finger.

"Now which causes which—the result or its cause?"

He took off his glasses, blinked, fitted them back on.

"You see," he said carefully, "some of the things that have happened to us are a little bit incredible. There is Lieutenant Crow's—*memory* of these events. He saw the skeleton and it brought back memories. From where? From the vast storehouse of the past? That does not seem possible. Thus far it is the major mystery, how he *knew* that the skeleton existed before the human race.

"Other things are perhaps more incredible. Three shipwrecks! Incredible coincidence! Then there is the incident of the ring. It is—a ring of death. I say it who thought I would never say it. Lieutenant Crow even had some difficulty throwing it into the river. A fish swallowed it and it came back to me. Then my daughter stole it from me. And she refused to give it up, or let us know what her plans for disposition of it are.

"I do not know whether we are shaping a future that is, or whether a future that is is shaping us.

"And finally we come to the most momentous occurrence of this whole madness. An utterly ridiculous thing like two hundred or two hundred and fifty pounds.

"So we must provide a skeleton. The future that *is* says so."

Silence held. The roar of the river, and the growing violence of the tidal wind rushed in at them. Braker's breath broke loose.

"He's right. Somebody has to get off—and stay off! And it isn't going to be the old man, him being the only one knows how to get us back."

"That's right," said Yates. "It ain't going to be the old man."

Masters shrank back. "Well, don't look at me!" he snarled.

"I wasn't looking at you," Yates said mildly.

Tony's stomach turned rigid. This was what you had to go through to choose a skeleton to die on an asteroid, its skin and flesh to wear and evaporate away and finally wind up millions of years later as a skeleton in a cave with a ring on its finger. These were some of the things you had to go through before you became that skeleton yourself—

"Laurette," he said, "isn't in this lottery."

Braker turned on him. "The hell she isn't!"

Laurette said, voice edged, "I'm in. I might be the straw that broke the camel's back."

Overland said painfully, "Minus a hundred and five might take us over the escarpment. Gentlemen, I'll arrange this lottery, being the only nonparticipant."

Masters snarled, eyes glittering, "You're prejudiced in favor of your daughter!"

Overland looked at him mildly, curiously, as he would some insect. He made a clicking sound with his lips.

Masters pursued his accusation.

"We'll cut for high man, low card to take the rap!"

"Yah!" jeered Yates. "With your deck, I suppose."

"Anybody's deck!" said Masters.

"All the cards were thrown out. Why weren't yours?"

"Because I knew it would come to this."

"Gentlemen," said Overland wearily. "It won't be a deck. Laurette, the ring."

She started, paled. She said, "I haven't got it."

"Then," said her father, without surprise, "we'll wait around until it shows up."

Braker whirled on him. "You're crazy! We'll draw lots anyway. Better still, we'll find where she put the ring."

"I buried it," said the girl, and her eyes fluttered faintly. "You better leave it buried. You're just proving—"

"Buried it!" blasted Masters. "When she could have used a hammer on it. When she could have melted it in an oxyacety-lene torch. When she could—"

"When she could have thrown it in the river and have a fish bring it back! Shut up, Masters." Braker's jawline turned ominous. "Where's the ring? The skeleton's got to have a ring and it's going to have one."

"I'm not going to tell you." She made a violent motion with her hand. "This whole thing is driving me crazy. We don't need the ring for the lottery. Leave it there, can't you?" Her eyes were suddenly pleading. "If you dig it up again, you'll just complete a chain of coincidence that couldn't pos-sibly—"

Overland said, "We won't use the ring in the lottery. It'll turn up later and the skeleton will wear it. We don't have to worry about it, Braker."

Yates said, "Now we're *worrying* about it!"

"Well, it has to be there, doesn't it?" Braker charged.

Tony interrupted by striking a match. He applied flame to a cigarette, sucked in the nerve-soothing smoke.

His eyes were hard, watchful. "Ten hours to get out of range of the collision," his lips said.

"Then we'll hold the lottery now," said Overland. He turned and left the room. Tony heard his heavy steps drag-ging up the ramp.

The five stood statuesque until he came back. He had a book in one hand. Five straws stuck out from between the pages, their ends making an even line parallel with the book.

Overland's extended hand trembled slightly.

"Draw," he said. "My daughter may draw last, so you may be sure I am not tricking anybody. Lieutenant? Braker? Any-body. And the short straw loses."

Tony pulled a straw.

"Put it down on the floor at your feet," said Overland, "since someone may have previously concealed a straw."

Tony put it down, face stony.

The straw was as long as the book was wide.

Braker said, in an ugly tone, "Well, I'll be damned!"

Braker drew a shorter one. He put it down.

Yates drew a still shorter one. His smile of bravado vanished. Sweat stood suddenly on his pale forehead.

"Go ahead, Masters!" he grated. "The law of averages says you'll draw a long one."

"I don't believe in the law of averages," said Masters sulkily. "Not on this planet, anyway— I'll relinquish the chance to Laurette."

"That," said Laurette, "is sweet of you."

She took a straw without hesitation.

Masters said nervously, "It's short, isn't it?"

"Shorter than mine." Yates breath came out in a long sigh. "Go ahead, Masters. Only one straw left, so you don't have to make a decision."

Masters jerked it out.

He put it on the floor. It was long.

A cry burst from Overland's lips. "Laurette!"

She faced their silent stares with curled lips.

"That's that. I hope my hundred and five helps."

Tony dropped his cigarette. "It won't," he snapped. "We were fools for including you."

Suddenly he was watching Braker out of the corner of his eye, his nerves tense.

Overland said in a whisper, "How could I suggest leaving my daughter out? I said a hundred pounds *might* be the margin. If I'd have suggested leaving her out, you'd have accused me of favoritism."

Braker said casually, "There's only going to be one lottery held here."

Yates looked dumfounded. "Why, you blasted fool," he said. "What if we're stuck back here before the human race and there ain't any women?"

"That's what I mean. I thought we'd include the girl. If she was drawn, then we could ask some gentleman to volunteer in her place."

He made a sudden motion. Tony made a faster one. His Hampton came out and up.

"Drop it!" he rasped. "I said—*drop it!*"

Braker's eyes bulged. He looked at the Hampton as if he were unable to comprehend it. He cursed rackingly and dropped the automatic as if it were infested with a radioactive element. It clattered on the metal grating of the denuded floor.

A smile froze on Tony's lips. "Now you can explain where you got that automatic."

Braker, eyes fuming like those of a trapped animal, involuntarily shot a glance at Masters.

Tony turned his head slightly toward Masters. "It would be you," he said bitterly.

He whirled—too late. Yates hurtled toward him, struck him in a flying tackle. Tony fell audibly. He tangled furiously with Yates. No good! Braker, face contorted with glee, leaped on top of him, struggled mightily, and then with the main force of his two gloved hands wrenched the Hampton away, rolled from Tony's reach, then snapped himself to his feet, panting.

"Thanks, Yates!" he exclaimed. "Now get up, Crow. Get up. What a man. What a big hulking man. Weighs two hundred if he weighs an ounce." His lips curled vengefully. "Now get up and get out!"

Overland made a step forward, falteringly.

Braker waved the weapon all-inclusively.

"Back, you," he snarled. "This is my party, and it's a bad-taste party, too. Yates, corner the girl. Masters, stand still—you're my friend if you want to be. All right, lieutenant, get going—and dig! For the ring!" His face screwed up sadistically. "Can't disappoint that skeleton, can we?"

Tony came to his feet slowly, heart pounding with what seemed like long-spaced blows against his ribs. Painfully, his eyes ran from face to face, finally centered on Laurette's.

She surged forward against Yates' retaining grip.

"Don't let them do it, lieutenant," she cried. "It's a dirty trick. You're the one person out of the four who doesn't deserve it. I'll—" She slumped back, her voice fading, her eyes burning. She laughed jerkily. "I was just remembering what you did when all the Christmas packages came tumbling down on us. You kissed me, and I slapped you, but I really wanted you to kiss me again."

Yates laughed nastily. "Well, would you listen to that. Masters, you going to stand there and watch them two making love?"

Masters shuddered, his face graying. He whispered, "It's all right. I wish—"

"Cut out the talk!" Braker broke in irritably.

Tony said, as if the other conversation had not intervened, "I wanted to kiss you again, too." He held her wide, unbelieving eyes for a long moment, then dropped his and bit at his shuddering lower lip. It seemed impossible to stand here and realize that this was defeat and that there was no defense against it! He shivered with an unnatural jerk of the shoulders.

"All right," Braker said caustically, "get going."

Tony stood where he was. Braker and everybody else except Laurette Overland faded. Her face came out of the mist, wild, tense, lovely and lovable. Tears were coming from her eyes, and her racking sobs were muted. For a long moment, he hungrily drank in that last glimpse of her.

"Lieutenant!"

He said dully, his eyes adding what his lips did not, "Good-bye, Laurette."

He turned, went toward the air lock with dragging feet, like a man who leaves the death house only to walk toward a worse fate. He stopped at the air lock. Braker's gun prodded him.

He stood faintly in the air lock until Braker said, "Out, copper! Get moving."

And then he stepped through, the night and the wild wind enclosing him, the baleful light of the invading planet washing at him.

Faintly he heard Braker's jeering voice, "So long, copper." Then, with grim, ponderous finality, came the wheeze of the closing air lock.

He wandered into the night for a hundred feet, somehow toward the vast pile that had been extracted from the ship's interior. He seemed lost in unreality. This was the pain that went beyond all pains, and therefore numbed.

He turned. A blast of livid flame burst from the ship's main tube. Smaller parallels of fire suddenly ringed it. The ship moved. It slid along the plain on its runners, hugged the ground for two hundred feet, plummeting down the slope. Tony found himself tense, praying staccato curses. Another hundred feet. The escarpment loomed.

He thrust his arms forcefully upward.

"Lift!" he screamed. *"Lift!"*

The ship's nose turned up, as her short wings caught the force of the wind. Then it roared up from the plain, cleared the escarpment by a scant dozen feet. The echoes of the blast muted the very howl of the wind. The echoes died. Then there was nothing but a bright jewel of light receding. Then there was—nothing.

Tony looked after it, conscious that the skin was stretched dry and tight across his cheekbones. His upflung arms dropped. A little laugh escaped his lips. He turned on his heels. The wind was so furious he could lean against it. It was night, and though the small moon this before-the-asteroids world boasted was invisible, the heavens overflowed with the baleful, pale-white glow of the invading planet.

It was still crescent. He could clearly see the ponderous immensity the lighted horns embraced. The leftward sky was occluded a full two-fifths by the falling monster, and down in the seas the shores would be overborne by tidal waves.

He stood motionless. He was at a loss in which direction to turn. An infinity of directions, and there could be no purpose in any. What type of mind could choose a direction?

That thought was lost. He moved toward the last link he had with humanity—with Laurette. He stood near the trembling pile. There was a cardboard carton, addressed to Professor Henry Overland, a short chain of canceled stamps staring up at him, pointing to the nonexistence of everything that would be. America and Christmas and the post office.

He grinned lopsidedly. The grin was lost. It was even hard to know what to do with one's face. He was the last man on a lost world. And even though he was doomed to death in this unimaginably furious crack-up, he should have some goal, something to live for up to the very moment of death!

He uttered a soft, trapped cry, dashed his gloves to his helmeted face. Then a thought simmered. Of course! The ring! He had to find that ring, and he would. The ring went with the skeleton. And the skeleton went with the ring. Lieutenant Tony Crow—and there could be no doubt of this whatsoever—was to be that skeleton which had grinned up at him so many years ago—no, not ago, acome.

A useless task, of course. The hours went past, and he wandered across the tumbled, howling plain, traversing each square foot, hunting for a telltale, freshly turned mound of earth. He went to the very brink of the river gorge, was immersed in leaping spumes of water. Of the ring that he must have there was no trace.

Where would she have buried it? How would her mind work? Surely, she could not have heartlessly buried the ring, hiding it forever, when Tony Crow needed it for the skeleton he was to turn into!

He knew the hours were flying. Yet, better to go mad with this tangible, positive purpose, than with the intangible, negative one of waiting spinelessly for death from the lowering monster who now owned the heavens.

How convenient this was. One time-traveled. One witness to the origin of the asteroids. Similarly, one might time-travel and understand at last the unimaginable, utterly baffling process by which the solar system came into being. Nothing as simple as a collision. Or a binary sweeping past a single. Or a whirling nebula. It would be connected with the expanding universe, in some outrageously simple manner. But everything was simple once one knew the answer. For instance—

The ring! Yes, it was as simple as that. Even Laurette Overland would be forced to yield to the result that was influencing its own cause!

Tenseness gave way to relief. One could not baffle the future. Naturally, she'd buried the ring in the cave. Unless she wanted to be perverse. But she would *not* be perverse in a matter like this. Future and present demanded co-operation, if there was to be a logical future!

Forcing himself against a wind that blew indiscriminately, he reached the funnel in the mountainside. The skeleton was not here, naturally. But it would be—with the necessary ring on its finger. Unbelievable how the future shapes its own past! It was as if his own skeleton, which existed millions of years *acome*, on which his own healthy flesh rode *now*, were plainly telling him what he should do.

He dug with a cold methodicity, starting from the rear of the cave. No sign of the ring, and no sign of recently turned earth. He discarded his gloves, placed them carefully to one side, and dug with a sharp rock.

No sign of the ring! The hours passed. What was he to do? His thoughts sharpened with desperation. An hour, little more, remained. Then would come the smash—and death.

He was in the cave! He, the skeleton!

He lay on his back, head propped up in locked hands. Trees and limbs and leaves hurtled by in a tempestuous wind. Soon, out in the sky, would float the remnants of this very substantial world. The millions of years would pass. A Lieutenant Tony Crow, on the trail of three criminals, would land here, look into this cave, and see his own skeleton—only he would not know it.

He lay there, tense, waiting. The wind would dig up the ring, whip it through the air. He would hear a tinkling sound. That would be the ring, striking against the wall of the cave. He would pick it up and put it on his finger. In a few moments after that would come the sound—the heavy vibration—the ear-splitting concussion—the cosmic clash—the . . . the . . . *bang* of a world breaking up. *Bang!*

He listened, waiting for the ring.

He listened, and heard a voice, screaming down the wind.

He impelled himself to his feet, in one surge of motion. He stood there, blood pounding against his temples, his lips parted and trembling. There could be no sound like that. Not when he was the last human being on this world. Not when the scream could be that of Laurette Overland, calling to him.

Of course, it was not she. Of course, it could not be. This was merely one of those things previewing the preparation of a skeleton with a ring in a— *Stop!*

He moved from the cave, out into the wind, and stood there. He heard nothing—did he? A pound of feet—such as death running might make.

A scream!

He ran around the shoulder of the mountain, stood there, panting, clasping his helmeted head between his trembling, cold hands.

"Lieutenant!"

A voice, whipped into his imagination by the ungodly wind!

He would not believe it.

A form, stumbling out of the pale night! Running toward him, its lips moving, saying words that the wind took away. And it was Laurette Overland, forming in his imagination now that he had gone completely mad.

He waited there, in cold amusement. There was small use in allowing himself to be fooled. And yet—and yet—the ring had to come back; to him. This was Laurette Overland, and she was bringing it—for him to wear. That was selfish of her. If *she* had the ring, if *she* had dug it up, why didn't *she* wear it?

Then she would be the skeleton.

Then there would be two skeletons!

His mind froze, then surged forward into life and sanity. A cold cry of agony escaped him. He stumbled forward and caught the girl up in his arms. He could feel the supple firmness of her body even through the folds of her undistended pressure suit.

Laurette's lips, red and full against the ghastly induced paleness of her face, parted and words came out. Yet he could make no sense of it, for the unimaginable wind, and the cold horror lancing through his mind occluded words and sentences.

"—had to . . . out. A hundred pounds." He felt her hysterical laugh. So the ship had started to fall. She had bailed out, had swept to solid ground on streams of flame shooting from the rocket jets in the shoulders of her suit. This much he knew. Hours and hours she had fought her way—toward the plain. Because she remembered something. The ship was gone. Safe. She remembered something that was important and it had to do with the skeleton and the ring. She had to get out. It was her part in the ghastly across-the-millions-of-years stage play. She had to dig up the ring.

He held her out at arm's length and looked down at her gloved hands. Yes, there was mud on them. So the ring had not been in the cave.

His eyes shuddered upward to hers.

"Give me the ring." His lips formed the words slowly.

"No, no, lieutenant," she blurted out. "It's not going to be *that* way. Don't you see? It's Amos! Amos!"

"You must be crazy to have come back!" he panted. He shook in sudden overwhelming, maddening fury. "You're crazy anyway!"

He suddenly wrenched at her hands, forced them open. But there was no ring. He shook her madly.

"Where's the ring? Give it to me, you damned little fool! If you're wearing it—if you think for one moment—you can't do this—"

The wind whipped the words away from her, she knew, even as that which she was saying was lost to him.

He stopped talking, and with a cold ferocity wrapped one arm around her, and with the other started to unbuckle her gloves with his own bare hands. She struggled suddenly, tigerishly. She wrenched herself away from him. She ran backward three steps. She looked up into the sky for one brief second, at the growing monster. He could see the cold, frantic horror settling on her face. Collision! And it was a matter of moments! And he, the true skeleton, did not have the ring!

He moved toward her, one slow step at a time, his eyes wild, his jaw set with purpose.

She darted past him. He whirled, panting, went frantically after her. And every step he took grew more leaden, for the moment was here. The collision was about to occur. And the girl was running toward the cave.

Laurette vanished around the shoulder of the mountain. The cave swallowed her. His steps slowed down. He stood there, drew a deep, tremulous breath. Then he entered the cave, and stood facing her, the wind's howl diminishing.

She said, coldly, "We haven't much time to talk or fight, lieutenant. You're acting like a madman. Here." She stooped and picked up his gloves. She held them out. "Put these on."

He said, "Give me the ring."

She stared at him through the gloom, at his preternaturally wide eyes.

"All right," she said. She unbuckled the glove of her right hand. She moved close to him, holding his eyes with her own. "If you want to be the skeleton, you may."

He felt her fingers touch his right hand. He felt something cold traveling up his fingers. He felt the ring enclosing his finger. Yes, the ring was on there, where it should be. He felt it—coldly. It could not very well be his imagination—could it? Of course not. She would not try to fool him. Yet her eyes were hypnotic, and he was in a daze. Feebly, he knew he should resist. But she forced his glove over his right hand, and he heard the buckles click. Then the left hand glove went on, and was buckled.

Her arms crept up around his neck. Tears glinted unashamedly in her eyes.

"Hold me tight, lieutenant," she whispered huskily. "You know . . . you know, there may be a chance."

"No, there isn't, Laurette. There can't be. I've got the ring on my finger."

He could feel her drawing a deep breath. "Of course—you've got the ring on your finger! I think it can't be very far away, lieutenant. Hold me." Her voice was a whimper. "Maybe we'll live."

"Not I. Perhaps you."

"This cave, this very mountain, lived through the holocaust. And perhaps we will, too. Both of us."

She was being illogical, he knew. But he had sunk into a dull, apathetic state of mind. Let her try to believe what was impossible. He had the ring on his finger. He *did*.

Did he?

He jerked. He had felt the cold of its metal encircling his finger. He had *thought* he had felt it! His fingers moved. A dull, sickening sense of utter defeat engulfed him. This was defeat. *She* had the ring! *She* was the skeleton!

And there was no time to change it. There would be no time. The blood rushed in his head, giddily. He caught her eyes, and held them, and tried to let her know in that last moment that he knew what she had done. She bit her lip and smiled. Then—her face clouded. Clouded as his thoughts clouded. It was like that.

He heard no monstrous sound, for here was sound that was no sound. It was simply the ponderous headlong meeting of two planets. They had struck. They were flattening out against each other, in the immeasurable second when consciousness was whipped away, and fragments of rock, some large, some small, were dribbling out in a fine frothy motion from underneath the circle of collision. The planet was yawning mightily. A jigsaw of pieces, a Humpty Dumpty that all the king's horses and all the king's men could never put together again. This was the mighty prelude to the forming of an asteroid belt, and of a girl skeleton on Asteroid No. 1007.

He was alive.
Alive and thinking.
It did not seem possible.
He was wedged into the back of the cave. A boulder shut off light, and a projecting spur of it reached out and pinioned him with gentle touch against the wall at his back. He was breathing. His suit was inflated with ten pounds of pressure. Electric coils were keeping his body warm. He was alive and the thoughts were beginning in his brain. Slow, senseless thoughts. Thoughts that were illogical. He could not even bring himself to feel emotion. He was pinioned here in the darkness, and out there was an asteroid of no air, small gravity, and a twenty-mile altitude.

Laurette Overland would be dead, and she would be wearing the ring. Tears, unashamed, burned at his eyes.

How long had he been here, wedged in like this: minutes, hours, days? Where were Overland, Masters, Braker and Yates? Would they land and move this boulder away?

Something suddenly seemed to shake the mountain. He felt the vibration rolling through his body. What had caused that? Some internal explosion, an aftermath of the collision? That did not seem likely, for the vibration had been brief, barely perceptible.

He stood there, wedged, his thoughts refusing to work except with a monotonous regularity. Mostly he thought of the skeleton; so that skeleton *had* existed before the human race!

After a while, it might have been five minutes or an hour or more, he became aware of arms and legs and a sluggishly beating heart. He raised his arms slowly, like an automaton that has come to life after ages of motionlessness, and pushed against the boulder that hemmed him in. It seemed to move away from him easily. He stepped to one side and imparted a ponderous, rocking motion to the boulder. It fell forward and stopped. Light, palely emanating from the starry, black night that overhung Asteroid No. 1007, burst through over the top of the boulder. Good. There was plenty of room to crawl through—after a while. He leaned against the boulder, blood surging weakly in his veins.

He felt a vibration so small that it might have been imagination. Then again, it might have been the ship, landing on the asteroid. At least, there was enough likelihood of that to warrant turning his headset receiver on.

He listened, and heard the dull undertone of a carrier wave; or was that the dull throb of blood against his temples? No, it couldn't be. He strained to listen, coherent thoughts at last making headway in his mind.

Then:

"Go on, professor—Masters." That was Braker's voice! "We'll all go crazy if we don't find out who the skeleton is."

Then Braker had landed the ship, after escaping the holocaust that had shattered that before-the-asteroids world! Tony almost let loose a hoarse breath, then withheld it, savagely. If Braker heard that, he might suspect something. Whatever other purpose Tony had in life now, the first and most important was to get the Hampton away from Braker.

Overland muttered, his voice lifeless, "If it's my daughter, I'd rather you'd go first, Braker."

Masters spoke. "I'll go ahead, professor. I'd do anything to—" His voice broke.

Overland muttered, "Don't take it so hard, son. We all have our bad moments. It couldn't be a skeleton, anyway."

"Why not?" That was Yates. Then, "Oh, hell, yes! It couldn't be, could it, professor? You know, this is just about the flukiest thing that has ever happened I guess. Sometimes it makes me laugh! On again, off again!"

"Finnegan," finished Braker absently. "Say, I don't get it. This time business. You say the gravity of that planet was holding us back in time like a rubber band stretched tight. When the planet went, the rubber band broke—there wasn't that gravity any more. And then we snapped back to our real time. But what if Crow and your daughter weren't released like that? Then we ought to find the skeleton—maybe two of 'em."

"The gravity of the asteroid would not be enough to hold them back," Overland said wearily.

"Then I don't get it," Braker snapped with exasperation. "This is the present, our real present. Back there is the ledge that cracked our ship up, so it has to be the present. Then how come Crow said he saw a skeleton? Say," he added, in a burst of anger, "do you think that copper was pulling the wool over our eyes? Well, I'll be—"

Yates said, "Grow up! Crow was telling the truth."

Overland said, "The skeleton will be there. The lieutenant saw it."

Masters: "Maybe he saw his own skeleton."

Yates: "Say, that's right!"

Braker: "Well, why not? The same ring was in two different places at the same time, so I guess the same skeleton could be in Crow at the same time as in the cave. It's a fact, and you don't talk yourself out of it."

Tony's head was whirling. What in heaven were they talking about? Were they intimating that the release of gravity, when the planet broke up, released everything back to the real present, as if some sort of bond had been broken? His hands started to tremble. Of course. It was possible. The escapage of gravitons had thrust them back into the past. Gravitons, the very stuff of gravity, had held them there. And when that one and a half gravity had dispersed, when the gravitons were so far distant that they no longer exerted that tension, everything had snapped back—to the present!

Everything! His thoughts turned cold. Somewhere, somehow, something was terribly wrong. His head ached. He clenched his hands, and listened again. For a full minute, there was no voice. Tony could envision them walking along, Masters and Overland in front, Braker and Yates behind, making their slow way to the cave, Overland dreading what he was to find there.

Then: "Hurry it up, professor. Should be right around here."

Overland whispered, throatily, "There it is, Braker. My God!" He sounded as if he were going all to pieces.

"The skeleton!" Yates blurted out, burrs in his voice. "Ye gods, professor, d'you suppose— Why sure—they just weren't snapped back."

Shaking, pasty white of face, Tony clawed his way halfway up the boulder. He hung there, just able to look outside. The whole floor of the cave was visible. And the skeleton lay there, gleaming white, and the ring shone on its tapering finger!

Laurette.

He lifted his head, conscious that his eyes were smarting painfully. Through a blur, he saw Braker, Yates, Masters and

Overland, standing about thirty feet distant from the cave, silent, speechless, staring at the skeleton.

Braker said, his voice unsteady, "It's damned strange, isn't it? We knew it was going to be there, and there it is, and it robs you of your breath."

Yates cleared his throat, and said firmly, "Yeah, but who is it? Crow or the girl?"

Overland took a step forward, his weak eyes straining.

"It's not a very long skeleton, is it?" he whispered.

Braker said, harshly, "Now don't try talking yourself into anything, professor. You can't see the skeleton well enough from here to tell who it is. Masters, stop shaking." His words were implicit with scorn. "Move over there and don't try any funny stuff like you did on the ship a while ago. I should have blasted you then. I'm going to take a look at that skeleton."

He went forward sideways, hand on his right hip where the Hampton was holstered.

He came up to the mouth of the cave, stood looking down on the skeleton, frowning. Then he knelt. Tony could see his face working with revulsion, but still he knelt there, as if fascinated.

Tony's lips stretched back from his teeth. Here's where Braker got his! He worked his way up to the top of the boulder, tensed, slid over to the other side on his feet. He took one step forward and bent his knees.

Braker raised his head.

His face contorted into a sudden mask of horror.

"*You!*" he screamed. His eyes bulged.

Tony leaped.

Braker fell backward, face deathly pale, clawing at the Hampton. Tony was on top of him before he could use it. He pinned Braker down, going for the Hampton with hands, feet, and blistering curses. His helmet was a sudden madhouse of consternated voices. Overland, Masters, and Yates swept across his vision. And Yates was coming forward.

He caught hold of the weapon, strained at it mightily, the muscles of his stomach going rigid under the exertion.

Braker kicked at Tony's midriff with heavy boots, striving to puncture the pressure suit. Tony was forced over on his back, saw Braker's sweating face grinning mirthlessly into his.

Stars were suddenly occluded by Yates' body. The man fell to his knees, pinned Tony down, and with Braker's help broke Tony's hold on the Hampton.

"Give it to me!" That was Masters' voice, blasting out shrilly. By sheer surprise, he wrenched the weapon from Yates. Tony flung himself to his feet as the outlaw hurled himself at Masters with a snarl, made a grab for Yates' foot. Yates tried to shake him off, hopped futilely, then stumbled forward, falling. But he struck against Masters. Masters' hold on the weapon was weak. It went sailing away in an arc, fell at the mouth of the cave.

"Get it!" Braker's voice blasted out as he struggled to his feet. Masters was ahead of him. Wildly, he thrust Braker aside. Yates reached out, tripped Masters. Braker went forward toward the Hampton, and then stopped, stock-still.

A figure stepped from the cave, picked up the weapon, and said, in cold, unmistakable tones, "Up with them. You, Braker. Yates!"

Braker's breath released in a long shuddering sigh, and he dropped weakly, helplessly to his knees.

His voice was horrible. "I'm crazy," he said simply, and continued to kneel there and continued to look up at the figure as if it were a dead figure come to life at which he stared.

The blood drummed upward in Tony's temples, until it was a wild, crazy, diapason. His shuddering hands raised to clasp his helmet.

Then:

"Laurette," he whispered brokenly. *"Laurette!"*

There were six human beings here.

And *one skeleton on the floor of the cave.*

How long that tableau held, Tony had no way of knowing. Professor Overland, standing off to Tony's left, arms half raised, a tortured, uncomprehending look on his face. Masters, full length on his stomach, pushing at the ground with his clawed hands to raise his head upward. Yates, in nearly the same position, turned to stone. Braker, his breath beginning to sound out in little, bottled-up rasps.

And the girl, Laurette, she who should have been the skeleton, standing there at the mouth of the cave, her face indescribably pale, as she centered the Hampton on Braker and Yates.

Her voice edged into the aching silence.

"It's Amos," she said. She was silent, looking at her father's haggard face, smiling twistedly.

"Amos," said Overland hoarsely, saying nothing else, but in that one word showing his utter, dismaying comprehension. He stumbled forward three steps. "We thought— We thought—" He seemed unable to go on. Tears sounded in his voice. He said humbly, "We thought you were the— But no. It's Amos!" His voice went upward hysterically.

"Stop it!" Laurette's voice lashed out. She added softly, tenderly, "No, I'm not the skeleton. Far from it, Daddy. Amos is the skeleton. He was the skeleton all along. I didn't realize it might be that way until the ship lifted. Then it seemed that the ship was going to fall and I thought my hundred and five might help after all and anyway, I decided that the lieutenant was all alone down there. And that somehow made me think of the time all the Christmas packages tumbled down on him and how I slapped him." She laughed unsteadily. "That made me remember that the university sent your present with a 'Do Not Open Before Christmas' sticker on it. I remembered you were leaving the university and they were giving you a combination farewell gift and Christmas present. You didn't know, but I did, that the professors decided you couldn't possibly be back before Christmas and so they sent it to the ship. You had always told them you admired—Amos. He hung on the biology classroom wall. It seemed I suddenly knew how things *had* to be. I put two and two together and I took a chance on it."

She fell silent, and the silence held for another full, shocking minute. She went on, as if with an effort.

"We threw everything out of the ship, remember? The Christmas presents, too. When I dropped from the ship later, I reached the plain and I broke open the carton with the 'Do Not Open' sticker on it, and there was Amos, as peaceful as you please. I put the ring on his finger and left him there, because I knew that some way the wind or crack-up or *something* would drop him in the cave. He *had* to turn up in the cave.

"Anyway," she added, her lips quirking roguishly, "by our time, back there, it was December 25th."

Masters clawed his way to his knees, his lips parted unnaturally.

"A Christmas present!" he croaked. "A Christmas present!" His face went white.

The girl said unsteadily, "Cut it out, Erle!"

She leaned weakly against the wall of the cave. "Now come up here, lieutenant, and take this gun out of my hands and don't stare at me as if you've lost your senses."

Tony forced himself to his feet, and like an automaton skirted around Braker and Yates and took the suddenly shaking weapon from her.

She uttered a weary sigh, smiled at him faintly, bemusedly, and whispered, "Merry Christmas, lieutenant!" She slumped slowly to the ground.

Tony gestured soundlessly at Masters. Masters, face abject and ashamed, picked her up in tender arms.

"Come up here, professor," Tony said dully. He felt as if all the life had been pumped from his bones.

Overland came forward, shaking his head with emotion. "Amos!" he whispered. He broke in a half-hysterical chuckle, stopped himself. He hovered around Laurette, watching her tired face. "At least my girl lives," he whispered brokenly.

"Get up, Braker," said Tony. "You, too, Yates."

Yates rose, vaguely brushing dust from his pressure suit, his lips working over words that refused to emerge.

Braker's voice was a hoarse, unbelieving whisper. His eyes were abnormally wide and fixed hypnotically on the skeleton. "So that's what we went through—for a damned classroom skeleton." He repeated it. "For a damned classroom skeleton!"

He came to his feet, fighting to mold his strained face back to normal. "Just about back where we started, eh? Well," he added in a shaking, bitter tone, "Merry Christmas." He forced his lips into half-hearted cynicism.

Tony's face relaxed. He drew in a full, much-needed breath of air. "Sure. Sure— Merry Christmas. Everybody. Including Amos—whoever he used to be."

Nobody seemed to have anything to say. Or perhaps their thoughts were going back for the moment to a pre-asteroid world. Remembering. At least Masters was remembering, if the suffering, remorseful look on his face meant anything.

Tony broke it. "That's that, isn't it? Now we can go back to the ship. From there to Earth. Professor—Masters—start off." He made a tired gesture.

Masters went ahead, without a backward look, carrying the gently breathing, but still unconscious girl. Overland stole a last look at the skeleton, at Amos, where he lay, unknowing of the chaos the mere fact of his being there, white and perfect and wired together, and with a ring on his perfect tapering finger, had caused. Overland walked away hurriedly after Masters. Amos would stay where he was.

Tony smiled grimly at Braker. He pointed with his free hand.

"Want your ring back, Braker?"

Braker's head jerked minutely. He stared at the ring, then back at Tony. His fists clenched at his sides. *"No!"*

Tony grinned—for the first time in three weeks.

"Then let's get going."

He made a gesture. Braker and Yates, walking side by side, went slowly for the ship, Tony following behind. He turned only once, and that was to look at his wrecked patrol ship, where it lay against the base of the mountain. A shudder passed down his spine. There was but one mystery that remained now. And its solution was coming to Tony Crow, in spite of his effort to shove its sheerly maddening implications into the back of his mind—

Professor Overland and Masters took Laurette to her room. Tony took the two outlaws to the lounge, wondering how he was going to secure them. Masters solved his problem by entering with a length of insulated electric wire. He said nothing, but wordlessly went to work securing Braker and Yates to the guide rail while Tony held the Hampton on them. After he had finished, Tony bluntly inspected the job. Masters winced, but he said nothing.

After they were out in the hall, going toward Laurette's room, Masters stopped him. His face was white, strained in the half-darkness.

"I don't know how to say this," he began huskily.

"Say what?"

Masters' eyes shifted, then, as if by a deliberate effort of will, came back.

"That I'm sorry."

Tony studied him, noted the lines of suffering around his mouth, the shuddering pain in his eyes.

"Yeah, I know how you feel," he muttered. "But I guess you made up for it when you tackled Braker and Yates. They might have been using electric wire on us by now." He grinned lopsidedly, and clapped Masters on the arm. "Forget it, Masters. I'm with you all the way."

Masters managed a smile, and let loose a long breath. He fell into step beside Tony's hurrying stride. "Laurette's O. K."

"Well, lieutenant," said Laurette, stretching lazily, and smiling up at him, "I guess I got weak in the knees at the last minute."

"Didn't we all!" He smiled ruefully. He dropped to his knees. She was still in her pressure suit and lying on the floor. He helped her to a sitting position, and then to her feet.

Overland chuckled, though there was a note of uneasy

reminiscence in his tone. "Wait till I tell the boys at Lipton U. about this."

"You'd better not," Laurette warned. She added, "You broke down and admitted the ring was an omen. When a scientist gets superstitious—"

Tony broke in. "Weren't we all?"

Masters said, dropping his eyes, "I guess we had good enough reason to be superstitious about it." His hand went absently upward to his shoulder.

Overland frowned, and, hands behind his back, walked to the empty porthole. "All that work DeTosque, the Farr brothers, Morrell, and myself put in. There's no reason to patch up the asteroids and try to prove they were all one world. But at the same time, there's no proof—no absolute proof—" He clicked his tongue. Then he swung on Tony, biting speculatively at his lower lip, his eyes sharpening.

"There's one thing that needs explaining which probably never will be explained, I guess. It's too bad. Memory? Bah! That's not the answer, lieutenant. You stood in the cave there, and you saw the skeleton, and somehow you *knew* it had existed before the human race, but was not *older* than the human race. It's something else. You didn't pick up the memory from the past—not over a hundred million years. What then?" He turned away, shaking his head, came back abruptly as Tony spoke, eyes sharpening.

"I'll tell you why," Tony said evenly.

His head moved up and down slowly, and his half-lidded eyes looked lingeringly out the porthole toward the mountain where his wrecked patrol ship lay. "Yes, I'll tell you why."

Laurette, Masters and Overland were caught up in tense silence by the strangeness of his tone.

He said faintly: "Laurette and I were trapped alive in the back of the cave when the two worlds crashed. We lived through it. I didn't know she was back there, of course; she recovered consciousness later—at the right time, I'd say!" He grinned at her obliquely, then sobered again. "I saw the skeleton and somehow I was too dazed to realize it couldn't be Laurette. Because when the gravity was dispersed, the tension holding everything back in time was released, and everything went back to the present—just a little less than the present. I'll explain that later."

He drew a long breath.

"This is hard to say. I was in the back of the cave. I felt something strike the mountainside.

"That was my patrol ship—with me in it."

His glance roved around. Overland's breath sucked in audibly.

"Careful now, boy," he rumbled warningly, alarm in his eyes.

Tony's lips twisted. "It happens to be the truth. After my ship crashed I got out. A few minutes later I stood at the mouth of the cave, looking at the skeleton. For a minute, I—remembered. Fragmentary things. The skeleton was—horror.

"And why not? I was also in the back of the cave, thinking that Laurette was dead and that she was the skeleton. The Tony Crow at the mouth of the cave and the Tony Crow trapped in the rear of the cave were *en rapport* to an infinite degree. They were the same person, in two different places at the same time, and their brains were the same."

He stopped.

Masters whispered through his clenched teeth, "Two Tony Crows. It couldn't be."

Tony leaned back against the wall. "There were two rings, at the same time. There were two skeletons, at the same time. Braker had the skeleton's ring on his finger. Amos was wrapped up in a carton with a Christmas sticker on it. They were both some place else. You all know that and admit it. Well, there were two Tony Crows, and if I think about it much longer, it'll drive me—"

"Hold it, boy!" Overland's tone was sharp. Then he said mildly, "It's nothing to get excited about. The mere fact of time-travel presupposes duplicity of existence. Our ship and everything in it was made of electrons that existed somewhere else at the same time—a hundred million years ago, on the pre-asteroid world. You can't get away from it. And you don't have to get scared just because two Tony Crows were a few feet distant from each other. Remember that all the rest of us were duplicated, too. Ship A was thrust *back* into time just an hour or so before Ship B landed here after being thrust *forward*. You see?"

Laurette shuddered. "It's clear, but it's—" She made a confused motion.

Overland's tired, haggard eyes twinkled. "Anyway, there's no danger of us running across ourselves again. The past is done for. That's the main thing."

Neither Laurette nor Tony said anything. They were studying each other, and a smile was beginning at the corner of Laurette's lips. Erle Masters squirmed uncomfortably.

Overland continued, speculatively: "There was an energy loss some place. We weren't snapped back to the real present at all. We should have come back to the present that we left, *plus* the three weeks we stayed back in time. Back there it was Christmas—and Laurette was quite correct when she broke open my package." He grinned crookedly. "But it's still more than three weeks to Christmas here. It was a simple energy loss, I guess. If I had a penc—"

Erle Masters broke in on him, coughing uncomfortably and grinning wryly at the same time. "We'd better get down to the control room and plot out our course, professor."

"What?" Overland's eyes widened. He looked around at the man and girl. "Oh." He studied them, then turned, and clapped Masters on the back. "You're dead right, son. Let's get out!"

"I'm glad you weren't Amos," Tony told the girl.

"I couldn't very well have been, lieutenant."

He grinned, coloring slightly.

Then he took her hands in his, and put his head as close to hers as the helmets would allow.

He said, "When we get back to Earth, I'm going to put a r—" He stopped, biting at his lip. Remembrances of another time, on a pre-asteroid world, flooded back with the thought.

She started, paled. Involuntarily, her eyes turned to the open port, beyond which was a mountain, a cave, a skeleton, a ring.

She nodded, slowly, faintly. "It's a good idea," she murmured. She managed a smile. "But not—an emerald."

1941

THE WORDS OF GURU

Stirring Science Stories
June

by C. M. Kornbluth

Another short but wonderful story by the very young Kornbluth. It appeared in Stirring Science Stories, *a short-lived but exciting magazine edited by Cyril's friend Donald A. Wollheim, which was a major market for a number of young New York fans-to-be-writers. Many of the stories in its pages were collaborations (regardless of whose name was on them) but this one was Kornbluth's.*

(When Don Wollheim edited *Stirring* and its companion magazine *Cosmic*, he had an operating budget that included zero dollars for writers—if I recall correctly. He had to call upon the members of the Futurians therefore to supply him with the material to keep going till the magazines caught on and he could afford to pay. Even I submitted a story called "The Secret Sense"—one of my lesser works, I think. Cyril was by far the most active contributor, I think, and the best. It wasn't Don's fault that the combination of no budget *and* World War II made continuation impossible. And, by the way, since I whined in the previous introduction about being only 20 as an excuse for imperfection, *this* story appeared when Cyril was only 18.—I.A.)

Yesterday, when I was going to meet Guru in the woods a man stopped me and said: "Child, what are you doing out at one in the morning? Does your mother know where you are? How old are you, walking around this late?"

I looked at him, and saw that he was white-haired, so I laughed. Old men never see; in fact men hardly see at all. Sometimes young women see part, but men rarely ever see at all. "I'm twelve on my next birthday," I said. And then, because I would not let him live to tell people, I said, "and I'm out this late to see Guru."

203

"Guru?" he asked. "Who is Guru? Some foreigner, I suppose? Bad business mixing with foreigners, young fellow. Who is Guru?"

So I told him who Guru was, and just as he began talking about cheap magazines and fairy tales I said one of the words that Guru taught me and he stopped talking. Because he was an old man and his joints were stiff he didn't crumple up but fell in one piece, hitting his head on the stone. Then I went on.

Even though I'm going to be only twelve on my next birthday I know many things that old people don't. And I remember things that other boys can't. I remember being born out of darkness, and I remember the noises that people made about me. Then when I was two months old I began to understand that the noises meant things like the things that were going on inside my head. I found out that I could make the noises too, and everybody was very much surprised. "Talking!" they said, again and again. "And so very young! Clara, what do you make of it?" Clara was my mother.

And Clara would say: "I'm sure I don't know. There never was any genius in my family, and I'm sure there was none in Joe's." Joe was my father.

Once Clara showed me a man I had never seen before, and told me that he was a reporter—that he wrote things in newspapers. The reporter tried to talk to me as if I were an ordinary baby; I didn't even answer him, but just kept looking at him until his eyes fell and he went away. Later Clara scolded me and read me a little piece in the reporter's newspaper that was supposed to be funny—about the reporter asking me very complicated questions and me answering with baby noises. It was not true, of course. I didn't say a word to the reporter, and he didn't ask me even one of the questions.

I heard her read the little piece, but while I listened I was watching the slug crawling on the wall. When Clara was finished I asked her: "What is that gray thing?"

She looked where I pointed, but couldn't see it. "What gray thing, Peter?" she asked. I had her call me by my whole name, Peter, instead of anything silly like Petey. "What gray thing?"

"It's as big as your hand, Clara, but soft. I don't think it has any bones at all. It's crawling up, but I don't see any face on the topwards side. And there aren't any legs."

I think she was worried, but she tried to baby me by putting her hand on the wall and trying to find out where it was. I called out whether she was right or left of the thing. Finally she put her hand right through the slug. And then I realized that she really couldn't see it, and didn't believe it was there. I stopped talking about it then and only asked her a few days later: "Clara, what do you call a thing which one person can see and another person can't?"

"An illusion, Peter," she said. "If that's what you mean." I said nothing, but let her put me to bed as usual, but when she turned out the light and went away I waited a little while and then called out softly. "Illusion! Illusion!"

At once Guru came for the first time. He bowed, the way he always has since, and said: "I have been waiting."

"I didn't know that was the way to call you," I said.

"Whenever you want me I will be ready. I will teach you, Peter—if you want to learn. Do you know what I will teach you?"

"If you will teach me about the gray thing on the wall," I said, "I will listen. And if you will teach me about real things and unreal things I will listen."

"These things," he said thoughtfully, "very few wish to learn. And there are some things that nobody ever wished to learn. And there are some things that I will not teach."

Then I said: "The things nobody has ever wished to learn I will learn. And I will even learn the things you do not wish to teach."

He smiled mockingly. "A master has come," he said, half-laughing. "A master of Guru."

That was how I learned his name. And that night he taught me a word which would do little things, like spoiling food.

From that day to the time I saw him last night he has not changed at all, though now I am as tall as he is. His skin is still as dry and shiny as ever it was, and his face is still bony, crowned by a head of very coarse, black hair.

When I was ten years old I went to bed one night only long enough to make Joe and Clara suppose I was fast asleep. I left in my place something which appears when you say one of the words of Guru and went down the drainpipe outside my window. It always was easy to climb down and up, ever since I was eight years old.

I met Guru in Inwood Hill Park. "You're late," he said.

"Not too late," I answered. "I know it's never too late for one of these things."

"How do you know?" he asked sharply. "This is your first."

"And maybe my last," I replied. "I don't like the idea of it.

If I have nothing more to learn from my second than my first I shan't go to another."

"You don't know," he said. "You don't know what it's like—the voices, and the bodies slick with unguent, leaping flames; mind-filling ritual! You can have no idea at all until you've taken part."

"We'll see," I said. "Can we leave from here?"

"Yes," he said. Then he taught me the word I would need to know, and we both said it together.

The place we were in next was lit with red lights, and I think that the walls were of rock. Though of course there was no real seeing there, and so the lights only seemed to be red, and it was not real rock.

As we were going to the fire one of them stopped us. "Who's with you?" she asked, calling Guru by another name. I did not know that he was also the person bearing that name, for it was a very powerful one.

He cast a hasty, sidewise glance at me and then said: "This is Peter of whom I have often told you."

She looked at me then and smiled, stretching out her oily arms. "Ah," she said, softly, like the cats when they talk at night to me. "Ah, this is Peter. Will you come to me when I call you, Peter? And sometimes call for me—in the dark—when you are alone?"

"Don't do that!" said Guru, angrily pushing past her. "He's very young—you might spoil him for his work."

She screeched at our backs: "Guru and his pupil—fine pair! Boy, he's no more real than I am—you're the only real thing here!"

"Don't listen to her," said Guru. "She's wild and raving. They're always tight-strung when this time comes around."

We came near the fires then, and sat down on rocks. They were killing animals and birds and doing things with their bodies. The blood was being collected in a basin of stone, which passed through the crowd. The one to my left handed it to me. "Drink," she said, grinning to show me her fine, white teeth. I swallowed twice from it and passed it to Guru.

When the bowl had passed all around we took off our clothes. Some, like Guru, did not wear them, but many did. The one to my left sat closer to me, breathing heavily at my face. I moved away. "Tell her to stop, Guru," I said. "This isn't part of it, I know."

Guru spoke to her sharply in their own language, and she changed her seat, snarling.

Then we all began to chant, clapping our hands and

beating our thighs. One of them rose slowly and circled about the fires in a slow pace, her eyes rolling wildly. She worked her jaws and flung her arms about so sharply that I could hear the elbows crack. Still shuffling her feet against the rock floor she bent her body backwards down to her feet. Her belly muscles were bands nearly standing out from her skin, and the oil rolled down her body and legs. As the palms of her hands touched the ground, she collapsed in a twitching heap and began to set up a thin wailing noise against the steady chant and hand beat that the rest of us were keeping up. Another of them did the same as the first, and we chanted louder for her and still louder for the third. Then, while we still beat our hands and thighs, one of them took up the third, laid her across the altar, and made her ready with a stone knife. The fire's light gleamed off the chipped edge of obsidian. As her blood drained down the groove, cut as a gutter into the rock of the altar, we stopped our chant and the fires were snuffed out.

But still we could see what was going on, for these things were, of course, not happening at all—only seeming to happen, really, just as all the people and things there only seemed to be what they were. Only I was real. That must be why they desired me so.

As the last of the fires died Guru excitedly whispered: "The Presence!" He was very deeply moved.

From the pool of blood from the third dancer's body there issued the Presence. It was the tallest one there, and when it spoke its voice was deeper, and when it commanded its commands were obeyed.

"Let blood!" it commanded, and we gashed ourselves with flints. It smiled and showed teeth bigger and sharper and whiter than any of the others.

"Make water!" it commanded, and we all spat on each other. It flapped its wings and rolled its eyes, which were bigger and redder than any of the others.

"Pass flame!" it commanded, and we breathed smoke and fire on our limbs. It stamped its feet, let blue flames roar from its mouth, and they were bigger and wilder than any of the others.

Then it returned to the pool of blood and we lit the fires again. Guru was staring straight before him; I tugged his arm. He bowed as though we were meeting for the first time that night.

"What are you thinking of?" I asked. "We shall go now."

"Yes," he said heavily. "Now we shall go." Then we said the word that had brought us there.

The first man I killed was Brother Paul, at the school where I went to learn the things that Guru did not teach me.

It was less than a year ago, but it seems like a very long time. I have killed so many times since then.

"You're a very bright boy, Peter," said the brother.

"Thank you, brother."

"But there are things about you that I don't understand. Normally I'd ask your parents but—I feel that they don't understand either. You were an infant prodigy, weren't you?"

"Yes, brother."

"There's nothing very unusual about that—glands, I'm told. You know what glands are?"

Then I was alarmed. I had heard of them, but I was not certain whether they were the short, thick green men who wear only metal or the things with many legs with whom I talked in the woods.

"How did you find out?" I asked him.

"But Peter! You look positively frightened, lad! I don't know a thing about them myself, but Father Frederick does. He has whole books about them, though I sometimes doubt whether he believes them himself."

"They aren't good books, brother," I said. "They ought to be burned."

"That's a savage thought, my son. But to return to your own problem—"

I could not let him go any further knowing what he did about me. I said one of the words Guru taught me and he looked at first very surprised and then seemed to be in great pain. He dropped across his desk and I felt his wrist to make sure, for I had not used that word before. But he was dead.

There was a heavy step outside and I made myself invisible. Stout Father Frederick entered, and I nearly killed him too with the word, but I knew that that would be very curious. I decided to wait, and went through the door as Father Frederick bent over the dead monk. He thought he was asleep.

I went down the corridor to the book-lined office of the stout priest and, working quickly, piled all his books in the center of the room and lit them with my breath. Then I went down to the schoolyard and made myself visible again when there was nobody looking. It was very easy. I killed a man I passed on the street the next day.

There was a girl named Mary who lived near us. She was

fourteen then, and I desired her as those in the Cavern out of Time and Space had desired me.

So when I saw Guru and he had bowed, I told him of it, and he looked at me in great surprise. "You are growing older, Peter," he said.

"I am, Guru. And there will come a time when your words will not be strong enough for me."

He laughed. "Come, Peter," he said. "Follow me if you wish. There is something that is going to be done—" He licked his thin, purple lips and said: "I have told you what it will be like."

"I shall come," I said. "Teach me the word." So he taught me the word and we said it together.

The place we were in next was not like any of the other places I had been to before with Guru. It was No-place. Always before there had been the seeming passage of time and matter, but here there was not even that. Here Guru and the others cast off their forms and were what they were, and No-place was the only place where they could do this.

It was not like the Cavern, for the Cavern had been out of Time and Space, and this place was not enough of a place even for that. It was No-place.

What happened there does not bear telling, but I was made known to certain ones who never departed from there. All came to them as they existed. They had not color or the seeming of color, or any seeming of shape.

There I learned that eventually I would join with them; that I had been selected as the one of my planet who was to dwell without being forever in that No-place.

Guru and I left, having said the word.

"Well?" demanded Guru, staring me in the eye.

"I am willing," I said. "But teach me one word now—"

"Ah," he said grinning. "The girl?"

"Yes," I said. "The word that will mean much to her."

Still grinning, he taught me the word.

Mary, who had been fourteen, is now fifteen and what they call incurably mad.

Last night I saw Guru again and for the last time. He bowed as I approached him. "Peter," he said warmly.

"Teach me the word," said I.

"It is not too late."

"Teach me the word."

"You can withdraw—with what you master you can master also this world. Gold without reckoning; sardonyx and gems, Peter! Rich crushed velvet—stiff, scraping, embroidered tapestries!"

"Teach me the word."

"Think, Peter, of the house you could build. It could be of white marble, and every slab centered by a winking ruby. Its gate could be of beaten gold within and without and it could be built about one slender tower of carven ivory, rising mile after mile into the turquoise sky. You could see the clouds float underneath your eyes."

"Teach me the word."

"Your tongue could crush the grapes that taste like melted silver. You could hear always the song of the bulbul and the lark that sounds like the dawnstar made musical. Spikenard that will bloom a thousand thousand years could be ever in your nostrils. Your hands could feel the down of purple Himalayan swans that is softer than a sunset cloud."

"Teach me the word."

"You could have women whose skin would be from the black of ebony to the white of snow. You could have women who would be as hard as flints or as soft as a sunset cloud."

"Teach me the word."

Guru grinned and said the word.

Now, I do not know whether I will say that word, which was the last that Guru taught me, today or tomorrow or until a year has passed.

It is a word that will explode this planet like a stick of dynamite in a rotten apple.

THE SEESAW

Astounding Science Fiction
July

by A. E. van Vogt (1912-   )

> *This is a good story, one of the best of 1941, but it is also important for what it led to. "The Seesaw" became* The Weapon Makers, *which led to* The Weapon Shops of Isher.
>
> *The slogan in the story, "The Right to Buy Weapons Is the Right to be Free," found few dissenters in that war-torn year of 1941. Van Vogt remains one of the field's most influential and least understood practitioners.*

(I shouldn't allow my personal opinions to intrude too much in this series of anthologies, for we are selecting stories that are not so much our favorites—although most of them are—but stories that are of historic significance in the development of science fiction. I liked "The Seesaw" enormously, but looking back on van Vogt's writing now, it seems to me that "The Seesaw" was almost the last piece I worshipped. I found that as the years of World War II progressed his stories got progressively more difficult to follow. I think he was trying to top himself each time and make each story successively more complex. This can be dangerous. E. E. Smith fell into the trap and in the case of the *Foundation Stories,* I stopped when I thought there was no longer any way I could avoid falling into the trap myself.—I. A.)

MAGICIAN BELIEVED TO HAVE
HYPNOTIZED CROWD!

June 11, 1941—Police and newspapermen believe that Middle City will shortly be advertised as the next stopping place of a master magician, and they are prepared to extend him a hearty welcome if he will condescend to explain exactly how he fooled hundreds of people into believing they saw a strange building, apparently a kind of gun shop.

The building seemed to appear on the space formerly, and still, occupied by Aunt Sally's Lunch and Patterson Tailors. Only employees were inside the two aforementioned shops, and none noticed any untoward event. A large, brightly shining sign featured the front of the gun shop, which had been so miraculously conjured out of nothingness; and the sign constituted the first evidence that the entire scene was nothing but a masterly illusion. For from whichever angle one gazed at it, one seemed to be staring straight at the words, which read:

FINE WEAPONS
THE RIGHT TO BUY WEAPONS
IS THE RIGHT TO BE FREE

The window display was made up of an assortment of rather curiously shaped guns, rifles as well as small arms; and a glowing sign in the window stated:

THE FINEST ENERGY WEAPONS
IN THE KNOWN UNIVERSE

Inspector Clayton of the Investigation Branch attempted to enter the shop, but the door seemed to be locked; a few moments later, C. J. (Chris) McAllister, reporter of the *Gazette-Bulletin*, tried the door, found it opened, and entered.

Inspector Clayton attempted to follow him, but discovered that the door was again locked. McAllister emerged after some time, and was seen to be in a dazed condition. All memory of the action had apparently been hypnotized out of him, for he could make no answer to the questions of the police and spectators.

Simultaneous with his reappearance, the strange building vanished as abruptly as it had appeared.

Police state they are baffled as to how the master magician created so detailed an illusion for so long a period before so large a crowd. They are prepared to recommend his show, when it comes, without reservation.

Author's Note: The foregoing account did not mention that the police, dissatisfied with the affair, attempted to contact McAllister for a further interview, but were unable to locate him. Weeks passed, and he was still not to be found.

Herewith follows the story of what happened to McAllister from the instant that he found the door of the gun shop unlocked.

There was a curious quality about the gun shop door. It was not so much that it opened at his first touch as that, when he pulled, it came away like a weightless thing. For a bare instant, McAllister had the impression that the knob had freed itself into his palm.

He stood quite still, startled. The thought that came finally had to do with Inspector Clayton, who a minute earlier had found the door locked.

The thought was like a signal. From behind him boomed the voice of the inspector: "Ah, McAllister, I'll handle this now."

It was dark inside the shop beyond the door, too dark to see anything, and somehow his eyes wouldn't accustom themselves to the intense gloom. . . .

Pure reporter's instinct made him step forward toward the blackness that pressed from beyond the rectangle of door. Out of the corner of one eye, he saw Inspector Clayton's hand reaching for the door handle that his own fingers had let go a moment before; and quite simply he knew that if the police officer could prevent it, no reporter would get inside that building.

His head was still turned, his gaze more on the police inspector than on the darkness in front; and it was as he began another step forward that the remarkable thing happened.

The door handle would not allow Inspector Clayton to touch it. It twisted in some queer way, in some *energy* way, for it was still there, a strange, blurred shape. The door itself, without visible movement, so swift it was, was suddenly touching McAllister's heel.

Light, almost weightless, was that touch; and then, before he could think or react to what had happened, the momentum of his forward movement had carried him inside.

As he breasted the darkness, there was a sudden, enormous tensing along his nerves. Then the door shut tight, the brief, incredible agony faded. Ahead was a brightly lit shop; behind—were unbelievable things!

For McAllister, the moment that followed was one of blank impression. He stood, body twisted awkwardly, only vaguely conscious of the shop's interior, but tremendously aware, in the brief moment before he was interrupted, of what lay beyond the transparent panels of the door through which he had just come.

There was no unyielding blackness anywhere, no Inspector Clayton, no muttering crowd of gaping spectators, no dingy row of shops across the way.

It wasn't even remotely the same street. There was *no* street.

Instead, a peaceful park spread there. Beyond it, brilliant under a noon sun, glowed a city of minarets and stately towers—

From behind him, a husky, musical, woman's voice said, "You will be wanting a gun?"

McAllister turned. It wasn't that he was ready to stop feasting his eyes on the vision of the city. The movement was automatic reaction to a sound. And because the whole affair was still like a dream, the city scene faded almost instantly; his mind focused on the young woman who was advancing slowly from the rear section of the store.

Briefly, his thought wouldn't come clear. A conviction that he ought to say something was tangled with first impressions of the girl's appearance. She had a slender, well-shaped body; her face was creased into a pleasant smile. She had brown eyes, neat, wavy brown hair. Her simple frock and sandals seemed so normal at first glance that he gave them no other thought.

He was able to say: "What I can't understand is why the police officer who tried to follow me couldn't get in. And where is he now?"

To his surprise, the girl's smile became faintly apologetic. "We know that people consider it silly of us to keep harping on that ancient feud."

Her voice grew firmer: "We even know how clever the propaganda is that stresses the silliness of our stand. Meanwhile, we never allow any of *her* men in here. We continue to take our principles very seriously."

She paused as if she expected dawning comprehension from him, but McAllister saw from the slow puzzlement creeping into her eyes that his face must look as limp as were the thoughts behind it.

Her men! The girl had spoken the word as if she were referring to some personage, and in direct reply to his use of the words, police officer. That meant *her* men, whoever she was, were policemen; and they weren't allowed in this gun shop. So the door was hostile, and wouldn't admit them.

A strange emptiness struck into McAllister's mind, matching the hollowness that was beginning to afflict the pit of his stomach, a sense of unplumbed depths, the first, staggering conviction that all was not as it should be.

The girl was speaking in sharper tone: "You mean you know nothing of all this, that for generations the gunmaker's guild has existed in this age of devastating energies as the common man's only protection against enslavement. The right to buy guns—"

She stopped again, her narrowed eyes searching him; then: "Come to think of it, there's something very illogical about you. Your outlandish clothes—you're not from the northern farm plains, are you?"

He shook his head dumbly, more annoyed with his reactions every passing second. But he couldn't help it. A tightness was growing in him, becoming more unbearable instant by instant, as if somewhere a vital mainspring were being wound to the breaking point.

The young woman went on more swiftly: "And come to think of it, it is astounding that a policeman should have tried the door and there was no alarm."

Her hand moved; metal flashed in it, metal as bright as steel in blinding sunlight. There was not the faintest hint of the apologetic in her voice as she said, "You will stay where you are, sir, till I have called my father. In our business, with our responsibility, we never take chances. Something is very wrong here."

Curiously, it was at that point that McAllister's mind began to function clearly; the thought that came paralleled hers: How had this gun shop appeared on a 1941 street? How had he come here into this fantastic world?

Something was very wrong indeed!

It was the gun that held his attention. A tiny thing it was, shaped like a pistol, but with three cubes projecting in a little half circle from the top of the slightly bulbous firing chamber.

And as he stared, his mind began to quiver on its base; for that wicked little instrument, glittering there in her browned fingers, was as real as she herself.

"Good Heaven!" he whispered. "What the devil kind of gun is it? Lower that thing and let's try to find out what all this is about."

She seemed not to be listening; and abruptly he noticed that her gaze was flicking to a point on the wall somewhat to his left. He followed her look—in time to see seven miniature white lights flash on.

Curious lights! Briefly, he was fascinated by the play of light and shade, the waxing and waning from one tiny globe to the next, a rippling movement of infinitesimal increments and decrements, an incredibly delicate effect of instantaneous reaction to some supersensitive barometer.

The lights steadied; his gaze reverted to the girl. To his surprise, she was putting away her gun. She must have noticed his expression.

"It's all right," she said coolly. "The automatics are on you now. If we're wrong about you, we'll be glad to apologize. Meanwhile, if you're still interested in buying a gun, I'll be happy to demonstrate."

So the automatics were on him, McAllister thought ironically. He felt no relief at the information. Whatever the automatics were, they wouldn't be working in his favor; and the fact that the young woman could put away her gun in spite of her suspicions spoke volumes for the efficiency of the new watchdogs.

There was absolutely nothing he could do but play out this increasingly grim and inexplicable farce. Either he was mad, or else he was no longer on Earth, at least not the Earth of 1941—which was utter nonsense.

He'd have to get out of this place, of course. Meanwhile, the girl was assuming that a man who came into a gun shop would, under ordinary circumstances, want to buy a gun.

It struck him suddenly that, of all the things he could think of, what he wanted to see was one of those strange guns. There were implications of incredible things in the very shape of the instruments. Aloud he said, "Yes, by all means show me."

Another thought occurred to him. He added: "I have no doubt your father is somewhere in the background making some sort of study of me."

The young woman made no move to lead him anywhere. Her eyes were dark pools of puzzlement, staring at him.

"You may not realize it," she said finally, slowly, "but you have already upset our entire establishment. The lights of the automatics should have gone on the moment father pressed the buttons, as he did when I called to him. They didn't! That's unnatural, that's alien.

"And yet"—her frown deepened—"if you were one of

them, how did you get through that door? Is it possible that *her* scientists have discovered human beings who do not affect the sensitive energies? And that you are one of many such, sent as an experiment to determine whether or not entrance could be gained?

"Yet that doesn't make logic either.

"If they had even a hope of success, they would not risk so lightly the chance of an overwhelming surprise. Instead you would be the entering wedge of an attack on a vast scale. She is ruthless, she's brilliant; and she craves all power during her lifetime over poor saps like you who have no more sense than to worship her amazing beauty and the splendor of the Imperial Court."

The young woman paused, with the faintest of smiles. "There I go again, off on a political speech. But you can see that there are at least a few reasons why we should be careful about you."

There was a chair over in one corner; McAllister started for it. His mind was calmer, cooler.

"Look," he began, "I don't know what you're talking about. I don't even know how I came to be in this shop. I agree with you that the whole thing requires explanation, but I mean that differently than you do. In fact . . ."

His voice trailed. He had been half lowered over the chair, but instead of sinking into it, he came erect like an old, old man. His eyes fixed on lettering that shone above a glass case of guns behind her. He said hoarsely, "Is that—a calendar?"

She followed his gaze, puzzled: "Yes, it's June third. What's wrong?"

"I don't mean that. I mean—" He caught himself with a horrible effort. "I mean those figures above that. I mean—what year is this?"

The girl looked surprised. She started to say something, then stopped and backed away. Finally: "Don't look like that! There's nothing wrong. This is eighty-four of the four thousand seven hundredth year of the Imperial House of the Isher. It's quite all right."

There was no real feeling in him. Quite deliberately he sat down, and the conscious wonder came: exactly how *should* he feel?

Not even surprise came to his aid. Quite simply, the whole pattern of events began to make a sort of distorted logic.

The building front superimposed on those two 1941 shops; the way the door had acted; the great exterior sign with its odd linking of freedom with the right to buy weapons; the actual display of weapons in the window, *the finest energy weapons in the known universe!*

He grew aware that minutes had passed while he sat there in slow, dumb thought. And that the girl was talking earnestly with a tall, gray-haired man who was standing on the open threshold of the door through which she had originally come.

There was an odd, straining tenseness in the way they were talking. Their low-spoken words made a curious blur of sound in his ears, strangely unsettling in effect—McAllister could not quite analyze the meaning of it until the girl turned; and, in a voice dark with urgency, said, "Mr. McAllister, my father wants to know what year you're from!"

Briefly, the sense of the sentence was overshadowed by that stark urgency; then: "Huh!" said McAllister. "Do you mean that you're responsible for— And how the devil did you know my name?"

The older man shook his head. "No, we're not responsible." His voice quickened but lost none of its gravity. "There's no time to explain. What has happened is what we gunmakers have feared for generations: that sooner or later would come one who lusted for unlimited power; and who, to attain tyranny, must necessarily seek first to destroy us.

"Your presence here is a manifestation of the energy force that she has turned against us—something so new that we did not even suspect it was being used against us. But now—I have no time to waste. Get all the information you can, Lystra, and warn him of his own personal danger."

The man turned. The door closed noiselessly behind his tall figure.

McAllister asked, "What did he mean—personal danger?"

He saw that the girl's brown eyes were uneasy as they rested on him.

"It's hard to explain," she began in an uncomfortable voice. "First of all, come to the window, and I'll try to make everything clear. It's all very confusing to you, I suppose."

McAllister drew a deep breath. "Now we're getting somewhere."

His alarm was gone. The older man seemed to know what it was all about; that meant there should be no difficulty getting home again. As for all this danger to the gunmakers' guild, that was their worry, not his. Meanwhile—

He stepped forward, closer to the girl. To his amazement, she cringed away as if he had struck at her.

As he stared blankly, she turned, and laughed a humorless,

uncertain laugh; finally she breathed, "Don't think I'm being silly, don't be offended—but for your life's sake don't touch any human body you might come into contact with."

McAllister was conscious of a chill. It struck him with a sudden, sharp dismay that the expression of uneasiness in the girl's face was—fear!

His own fear fled before a wave of impatience. He controlled himself with an effort.

"Now, look," he began. "I want to get things clear. We can talk here without danger, providing I don't touch you or come near you. Is that straight?"

She nodded. "The floor, the walls, every piece of furniture, in fact the entire shop is made of perfect nonconducting material."

McAllister had a sudden sense of being balanced on a tightrope over a bottomless abyss. The way this girl could imply danger without making it clear what the danger was almost petrified him.

He forced calm into his mind. "Let's start," he said, "at the beginning. How did you and your father know my name, and that I was not of"—he paused before the odd phrase, then went on—"of this time?"

"Father X-rayed you," the girl said, her voice as stiff as her body. "He X-rayed the contents of your pockets. That was how he first found out what was the matter. You see, the X-rays themselves became carriers of the energy with which you're charged. That's what was the matter; that's why the automatics wouldn't focus on you, and—"

"Just a minute!" said McAllister. His brain was a spinning world. "Energy—charged?"

The girl was staring at him. "Don't you understand?" she gasped. "You've come across five thousand years of time; and of all the energies in the universe, time is the most potent. You're charged with trillions of trillions of time-energy units. If you should step outside this shop, you'd blow up this city of the Isher and half a hundred miles of land beyond.

"You"—she finished on an unsteady, upward surge of her voice—"you could conceivably destroy the Earth!"

He hadn't noticed the mirror before; funny, too, because it was large enough, at least eight feet high, and directly in front of him on the wall where a minute before—he could have sworn—had been solid metal.

"Look at yourself," the girl was saying soothingly. "There's nothing so steadying as one's own image. Actually your body is taking the mental shock very well."

It was! He stared in dimly gathering surprise at his image. There was a paleness in the lean face that stared back at him; but the body was not actually shaking as the whirling in his mind had suggested.

He grew aware again of the girl. She was standing with one finger on one of a series of wall switches. Abruptly, he felt better.

"Thank you," he said quietly. "I certainly needed that."

She smiled encouragingly; and he was able now to be amazed at her conflicting personality. There had been on the one hand her complete inability a few minutes earlier to get to the point of his danger, a distinct incapacity for explaining things with words; yet obviously her action with the mirror showed a keen understanding of human psychology. He said, "The problem now is, from your point of view, to circumvent this—Isher—woman, and to get me back to 1941 before I blow up the Earth of . . . of whatever year this is."

The girl nodded. "Father says that you can be sent back, but—as for the rest: watch!"

He had no time for relief at the knowledge that he could be returned to his own time. She pressed another button. Instantly the mirror was gone into the metallic wall. Another button clicked—and the wall vanished.

Literally vanished. Before him stretched a park similar to the one he had already seen through the front door—obviously an extension of the same garden-like vista. Trees were there, and flowers, and green, green grass in the sun.

There was also the city again, nearer from this side, but not so pretty, immeasurably grimmer.

One vast building, as high as it was long, massively dark against the sky, dominated the entire horizon. It was a good quarter-mile away; and incredibly, it was at least that long and that high.

Neither near that monstrous building nor in the park was a living person visible. Everywhere was evidence of man's dynamic labor—but no men, not a movement; even the trees stood motionless in that strangely breathless sunlit day.

"Watch!" said the girl again, more softly.

There was no click this time. She made an adjustment on one of the buttons; and suddenly the view was no longer so clear. It wasn't that the sun had dimmed its bright intensity. It wasn't even that glass was visible where a moment before there had been nothing.

There was still no apparent substance between them and the gemlike park. But—

The park was no longer deserted!

Scores of men and machines swarmed out there. McAllister stared in frank amazement; and then as the sense of illusion faded, and the dark menace of those men penetrated, his emotion changed to dismay.

"Why," he said at last, "those men are soldiers, and the machines are—"

"Energy guns!" she said. "That's always been their problem: how to get their weapons close enough to our shops to destroy us. It isn't that the guns are not powerful over a very great distance. Even the rifles we sell can kill unprotected life over a distance of miles; but our gun shops are so heavily fortified that, to destroy us, they must use their biggest cannon at point-blank range.

"In the past, they could never do that because we own the surrounding park; and our alarm system was perfect—until now. The new energy they're using affects none of our protective instruments; and—what is infinitely worse—affords them a perfect shield against our own guns. Invisibility, of course, has long been known; but if you hadn't come, we would have been destroyed without ever knowing what happened."

"But," McAllister exclaimed sharply, "what are you going to do? They're still out there working—"

Her brown eyes burned with a fierce, yellow flame. "Where do you think Father is?" she asked. "He's warned the guild; and every member has now discovered that similar invisible guns are being set up outside his place by invisible men. Every member is working at top speed for some solution. They haven't found it yet."

She finished quietly: "I thought I'd tell you."

McAllister cleared his throat, parted his lips to speak—then closed them as he realized that no words were even near his lips. Fascinated, he watched the soldiers connecting what must have been invisible cables that led to the vast building in the background: foot-thick cables that told of the titanic power that was to be unleashed on the tiny weapon shop.

There was actually nothing to be said. The deadly reality out there overshadowed all conceivable sentences and phrases. Of all the people here, he was the most useless, his opinion the least worthwhile.

Oddly, he must have spoken aloud, but he did not realize that until the familiar voice of the girl's father came from one side of him. The older man said, "You're quite mistaken, McAllister. Of all the people here you are the *most* valuable.

Through you we discovered that the Isher were actually attacking us. Furthermore, our enemies do not know of your existence, therefore have not yet realized the full effect produced by the new blanketing energy they have used.

"You, accordingly, constitute the unknown factor—our only hope, for the time left to us is incredibly short. Unless we can make immediate use of the unknown quantity you represent, all is lost!"

The man looked older, McAllister thought; there were lines of strain in his lean, sallow face as he turned toward his daughter; and his voice, when he spoke, was edged with harshness: "Lystra, number seven!"

As the girl's fingers touched the seventh button, her father explained swiftly to McAllister: "The guild supreme council is holding an immediate emergency session. We must choose the most likely method of attacking the problem, and concentrate individually and collectively on that method. Regional conversations are already in progress, but only one important idea has been put forward as yet . . . ah, gentlemen!"

He spoke past McAllister, who turned with a start, then froze.

Men were coming out of the solid wall, lightly, easily, as if it were a door and they were stepping across a threshold. One, two, three—twelve.

They were grim-faced men, all except one who glanced at McAllister, started to walk past, then stopped with a half-amused smile.

"Don't look so blank. How else do you think we could have survived these many years if we hadn't been able to transmit material objects through space? The Isher police have always been only too eager to blockade our sources of supply. Incidentally, my name is Cadron—Peter Cadron!"

McAllister nodded in a perfunctory manner. He was no longer genuinely impressed by the new machines. Here were endless products of the machine age; science and invention so stupendously advanced that men made scarcely a move that did not involve a machine. He grew aware that a heavy-faced man near him was about to speak.

The man began: "We are gathered here because it is obvious that the source of the new energy is the great building just outside this shop—"

He motioned toward the wall where the mirror had been a few minutes previously, and the window through which McAllister had gazed at the monstrous structure in question.

The speaker went on: "We've known, ever since that build-

ing was completed five years ago, that it was a power building aimed against us; and now from it new energy has flown
out to engulf the world, immensely potent energy, so strong
that it broke the very tension of time, fortunately only at this
nearest gun shop. Apparently it weakens when transmitted
over distance. It—"

"Look, Dresley!" came a curt interruption from a small,
thin man. "What good is all this preamble? You have been
examining the various plans put forward by regional groups.
Is there, or isn't there, a decent one among them?"

Dresley hesitated. To McAllister's surprise, the man's eyes
fixed doubtfully on him, his heavy face worked for a moment, then hardened.

"Yes, there is a method, but it depends on compelling our
friend from the past to take a great risk. You all know what
I'm referring to. It will gain us the time we need so desperately."

"Eh!" said McAllister, and stood stunned as all eyes turned
to stare at him.

The seconds fled; and it struck McAllister that what he
really needed again was the mirror—to prove to him that his
body was putting up a good front. Something, he thought,
something to steady him.

His gaze flicked over the faces of the men. The gunmakers
made a curious, confusing pattern in the way they sat, or
stood, or leaned against glass cases of shining guns; and there
seemed to be fewer than he had previously counted. One,
two—ten, including the girl. He could have sworn there had
been fourteen.

His eyes moved on, just in time to see the door of the back
room closing. Four of the men had obviously gone to the laboratory or whatever lay beyond the door. Satisfied, he forgot
them.

Still, he felt unsettled; and briefly his eyes were held by the
purely mechanical wonder of this shop, here in this vastly future world, a shop that was an intricate machine in itself
and—

He discovered that he was lighting a cigarette; and
abruptly realized that that was what he needed most. The first
puff tingled deliciously along his nerves. His mind grew calm;
his eyes played thoughtfully over the faces before him.

He said, "I can't understand how any one of you could
even think of compulsion. According to you, I'm loaded with
energy. I may be wrong, but if any of you should try to

thrust me back down the chute of time, or even touch me, that energy in me would do devastating things—"

"You're damned right!" chimed in a young man. He barked irritably at Dresley: "How the devil did you ever come to make such a psychological blunder? You know that McAllister will have to do as we want, to save himself; and he'll have to do it fast!"

Dresley grunted under the sharp attack. "Hell," he said, "the truth is we have no time to waste, and I just figured there wasn't time to explain, and that he might scare easily. I see, however, that we're dealing with an intelligent man."

McAllister's eyes narrowed over the group. There was something phony here. They were talking too much, wasting the very time they needed, as if they were marking time, waiting for something to happen.

He said sharply, "And don't give me any soft soap about being intelligent. You fellows are sweating blood. You'd shoot your own grandmothers and trick me into the bargain, because the world you think right is at stake. What's this plan of yours that you were going to compel me to participate in?"

It was the young man who replied: "You are to be given insulated clothes and sent back into your own time—"

He paused. McAllister said, "That sounds okay, so far. What's the catch?"

"There is no catch!"

McAllister stared. "Now, look here," he began, "don't give me any of that. If it's as simple as that, how the devil am I going to be helping you against the Isher energy?"

The young man scowled blackly at Dresley. "You see," he said to the other, "you've made him suspicious with the talk of yours about compulsion."

He faced McAllister. "What we have in mind is an application of a sort of an energy lever and fulcrum principle. You are to be a 'weight' at the long end of a kind of energy 'crowbar,' which lifts the greater 'weight' at the short end. You will go back five thousand years in time; the machine in the great building to which your body is tuned, and which has caused all this trouble, will move ahead in time about two weeks."

"In that way," interrupted another man before McAllister could speak, "we shall have time to find a counteragent. There must be a solution, else our enemies would not have acted so secretly. Well, what do you think?"

McAllister walked slowly over to the chair that he had occupied previously. His mind was turning at furious speed, but he knew with a grim foreboding that he hadn't a fraction of the technical knowledge necessary to safeguard his interests.

He said slowly, "As I see it, this is supposed to work something like a pump handle. The lever principle, the old idea that if you had a lever long enough, and a suitable fulcrum, you could move the Earth out of its orbit."

"Exactly!" It was the heavy-faced Dresley who spoke. "Only this works in time. You go five thousand years, the building goes a few wee . . ."

His voice faded, his eagerness drained from him as he caught the expression on McAllister's face.

"Look!" said McAllister, "there's nothing more pitiful than a bunch of honest men engaged in their first act of dishonesty. You're strong men, the intellectual type, who've spent your lives enforcing an idealistic conception. You've always told yourself that if the occasion should ever require it, you would not hesitate to make drastic sacrifices. But you're not fooling anybody. *What's the catch?*"

It was quite startling to have the suit thrust at him. He hadn't observed the men emerge from the back room; and it came as a distinct shock to realize that they had actually gone for the insulated clothes before they could have known that he would use them.

McAllister stared grimly at Peter Cadron, who held the dull, grayish, limp thing toward him. A very flame of abrupt rage held him choked; before he could speak, Cadron said in a tight voice, "Get into this, and get going! It's a matter of minutes, man! When those guns out there start spraying energy, you won't be alive to argue about our honesty."

Still he hesitated; the room seemed insufferably hot; and he was sick—sick with the deadly uncertainty. Perspiration streaked stingingly down his cheeks. His frantic gaze fell on the girl, standing silent and subdued in the background, near the front door.

He strode toward her; and either his glare or presence was incredibly frightening, for she cringed and turned white as a sheet.

"Look!" he said. "I'm in this as deep as hell. What's the risk in this thing? I've got to feel that I have some chance. Tell me, what's the catch?"

The girl was gray now, almost as gray and dead-looking as the suit Peter Cadron was holding. "It's the friction," she mumbled finally, "you may not get all the way back to 1941. You see, you'll be a sort of 'weight' and—"

McAllister whirled away from her. He climbed into the soft, almost flimsy suit, crowding the overall-like shape over his neatly pressed clothes. "It comes tight over the head, doesn't it?" he asked.

"Yes!" It was Lystra's father who answered. "As soon as you pull that zipper shut, the suit will become completely invisible. To outsiders it will seem just as if you have your ordinary clothes on. The suit is fully equipped. You could live on the moon inside it."

"What I don't get," complained McAllister, "is why I have to wear it. I got here all right without it."

He frowned. His words had been automatic, but abruptly a thought came: "Just a minute. What becomes of the energy with which I'm charged when I'm bottled up in this insulation?"

He saw by the stiffening expressions of those around him that he had touched on a vast subject.

"So that's it!" he snapped. "The insulation is to prevent me losing any of that energy. That's how it can make a 'weight.' I have no doubt there's a connection from this suit to that other machine. Well, it's not too late. It's—"

With a desperate twist, he tried to jerk aside, to evade the clutching hands of the four men who leaped at him. Hopeless movement! They had him instantly; and their grips on him were strong beyond his power to break.

The fingers of Peter Cadron jerked the zipper tight, and Peter Cadron said, "Sorry, but when we went into that back room, we also dressed in insulated clothing. That's why you couldn't hurt us. Sorry, again!

"And remember this: There's no certainty that you are being sacrificed. The fact that there is no crater in *our* Earth proves that you did not explode in the past, and that you solved the problem in some other way. *Now, somebody open the door, quick!*"

Irresistibly he was carried forward. And then—

"Wait!"

It was the girl. The colorless gray in her face was a livid thing. Her eyes glittered like dark jewels; and in her fingers was the tiny, mirror-bright gun she had pointed in the beginning at McAllister.

The little group hustling McAllister stopped as if they had been struck. He was scarcely aware; for him there was only the girl, and the way the muscles of her lips were working, and the way her voice suddenly flamed: "This is utter outrage. Are we such cowards—is it possible that the spirit of liberty can survive only through a shoddy act of murder and gross defiance of the rights of the individual? I say no! Mr. McAllister must have the protection of the hypnotism treatment, even if we die during the wasted minutes."

"Lystra!" It was her father; and McAllister realized in the swift movement of the older man what a brilliant mind was there, and how quickly the older man grasped every aspect of the situation.

He stepped forward and took the gun from his daughter's fingers—the only man in the room, McAllister thought flashingly, who could dare approach her in that moment with the certainty she would not fire. For hysteria was in every line of her face, and the racking tears that followed showed how dangerous her stand might have been against the others.

Strangely, not for a moment had hope come. The entire action seemed divorced from his life and his thought; there was only the observation of it. He stood there for a seeming eternity and, when emotion finally came, it was surprise that he was not being hustled to his doom. With the surprise came awareness that Peter Cadron had let go his arm and stepped clear of him.

The man's eyes were calm, his head held proudly erect; he said, "Your daughter is right, sir. At this point we rise above our petty fears, and we say to this unhappy man: 'Have courage! You will not be forgotten. We can guarantee nothing, cannot even state exactly what will happen to you. But we say: if it lies in our power to help you, that help you shall have.' And now—we must protect you from the devastating psychological pressures that would otherwise destroy you, simply but effectively."

Too late, McAllister noticed that the others had turned faces away from that extraordinary wall—the wall that had already displayed so vast a versatility. He did not even see who pressed the activating button for what followed.

There was a flash of dazzling light. For an instant he felt as if his mind had been laid bare; and against that nakedness the voice of Peter Cadron pressed like some ineradicable engraving stamp: "To retain your self-control and your sanity—this is your hope: this you will do in spite of everything! And, for your sake, speak of your experience only to scientists or to those in authority who you feel will understand and help. Good luck!"

So strong remained the effect of that brief flaring light that he felt only vaguely the touch of their hands on him, propelling him. He must have fallen, but there was no pain—

He grew aware that he was lying on a sidewalk. The deep, familiar voice of Police Inspector Clayton boomed over him: "Clear the way; no crowding now!"

McAllister climbed to his feet. A pall of curious faces gawked at him; and there was no park, no gorgeous city. Instead, a bleak row of one-story shops made a dull pattern on either side of the street.

He'd have to get away from here. These people didn't understand. Somewhere on Earth must be a scientist who could help him. After all, the record was that he hadn't exploded. Therefore, somewhere, somehow—

He mumbled answers at the questions that beat at him; and then he was clear of the disappointed crowd. There followed purposeless minutes of breakneck walking; the streets ahead grew narrower, dirtier—

He stopped, shaken. What was happening?

It was night, in a brilliant, glowing city. He was standing on an avenue that stretched jewel-like into remote distance.

A street that lived, flaming with a soft light that gleamed up from its surface—a road of light, like a river flowing under a sun that shone nowhere else, straight and smooth and—

He walked along for uncomprehending minutes, watching the cars that streamed past—and wild hope came!

Was this again the age of the Isher and the gunmakers? It could be; it looked right, and it meant they had brought him back. After all, they were not evil, and they would save him if they could. For all he knew, weeks had passed in their time and—

Abruptly, he was in the center of a blinding snowstorm. He staggered from the first, mighty, unexpected blow of that untamed wind, then, bracing himself, fought for mental and physical calm.

The shining, wondrous night city was gone; gone too the glowing road—both vanished, transformed into this deadly, wilderness world.

He peered through the driving snow. It was daylight; and he could make out the dim shadows of trees that reared up through the white mist of blizzard less than fifty feet away.

Instinctively he pressed toward their shelter, and stood finally out of that blowing, pressing wind.

He thought: One minute in the distant future; the next—where?

There was certainly no city. Only trees, an uninhabited forest and winter—

The blizzard was gone. And the trees. He stood on a sandy beach; before him stretched a blue, sunlit sea that rippled over broken white buildings. All around, scattered far into that shallow, lovely sea, far up into the weed-grown hills, were the remnants of a once tremendous city. Over all clung an aura of incredible age; and the silence of the long-dead was broken only by the gentle, timeless lapping of the waves—

Again came that instantaneous change. More prepared this time, he nevertheless sank twice under the surface of the vast, swift river that carried him on and on. It was hard swimming, but the insulated suit was buoyant with the air it manufactured each passing second; and, after a moment, he began to struggle purposefully toward the tree-lined shore a hundred feet to his right.

A thought came, and he stopped swimming. "What's the use!"

The truth was as simple as it was terrible. He was being shunted from the past to the future; he was the "weight" on the long end of an energy seesaw; and in some way he was slipping farther ahead and farther back each time. Only that could explain the catastrophic changes he had already witnessed. In a minute would come another change and—

It came! He was lying face downward on green grass, but there was no curiosity in him. He did not look up, but lay there hour after hour as the seesaw jerked on: past—future—past—future—

Beyond doubt, the gunmakers had won their respite; for at the far end of this dizzy teeter-totter was the machine that had been used by the Isher soldiers as an activating force; it too teetered up, then down, in a mad seesaw.

There remained the gunmakers' promise to help him, vain now; for they could not know what had happened. They could not find him even in this maze of time.

There remained the mechanical law that forces must balance.

Somewhere, sometime, a balance would be struck, probably in the future—because there was still the fact that he hadn't exploded in the past. Yes, somewhere would come the balance when he would again face *that* problem. But now—

On, on, on the seesaw flashed; the world on the one hand grew bright with youth, and on the other dark with fantastic age.

Infinity yawned blackly ahead.

Quite suddenly it came to him that he knew where the seesaw would stop. It would end in the very remote past, with the release of the stupendous temporal energy he had been accumulating with each of those monstrous swings.

He would not witness, but he would cause, the formation of the planets.

ARMAGEDDON

Unknown
August

by Fredric Brown (1906-1972)

Fredric Brown was one of the most talented professionals in the history of science fiction. A well known mystery writer (he was a winner of the Edgar Award of the MWA), in the sf field he is best remembered for his short-shorts, but he produced excellent work at all lengths. His novel What Mad Universe *(book form, 1949) remains one of the outstanding satires on the science fiction field—and much of it still hurts!*

There have been too many end-of-the-world stories. Here is a beautiful example of the rare almost-the-end-of-the-world tale, told as only Brown could tell it—with his tongue firmly in his cheek.

(I suppose Fred Brown is the acknowledged master of the short-short. When Marty and I, along with Joe Olander, put out our recent *One Hundred S. F. Short Short Stories*, there were none included by Fred Brown for the simple reason that we could not get permissions for any. —That was the reason, wasn't it, Marty?—In any case, more than one reviewer shook his head over the omission, feeling it was a measure of our lack of good taste, and I couldn't help but feel that that was the way it indeed looked.—I. A.)

It happened—of all places—in Cincinnati. Not that there is anything wrong with Cincinnati, save that it is not the center of the Universe, nor even of the State of Ohio. It's a nice old town and, in its way, second to none. But even its Chamber of Commerce would admit that it lacks cosmic significance. It must have been mere coincidence that Gerber the Great—what a name!—was playing Cincinnati when things slipped elsewhere.

Of course, if the episode had become known, Cincinnati would be the most famous city of the world, and little Herbie would be hailed as a modern St. George and get more acclaim than a quiz kid. But no member of that audience in the Bijou Theater remembers a thing about it. Not even little Herbie Westerman, although he had the water pistol to show for it.

He wasn't thinking about the water pistol in his pocket as he sat looking up at the prestidigitator on the other side of the footlights. It was a new water pistol, bought en route to the theater when he'd inveigled his parents into a side trip into the five-and-dime on Vine Street, but at the moment, Herbie was much more interested in what went on upon the stage.

His expression registered qualified approval. The front-and-back palm was no mystery to Herbie. He could do it himself. True, he had to use pony-sized cards that came with his magic set and were just right for his nine-year-old hands. And true, anyone watching could see the card flutter from the front-palm position to the back as he turned his hand. But that was a detail.

He knew, though, that front-and-back palming seven cards at a time required great finger strength as well as dexterity, and that was what Gerber the Great was doing. There wasn't a telltale click in the shift, either, and Herbie nodded approbation. Then he remembered what was coming next.

He nudged his mother and said, "Ma, ask Pop if he's gotta extra handkerchief."

Out of the corner of his eyes, Herbie saw his mother turn her head and in less time than it would take to say, "Presto," Herbie was out of his seat and skinning down the aisle. It had been, he felt, a beautiful piece of misdirection and his timing had been perfect.

It was at this stage of the performance—which Herbie had seen before, alone—that Gerber the Great asked if some little boy from the audience would step to the stage. He was asking it now.

Herbie Westerman had jumped the gun. He was well in motion before the magician had asked the question. At the previous performance, he'd been a bad tenth in reaching the steps from aisle to stage. This time he'd been ready, and he hadn't taken any chances with parental restraint. Perhaps his mother would have let him go and perhaps not; it had seemed wiser to see that she was looking the other way. You couldn't trust parents on things like that. They had funny ideas sometimes.

"—will please step up on the stage?" And Herbie's foot

touched the first of the steps upward right smack on the interrogation point of that sentence. He heard the disappointed scuffle of other feet behind him, and grinned smugly as he went on up across the footlights.

It was the three-pigeon trick, Herbie knew from the previous performance, that required an assistant from the audience. It was almost the only trick he hadn't been able to figure out. There *must*, he knew, have been a concealed compartment somewhere in that box, but where it could be he couldn't even guess. But this time he'd be holding the box himself. If from that range he couldn't spot the gimmick, he'd better go back to stamp collecting.

He grinned confidently up at the magician. Not that he, Herbie, would give him away. He was a magician, too, and he understood that there was a freemasonry among magicians and that one never gave away the tricks of another.

He felt a little chilled, though, and the grin faded as he caught the magician's eyes. Gerber the Great, at close range, seemed much older than he had seemed from the other side of the footlights. And somehow different. Much taller, for one thing.

Anyway, here came the box for the pigeon trick. Gerber's regular assistant was bringing it in on a tray. Herbie looked away from the magician's eyes and he felt better. He remembered, even, his reason for being on the stage. The servant limped. Herbie ducked his head to catch a glimpse of the under side of the tray, just in case. Nothing there.

Gerber took the box. The servant limped away and Herbie's eyes followed him suspiciously. Was the limp genuine or was it a piece of misdirection?

The box folded out flat as the proverbial pancake. All four sides hinged to the bottom, the top hinged to one of the sides. There were little brass catches.

Herbie took a quick step back so he could see behind it while the front was displayed to the audience. Yes, he saw it now. A triangular compartment built against one side of the lid, mirror-covered, angles calculated to achieve invisibility. Old stuff. Herbie felt a little disappointed.

The prestidigitator folded the box, mirror-concealed compartment inside. He turned slightly. "Now, my fine young man—"

What happened in Tibet wasn't the only factor; it was merely the final link of a chain.

The Tibetan weather had been unusual that week, highly unusual. It had been warm. More snow succumbed to the gentle warmth than had melted in more years than man could count. The streams ran high, they ran wide and fast.

Along the streams some prayer wheels whirled faster than they had ever whirled. Others, submerged, stopped altogether. The priests, knee-deep in the cold water, worked frantically, moving the wheels nearer to shore where again the rushing torrent would turn them.

There was one small wheel, a very old one that had revolved without cease for longer than any man knew. So long had it been there that no living lama recalled what had been inscribed upon its prayer plate, nor what had been the purpose of that prayer.

The rushing water had neared its axle when the lama Klarath reached for it to move it to safety. Just too late. His foot slid in the slippery mud and the back of his hand touched the wheel as he fell. Knocked loose from its moorings, it swirled down with the flood, rolling along the bottom of the stream, into deeper and deeper waters.

While it rolled, all was well.

The lama rose, shivering from his momentary immersion, and went after other of the spinning wheels. What, he thought, could one small wheel matter? He didn't know that—now that other links had broken—only that tiny thing stood between Earth and Armageddon.

The prayer wheel of Wangur Ul rolled on, and on, until— a mile farther down—it struck a ledge, and stopped. That was the moment.

"And now, my fine young man—"

Herbie Westerman—we're back in Cincinnati now—looked up, wondering why the prestidigitator had stopped in mid-sentence. He saw the face of Gerber the Great contorted as though by a great shock. Without moving, without changing, his face began to change. Without appearing different, it became different.

Quietly, then, the magician began to chuckle. In the overtones of that soft laughter was all of evil. No one who heard it could have doubted who he was. No one did doubt. The audience, every member of it, knew in that awful moment who stood before them, knew it—even the most skeptical among them—beyond shadow of doubt.

No one moved, no one spoke, none drew a shuddering breath. There are things beyond fear. Only uncertainty causes fear, and the Bijou Theater was filled, then, with a dreadful certainty.

The laughter grew. Crescendo, it reverberated into the far dusty corners of the gallery. Nothing—not a fly on the ceiling—moved.

Satan spoke.

"I thank you for your kind attention to a poor magician." He bowed, ironically low. "The performance is ended."

He smiled. "All performances are ended."

Somehow the theater seemed to darken, although the electric lights still burned. In dead silence, there seemed to be the sound of wings, leathery wings, as though invisible Things were gathering.

On the stage was a dim red radiance. From the head and from each shoulder of the tall figure of the magician there sprang a tiny flame. A naked flame.

There were other flames. They flickered along the proscenium of the stage, along the footlights. One sprang from the lid of the folded box little Herbie Westerman still held in his hands.

Herbie dropped the box.

Did I mention that Herbie Westerman was a Safety Cadet? It was purely a reflex action. A boy of nine doesn't know much about things like Armageddon, but Herbie Westerman should have known that water would never have put out that fire.

But, as I said, it was purely a reflex action. He yanked out his new water pistol and squirted it at the box of the pigeon trick. And the fire *did* vanish, even as a spray from the stream of water ricocheted and dampened the trouser leg of Gerber the Great, who had been facing the other way.

There was a sudden, brief hissing sound. The lights were growing bright again, and all the other flames were dying, and the sound of wings faded, blended into another sound—rustling of the audience.

The eyes of the prestidigitator were closed. His voice sounded strangely strained as he said: "This much power I retain. None of you will remember this."

Then, slowly, he turned and picked up the fallen box. He held it out to Herbie Westerman. "You must be more careful, boy," he said. "Now hold it so."

He tapped the top lightly with his wand. The door fell open. Three white pigeons flew out of the box. The rustle of their wings was not leathery.

Herbie Westerman's father came down the stairs and, with

a purposeful air, took his razor strop off the hook on the kitchen wall.

Mrs. Westerman looked up from stirring the soup on the stove. "Why, Henry," she asked, "are you really going to punish him with that—just for squirting a little water out of the window of the car on the way home?"

Her husband shook his head grimly. "Not for that, Marge. But don't you remember we bought him that water gun on the way downtown, and that he wasn't near a water faucet after that? Where do you think he filled it?"

He didn't wait for an answer. "When we stopped in at the cathedral to talk to Father Ryan about his confirmation, that's when the little brat filled it. Out of the baptismal font! Holy water he uses in his water pistol!"

He clumped heavily up the stairs, strop in hand.

Rhythmic thwacks and wails of pain floated down the staircase. Herbie—who had saved the world—was having his reward.

ADAM AND NO EVE

Astounding Science Fiction
September

by Alfred Bester (1913-   )

Alfred Bester really came into his own after World War II, with stories like "The Men Who Murdered Mohammed," "Time Is the Traitor," and the spectacular novels, The Demolished Man *(in* Galaxy, *1952) and* The Stars My Destination *(1956), both considered among the finest in modern science fiction. Bester had (he is still writing) a varied career, dropping in and out of the sf field while working for the comics, television, and Holiday magazine. An astute observer of science fiction, he was one of the field's best critics as book reviewer for* The Magazine of Fantasy and Science Fiction *from 1960 to 1962. Alfred Bester was a "New Wave" writer long before the term became fashionable.*

"Adam and No Eve" remains one of his best stories, and one of the finest early tales of "inner space."

(I didn't meet Alfie Bester till long after this story was written—and goodness, how it impressed me. I can still quote the formula. When I did meet him, I instantly found he could be classified into the group of "Writers who have personalities like the stories they write." Others are L. Sprague de Camp and Lester del Rey. Of course, there is the group of "Writers who don't have personalities like the stories they write," such as Fredric Brown and Theodore Sturgeon. Naturally, I realize that this is subjective and that other people will group different writers into each of the two groups. I don't know in which group I belong, by the way.—I.A.)

Crane knew this must be the seacoast. Instinct told him; but more than instinct, the few shreds of knowledge that clung to his torn, feverish brain told him; the stars that had shown at night through the rare breaks in the clouds, and his compass that still pointed a trembling finger north. That was strangest of all, Crane thought. Though a welter of chaos, the Earth still retained its polarity.

It was no longer a coast; there was no longer any sea. Only the faint line of what had been a cliff, stretching north and south for endless miles. A line of gray ash. The same gray ash and cinders that lay behind him; the same gray ash that stretched before him. Fine silt, knee-deep, that swirled up at every motion and choked him. Cinders that scudded in dense mighty clouds when the mad winds blew. Cinders that were churned to viscous mud when the frequent rains fell.

The sky was jet overhead. The black clouds rode high and were pierced with shafts of sunlight that marched swiftly over the Earth. Where the light struck a cinder storm, it was filled with gusts of dancing, gleaming particles. Where it played through rain it brought the arches of rainbows into being. Rain fell; cinder storms blew; light thrust down—together, alternately and continually in a jigsaw of black and white violence. So it had been for months. So it was over every mile of the broad Earth.

Crane passed the edge of the ashen cliffs and began crawling down the even slope that had once been the ocean bed. He had been traveling so long that all sense of pain had left him. He braced elbows and dragged his body forward. Then he brought his right knee under him and reached forward with elbows again. Elbows, knee, elbows, knee— He had forgotten what it was to walk.

Life, he thought dazedly, is wonderful. It adapts itself to anything. If it must crawl, it crawls. Callus forms on the elbows and knees. The neck and shoulders toughen. The nostrils learn to snort away the ashes before they inhale. The bad leg swells and festers. It numbs, and presently it will rot and fall off.

"I beg pardon," Crane said, "I didn't quite get that—"

He peered up at the tall figure before him and tried to understand the words. It was Hallmyer. He wore his stained lab jacket and his gray hair was awry. Hallmyer stood delicately on top of the ashes and Crane wondered why he could see the scudding cinder clouds through his body.

"How do you like your world, Stephen?" Hallmyer asked.

Crane shook his head miserably.

"Not very pretty, eh?" said Hallmyer. "Look around you.

Dust, that's all; dust and ashes. Crawl, Stephen, crawl. You'll find nothing but dust and ashes—"

Hallmyer produced a goblet of water from nowhere. It was clear and cold. Crane could see the fine mist of dew on its surface and his mouth was suddenly coated with dry grit.

"Hallmyer!" he cried. He tried to get to his feet and reach for the water, but the jolt of pain in his right leg warned him. He crouched back.

Hallmyer sipped and then spat in his face. The water felt warm.

"Keep crawling," said Hallmyer bitterly. "Crawl round and round the face of the Earth. You'll find nothing but dust and ashes—" He emptied the goblet on the ground before Crane. "Keep crawling. How many miles? Figure it out for yourself. Pi-R-Square. The radius is eight thousand or so—"

He was gone, jacket and goblet. Crane realized that rain was falling again. He pressed his face into the warm sodden cinder mud, opened his mouth and tried to suck the moisture. He groaned and presently began crawling.

There was an instinct that drove him on. He had to get somewhere. It was associated, he knew, with the sea—with the edge of the sea. At the shore of the sea something waited for him. Something that would help him understand all this. He had to get to the sea—that is, if there was a sea any more.

The thundering rain beat his back like heavy planks. Crane paused and yanked the knapsack around to his side where he probed in it with one hand. It contained exactly three things. A pistol, a bar of chocolate and a can of peaches. All that was left of two months' supplies. The chocolate was pulpy and spoiled. Crane knew he had best eat it before all value rotted away. But in another day he would lack the strength to open the can. He pulled it out and attacked it with the opener. By the time he had pierced and pried away a flap of tin, the rain had passed.

As he munched the fruit and sipped the juice, he watched the wall of rain marching before him down the slope of the ocean bed. Torrents of water were gushing through the mud. Small channels had already been cut—channels that would be new rivers some day. A day he would never see. A day that no living thing would ever see. As he flipped the empty can aside, Crane thought: The last living thing on Earth eats its last meal. Metabolism plays its last act.

Wind would follow the rain. In the endless weeks that he

had been crawling, he had learned that. Wind would come in a few minutes and flog him with its clouds of cinders and ashes. He crawled forward, bleary eyes searching the flat gray miles for cover.

Evelyn tapped his shoulder.

Crane knew it was she before he turned his head. She stood alongside, fresh and gay in her bright dress, but her lovely face was puckered with alarm.

"Stephen," she cried, "you've got to hurry!"

He could only admire the way her smooth honey hair waved to her shoulders.

"Oh, darling!" she said, "you've been hurt!" Her quick gentle hands touched his legs and back. Crane nodded.

"Got it landing," he said. "I wasn't used to a parachute. I always thought you came down gently—like plumping onto a bed. But the gray earth came up at me like a fist—And Umber was fighting around in my arms. I couldn't let him drop, could I?"

"Of course not, dear—" Evelyn said.

"So I just held on to him and tried to get my legs under me," Crane said. "And then something smashed my legs and side—"

He paused, wondering how much she knew of what really had happened. He didn't want to frighten her.

"Evelyn, darling—" he said, trying to reach up his arms.

"No dear," she said. She looked back in fright. "You've got to hurry. You've got to watch out behind!"

"The cinder storms?" He grimaced. "I've been through them before."

"Not the storms!" Evelyn cried. "Something else. Oh, Stephen—"

Then she was gone, but Crane knew she had spoken the truth. There was something behind—something that had been following him all those weeks. Far in the back of his mind he had sensed the menace. It was closing in on him like a shroud. He shook his head. Somehow that was impossible. He was the last living thing on Earth. How could there be a menace?

The wind roared behind him, and an instant later came the heavy clouds of cinders and ashes. They lashed over him, biting his skin. With dimming eyes, he saw the way they coated the mud and covered it with a fine dry carpet. Crane drew his knees under him and covered his head with his arms. With the knapsack as a pillow, he prepared to wait out the storm. It would pass as quickly as the rain.

The storm whipped up a great bewilderment in his sick head. Like a child he pushed at the pieces of his memory, trying to fit them together. Why was Hallmyer so bitter toward him? It couldn't have been that argument, could it?

What argument?

Why, that one before all this happened.

Oh, that!

Abruptly, the pieces fit themselves together.

Crane stood alongside the sleek lines of his ship and admired it tremendously. The roof of the shed had been removed and the nose of the ship hoisted so that it rested on a cradle pointed toward the sky. A workman was carefully burnishing the inner surfaces of the rocket jets.

The muffled sounds of an argument came from within the ship and then a heavy clanking. Crane ran up the short iron ladder to the port and thrust his head inside. A few feet beneath him, two men were buckling the long tanks of ferrous solution into place.

"Easy there," Crane called. "Want to knock the ship apart?"

One looked up and grinned. Crane knew what he was thinking. That the ship would tear itself apart. Everyone said that. Everyone except Evelyn. She had faith in him. Hallmyer never said it either. But Hallmyer thought he was crazy in another way. As he descended the ladder, Crane saw Hallmyer come into the shed, lab jacket flying.

"Speak of the devil!" Crane muttered.

Hallmyer began shouting as soon as he saw Crane. "Now listen—"

"Not all over again," Crane said.

Hallmyer dug a sheaf of papers out of his pocket and waved it under Crane's nose.

"I've been up half the night," he said, "working it through again. I tell you I'm right. I'm absolutely right—"

Crane looked at the tight-written equations and then at Hallmyer's bloodshot eyes. The man was half mad with fear.

"For the last time," Hallmyer went on. "You're using your new catalyst on iron solution. All right. I grant that it's a miraculous discovery. I give you credit for that."

Miraculous was hardly the word for it. Crane knew that without conceit, for he realized he'd only stumbled on it. You had to stumble on a catalyst that would induce atomic disintegration of iron and give 10×10^{10} foot-pounds of energy for every gram of fuel. No man was smart enough to think all that up by himself.

"You don't think I'll make it?" Crane asked.

"To the moon? Around the moon? Maybe. You've got a fifty-fifty chance." Hallmyer ran fingers through his lank hair. "But for God's sake, Stephen, I'm not worried about you. If you want to kill yourself, that's your own affair. It's the Earth I'm worried about—"

"Nonsense. Go home and sleep it off."

"Look"—Hallmyer pointed to the sheets of paper with a shaky hand—"no matter how you work the feed and mixing system you can't get one hundred percent efficiency in the mixing and discharge."

"That's what makes it a fifty-fifty chance," Crane said. "So what's bothering you?"

"The catalyst that will escape through the rocket tubes. Do you realize what it'll do if a drop hits the Earth? It'll start a chain of iron disintegrations that'll envelope the globe. It'll reach out to every iron atom—and there's iron everywhere. There won't be any Earth left for you to return to—"

"Listen," Crane said wearily, "we've been through all this before."

He took Hallmyer to the base of the rocket cradle. Beneath the iron framework was a two-hundred-foot pit, fifty feet wide and lined with firebrick.

"That's for the initial discharge flames. If any of the catalyst goes through, it'll be trapped in this pit and taken care of by the secondary reactions. Satisfied now?"

"But while you're in flight," Hallmyer persisted, "you'll be endangering the Earth until you're beyond Roche's limit. Every drop of non-activated catalyst will eventually sink back to the ground and—"

"For the very last time," Crane said grimly, "the flame of the rocket discharge takes care of that. It will envelop any escaped particles and destroy them. Now get out. I've got work to do."

As he pushed him to the door, Hallmyer screamed and waved his arms. "I won't let you do it!" he repeated over and over. "I'll find some way to stop you. I won't let you do it—"

Work? No, it was sheer intoxication to labor over the ship. It had the fine beauty of a well-made thing. The beauty of polished armor, of a balanced swept-hilt rapier, of a pair of matched guns. There was no thought of danger and death in Crane's mind as he wiped his hands with waste after the last touches were finished.

She lay in the cradle ready to pierce the skies. Fifty feet of slender steel, the rivet heads gleaming like jewels. Thirty feet were given over to fuel the catalyst. Most of the forward compartment contained the spring hammock Crane had devised to take up the initial acceleration shock. The ship's nose was a solid mass of natural quartz that stared upward like a cyclopian eye.

Crane thought: She'll die after this trip. She'll return to the Earth and smash in a blaze of fire and thunder, for there's no way yet of devising a safe landing for a rocket ship. But it's worth it. She'll have had her one great flight, and that's all any of us should want. One great beautiful flight into the un-known—

As he locked the workshop door, Crane heard Hallmyer shouting from the cottage across the fields. Through the evening gloom he could see him waving frantically. He trotted through the crisp stubble, breathing the sharp air deeply, grateful to be alive.

"It's Evelyn on the phone," Hallmyer said.

Crane stared at him. Hallmyer was acting peculiarly. He refused to meet his eyes.

"What's the idea?" Crane asked. "I thought we agreed that she wasn't to call—wasn't to get in touch with me until I was ready to start? You been putting ideas into her head? Is this the way you're going to stop me?"

Hallmyer said, "No—" and studiously examined the indigo horizon.

Crane went into his study and picked up the phone.

"Now, listen, darling," he said without preamble, "there's no sense getting alarmed now. I explained everything very carefully. Just before the ship crashes, I take to a parachute and float down as happy and gentle as Wynken, Blynken and Nod. I love you very much and I'll see you Wednesday when I start. So long—"

"Good-bye, sweetheart," Evelyn's clear voice said, "and is that what you called me for?"

"Called you!"

A brown hulk disengaged itself from the hearth rug and lifted itself to strong legs. Umber, Crane's Great Dane, sniffed and cocked an ear. Then he whined.

"Did you say I called you?" Crane shouted.

Umber's throat suddenly poured forth a bellow. He reached Crane in a single bound, looked up into his face and whined and roared all at once.

"Shut up, you monster!" Crane said. He pushed Umber away with his foot.

"Give Umber a kick for me," Evelyn laughed. "Yes, dear. Someone called and said you wanted to speak to me."

"They did, eh? Look, honey, I'll call you back—"

Crane hung up. He arose doubtfully and watched Umber's uneasy actions. Through the windows, the late evening glow sent flickering shadows of orange light. Umber gazed at the light, sniffed and bellowed again. Suddenly struck, Crane leaped to the window.

Across the fields a solid mass of flame thrust high into the air, and within it was the fast-crumbling walls of the workshop. Silhouetted against the blaze, the figure of half a dozen men darted and ran.

"Good heavens!" Crane cried.

He shot out of the cottage and with Umber hard at his heels, sprinted toward the shed. As he ran he could see the graceful nose of the spaceship within the core of heat, still looking cool and untouched. If only he could reach it before the flames softened its metal and started the rivets.

The workmen trotted up to him, grimy and panting. Crane gaped at them in a mixture of fury and bewilderment.

"Hallmyer!" he shouted. "Hallmyer!"

Hallmyer pushed through the crowd. His eyes were wild and gleamed with triumph.

"Too bad," he said. "I'm sorry, Stephen—"

"You swine!" Crane shouted. "You frightened old man!" He grasped Hallmyer by the lapels and shook him just once. Then he dropped him and started into the shed.

Hallmyer cried something and an instant later a body hurtled against Crane's calves and spilled him to the ground. He lurched to his feet, fists swinging. Umber was alongside, growling over the roar of the flames. Crane smashed a man in the face, and saw him stagger back against a second. He lifted a knee in a vicious drive that sent the last man crumpling to the ground. Then he ducked his head and plunged into the shop.

The scorch felt cool at first, but when he reached the ladder and began mounting to the port, he screamed with the agony of his burns. Umber was howling at the foot of the ladder, and Crane realized that the dog could never escape from the rocket blasts. He reached down and hauled Umber into the ship.

Crane was reeling as he closed and locked the port. He retained consciousness barely long enough to settle himself in the spring hammock. Then instinct alone prompted his hands to reach out toward the control board. Instinct and the frenzied refusal to let his beautiful ship waste itself in the flames. He would fail— Yes. But he would fail, trying.

His fingers tripped the switches. The ship shuddered and roared. And blackness descended over him.

How long was he unconscious? There was no telling. Crane awoke with cold pressing against his face and body, and the sound of frightened yelps in his ears. Crane looked up and saw Umber tangled in the springs and straps of the hammock. His first impulse was to laugh; then suddenly he realized. He had looked *up!* He had looked up at the hammock.

He was lying curled in the cup of the quartz nose. The ship had risen high—perhaps almost to Roche's zone, to the limit of the Earth's gravitational attraction, but then without guiding hands at the controls to continue its flight, had turned and was dropping back toward Earth. Crane peered through the crystal and gasped.

Below him was the ball of the Earth. It looked three times the size of the moon. And it was no longer his Earth. It was a globe of fire mottled with black clouds. At the northernmost pole there was a tiny patch of white, and even as Crane watched, it was suddenly blotted over with hazy tones of red, scarlet and crimson. Hallmyer had been right.

He lay frozen in the cup of the nose for hours as the ship descended, watching the flames gradually fade away to leave nothing but the dense blanket of black around the Earth. He lay numb with horror, unable to understand—unable to reckon up a billion people snuffed out, a green fair planet reduced to ashes and cinders. His family, home, friends, everything that was once dear and close to him—gone. He could not think of Evelyn.

Air, whistling outside, awoke some instinct in him. The few shreds of reason left told him to go down with his ship and forget everything in the thunder and destruction, but the instinct of life forced him to his feet. He climbed up to the store chest and prepared for the landing. Parachute, a small oxygen tank—a knapsack of supplies. Only half aware of what he was doing he dressed for the descent, buckled on the 'chute and opened the port. Umber whined pathetically, and he took the heavy dog in his arms and stepped out into space.

But space hadn't been so clogged, the way it was now. Then it had been difficult to breathe. But that was because the air had been rare—not filled with dry clogging grit like now.

Every breath was a lungful of ground glass—or ashes—or cinders—

The pieces of memory sagged apart. Abruptly he was in the present again—a dense black present that hugged him with soft weight and made him fight for breath. Crane struggled in mad panic, and then relaxed.

It had happened before. A long time past he'd been buried deep under ashes when he'd stopped to remember. Weeks ago—or days—or months. Crane clawed with his hands, inching forward through the mound of cinders that the wind had thrown over him. Presently he emerged into the light again. The wind had died away. It was time to begin his crawl to the sea once more.

The vivid pictures of his memory scattered again before the grim vista that stretched out ahead. Crane scowled. He remembered too much, and too often. He had the vague hope that if he remembered hard enough, he might change one of the things he had done—just a very little thing—and then all this would become untrue. He thought: It might help if everyone remembered and wished at the same time—but there isn't any more everyone. I'm the only one. I'm the last memory on Earth. I'm the last life.

He crawled. Elbows, knee, elbows, knee— And then Hallmyer was crawling alongside and making a great game of it. He chortled and plunged in the cinders like a happy sea lion.

Crane said; "But why do we have to get to the sea?"

Hallmyer blew a spume of ashes.

"Ask her," he said, pointing to Crane's other side.

Evelyn was there, crawling seriously, intently; mimicking Crane's smallest action.

"It's because of our house," she said. "You remember our house, darling? High on the cliff. We were going to live there forever and ever, breathing the ozone and taking morning dips. I was there when you left. Now you're coming back to the house at the edge of the sea. Your beautiful flight is over, dear, and you're coming back to me. We'll live together, just we two, like Adam and Eve—"

Crane said: "That's nice."

Then Evelyn turned her head and screamed: "Oh, Stephen! Watch out!" and Crane felt the menace closing in on him again. Still crawling, he stared back at the vast gray plains of ash, and saw nothing. When he looked at Evelyn again he saw only his shadow, sharp and black. Presently, it, too, faded away as the marching shaft of sunlight passed.

But the dread remained. Evelyn had warned him twice, and she was always right. Crane stopped and turned, and settled himself to watch. If he was really being followed, he would see whatever it was, coming along his tracks.

There was a painful moment of lucidity. It cleaved through his fever and bewilderment, bringing with it the sharpness and strength of a knife.

I'm going mad, he thought. The corruption in my leg has spread to my brain. There is no Evelyn, no Hallmyer, no menace. In all this land there is no life but mine—and even ghosts and spirits of the underworld must have perished in the inferno that girdled the planet. No—there is nothing but me and my sickness. I'm dying—and when I perish, everything will perish. Only a mass of lifeless cinders will go on.

But there was a movement.

Instinct again. Crane dropped his head and played dead. Through slitted eyes he watched the ashen plains, wondering if death was playing tricks with his eyes. Another façade of rain was beating down toward him, and he hoped he could make sure before all vision was obliterated.

Yes. There.

A quarter mile back, a gray-brown shape was flitting along the gray surface. Despite the drone of the distant rain, Crane could hear the whisper of trodden cinders and see the little clouds kicking up. Stealthily he groped for the revolver in the knapsack as his mind reached feebly for explanations and recoiled from fear.

The thing approached, and suddenly Crane squinted and understood. He recalled Umber kicking with fear and springing away from him when the 'chute landed them on the ashen face of the Earth.

"Why, it's Umber," he murmured. He raised himself. The dog halted. "Here boy!" Crane croaked gayly. "Here, boy!"

He was overcome with joy. He realized that a miserable loneliness had hung over him, almost a horrible sensation of oneness in emptiness. Now his was not the only life. There was another. A friendly life that could offer love and companionship. Hope kindled again.

"Here, boy!" he repeated. "Come on, boy—"

After a while he stopped trying to snap his fingers. The Great Dane hung back, showing fangs and a lolling tongue. The dog was emaciated to a skeleton and its eyes gleamed red and ugly in the dusk. As Crane called once more, mechanically, the dog snarled. Puffs of ash leaped beneath its nostrils.

He's hungry, Crane thought, that's all. He reached into the knapsack and at the gesture the dog snarled again. Crane withdrew the chocolate bar and laboriously peeled off the paper and silver foil. Weakly he tossed it toward Umber. It fell far short. After a minute of savage uncertainty, the dog advanced slowly and gobbled up the food. Ashes powdered its muzzle. It licked its chops ceaselessly and continued to advance on Crane.

Panic jerked within him. A voice persisted: This is no friend. He has no love or companionship for you. Love and companionship have vanished from the land along with life. Now there is nothing left but hunger.

"No—" Crane whispered. "That isn't right. We're the last of life on Earth. It isn't right that we should tear at each other and seek to devour—"

But Umber was advancing with a slinking sidle, and his teeth showed sharp and white. And even as Crane stared at him, the dog snarled and lunged.

Crane thrust up an arm under the dog's muzzle, but the weight of the charge carried him backward. He cried out in agony as his broken, swollen leg was struck by the weight of the dog. With his free right hand he struck weakly, again and again, scarcely feeling the grind of teeth gnawing his left arm. Then something metallic was pressed under him and he realized he was lying on the revolver he had let fall.

He groped for it and prayed the cinders had not clogged its mechanism. As Umber let go his arm and tore at his throat, Crane brought the gun up and jabbed the muzzle blindly against the dog's body. He pulled and pulled the trigger until the roars died away and only empty clicks sounded. Umber shuddered in the ashes before him, his body nearly shot in two. Thick scarlet stained the gray.

Evelyn and Hallmyer looked down sadly at the broken animal. Evelyn was crying, and Hallmyer reached nervous fingers through his hair in the same old gesture.

"This is the finish, Stephen," he said. "You've killed part of yourself. Oh—you'll go on living, but not all of you. You'd best bury that corpse, Stephen. It's the corpse of your soul."

"I can't," Crane said. "The wind will blow the ashes away."

"Then burn it—"

It seemed that they helped him thrust the dead dog into his

knapsack. They helped him take off his clothes and pack them underneath. They cupped their hands around the matches until the cloth caught fire, and blew on the weak flame until it sputtered and burned limply. Crane crouched by the fire and nursed it until nothing was left but more gray ash. Then he turned and once again began crawling down the ocean bed. He was naked now. There was nothing left of what-had-been but his flickering little life.

He was too heavy with sorrow to notice the furious rain that slammed and buffeted him, or the searing pains that were shooting through his blackened leg and up his hip. He crawled. Elbows, knee, elbows, knee— Woodenly, mechanically, apathetic to everything. To the latticed skies, the dreary ashen plains and even the dull glint of water that lay far ahead.

He knew it was the sea—what was left of the old, or a new one in the making. But it would be an empty, lifeless sea that some day would lap against a dry lifeless shore. This would be a planet of rock and stone, of metal and snow and ice and water, but that would be all. No more life. He, alone, was useless. He was Adam, but there was no Eve.

Evelyn waved gayly to him from the shore. She was standing alongside the white cottage with the wind snapping her dress to show the clean, slender lines of her figure. And when he came a little closer, she ran out to him and helped him. She said nothing—only placed her hands under his shoulders and helped him lift the weight of his heavy pain-ridden body. And so at last he reached the sea.

It was real. He understood that. For even after Evelyn and the cottage had vanished, he felt the cool waters bathe his face. Quietly— Calmly—

Here's the sea, Crane thought, and here am I. Adam and no Eve. It's hopeless.

He rolled a little farther into the waters. They laved his torn body. Quietly— Calmly—

He lay with face to the sky, peering at the high menacing heavens, and the bitterness within him welled up.

"It's not right!" he cried. "It's not right that all this should pass away. Life is too beautiful to perish at the mad act of one mad creature—"

Quietly the waters laved him. Quietly— Calmly—

The sea rocked him gently, and even the agony that was reaching up toward his heart was no more than a gloved hand. Suddenly the skies split apart—for the first time in all those months—and Crane stared up at the stars.

Then he knew. This was not the end of life. There could never be an end to life. Within his body, within the rotting tissues that were rocking gently in the sea was the source of ten million-million lives. Cells—tissues—bacteria—endamœba— Countless infinities of life that would take new root in the waters and live long after he was gone.

They would live on his rotting remains. They would feed on each other. They would adapt themselves to the new environment and feed on the minerals and sediments washed into this new sea. They would grow, burgeon, evolve. Life would reach out to the lands once more. It would begin again the same old re-repeated cycle that had begun perhaps with the rotting corpse of some last survivor of interstellar travel. It would happen over and over in the future ages.

And then he knew what had brought him back to the sea. There need be no Adam—no Eve. Only the sea, the great mother of life was needed. The sea had called him back to her depths that presently life might emerge once more, and he was content.

Quietly the waters rocked him. Quietly—Calmly—the mother of life rocked the last-born of the old cycle who would become the first-born of the new. And with glazing eyes Stephen Crane smiled up at the stars, stars that were sprinkled evenly across the sky. Stars that had not yet formed into the familiar constellations, nor would not for another hundred million centuries.

SOLAR PLEXUS

Astonishing Stories
September

by James Blish (1921-1975)

The late James Blish made several notable con-
tributions to science fiction. As a writer, his novel
A Case of Conscience *(1958) remains one of the*
most fascinating and provoking treatments of reli-
gion in sf. His "Okie" series (collected as Cities in
Flight, *1969) was a most original contribution to*
the classic quest theme, while his "Pantropy" stories
were uniformly excellent accounts of human and
more-than-human biological change.

As a commentator, Blish was among the pioneer
critical voices from within the genre, and his two
collections The Issue at Hand *and* More Issues at
Hand *(both published as "William Atheling, Jr.")*
are insightful and perceptive. Finally, Blish was a
creative editor—the one and only issue of Van-
guard Science Fiction *produced under his editorship*
is one of the most sought after collector's items in
sf while New Dreams This Morning *(1966) is still*
the definitive anthology on the portrayal of the arts
in science fiction.

"Solar Plexus" is one of his earliest stories, and
the best early discussion of what a cyborg might be
like, and what the effect on the human component
might be.

(Jim Blish is one of the most endearing of all the science
fiction writers. Indeed, a photograph exists—which Jay Kay
Klein shows at all available opportunities, of him planting a
juicy kiss right on my cheek. I must admit, though, that my
fondness for him was shaken when I discovered he was
William Atheling, Jr. I don't particularly like critics and
Atheling hadn't always been kind to me.—However, I recovered and decided I would forgive that rat, Atheling, for Jim's
sake. —I.A.)

Brant Kittinger did not hear the alarm begin to ring. Indeed, it was only after a soft blow had jarred his free-floating observatory that he looked up in sudden awareness from the interferometer. Then the sound of the warning bell reached his consciousness.

Brant was an astronomer, not a spaceman, but he knew that the bell could mean nothing but the arrival of another ship in the vicinity. There would be no point in ringing a bell for a meteor—the thing could be through and past you during the first cycle of the clapper. Only an approaching ship would be likely to trip the detector, and it would have to be close.

A second dull jolt told him how close it was. The rasp of metal which followed, as the other ship slid along the side of his own, drove the fog of tensors completely from his brain. He dropped his pencil and straightened up.

His first thought was that his year in the orbit around the new trans-Plutonian planet was up, and that the Institute's tug had arrived to tow him home, telescope and all. A glance at the clock reassured him at first, then puzzled him still further. He still had the better part of four months.

No commercial vessel, of course, could have wandered this far from the inner planets; and the UN's police cruisers didn't travel far outside the commercial lanes. Besides, it would have been impossible for anyone to find Brant's orbital observatory by accident.

He settled his glasses more firmly on his nose, clambered awkwardly backwards out of the prime focus chamber and down the wall net to the control desk on the observation floor. A quick glance over the boards revealed that there was a magnetic field of some strength nearby, one that didn't belong to the invisible gas giant revolving half a million miles away.

The strange ship was locked to him magnetically; it was an old ship, then, for that method of grappling had been discarded years ago as too hard on delicate instruments. And the strength of the field meant a big ship.

Too big. The only ship of that period that could mount generators that size, as far as Brant could remember, was the Cybernetics Foundation's *Astrid*. Brant could remember well the Foundation's regretful announcement that Murray Bennett had destroyed both himself and the *Astrid* rather than turn the ship in to some UN inspection team. It had happened only eight years ago. Some scandal or other . . .

Well, who then?

He turned the radio on. Nothing came out of it. It was a simple transistor set tuned to the Institute's frequency, and since the ship outside plainly did not belong to the Institute, he had expected nothing else. Of course he had a photophone also, but it had been designed for communication over a reasonable distance, not for cheek-to-cheek whispers.

As an afterthought, he turned off the persistent alarm bell. At once another sound came through: a delicate, rhythmic tapping on the hull of the observatory. Someone wanted to get in.

He could think of no reason to refuse entrance, except for a vague and utterly unreasonable wonder as to whether or not the stranger was a friend. He had no enemies, and the notion that some outlaw might have happened upon him out here was ridiculous. Nevertheless, there was something about the anonymous, voiceless ship just outside which made him uneasy.

The gentle tapping stopped, and then began again, with an even, mechanical insistence. For a moment Brant wondered whether or not he should try to tear free with the observatory's few maneuvering rockets—but even should he win so uneven a struggle, he would throw the observatory out of the orbit where the Institute expected to find it, and he was not astronaut enough to get it back there again.

Tap, tap. Tap, tap.

"All right," he said irritably. He pushed the button which set the airlock to cycling. The tapping stopped. He left the outer door open more than long enough for anyone to enter and push the button in the lock which reversed the process; but nothing happened.

After what seemed to be a long wait, he pushed his button again. The outer door closed, the pumps filled the chamber with air, the inner door swung open. No ghost drifted out of it; there was nobody in the lock at all.

Tap, tap. Tap, tap.

Absently he polished his glasses on his sleeve. If they didn't want to come into the observatory, they must want him to come out of it. That was possible: although the telescope had a Coudé focus which allowed him to work in the ship's air most of the time, it was occasionally necessary for him to exhaust the dome, and for that purpose he had a space suit. But he had never been outside the hull in it, and the thought alarmed him. Brant was nobody's spaceman.

Be damned to them. He clapped his glasses back into place and took one more look into the empty airlock. It was still empty, with the outer door now moving open very slowly. . . .

A spaceman would have known that he was already dead, but Brant's reactions were not quite as fast. His first move was to try to jam the inner door shut by sheer muscle-power, but it would not stir. Then he simply clung to the nearest stanchion, waiting for the air to rush out of the observatory, and his life after it.

The outer door of the airlock continued to open, placidly, and still there was no rush of air—only a kind of faint, unticketable inwash of odor, as if Brant's air were mixing with someone else's. When both doors of the lock finally stood wide apart from each other, Brant found himself looking down the inside of a flexible, airtight tube, such as he had once seen used for the transfer of a small freight-load from a ship to one of Earth's several space stations. It connected the airlock of the observatory with that of the other ship. At the other end of it, lights gleamed yellowly, with the unmistakable, dismal sheen of incandescent overheads.

That was an old ship, all right.

Tap. Tap.

"Go to hell," he said aloud. There was no answer.

Tap. Tap.

"Go to hell," he said. He walked out into the tube, which flexed sinuously as his body pressed aside the static air. In the airlock of the stranger, he paused and looked back. He was not much surprised to see the outer door of his own airlock swinging snugly shut against him. Then the airlock of the stranger began to cycle; he skipped on into the ship barely in time.

There was a bare metal corridor ahead of him. While he watched, the first light bulb over his head blinked out. Then the second. Then the third. As the fourth one went out, the first came on again, so that now there was a slow ribbon of darkness moving away from him down the corridor. Clearly, he was being asked to follow the line of darkening bulbs down the corridor.

He had no choice, now that he had come this far. He followed the blinking lights.

The trail led directly to the control room of the ship. There was nobody there, either.

The whole place was oppressively silent. He could hear the soft hum of generators—a louder noise than he ever heard on board the observatory—but no ship should be this quiet. There should be muffled human voices, the chittering of communications systems, the impacts of soles on metal. Someone had to operate a proper ship—not only its airlocks, but its motors—and its brains. The observatory was only a barge, and needed no crew but Brant, but a real ship had to be manned.

He scanned the bare metal compartment, noting the apparent age of the equipment. Most of it was manual, but there were no hands to man it.

A ghost ship for true.

"All right," he said. His voice sounded flat and loud to him. "Come on out. You wanted me here—why are you hiding?"

Immediately there was a noise in the close, still air, a thin, electrical sigh. Then a quiet voice said, "You're Brant Kittinger."

"Certainly," Brant said, swiveling fruitlessly toward the apparent source of the voice. "You know who I am. You couldn't have found me by accident. Will you come out? I've no time to play games."

"I'm not playing games," the voice said calmly. "And I can't come out, since I'm not hiding from you. I can't see you; I needed to hear your voice before I could be sure of you."

"Why?"

"Because I can't see inside the ship. I could find your observation boat well enough, but until I heard you speak I couldn't be sure that you were the one aboard it. Now I know."

"All right," Brant said suspiciously. "I still don't see why you're hiding. Where are you?"

"Right here," said the voice. "All around you."

Brant looked all around himself. His scalp began to creep. "What kind of nonsense is that?" he said.

"You aren't seeing what you're looking at, Brant. You're looking directly at me, no matter where you look. *I am the ship.*"

"Oh," Brant said softly. "So that's it. You're one of Murray Bennett's computer-driven ships. Are you the *Astrid*, after all?"

"This is the *Astrid*," the voice said. "But you miss my point. I am Murray Bennett, also."

Brant's jaw dropped open. "Where are you?" he said after a time.

"Here," the voice said impatiently. "I am the *Astrid*. I am also Murray Bennett. Bennett is dead, so he can't very well come into the cabin and shake your hand. I am now Murray

Bennett; I remember you very well, Brant. I need your help, so I sought you out. I'm not as much Murray Bennett as I'd like to be."

Brant sat down in the empty pilot's seat.

"You're a computer," he said shakily. "Isn't that so?"

"It is and it isn't. No computer can duplicate the performance of a human brain. I tried to introduce real human neural mechanisms into computers, specifically to fly ships, and was outlawed for my trouble. I don't think I was treated fairly. It took enormous surgical skill to make the hundreds and hundreds of nerve-to-circuit connections that were needed—and before I was half through, the UN decided that what I was doing was human vivisection. They outlawed me, and the Foundation said I'd have to destroy myself; what could I do after that?

"I did destroy myself. I transferred most of my own nervous system into the computers of the *Astrid,* working at the end through drugged assistants under telepathic control, and finally relying upon the computers to seal the last connections. No such surgery ever existed before, but I brought it into existence. It worked. Now I'm the *Astrid*—and still Murray Bennett too, though Bennett is dead."

Brant locked his hands together carefully on the edge of the dead control board. "What good did that do you?" he said.

"It proved my point. I was trying to build an almost living spaceship. I had to build part of myself into it to do it—since they made me an outlaw to stop my using any other human being as a source of parts. But here is the *Astrid,* Brant, as almost alive as I could ask. I'm as immune to a dead spaceship—a UN cruiser, for instance—as you would be to an infuriated wheelbarrow. My reflexes are human-fast. I feel things directly, not through instruments. I fly myself: I am what I sought—the ship that almost thinks for itself."

"You keep saying 'almost,' " Brant said.

"That's why I came to you," the voice said. "I don't have enough of Murray Bennett here to know what I should do next. You knew me well. Was I out to try to use human brains more and more, and computer-mechanisms less and less? It seems to me that I was. I can pick up the brains easily enough, just as I picked you up. The solar system is full of people isolated on research boats who could be plucked off them and incorporated into efficient machines like the *Astrid.* But I don't know. I seem to have lost my creativity. I have a base where I have some other ships with beautiful computers in them, and with a few people to use as research animals I could make even better ships of them than the *Astrid* is. But is that what I want to do? Is that what I set out to do? I no longer know, Brant. Advise me."

The machine with the human nerves would have been touching had it not been so much like Bennett had been. The combination of the two was flatly horrible.

"You've made a bad job of yourself, Murray," he said. "You've let me inside your brain without taking any real thought of the danger. What's to prevent me from stationing myself at your old manual controls and flying you to the nearest UN post?"

"You can't fly a ship."

"How do you know?"

"By simple computation. And there are other reasons. What's to prevent me from making you cut your own throat? The answer's the same. You're in control of your body; I'm in control of mine. My body is the *Astrid*. The controls are useless, unless I actuate them. The nerves through which I do so are sheathed in excellent steel. The only way in which you could destroy my control would be to break something necessary to the running of the ship. That, in a sense, would kill me, as destroying your heart or your lungs would kill you. But that would be pointless, for then you could no more navigate the ship than I. And if you made repairs, I would be— well, resurrected."

The voice fell silent a moment. Then it added, matter-of-factly, "Of course, I can protect myself."

Brant made no reply. His eyes were narrowed to the squint he more usually directed at a problem in Milne transformations.

"I never sleep," the voice went on, "but much of my navigating and piloting is done by an autopilot without requiring my conscious attention. It is the same old Nelson autopilot which was originally on board the *Astrid,* though, so it has to be monitored. If you touch the controls while the autopilot is running, it switches itself off and I resume direction myself."

Brant was surprised and instinctively repelled by the steady flow of information. It was a forcible reminder of how much of the computer there was in the intelligence that called itself Murray Bennett. It was answering a question with the almost mindless wealth of detail of a public-library selector—and there was no "Enough" button for Brant to push.

"Are you going to answer my question?" the voice said suddenly.

"Yes," Brant said. "I advise you to turn yourself in. The *Astrid* proves your point—and also proves that your research was a blind alley. There's no point in your proceeding to make more *Astrids;* you're aware yourself that you're incapable of improving on the model now."

"That's contrary to what I have recorded," the voice said. "My ultimate purpose as a man was to build machines like this. I can't accept your answer: it conflicts with my primary directive. Please follow the lights to your quarters."

"What are you going to do with me?"

"Take you to the base."

"What for?" Brant said.

"As a stock of parts," said the voice. "Please follow the lights, or I'll have to use force."

Brant followed the lights. As he entered the cabin to which they led him, a disheveled figure arose from one of the two cots. He started back in alarm. The figure chuckled wryly and displayed a frayed bit of gold braid on its sleeve.

"I'm not as terrifying as I look," he said. "Lt. Powell of the UN scout *Iapetus*, at your service."

"I'm Brant Kittinger, Planetary Institute astrophysicist. You're just the faintest bit battered, all right. Did you tangle with Bennett?"

"Is that his name?" the UN patrolman nodded glumly. "Yes. There's some whoppers of guns mounted on this old tub. I challenged it, and it cut my ship to pieces before I could lift a hand. I barely got into my suit in time—and I'm beginning to wish I hadn't."

"I don't blame you. You know what he plans to use us for, I judge."

"Yes," the pilot said. "He seems to take pleasure in bragging about his achievements—God knows they're amazing enough, if even half of what he says is true."

"It's all true," Brant said. "He's essentially a machine, you know, and as such I doubt that he can lie."

Powell looked startled. "That makes it worse. I've been trying to figure a way out—"

Brant raised one hand sharply, and with the other he patted his pockets in search of a pencil. "If you've found anything, write it down, don't talk about it. I think he can hear us. Is that so, Bennett?"

"Yes," said the voice in the air. Powell jumped. "My hearing extends throughout the ship."

There was silence again. Powell, grim as death, scribbled on a tattered UN trip ticket.

Doesn't matter, can't think of a thing.

Where's the main computer? Brant wrote. *There's where personality residues must lie.*

Down below. Not a chance without blaster. Must be 8" of steel around it. Control nerves the same.

They sat hopelessly on the lower cot. Brant chewed on the pencil. "How far is his home base from here?" he asked at length.

"Where's here?"

"In the orbit of the new planet."

Powell whistled. "In that case, his base can't be more than three days away. I came on board from just off Titan, and he hasn't touched his base since, so his fuel won't last much longer. I know this type of ship well enough. And from what I've seen of the drivers, they haven't been altered."

"Umm," Brant said. "That checks. If Bennett in person never got around to altering the drive, this ersatz Bennett we have here will never get around to it, either." He found it easier to ignore the listening presence while talking; to monitor his speech constantly with Bennett in mind was too hard on the nerves. "That gives us three days to get out, then. Or less."

For at least twenty minutes Brant said nothing more, while the UN pilot squirmed and watched his face hopefully. Finally the astronomer picked up the piece of paper again.

Can you pilot this ship? he wrote.

The pilot nodded and scribbled: *Why?*

Without replying, Brant lay back on the bunk, swiveled himself around so that his head was toward the center of the cabin, doubled up his knees, and let fly with both feet. They crashed hard against the hull, the magnetic studs in his shoes leaving bright scars on the metal. The impact sent him sailing like an ungainly fish across the cabin.

"What was that for?" Powell and the voice in the air asked simultaneously. Their captor's tone was faintly curious, but not alarmed.

Brant had his answer already prepared. "It's part of a question I want to ask," he said. He brought up against the far wall and struggled to get his feet back to the desk. "Can you tell me what I did then, Bennett?"

"Why, not specifically. As I told you, I can't see inside the ship. But I get a tactual jar from the nerves of the controls, the lights, the floors, the ventilation system, and so on, and also a ringing sound from the audios. These things tell me that you either stamped on the floor or pounded on the wall.

From the intensity of all the impressions, I compute that you stamped."

"You hear and you feel, eh?"

"That's correct," the voice said. "Also I can pick up your body heat from the receptors in the ship's temperature control system—a form of seeing, but without any definition."

Very quietly, Brant retrieved the worn trip ticket and wrote on it: *Follow me.*

He went out into the corridor and started down it toward the control room, Powell at his heels. The living ship remained silent only for a moment.

"Return to your cabin," the voice said.

Brant walked a little faster. How would Bennett's vicious brain child enforce his orders?

"I said, go back to your cabin," the voice said. Its tone was now loud and harsh, and without a trace of feeling; for the first time, Brant was able to tell that it came from a voder, rather than from a tape-vocabulary of Bennett's own voice. Brant gritted his teeth and marched forward.

"I don't want to have to spoil you," the voice said. "For the last time—"

An instant later Brant received a powerful blow in the small of his back. It felled him like a tree and sent him skimming along the corridor deck like a flat stone. A bare fraction of a second later there was a hiss and a flash, and the air was abruptly hot and choking with the sharp odor of ozone.

"Close," Powell's voice said calmly. "Some of these rivet heads in the walls evidently are high-tension electrodes. Lucky I saw the nimbus collecting on that one. Crawl, and make it snappy."

Crawling in a gravity-free corridor was a good deal more difficult to manage than walking. Determinedly, Brant squirmed into the control room, calling into play every trick he had ever learned in space to stick to the floor. He could hear Powell wriggling along behind him.

"He doesn't know what I'm up to," Brant said aloud. "Do you, Bennett?"

"No," the voice in the air said. "But I know of nothing you can do that's dangerous while you're lying on your belly. When you get up, I'll destroy you, Brant."

"Hmmm," Brant said. He adjusted his glasses, which he had nearly lost during his brief, skipping carom along the deck. The voice had summarized the situation with deadly precision. He pulled the now nearly pulped trip ticket out of his shirt pocket, wrote on it, and shoved it across the desk to Powell.

How can we reach the autopilot? Got to smash it.

Powell propped himself up on one elbow and studied the scrap of paper, frowning. Down below, beneath the deck, there was an abrupt sound of power, and Brant felt the cold metal on which he was lying sink beneath him. Bennett was changing course, trying to throw them within range of his defenses. Both men began to slide sidewise.

Powell did not appear to be worried; evidently he knew just how long it took to turn a ship of this size and period. He pushed the piece of paper back. On the last free space on it, in cramped letters, was: *Throw something at it.*

"Ah," said Brant. Still sliding, he drew off one of his heavy shoes and hefted it critically. It would do. With a sudden convulsion of motion he hurled it.

Fat, crackling sparks criss-crossed the room; the noise was ear-splitting. While Bennett could have had no idea what Brant was doing, he evidently had sensed the sudden stir of movement and had triggered the high-tension current out of general caution. But he was too late. The flying shoe plowed heel-foremost into the autopilot with a rending smash.

There was an unfocused blare of sound from the voder— more like the noise of a siren than like a human cry. The *Astrid* rolled wildly, once. Then there was silence.

"All right," said Brant, getting to his knees. "Try the controls, Powell."

The UN pilot arose cautiously. No sparks flew. When he touched the boards, the ship responded with an immediate purr of power.

"She runs," he said. "Now, how the hell did you know what to do?"

"It wasn't difficult," Brant said complacently, retrieving his shoe. "But we're not out of the woods yet. We have to get to the stores fast and find a couple of torches. I want to cut through every nerve-channel we can find. Are you with me?"

"Sure."

The job was more quickly done than Brant had dared to hope. Evidently the living ship had never thought of lightening itself by jettisoning all the equipment its human crew had once needed. While Brant and Powell cut their way enthusiastically through the jungle of efferent nerve-trunks running from the central computer, the astronomer said:

"He gave us too much information. He told me that he had connected the artificial nerves of the ship, the control nerves, to the nerve-ends running from the parts of his own brain that he had used. And he said that he'd had to make *hundreds* of such connections. That's the trouble with allowing a computer to act as an independent agent—it doesn't know enough about interpersonal relationships to control its tongue. . . . There we are. He'll be coming to before long, but I don't think he'll be able to interfere with us now."

He set down his torch with a sigh. "I was saying? Oh, yes. About those nerve connections: if he had separated out the pain-carrying nerves from the other sensory nerves, he would have had to have made *thousands* of connections, not hundreds. Had it really been the living human being, Bennett, who had given me that cue, I would have discounted it, because he might have been using understatement. But since it was Bennett's double, a computer, I assumed that the figure was of the right order of magnitude. Computers don't understate.

"Besides, I didn't think Bennett could have made thousands of connections, especially not working telepathically through a proxy. There's a limit even to the most marvelous neurosurgery. Bennett had just made general connections, and had relied on the segments from his own brain which he had incorporated to sort out the impulses as they came in—as any human brain could do under like circumstances. That was one of the advantages of using parts from a human brain in the first place."

"And when you kicked the wall—" Powell said.

"Yes, you see the crux of the problem already. When I kicked the wall, I wanted to make sure that he could *feel* the impact of my shoes. If he could, then I could be sure that he hadn't eliminated the sensory nerves when he installed the motor nerves. And if he hadn't, then there were bound to be pain axons present, too."

"But what has the autopilot to do with it?" Powell asked plaintively.

"The autopilot," Brant said, grinning, "is a center of his nerve-mesh, an important one. He should have protected it as heavily as he protected the main computer. When I smashed it, it was like ramming a fist into a man's solar plexus. It hurt him."

Powell grinned too. "K.O.," he said.

NIGHTFALL

Astounding Science Fiction
September

by Isaac Asimov

(Well, here it is. "Nightfall" was my sixteenth published story, but the thirty-second I had written. I wrote it in March 1941, when I was 21¼ years old. It was the first story of mine that Campbell paid me a bonus for. It was the first story of mine that placed as the lead novelet in an issue of *Astounding*. It was the first story of mine that rated an *Astounding* cover.

It was a milestone for me, obviously.

I was not aware at the time just exactly how much of a milestone it was.

At the time, it was just another story I had written, and it didn't make a terribly big splash, but as the months and years passed, it seemed to get bigger and bigger in retrospect until now there is not only a general consensus that it is the best short piece I have ever written, but there seems to be a general consensus that it is the best short piece of science fiction ever written. At least it placed first in several polls, including one of the membership of the Science Fiction Writers of America.

I hasten to say that I disagree. In my own opinion I have written three short pieces that are better and I shall see to it that each is included in this series when the appropriate year is reached. In fact, I think "Nightfall" has serious flaws and crudities as far as writing style is concerned. However—after it appeared I never again wrote another science fiction story that remained unpublished, and very few that weren't accepted by the first editor to whom it was offered—so I guess "Nightfall," not quite three years after I had begun to submit stories for publication, marked the end of my apprenticeship—I.A.)

*"If the stars should appear one night in a thousand years,
how would men believe and adore, and preserve for many
generations the remembrance of the city of God!"—Emerson*

Aton 77, director of Saro University, thrust out a belligerent lower lip and glared at the young newspaperman in a hot fury.

Theremon 762 took that fury in his stride. In his earlier days, when his now widely syndicated column was only a mad idea in a cub reporter's mind, he had specialized in "impossible" interviews. It had cost him bruises, black eyes, and broken bones; but it had given him an ample supply of coolness and self-confidence.

So he lowered the outthrust hand that had been so pointedly ignored and calmly waited for the aged director to get over the worst. Astronomers were queer ducks, anyway, and if Aton's actions of the last two months meant anything, this same Aton was the queer-duckiest of the lot.

Aton 77 found his voice, and though it trembled with restrained emotion, the careful, somewhat pedantic, phraseology for which the famous astronomer was noted, did not abandon him.

"Sir," he said, "you display an infernal gall in coming to me with that impudent proposition of yours."

The husky telephotographer of the Observatory, Beenay 25, thrust a tongue's tip across dry lips and interposed nervously, "Now, sir, after all—"

The director turned to him and lifted a white eyebrow. "Do not interfere, Beenay. I will credit you with good intentions in bringing this man here; but I will tolerate no insubordination now."

Theremon decided it was time to take a part. "Director Aton, if you'll let me finish what I started saying I think—"

"I don't believe, young man," retorted Aton, "that anything you could say now would count much as compared with your daily columns of these last two months. You have led a vast newspaper campaign against the efforts of myself and my colleagues to organize the world against the menace which it is now too late to avert. You have done your best with your highly personal attacks to make the staff of this Observatory objects of ridicule."

The director lifted the copy of the Saro City *Chronicle* on the table and shook it at Theremon furiously. "Even a person of your well-known impudence should have hesitated before coming to me with a request that he be allowed to cover today's events for his paper. Of all newsmen, you!"

Aton dashed the newspaper to the floor, strode to the window and clasped his arms behind his back.

"You may leave," he snapped over his shoulder. He stared moodily out at the skyline where Gamma, the brightest of the planet's six suns, was setting. It had already faded and yellowed into the horizon mists, and Aton knew he would never see it again as a sane man.

He whirled. "No, wait, come here!" He gestured peremptorily. "I'll give you your story."

The newsman had made no motion to leave, and now he approached the old man slowly. Aton gestured outward, "Of the six suns, only Beta is left in the sky. Do you see it?"

The question was rather unnecessary. Beta was almost at zenith; its ruddy light flooding the landscape to an unusual orange as the brilliant rays of setting Gamma died. Beta was at aphelion. It was small; smaller than Theremon had ever seen it before, and for the moment it was undisputed ruler of Lagash's sky.

Lagash's own sun, Alpha, the one about which it revolved, was at the antipodes; as were the two distant companion pairs. The red dwarf Beta—Alpha's immediate companion—was alone, grimly alone.

Aton's upturned face flushed redly in the sunlight. "In just under four hours," he said, "civilization, as we know it, comes to an end. It will do so because, as you see, Beta is the only sun in the sky." He smiled grimly. "Print that! There'll be no one to read it."

"But if it turns out that four hours pass—and another four—and nothing happens?" asked Theremon softly.

"Don't let that worry you. Enough will happen."

"Granted! And *still*—if nothing happens?"

For a second time, Beenay 25 spoke, "Sir, I think you ought to listen to him."

Theremon said, "Put it to a vote, Director Aton."

There was a stir among the remaining five members of the Observatory staff, who till now had maintained an attitude of wary neutrality.

"That," stated Aton flatly, "is not necessary." He drew out his pocket watch. "Since your good friend, Beenay, insists so urgently, I will give you five minutes. Talk away."

"Good! Now, just what difference would it make if you allowed me to take down an eyewitness account of what's to come? If your prediction comes true, my presence won't hurt; for in that case my column would never be written. On the other hand, if nothing comes of it, you will just have to expect ridicule or worse. It would be wise to leave that ridicule to friendly hands."

Aton snorted. "Do you mean yours when you speak of friendly hands?"

"Certainly!" Theremon sat down and crossed his legs. "My columns may have been a little rough at times, but I gave you people the benefit of the doubt every time. After all, this is not the century to preach 'the end of the world is at hand' to Lagash. You have to understand that people don't believe the 'Book of Revelations' any more, and it annoys them to have scientists turn about face and tell us the Cultists are right after all——"

"No such thing, young man," interrupted Aton. "While a great deal of our data has been supplied us by the Cult, our results contain none of the Cult's mysticism. Facts are facts, and the Cult's so-called 'mythology' *has* certain facts behind it. We've exposed them and ripped away their mystery. I assure you that the Cult hates us now worse than you do."

"I don't hate you. I'm just trying to tell you that the public is in an ugly humor. They're angry."

Aton twisted his mouth in derision. "Let them be angry."

"Yes, but what about tomorrow?"

"There'll be no tomorrow!"

"But if there is. Say that there is—just to see what happens. That anger might take shape into something serious. After all, you know, business has taken a nose dive these last two months. Investors don't really believe the world is coming to an end, but just the same they're being cagy with their money until it's all over. Johnny Public doesn't believe you, either, but the new spring furniture might as well wait a few months—just to make sure.

"You see the point. Just as soon as this is all over, the business interests will be after your hide. They'll say that if crackpots—begging your pardon—can upset the country's prosperity any time they want simply by making some cock-eyed prediction—it's up to the planet to prevent them. The sparks will fly, sir."

The director regarded the columnist sternly. "And just what were you proposing to do to help the situation?"

"Well," grinned Theremon, "I was proposing to take charge of the publicity. I can handle things so that only the ridiculous side will show. It would be hard to stand, I admit, because I'd have to make you all out to be a bunch of gibbering idiots, but if I can get people laughing at you, they might forget to be angry. In return for that, all my publisher asks is an exclusive story."

Beenay nodded and burst out, "Sir, the rest of us think he's right. These last two months we've considered everything but the million-to-one chance that there is an error somewhere in our theory or in our calculations. We ought to take care of that, too."

There was a murmur of agreement from the men grouped about the table, and Aton's expression became that of one who found his mouth full of something bitter and couldn't get rid of it.

"You may stay if you wish, then. You will kindly refrain, however, from hampering us in our duties in any way. You will also remember that I am in charge of all activities here, and in spite of your opinions as expressed in your columns, I will expect full co-operation and full respect—"

His hands were behind his back, and his wrinkled face thrust forward determinedly as he spoke. He might have continued indefinitely but for the intrusion of a new voice.

"Hello, hello, hello!" It came in a high tenor, and the plump cheeks of the newcomer expanded in a pleased smile. "What's this morgue-like atmosphere about here? No one's losing his nerve, I hope."

Aton started in consternation and said peevishly, "Now what the devil are you doing here, Sheerin? I thought you were going to stay behind in the Hideout."

Sheerin laughed and dropped his tubby figure into a chair. "Hideout be blowed! The place bored me. I wanted to be here, where things are getting hot. Don't you suppose I have my share of curiosity? I want to see these Stars the Cultists are forever speaking about." He rubbed his hands and added in a soberer tone. "It's freezing outside. The wind's enough to hang icicles on your nose. Beta doesn't seem to give any heat at all, at the distance it is."

The white-haired director ground his teeth in sudden exasperation, "Why do you go out of your way to do crazy things, Sheerin? What kind of good are you around here?"

"What kind of good am I around there?" Sheerin spread his palms in comical resignation. "A psychologist isn't worth his salt in the Hideout. They need men of action and strong, healthy women that can breed children. Me? I'm a hundred pounds too heavy for a man of action, and I wouldn't be a success at breeding children. So why bother them with an extra mouth to feed? I feel better over here."

Theremon spoke briskly, "Just what is the Hideout, sir?"

Sheerin seemed to see the columnist for the first time. He frowned and blew his ample cheeks out, "And just who in Lagash are you, redhead?"

Aton compressed his lips and then muttered sullenly, "That's Theremon 762, the newspaper fellow. I suppose you've heard of him."

The columnist offered his hand. "And, of course, you're Sheerin 501 of Saro University. I've heard of you." Then he repeated, "What is this Hideout, sir?"

"Well," said Sheerin, "we have managed to convince a few people of the validity of our prophecy of—er—doom, to be spectacular about it, and those few have taken proper measures. They consist mainly of the immediate members of the families of the Observatory staff, certain of the faculty of Saro University and a few outsiders. Altogether, they number about three hundred, but three quarters are women and children."

"I see! They're supposed to hide where the Darkness and the—er—Stars can't get at them, and then hold out when the rest of the world goes poof."

"If they can. It won't be easy. With all of mankind insane; with the great cities going up in flames—environment will not be conducive to survival. But they have food, water, shelter, and weapons—"

"They've got more," said Aton. "They've got all our records, except for what we will collect today. Those records will mean everything to the next cycle, and *that's* what must survive. The rest can go hang."

Theremon whistled a long, low whistle and sat brooding for several minutes. The men about the table had brought out a multichess board and started a six-member game. Moves were made rapidly and in silence. All eyes bent in furious concentration on the board. Theremon watched them intently and then rose and approached Aton, who sat apart in whispered conversation with Sheerin.

"Listen," he said, "let's go somewhere where we won't bother the rest of the fellows. I want to ask some questions."

The aged astronomer frowned sourly at him, but Sheerin chirped up, "Certainly. It will do me good to talk. It always does. Aton was telling me about your ideas concerning world reaction to a failure of the prediction—and I agree with you.

I read your column pretty regularly, by the way, and as a general thing I like your views."

"Please, Sheerin," growled Aton.

"Eh? Oh, all right. We'll go into the next room. It has softer chairs, anyway."

There *were* softer chairs in the next room. There were also thick red curtains on the windows and a maroon carpet on the floor. With the bricky light of Beta pouring in, the general effect was one of dried blood.

Theremon shuddered, "Say, I'd give ten credits for a decent dose of white light for just a second. I wish Gamma or Delta were in the sky."

"What are your questions?" asked Aton. "Please remember that our time is limited. In a little over an hour and a quarter we're going upstairs, and after that there will be no time for talk."

"Well, here it is." Theremon leaned back and folded his hands on his chest. "You people seem so all-fired serious about this that I'm beginning to believe you. Would you mind explaining what it's all about?"

Aton exploded, "Do you mean to sit there and tell me that you've been bombarding us with ridicule without even finding out what we've been trying to say?"

The columnist grinned sheepishly. "It's not that bad, sir. I've got the general idea. You say that there is going to be a world-wide Darkness in a few hours and that all mankind will go violently insane. What I want now is the science behind it."

"No, you don't. No, you don't," broke in Sheerin. "If you ask Aton for that—supposing him to be in the mood to answer at all—he'll trot out pages of figures and volumes of graphs. You won't make head or tail of it. Now if you were to ask *me*, I could give you the layman's standpoint."

"All right; I ask you."

"Then first I'd like a drink." He rubbed his hands and looked at Aton.

"Water?" grunted Aton.

"Don't be silly!"

"Don't you be silly. No alcohol today. It would be too easy to get my men drunk. I can't afford to tempt them."

The psychologist grumbled wordlessly. He turned to Theremon, impaled him with his sharp eyes, and began.

"You realize, of course, that the history of civilization on Lagash displays a cyclic character—but I mean, *cyclic!*"

"I know," replied Theremon cautiously, "that that is the current archeological theory. Has it been accepted as a fact?"

"Just about. In this last century it's been generally agreed upon. This cyclic character is—or, rather, was—one of *the* great mysteries. We've located series of civilizations, nine of them definitely, and indications of others as well, all of which have reached heights comparable to our own, and all of which, without exception, were destroyed by fire at the very height of their culture.

"And no one could tell why. All centers of culture were thoroughly gutted by fire, with nothing left behind to give a hint as to the cause."

Theremon was following closely. "Wasn't there a Stone Age, too?"

"Probably, but as yet, practically nothing is known of it, except that men of that age were little more than rather intelligent apes. We can forget about that."

"I see. Go on!"

"There have been explanations of these recurrent catastrophes, all of a more or less fantastic nature. Some say that there are periodic rains of fire; some that Lagash passes through a sun every so often; some even wilder things. But there is one theory, quite different from all of these, that has been handed down over a period of centuries."

"I know. You mean this myth of the 'Stars' that the Cultists have in their 'Book of Revelations.'"

"Exactly," rejoined Sheerin with satisfaction. "The Cultists said that every two thousand and fifty years Lagash entered a huge cave, so that all the suns disappeared, and there came *total darkness all over the world!* And then, they say, things called Stars appeared, which robbed men of their souls and left them unreasoning brutes, so that they destroyed the civilization they themselves had built up. Of course, they mix all this up with a lot of religio-mystic notions, but that's the central idea."

There was a short pause in which Sheerin drew a long breath. "And now we come to the Theory of Universal Gravitation." He pronounced the phrase so that the capital letters sounded—and at that point Aton turned from the window, snorted loudly, and stalked out of the room.

The two stared after him, and Theremon said, "What's wrong?"

"Nothing in particular," replied Sheerin. "Two of the men

were due several hours ago and haven't shown up yet. He's terrifically shorthanded, of course, because all but the really essential men have gone to the Hideout."

"You don't think the two deserted, do you?"

"Who? Faro and Yimot? Of course not. Still, if they're not back within the hour, things would be a little sticky." He got to his feet suddenly, and his eyes twinkled. "Anyway, as long as Aton is gone——"

Tiptoeing to the nearest window, he squatted, and from the low window box beneath withdrew a bottle of red liquid that gurgled suggestively when he shook it.

"I *thought* Aton didn't know about this," he remarked as he trotted back to the table. "Here! We've only got one glass so, as the guest, you can have it. I'll keep the bottle." And he filled the tiny cup with judicious care.

Theremon rose to protest, but Sheerin eyed him sternly. "Respect your elders, young man."

The newsman seated himself with a look of pain and anguish on his face. "Go ahead, then, you old villain."

The psychologist's Adam's apple wobbled as the bottle upended, and then, with a satisfied grunt and a smack of the lips, he began again.

"But what do you know about gravitation?"

"Nothing, except that it is a very recent development, not too well established, and that the math is so hard that only twelve men in Lagash are supposed to understand it."

"*Tcha!* Nonsense! Boloney! I can give you all the essential math in a sentence. The Law of Universal Gravitation states that there exists a cohesive force among all bodies of the universe, such that the amount of this force between any two given bodies is proportional to the product of their masses divided by the square of the distance between them."

"Is that all?"

"That's enough! It took four hundred years to develop it."

"Why that long? It sounded simple enough, the way you said it."

"Because great laws are not divined by flashes of inspiration, whatever you may think. It usually takes the combined work of a world full of scientists over a period of centuries. After Genovi 41 discovered that Lagash rotated about the sun Alpha, rather than vice versa—and that was four hundred years ago—astronomers have been working. The complex motions of the six suns were recorded and analyzed and unwoven. Theory after theory was advanced and checked and counterchecked and modified and abandoned and revived and converted to something else. It was a devil of a job."

Theremon nodded thoughtfully and held out his glass for more liquor. Sheerin grudgingly allowed a few ruby drops to leave the bottle.

"It was twenty years ago," he continued after remoistening his own throat, "that it was finally demonstrated that the Law of Universal Gravitation accounted exactly for the orbital motions of the six suns. It was a great triumph."

Sheerin stood up and walked to the window, still clutching his bottle, "And now we're getting to the point. In the last decade, the motions of Lagash about Alpha were computed according to gravity, and *it did not account for the orbit observed;* not even when all perturbations due to the other suns were included. Either the law was invalid, or there was another, as yet unknown, factor involved."

Theremon joined Sheerin at the window and gazed out past the wooded slopes to where the spires of Saro City gleamed bloodily on the horizon. The newsman felt the tension of uncertainty grow within him as he cast a short glance at Beta. It glowered redly at Zenith, dwarfed and evil.

"Go ahead, sir," he said softly.

Sheerin replied, "Astronomers stumbled about for years, each proposed theory more untenable than the one before—until Aton had the inspiration of calling in the Cult. The head of the Cult, Sor 5, had access to certain data that simplified the problem considerably. Aton set to work on a new track.

"What if there were another nonluminous planetary body such as Lagash? If there were, you know, it would shine only by reflected light, and if it were composed of bluish rock, as Lagash itself largely is, then, in the redness of the sky, the eternal blaze of the suns would make it invisible—drown it out completely."

Theremon whistled, "What a screwy idea!"

"You think *that's* screwy? Listen to this: Suppose this body rotated about Lagash at such a distance and in such an orbit and had such a mass that its attraction would exactly account for the deviations of Lagash's orbit from theory—do you know what would happen?"

The columnist shook his head.

"Well, sometimes this body would get in the way of a sun." And Sheerin emptied what remained in the bottle at a draft.

"And it does, I suppose," said Theremon flatly.

"Yes! But only one sun lies in its plane of revolutions." He jerked a thumb at the shrunken sun above. "Beta! And it has been shown that the eclipse will occur only when the arrangement of the suns is such that Beta is alone in its hemisphere and at maximum distance, at which time the moon is invariably at minimum distance. The eclipse that results, with the moon seven times the apparent diameter of Beta, covers all of Lagash and lasts well over half a day, so that no spot on the planet escapes the effects. *That eclipse comes once every two thousand and forty-nine years.*"

Theremon's face was drawn into an expressionless mask. "And that's my story?"

The psychologist nodded. "That's all of it. First the eclipse—which will start in three quarters of an hour—then universal Darkness, and, maybe, these mysterious Stars—then madness, and end of the cycle."

He brooded. "We had two months' leeway—we at the Observatory—and that wasn't enough time to persuade Lagash of the danger. Two centuries might not have been enough. But our records are at the Hideout, and today we photograph the eclipse. The next cycle will *start off* with the truth, and when the *next.* eclipse comes, mankind will at last be ready for it. Come to think of it, that's part of your story, too."

A thin wind ruffled the curtains at the window as Theremon opened it and leaned out. It played coldly with his hair as he stared at the crimson sunlight on his hand. Then he turned in sudden rebellion.

"What is there in Darkness to drive *me* mad?"

Sheerin smiled to himself as he spun the empty liquor bottle with abstracted motions of his hand. "Have you ever experienced Darkness, young man?"

The newsman leaned against the wall and considered. "No. Can't say I have. But I know what it is. Just—uh—" He made vague motions with his fingers, and then brightened. "Just no light. Like in caves."

"Have you ever been in a cave?"

"In a *cave!* Of course not!"

"I thought not. *I* tried last week—just to see—but I got out in a hurry. I went in until the mouth of the cave was just visible as a blur of light, with black everywhere else. I never thought a person my weight could run that fast."

Theremon's lip curled. "Well, if it comes to that, I guess I wouldn't have run, if I had been there."

The psychologist studied the young man with an annoyed frown.

"My, don't you talk big! I dare you to draw the curtain."

Theremon looked his surprise and said, "What for? If we had four or five suns out there we might want to cut the light down a bit for comfort, but now we haven't enough light as it is."

"That's the point. Just draw the curtain; then come here and sit down."

"All right." Theremon reached for the tasseled string and jerked. The red curtain slid across the wide window, the brass rings hissing their way along the crossbar, and a dusk-red shadow clamped down on the room.

Theremon's footsteps sounded hollowly in the silence as he made his way to the table, and then they stopped halfway. "I can't see you, sir," he whispered.

"Feel your way," ordered Sheerin in a strained voice.

"But I can't see you, sir." The newsman was breathing harshly. "I can't see anything."

"What did you expect?" came the grim reply. "Come here and sit down!"

The footsteps sounded again, waveringly, approaching slowly. There was the sound of someone fumbling with a chair. Theremon's voice came thinly, "Here I am. I feel . . . *ulp* . . . all right."

"You like it, do you?"

"N-no. It's pretty awful. The walls seem to be—" He paused. "They seem to be closing in on me. I keep wanting to push them away. But I'm not going *mad*! In fact, the feeling isn't as bad as it was."

"All right. Draw the curtain back again."

There were cautious footsteps through the dark, the rustle of Theremon's body against the curtain as he felt for the tassel, and then the triumphant *ro-o-o-osh* of the curtain slithering back. Red light flooded the room, and with a cry of joy Theremon looked up at the sun.

Sheerin wiped the moistness off his forehead with the back of a hand and said shakily, "And that was just a dark room."

"It can be stood," said Theremon lightly.

"Yes, a dark room can. But were you at the Jonglor Centennial Exposition two years ago?"

"No, it so happens I never got around to it. Six thousand miles was just a bit too much to travel, even for the exposition."

"Well, I was there. You remember hearing about the 'Tun-

nel of Mystery' that broke all records in the amusement
area—for the first month or so, anyway?"

"Yes. Wasn't there some fuss about it?"

"Very little. It was hushed up. You see, that Tunnel of
Mystery was just a mile-long tunnel—with no lights. You got
into a little open car and jolted along through Darkness for
fifteen minutes. It was very popular—while it lasted."

"Popular?"

"Certainly. There's a fascination in being frightened when
it's part of a game. A baby is born with three instinctive
fears: of loud noises, of falling, and of the absence of light.
That's why it's considered so funny to jump at someone and
shout 'Boo!' That's why it's such fun to ride a roller coaster.
And that's why that Tunnel of Mystery started cleaning up.
People came out of that Darkness shaking, breathless, half
dead with fear, but they kept on paying to get in."

"Wait a while, I remember now. Some people came out
dead, didn't they? There were rumors of that after it shut
down."

The psychologist snorted. "Bah! Two or three died. That
was nothing! They paid off the families of the dead ones and
argued the Jonglor City Council into forgetting it. After all,
they said, if people with weak hearts want to go through the
tunnel, it was at their own risk—and besides, it wouldn't happen again. So they put a doctor in the front office and had
every customer go through a physical examination before getting into the car. That actually *boosted* ticket sales."

"Well, then?"

"But, you see, there was something else. People sometimes
came out in perfect order, except that they refused to go into
buildings—any buildings; including palaces, mansions, apartment houses, tenements, cottages, huts, shacks, lean-tos, and
tents."

Theremon looked shocked. "You mean they refused to
come in out of the open. Where'd they sleep?"

"In the open."

"They should have forced them inside."

"Oh, they did, they did. Whereupon these people went into
violent hysterics and did their best to bat their brains out
against the nearest wall. Once you got them inside, you
couldn't keep them there without a strait jacket and a shot of
morphine."

"They must have been crazy."

"Which is exactly what they were. One person out of every
ten who went into that tunnel came out that way. They called

in the psychologists, and we did the only thing possible. We closed down the exhibit." He spread his hands.

"What was the matter with these people?" asked Theremon finally.

"Essentially the same thing that was the matter with you when you thought the walls of the room were crushing in on you in the dark. There is a psychological term for mankind's instinctive fear of the absence of light. We call it 'claustrophobia,' because the lack of light is always tied up with enclosed places, so that fear of one is fear of the other. You see?"

"And those people of the tunnel?"

"Those people of the tunnel consisted of those unfortunates whose mentality did not quite possess the resiliency to overcome the claustrophobia that overtook them in the Darkness. Fifteen minutes without light is a long time; you only had two or three minutes, and I believe you were fairly upset.

"The people of the tunnel had what is called a 'claustrophobic fixation.' Their latent fear of Darkness and enclosed places had crystallized and become active, and, as far as we can tell, permanent. *That's* what fifteen minutes in the dark will do."

There was a long silence, and Theremon's forehead wrinkled slowly into a frown. "I don't believe it's that bad."

"You mean you don't want to believe," snapped Sheerin. "You're afraid to believe. Look out the window!"

Theremon did so, and the psychologist continued without pausing. "Imagine Darkness—everywhere. No light, as far as you can see. The houses, the trees, the fields, the earth, the sky—*black!* And Stars thrown in, for all I know—whatever *they* are. Can you conceive it?"

"Yes, I can," declared Theremon truculently.

And Sheerin slammed his fist down upon the table in sudden passion. "You lie! You can't conceive that. Your brain wasn't built for the conception any more than it was built for the conception of infinity or of eternity. You can only talk about it. A fraction of the reality upsets you, and when the real thing comes, your brain is going to be presented with a phenomenon outside its limits of comprehension. You will go mad, completely and permanently! There is no question of it!"

He added sadly, "And another couple of millennia of painful struggle comes to nothing Tomorrow there won't be a city standing unharmed in all Lagash."

Theremon recovered part of his mental equilibrium. "That doesn't follow. I still don't see that I can go loony just because there isn't a sun in the sky—but even if I did, and everyone else did, how does that harm the cities? Are we going to blow them down?"

But Sheerin was angry, too. "If you were in Darkness, what would you want more than anything else; what would it be that every instinct would call for? Light, damn you, *light!*"

"Well?"

"And how would you get light?"

"I don't know," said Theremon flatly.

"What's the *only* way to get light, short of the sun?"

"How should I know?"

They were standing face to face and nose to nose.

Sheerin said, "You burn something, mister. Ever see a forest fire? Ever go camping and cook a stew over a wood fire? Heat isn't the only thing burning wood gives off, you know. It gives off light, and people know that. And when it's dark they want light, and they're going to *get it.*"

"So they burn wood?"

"So they burn whatever they can get. They've got to have light. They've got to burn something, and wood isn't handy—so they'll burn whatever is nearest. They'll have their light—and every center of habitation goes up in flames!"

Eyes held each other as though the whole matter were a personal affair of respective will powers, and then Theremon broke away wordlessly. His breathing was harsh and ragged, and he scarcely noted the sudden hubbub that came from the adjoining room behind the closed door.

Sheerin spoke, and it was with an effort that he made it sound matter-of-fact. "I think I heard Yimot's voice. He and Faro are probably back. Let's go in and see what kept them."

"Might as well!" muttered Theremon. He drew a long breath and seemed to shake himself. The tension was broken.

The room was in an uproar, with members of the staff clustering about two young men who were removing outer garments even as they parried the miscellany of questions being thrown at them.

Aton bustled through the crowd and faced the newcomers angrily. "Do you realize that it's less than half an hour before deadline? Where have you two been?"

Faro 24 seated himself and rubbed his hands. His cheeks were red with the outdoor chill. "Yimot and I have just finished carrying through a little crazy experiment of our own.

We've been trying to see if we couldn't construct an arrangement by which we could simulate the appearance of Darkness and Stars so as to get an advance notion as to how it looked."

There was a confused murmur from the listeners, and a sudden look of interest entered Aton's eyes. "There wasn't anything said of this before. How did you go about it?"

"Well," said Faro, "the idea came to Yimot and myself long ago, and we've been working it out in our spare time. Yimot knew of a low one-story house down in the city with a domed roof—it had once been used as a museum, I think. Anyway, we bought it—"

"Where did you get the money?" interrupted Aton peremptorily.

"Our bank accounts," grunted Yimot 70. "It cost two thousand credits." Then, defensively, "Well, what of it? Tomorrow, two thousand credits will be two thousand pieces of paper. That's all."

"Sure," agreed Faro. "We bought the place and rigged it up with black velvet from top to bottom so as to get as perfect a Darkness as possible. Then we punched tiny holes in the ceiling and through the roof and covered them with little metal caps, all of which could be shoved aside simultaneously at the close of a switch. At least, we didn't do that part ourselves; we got a carpenter and an electrician and some others—money didn't count. The point was that we could get the light to shine through those holes in the roof, so that we could get a starlike effect."

Not a breath was drawn during the pause that followed. Aton said stiffly:

"You had no right to make a private—"

Faro seemed abashed. "I know, sir—but, frankly, Yimot and I thought the experiment was a little dangerous. If the effect really worked, we half expected to go mad—from what Sheerin says about all this, we thought that would be rather likely. We wanted to take the risk ourselves. Of course, if we found we could retain sanity, it occurred to us that we might develop immunity to the real thing, and then expose the rest of you to the same thing. But things didn't work out at all—"

"Why, what happened?"

It was Yimot who answered. "We shut ourselves in and allowed our eyes to get accustomed to the dark. It's an extremely creepy feeling because the total Darkness makes you feel as if the walls and ceiling are crushing in on you. But we got over that and pulled the switch. The caps fell away and the roof glittered all over with little dots of light—"

"Well?"

"Well—nothing. That was the whacky part of it. Nothing happened. It was just a roof with holes in it, and that's just what it looked like. We tried it over and over again—that's what kept us so late—but there just isn't any effect at all."

There followed a shocked silence, and all eyes turned to Sheerin, who sat motionless, mouth open.

Theremon was the first to speak. "You know what this does to this whole theory you've built up, Sheerin, don't you?" He was grinning with relief.

But Sheerin raised his hand. "Now wait a while. Just let me think this through." And then he snapped his fingers, and when he lifted his head there was neither surprise nor uncertainty in his eyes. "Of course—"

He never finished. From somewhere up above there sounded a sharp clang, and Beenay, starting to his feet, dashed up the stairs with a "What the devil!"

The rest followed after.

Things happened quickly. Once up in the dome, Beenay cast one horrified glance at the shuttered photographic plates and at the man bending over them; and then hurled himself fiercely at the intruder, getting a death grip on his throat. There was a wild threshing, and as others of the staff joined in, the stranger was swallowed up and smothered under the weight of half a dozen angry men.

Aton came up last, breathing heavily. "Let him up!"

There was a reluctant unscrambling and the stranger, panting harshly, with his clothes torn and his forehead bruised, was hauled to his feet. He had a short yellow beard curled elaborately in the style affected by the Cultists.

Beenay shifted his hold to a collar grip and shook the man savagely. "All right, rat, what's the idea? These plates—"

"I wasn't after *them*," retorted the Cultist coldly. "That was an accident."

Beenay followed his glowering stare and snarled, "I see. You were after the cameras themselves. The accident with the plates was a stroke of luck for you, then. If you had touched Snapping Bertha or any of the others, you would have died by slow torture. As it is—" He drew his fist back.

Aton grabbed his sleeve. "Stop that! Let him go!"

The young technician wavered, and his arm dropped reluctantly. Aton pushed him aside and confronted the Cultist. "You're Latimer, aren't you?"

The Cultist bowed stiffly and indicated the symbol upon his hip. "I am Latimer 25, adjutant of the third class to his serenity, Sor 5."

"And"—Aton's white eyebrows lifted—"you were with his serenity when he visited me last week, weren't you?"

Latimer bowed a second time.

"Now, then, what do you want?"

"Nothing that you would give me of your own free will."

"Sor 5 sent you, I suppose—or is this your own idea?"

"I won't answer that question."

"Will there be any further visitors?"

"I won't answer that, either."

Aton glanced at his timepiece and scowled. "Now, man, what is it your master wants of me? I have fulfilled my end of the bargain."

Latimer smiled faintly, but said nothing.

"I asked him," continued Aton angrily, "for data only the Cult could supply, and it was given to me. For that, thank you. In return, I promised to prove the essential truth of the creed of the Cult."

"There was no need to prove that," came the proud retort. "It stands proven by the 'Book of Revelations.' "

"For the handful that constitute the Cult, yes. Don't pretend to mistake my meaning. I offered to present scientific backing for your beliefs. And I did!"

The Cultist's eyes narrowed bitterly. "Yes, you did—with a fox's subtlety, for your pretended explanation backed our beliefs, and at the same time removed all necessity for them. You made of the Darkness and of the Stars a natural phenomenon, and removed all its real significance. That was blasphemy."

"If so, the fault isn't mine. The facts exist. What can I do but state them?"

"Your 'facts' are a fraud and a delusion."

Aton stamped angrily. "How do you know?"

And the answer came with the certainty of absolute faith. "I *know!*"

The director purpled and Beenay whispered urgently. Aton waved him silent. "And what does Sor 5 want us to do? He still thinks, I suppose, that in trying to warn the world to take measures against the menace of madness, we are placing innumerable souls in jeopardy. We aren't succeeding, if that means anything to him."

"The attempt itself has done harm enough, and your vicious effort to gain information by means of your devilish instruments must be stopped. We obey the will of their Stars, and I only regret that my clumsiness prevented me from wrecking your infernal devices."

"It wouldn't have done you too much good," returned Aton. "All our data, except for the direct evidence we intend collecting right now, is already safely cached and well beyond possibility of harm." He smiled grimly. "But that does not affect your present status as an attempted burglar and criminal."

He turned to the men behind him. "Someone call the police at Saro City."

There was a cry of distaste from Sheerin. "Damn it, Aton, what's wrong with you? There's no time for that. Here"—he bustled his way forward—"let me handle this."

Aton stared down his nose at the psychologist. "This is not the time for your monkeyshines, Sheerin. Will you please let me handle this my own way? Right now you are a complete outsider here, and don't forget it."

Sheerin's mouth twisted eloquently. "Now why should we go to the impossible trouble of calling the police—with Beta's eclipse a matter of minutes from now—when this young man here is perfectly willing to pledge his word of honor to remain and cause no trouble whatsoever?"

The Cultist answered promptly, "I will do no such thing. You're free to do what you want, but it's only fair to warn you that just as soon as I get my chance I'm going to finish what I came out here to do. If it's my word of honor you're relying on, you'd better call the police."

Sheerin smiled in a friendly fashion. "You're a determined cuss, aren't you? Well, I'll explain something. Do you see that young man at the window? He's a strong, husky fellow, quite handy with his fists, and he's an outsider besides. Once the eclipse starts there will be nothing for him to do except keep an eye on you. Besides him, there will be myself—a little too stout for active fisticuffs, but still able to help."

"Well, what of it?" demanded Latimer frozenly.

"Listen and I'll tell you," was the reply. "Just as soon as the eclipse starts, we're going to take you, Theremon and I, and deposit you in a little closet with one door, to which is attached one giant lock and no windows. You will remain there for the duration."

"And afterward," breathed Latimer fiercely, "there'll be no

one to let me out. I know as well as you do what the coming
of the Stars means—I know it far better than you. With all
your minds gone, you are not likely to free me. Suffocation
or slow starvation, is it? About what I might have expected
from a group of scientists. But I don't give my word. It's a
matter of principle, and I won't discuss it further."

Aton seemed perturbed. His faded eyes were troubled.
"Really, Sheerin, locking him—"

"Please!" Sheerin motioned him impatiently to silence. "I
don't think for a moment things will go that far. Latimer has
just tried a clever little bluff, but I'm not a psychologist just
because I like the sound of the word." He grinned at the
Cultist. "Come now, you don't really think I'm trying anything as crude as slow starvation. My dear Latimer, if I lock
you in the closet, you are not going to see the Darkness, and
you are not going to see the Stars. It does not take much of a
knowledge of the fundamental creed of the Cult to realize
that for you to be hidden from the Stars when they appear
means the loss of your immortal soul. Now, I believe you to
be an honorable man. I'll accept your word of honor to make
no further effort to disrupt proceedings if you'll offer it."

A vein throbbed in Latimer's temple, and he seemed to
shrink within himself as he said thickly, "You have it!" And
then he added with swift fury, "But it is my consolation that
you will all be damned for your deeds of today." He turned
on his heel and stalked to the high three-legged stool by the
door.

Sheerin nodded to the columnist. "Take a seat next to him,
Theremon—just as a formality. Hey, Theremon!"

But the newspaperman didn't move. He had gone pale to
the lips. "Look at that!" The finger he pointed toward the sky
shook, and his voice was dry and cracked.

There was one simultaneous gasp as every eye followed the
pointing finger and, for one breathless moment, stared
frozenly.

Beta was chipped on one side!

The tiny bit of encroaching blackness was perhaps the
width of a fingernail, but to the staring watchers it magnified
itself into the crack of doom.

Only for a moment they watched, and after that there was
a shrieking confusion that was even shorter of duration and
which gave way to an orderly scurry of activity—each man
at his prescribed job. At the crucial moment there was no

time for emotion. The men were merely scientists with work to do. Even Aton had melted away.

Sheerin said prosaically, "First contact must have been made fifteen minutes ago. A little early, but pretty good considering the uncertainties involved in the calculation." He looked about him and then tiptoed to Theremon, who still remained staring out the window, and dragged him away gently.

"Aton is furious," he whispered, "so stay away. He missed first contact on account of this fuss with Latimer, and if you get in his way he'll have you thrown out the window."

Theremon nodded shortly and sat down. Sheerin stared in surprise at him.

"The devil, man," he exclaimed, "you're shaking."

"Eh?" Theremon licked dry lips and then tried to smile. "I don't feel very well, and that's a fact."

The psychologist's eyes hardened. "You're not losing your nerve?"

"No!" cried Theremon in a flash of indignation. "Give me a chance, will you? I haven't really believed this rigmarole—not way down beneath, anyway—till just this minute. Give me a chance to get used to the idea. You've been preparing yourself for two months or more."

"You're right, at that," replied Sheerin thoughtfully. "Listen! Have you got a family—parents, wife, children?"

Theremon shook his head. "You mean the Hideout, I suppose. No, you don't have to worry about that. I have a sister, but she's two thousand miles away. I don't even know her exact address."

"Well, then, what about yourself? You've got time to get there, and they're one short anyway, since I left. After all, you're not needed here, and you'd make a darned fine addition—"

Theremon looked at the other wearily. "You think I'm scared stiff, don't you? Well, get this, mister, I'm a newspaperman and I've been assigned to cover a story. I intend covering it."

There was a faint smile on the psychologist's face. "I see. Professional honor, is that it?"

"You might call it that. But, man, I'd give my right arm for another bottle of that sockeroo juice even half the size of the one you hogged. If ever a fellow needed a drink, I do."

He broke off. Sheerin was nudging him violently. "Do you hear that? Listen!"

Theremon followed the motion of the other's chin and

stared at the Cultist, who, oblivious to all about him, faced the window, a look of wild elation on his face, droning to himself the while in singsong fashion.

"What's he saying?" whispered the columnist.

"He's quoting 'Book of Revelations,' fifth chapter," replied Sheerin. Then, urgently, "Keep quiet and listen, I tell you."

The Cultist's voice had risen in a sudden increase of fervor:

" 'And it came to pass that in those days the sun, Beta, held lone vigil in the sky for ever longer periods as the revolutions passed; until such time as for full half a revolution, it alone, shrunken and cold, shone down upon Lagash.

" 'And men did assemble in the public squares and in the highways, there to debate and to marvel at the sight, for a strange depression had seized them. Their minds were troubled and their speech confused, for the souls of men awaited the coming of the Stars.

" 'And in the city of Trigon, at high noon, Vendret 2 came forth and said unto the men of Trigon, "Lo, ye sinners! Though ye scorn the ways of righteousness, yet will the time of reckoning come. Even now the Cave approaches to swallow Lagash; yea, and all it contains.

" 'And even as he spoke the lip of the Cave of Darkness passed the edge of Beta so that to all Lagash it was hidden from sight. Loud were the cries of men as it vanished, and great the fear of soul that fell upon them.

" 'It came to pass that the Darkness of the Cave fell upon Lagash, and there was no light on all the surface of Lagash. Men were even as blinded, nor could one man see his neighbor, though he felt his breath upon his face.

" 'And in this blackness there appeared the Stars, in countless numbers, and to the strains of ineffable music of a beauty so wondrous that the very leaves of the trees turned to tongues that cried out in wonder.

" 'And in that moment the souls of men departed from them, and their abandoned bodies became even as beasts; yea, even as brutes of the wild; so that through the blackened streets of the cities of Lagash they prowled with wild cries.

" 'From the Stars there then reached down the Heavenly Flame, and where it touched, the cities of Lagash flamed to utter destruction, so that of man and of the works of man nought remained.

" 'Even then—' "

There was a subtle change in Latimer's tone. His eyes had not shifted, but somehow he had become aware of the absorbed attention of the other two. Easily, without pausing for breath, the timbre of his voice shifted and the syllables became more liquid.

Theremon, caught by surprise, stared. The words seemed on the border of familiarity. There was an elusive shift in the accent, a tiny change in the vowel stress; nothing more—yet Latimer had become thoroughly unintelligible.

Sheerin smiled slyly. "He shifted to some old-cycle tongue, probably their traditional second cycle. That was the language in which the 'Book of Revelations' had originally been written, you know."

"It doesn't matter; I've heard enough." Theremon shoved his chair back and brushed his hair back with hands that no longer shook. "I feel much better now."

"You do?" Sheerin seemed mildly surprised.

"I'll say I do. I had a bad case of jitters just a while back. Listening to you and your gravitation and seeing that eclipse start almost finished me. But this"—he jerked a contemptuous thumb at the yellow-bearded Cultist—"*this* is the sort of thing my nurse used to tell me. I've been laughing at that sort of thing all my life. I'm not going to let it scare me *now*."

He drew a deep breath and said with a hectic gaiety, "But if I expect to keep on the good side of myself, I'm going to turn my chair away from the window."

Sheerin said, "Yes, but you'd better talk lower. Aton just lifted his head out of that box he's got it stuck into and gave you a look that should have killed you."

Theremon made a mouth. "I forgot about the old fellow." With elaborate care he turned the chair from the window, cast one distasteful look over his shoulder and said, "It has occurred to me that there must be considerable immunity against this Star madness."

The psychologist did not answer immediately. Beta was past its zenith now, and the square of bloody sunlight that outlined the window upon the floor had lifted into Sheerin's lap. He stared at its dusky color thoughtfully and then bent and squinted into the sun itself.

The chip in its side had grown to a black encroachment that covered a third of Beta. He shuddered, and when he straightened once more his florid cheeks did not contain quite as much color as they had had previously.

With a smile that was almost apologetic, he reversed his chair also. "There are probably two million people in Saro

City that are all trying to join the Cult at once in one gigantic revival." Then, ironically, "The Cult is in for an hour of
unexampled prosperity. I trust they'll make the most of it.
Now, what was it you said?"

"Just this. How do the Cultists manage to keep the 'Book
of Revelations' going from cycle to cycle, and how on Lagash
did it get written in the first place? There must have been
some sort of immunity, for if everyone had gone mad, who
would be left to write the book?"

Sheerin stared at his questioner ruefully. "Well, now,
young man, there isn't any eyewitness answer to that, but
we've got a few damned good notions as to what happened.
You see, there are three kinds of people who might remain
relatively unaffected. First, the very few who don't see the
Stars at all; the blind, those who drink themselves into a stupor at the beginning of the eclipse and remain so to the end.
We leave them out—because they aren't really witnesses.

"Then there are children below six, to whom the world as
a whole is too new and strange for them to be too frightened
at Stars and Darkness. They would be just another item in an
already surprising world. You see that, don't you?"

The other nodded doubtfully. "I suppose so."

"Lastly, there are those whose minds are too coarsely
grained to be entirely toppled. The very insensitive would be
scarcely affected—oh, such people as some of our older,
work-broken peasants. Well, the children would have fugitive
memories, and that, combined with the confused, incoherent
babblings of the half-mad morons, formed the basis for the
'Book of Revelations.'

"Naturally, the book was based, in the first place, on the
testimony of those least qualified to serve as historians; that
is, children and morons; and was probably extensively edited
and re-edited through the cycles."

"Do you suppose," broke in Theremon, "that they carried
the book through the cycles the way we're planning on handing on the secret of gravitation?"

Sheerin shrugged. "Perhaps, but their exact method is
unimportant. They do it, somehow. The point I was getting at
was that the book can't help but be a mass of distortion, even
if it is based on fact. For instance, do you remember the experiment with the holes in the roof that Faro and Yimot
tried—the one that didn't work?"

"Yes."

"You know why it didn't w—" He stopped and rose in

alarm, for Aton was approaching, his face a twisted mask of consternation. *"What's happened?"*

Aton drew him aside and Sheerin could feel the fingers on his elbow twitching.

"Not so loud!" Aton's voice was low and tortured. "I've just gotten word from the Hideout on the private line."

Sheerin broke in anxiously, "They are in trouble?"

"Not *they*." Aton stressed the pronoun significantly. "They sealed themselves off just a while ago, and they're going to stay buried till day after tomorrow. They're safe. But the city, Sheerin—it's a shambles. You have no idea—" He was having difficulty in speaking.

"Well?" snapped Sheerin impatiently. "What of it? It will get worse. What are you shaking about?" Then, suspiciously, "How do you feel?"

Aton's eyes sparkled angrily at the insinuation, and then faded to anxiety once more. "You don't understand. The Cultists are active. They're rousing the people to storm the Observatory—promising them immediate entrance into grace, promising them salvation, promising them anything. What are we to do, Sheerin?"

Sheerin's head bent, and he stared in long abstraction at his toes. He tapped his chin with one knuckle, then looked up and said crisply, "Do? What is there to do? Nothing at all! Do the men know of this?"

"No, of course not!"

"Good! Keep it that way. How long till totality?"

"Not quite an hour."

"There's nothing to do but gamble. It will take time to organize any really formidable mob, and it will take more time to get them out here. We're a good five miles from the city—"

He glared out the window, down the slopes to where the farmed patches gave way to clumps of white houses in the suburbs; down to where the metropolis itself was a blur on the horizon—a mist in the waning blaze of Beta.

He repeated without turning, "It will take time. Keep on working and pray that totality comes first."

Beta was cut in half, the line of division pushing a slight concavity into the still-bright portion of the Sun. It was like a gigantic eyelid shutting slantwise over the light of a world.

The faint clatter of the room in which he stood faded into oblivion, and he sensed only the thick silence of the fields outside. The very insects seemed frightened mute. And things were dim.

He jumped at the voice in his ear. Theremon said, "Is something wrong?"

"Eh? Er—no. Get back to the chair. We're in the way." They slipped back to their corner, but the psychologist did not speak for a time. He lifted a finger and loosened his collar. He twisted his neck back and forth but found no relief. He looked up suddenly.

"Are you having any difficulty in breathing?"

The newspaperman opened his eyes wide and drew two or three long breaths. "No. Why?"

"I looked out the window too long, I suppose. The dimness got me. Difficulty in breathing is one of the first symptoms of a claustrophobic attack."

Theremon drew another long breath. "Well, it hasn't got me yet. Say, here's another of the fellows."

Beenay had interposed his bulk between the light and the pair in the corner, and Sheerin squinted up at him anxiously. "Hello, Beenay."

The astronomer shifted his weight to the other foot and smiled feebly. "You won't mind if I sit down awhile and join in on the talk? My cameras are set, and there's nothing to do till totality." He paused and eyed the Cultist, who fifteen minutes earlier had drawn a small, skin-bound book from his sleeve and had been poring intently over it ever since. "That rat hasn't been making trouble, has he?"

Sheerin shook his head. His shoulders were thrown back and he frowned his concentration as he forced himself to breathe regularly. He said, "Have you had any trouble breathing, Beenay?"

Beenay sniffed the air in his turn. "It doesn't seem stuffy to me."

"A touch of claustrophobia," explained Sheerin apologetically.

"Oh-h-h! It worked itself differently with me. I get the impression that my eyes are going back on me. Things seem to blur and—well, nothing is clear. And it's cold, too."

"Oh, it's cold, all right. That's no illusion." Theremon grimaced. "My toes feel as if I'd been shipping them cross country in a refrigerating car."

"What we need," put in Sheerin, "is to keep our minds busy with extraneous affairs. I was telling you a while ago,

Theremon, why Faro's experiments with the holes in the roof came to nothing."

"You were just beginning," replied Theremon. He encircled a knee with both arms and nuzzled his chin against it.

"Well, as I started to say, they were misled by taking the 'Book of Revelations' literally. There probably wasn't any sense in attaching any physical significance to the Stars. It might be, you know, that in the presence of total Darkness, the mind finds it absolutely necessary to create light. This illusion of light might be all the Stars there really are."

"In other words," interposed Theremon, "you mean the Stars are the results of the madness and not one of the causes. Then, what good will Beenay's photographs be?"

"To prove that it is an illusion, maybe; or to prove the opposite, for all I know. Then again—"

But Beenay had drawn his chair closer, and there was an expression of sudden enthusiasm on his face. "Say, I'm glad you two got on to this subject." His eyes narrowed and he lifted one finger. "I've been thinking about these Stars and I've got a really cute notion. Of course, it's strictly ocean foam, and I'm not trying to advance it seriously, but I think it's interesting. Do you want to hear it?"

He seemed half reluctant, but Sheerin leaned back and said, "Go ahead! I'm listening."

"Well, then, supposing there were other suns in the universe." He broke off a little bashfully. "I mean suns that are so far away that they're too dim to see. It sounds as if I've been reading some of that fantastic fiction, I suppose."

"Not necessarily. Still, isn't that possibility eliminated by the fact that, according to the Law of Gravitation, they would make themselves evident by their attractive forces?"

"Not if they were far enough off," rejoined Beenay, "really far off—maybe as much as four light years, or even more. We'd never be able to detect perturbations then, because they'd be too small. Say that there were a lot of suns that far off; a dozen or two, maybe."

Theremon whistled melodiously. "What an idea for a good Sunday supplement article. Two dozen suns in a universe eight light years across. Wow! That would shrink our universe into insignificance. The readers would eat it up."

"Only an idea," said Beenay with a grin, "but you see the point. During eclipse, these dozen suns would become visible, because there'd be no *real* sunlight to drown them out. Since they're so far off, they'd appear small, like so many little marbles. Of course, the Cultists talk of millions of Stars, but that's probably exaggeration. There just isn't any place in the universe you could put a million suns—unless they touch one another."

Sheerin had listened with gradually increasing interest. "You've hit something there, Beenay. And exaggeration is just exactly what would happen. Our minds, as you probably know, can't grasp directly any number higher than five; above that there is only the concept of 'many.' A dozen would become a million just like that. A damn good idea!"

"And I've got another cute little notion," Beenay said. "Have you ever thought what a simple problem gravitation would be if only you had a sufficiently simple system? Supposing you had a universe in which there was a planet with only one sun. The planet would travel in a perfect eclipse and the exact nature of the gravitational force would be so evident it could be accepted as an axiom. Astronomers on such a world would start off with gravity probably before they even invent the telescope. Naked-eye observation would be enough."

"But would such a system be dynamically stable?" questioned Sheerin doubtfully.

"Sure! They call it the 'one-and-one' case. It's been worked out mathematically, but it's the philosophical implications that interest me."

"It's nice to think about," admitted Sheerin, "as a pretty abstraction—like a perfect gas or absolute zero."

"Of course," continued Beenay, "there's the catch that life would be impossible on such a planet. It wouldn't get enough heat and light, and if it rotated there would be total Darkness half of each day. You couldn't expect life—which is fundamentally dependent upon light—to develop under those conditions. Besides—"

Sheerin's chair went over backward as he sprang to his feet in a rude interruption. "Aton's brought out the lights."

Beenay said, "Huh," turned to stare, and then grinned half-way around his head in open relief.

There were half a dozen foot-long, inch-thick rods cradled in Aton's arms. He glared over them at the assembled staff members.

"Get back to work, all of you. Sheerin, come here and help me!"

Sheerin trotted to the older man's side and, one by one, in utter silence, the two adjusted the rods in makeshift metal holders suspended from the walls.

With the air of one carrying through the most sacred item of a religious ritual, Sheerin scraped a large, clumsy match into spluttering life and passed it to Aton, who carried the flame to the upper end of one of the rods.

It hesitated there a while, playing futilely about the tip, until a sudden, crackling flare cast Aton's lined face into yellow highlights. He withdrew the match and a spontaneous cheer rattled the window.

The rod was topped by six inches of wavering flame! Methodically, the other rods were lighted, until six independent fires turned the rear of the room yellow.

The light was dim, dimmer even than the tenuous sunlight. The flames reeled crazily, giving birth to drunken, swaying shadows. The torches smoked devilishly and smelled like a bad day in the kitchen. But they emitted yellow light.

There is something to yellow light—after four hours of somber, dimming Beta. Even Latimer had lifted his eyes from his book and stared in wonder.

Sheerin warmed his hands at the nearest, regardless of the soot that gathered upon them in a fine, gray powder, and muttered ecstatically to himself. "Beautiful! Beautiful! I never realized before what a wonderful color yellow is."

But Theremon regarded the torches suspiciously. He wrinkled his nose at the rancid odor, and said, "What are those things?"

"Wood," said Sheerin shortly.

"Oh, no, they're not. They aren't burning. The top inch is charred and the flame just keeps shooting up out of nothing."

"That's the beauty of it. This is a really efficient artificial-light mechanism. We made a few hundred of them, but most went to the Hideout, of course. You see"—he turned and wiped his blackened hands upon his handkerchief—"you take the pithy core of coarse water reeds, dry them thoroughly and soak them in animal grease. Then you set fire to it and the grease burns, little by little. These torches will burn for almost half an hour without stopping. Ingenious, isn't it? It was developed by one of our own young men at Saro University."

After the momentary sensation, the dome had quieted. Latimer had carried his chair directly beneath a torch and continued reading, lips moving in the monotonous recital of invocations to the Stars. Beenay had drifted away to his cameras once more, and Theremon seized the opportunity to add to his notes on the article he was going to write for the

Saro City *Chronicle* the next day—a procedure he had been following for the last two hours in a perfectly methodical, perfectly conscientious and, as he was well aware, perfectly meaningless fashion.

But, as the gleam of amusement in Sheerin's eyes indicated, careful note taking occupied his mind with something other than the fact that the sky was gradually turning a horrible deep purple-red, as if it were one gigantic, freshly peeled beet; and so it fulfilled its purpose.

The air grew, somehow, denser. Dusk, like a palpable entity, entered the room, and the dancing circle of yellow light about the torches etched itself into ever-sharper distinction against the gathering grayness beyond. There was the odor of smoke and the presence of little chuckling sounds that the torches made as they burned; the soft pad of one of the men circling the table at which he worked, on hesitant tiptoes; the occasional indrawn breath of someone trying to retain composure in a world that was retreating into the shadow.

It was Theremon who first heard the extraneous noise. It was a vague, unorganized *impression* of sound that would have gone unnoticed but for the dead silence that prevailed within the dome.

The newsman sat upright and replaced his notebook. He held his breath and listened; then, with considerable reluctance, threaded his way between the solarscope and one of Beenay's cameras and stood before the window.

The silence ripped to fragments at his startled shout:

"Sheerin!"

Work stopped! The psychologist was at his side in a moment. Aton joined him. Even Yimot 70, high in his little lean-back seat at the eyepiece of the gigantic solarscope, paused and looked downward.

Outside, Beta was a mere smoldering splinter, taking one last desperate look at Lagash. The eastern horizon, in the direction of the city was lost in Darkness, and the road from Saro to the Observatory was a dull-red line bordered on both sides by wooded tracts, the trees of which had somehow lost individuality and merged into a continuous shadowy mass.

But it was the highway itself that held attention, for along it there surged another, and infinitely menacing, shadowy mass.

Aton cried in a cracked voice, "The madmen from the city! They've come!"

"How long to totality?" demanded Sheerin.

"Fifteen minutes, but . . . but they'll be here in five."

"Never mind, keep the men working. We'll hold them off. This place is built like a fortress. Aton, keep an eye on our young Cultist just for luck. Theremon, come with me."

Sheerin was out the door, and Theremon was at his heels. The stairs stretched below them in tight, circular sweeps about the central shaft, fading into a dank and dreary grayness.

The first momentum of their rush had carried them fifty feet down, so that the dim, flickering yellow from the open door of the dome had disappeared and both up above and down below the same dusky shadow crushed in upon them.

Sheerin paused, and his pudgy hand clutched at his chest. His eyes bulged and his voice was a dry cough. "I can't . . . breathe . . . go down . . . yourself. Close all doors—"

Theremon took a few downward steps, then turned. "Wait! Can you hold out a minute?" He was panting himself. The air passed in and out his lungs like so much molasses, and there was a little germ of screeching panic in his mind at the thought of making his way into the mysterious Darkness below by himself.

Theremon, after all, was afraid of the dark!

"Stay here," he said. "I'll be back in a second." He dashed upward two steps at a time, heart pounding—not altogether from the exertion—tumbled into the dome and snatched a torch from its holder. It was foul smelling, and the smoke smarted his eyes almost blind, but he clutched that torch as if he wanted to kiss it for joy, and its flame streamed backward as he hurtled down the stairs again.

Sheerin opened his eyes and moaned as Theremon bent over him. Theremon shook him roughly. "All right, get a hold on yourself. We've got light."

He held the torch at tiptoe height and, propping the tottering psychologist by an elbow, made his way downward in the middle of the protecting circle of illumination.

The offices on the ground floor still possessed what light there was, and Theremon felt the horror about him relax.

"Here," he said brusquely, and passed the torch to Sheerin. "You can hear *them* outside."

And they could. Little scraps of hoarse, wordless shouts.

But Sheerin was right; the Observatory was built like a fortress. Erected in the last century, when the neo-Gavottian style of architecture was at its ugly height, it had been designed for stability and durability, rather than for beauty.

The windows were protected by the grillework of inch-thick iron bars sunk deep into the concrete sills. The walls were solid masonry that an earthquake couldn't have touched, and the main door was a huge oaken slab reinforced with iron at the strategic points. Theremon shot the bolts and they slid shut with a dull clang.

At the other end of the corridor, Sheerin cursed weakly. He pointed to the lock of the back door which had been neatly jimmied into uselessness.

"That must be how Latimer got in," he said.

"Well, don't stand there," cried Theremon impatiently. "Help drag up the furniture—and keep that torch out of my eyes. The smoke's killing me."

He slammed the heavy table up against the door as he spoke, and in two minutes had built a barricade which made up for what it lacked in beauty and symmetry by the sheer inertia of its massiveness.

Somewhere, dimly, far off, they could hear the battering of naked fists upon the door; and the screams and yells from outside had a sort of half reality.

That mob had set off from Saro City with only two things in mind: the attainment of Cultist salvation by the destruction of the Observatory, and a maddening fear that all but paralyzed them. There was no time to think of ground cars, or of weapons, or of leadership, or even of organization. They made for the Observatory on foot and assaulted it with bare hands.

And now that they were there, the last flash of Beta, the last ruby-red drop of flame, flickered feebly over a humanity that had left only stark, universal fear!

Theremon groaned, "Let's get back to the dome!"

In the dome, only Yimot, at the solarscope, had kept his place. The rest were clustered about the cameras, and Beenay was giving his instructions in a hoarse, strained voice.

"Get it straight, all of you. I'm snapping Beta just before totality and changing the plate. That will leave one of you to each camera. You all know about . . . about times of exposure—"

There was a breathless murmur of agreement.

Beenay passed a hand over his eyes. "Are the torches still burning? Never mind, I see them!" He was leaning hard against the back of a chair. "Now remember, don't . . . don't try to look for good shots. Don't waste time trying to get t-two stars at a time in the scope field. One is enough. And

. . . and if you feel yourself going, *get away from the camera.*"

At the door, Sheerin whispered to Theremon, "Take me to Aton. I don't see him."

The newsman did not answer immediately. The vague forms of the astronomers wavered and blurred, and the torches overhead had become only yellow splotches.

"It's dark," he whimpered.

Sheerin held out his hand, "Aton." He stumbled forward. "Aton!"

Theremon stepped after and seized his arm. "Wait, I'll take you." Somehow he made his way across the room. He closed his eyes against the Darkness and his mind against the chaos within it.

No one heard them or paid attention to them. Sheerin stumbled against the wall. "Aton!"

The psychologist felt shaking hands touching him, then withdrawing, and a voice muttering, "Is that you, Sheerin?"

"Aton!" He strove to breathe normally. "Don't worry about the mob. The place will hold them off."

Latimer, the Cultist, rose to his feet, and his face twisted in desperation. His word was pledged, and to break it would mean placing his soul in mortal peril. Yet that word had been forced from him and had not been given freely. The Stars would come soon; he could not stand by and allow— And yet his word was pledged.

Beenay's face was dimly flushed as it looked upward at Beta's last ray, and Latimer, seeing him bend over his camera, made his decision. His nails cut the flesh of his palms as he tensed himself.

He staggered crazily as he started his rush. There was nothing before him but shadows; the very floor beneath his feet lacked substance. And then someone was upon him and he went down with clutching fingers at his throat.

He doubled his knee and drove it hard into his assailant. "Let me up or I'll kill you."

Theremon cried out sharply and muttered through a blinding haze of pain, "You double-crossing rat!"

The newsman seemed conscious of everything at once. He heard Beenay croak, "I've got it. At your cameras, men!" and then there was the strange awareness that the last thread of sunlight had thinned out and snapped.

Simultaneously he heard one last choking gasp from Beenay, and a queer little cry from Sheerin, a hysterical giggle that cut off in a rasp—and a sudden silence, a strange, deadly silence from outside.

And Latimer had gone limp in his loosening grasp. Theremon peered into the Cultist's eyes and saw the blankness of them, staring upward, mirroring the feeble yellow of the torches. He saw the bubble of froth upon Latimer's lips and heard the low animal whimper in Latimer's throat.

With the slow fascination of fear, he lifted himself on one arm and turned his eyes toward the blood-curdling blackness of the window.

Through it shone the Stars!

Not Earth's feeble thirty-six hundred Stars visible to the eye—Lagash was in the center of a giant cluster. Thirty thousand mighty suns shown down in a soul-searing splendor that was more frighteningly cold in its awful indifference than the bitter wind that shivered across the cold, horribly bleak world.

Theremon staggered to his feet, his throat constricting him to breathlessness, all the muscles of his body writhing in a tensity of terror and sheer fear beyond bearing. He was going mad, and knew it, and somewhere deep inside a bit of sanity was screaming, struggling to fight off the hopeless flood of black terror. It was very horrible to go mad and know that you were doing mad—to know that in a little minute you would be here physically and yet all the real essence would be dead and drowned in the black madness. For this was the Dark—the Dark and the Cold and the Doom. The bright walls of the universe were shattered and their awful black fragments were falling down to crush and squeeze and obliterate him.

He jostled someone crawling on hands and knees, but stumbled somehow over him. Hands groping at his tortured throat, he limped toward the flame of the torches that filled all his mad vision.

"Light!" he screamed.

Aton, somewhere, was crying, whimpering horribly like a terribly frightened child. "Stars—all the Stars—we didn't know at all. We didn't know anything. We thought six stars is a universe is something the Stars didn't notice is Darkness forever and ever and ever and the walls are breaking in and we didn't know we couldn't know and anything—"

Someone clawed at the torch, and it fell and snuffed out. In the instant, the awful splendor of the indifferent Stars leaped nearer to them.

On the horizon outside the window, in the direction of Saro City, a crimson glow began growing, strengthening in brightness, that was not the glow of a sun.

The long night had come again.

A GNOME THERE WAS

Unknown
October

by Henry Kuttner (1914-1958)
and
C. L. Moore (1911-   )

> *After their marriage in 1940, it was impossible
> to tell who wrote what—it didn't matter what name
> they used—Kuttner, Moore, "Lewis Padgett," or
> "Lawrence O'Donnell." They didn't know them-
> selves, although there were a few exceptions. They
> produced some of the most important science fic-
> tion and fantasy of the forties, including this won-
> derful tale from that rich and lamented reservoir of
> riches, Unknown (a.k.a. Unknown Worlds).*
>
> *There is a book on the subject of Gnomes on the
> best-seller lists as these words are written, but it is
> doubtful if any of them are quite like the creatures
> in this delightful story.*

(Henry Kuttner died in February 1958, and Cyril
Kornbluth died a month later, and that double loss rocked
the science fiction world. There hasn't been such a pair of
deaths in successive months since and I hope there never is.
Kuttner was so different from Kornbluth. Kuttner was a
prime example of a man whose personality was *not* like his
stories and Kornbluth a man whose personality *was*. The coincidence of both having names starting with K was striking
and, considering the superstition that deaths come in threes, I
was told that Damon Knight passed an uncomfortable few
months there.—I.A.)

Tim Crockett should never have sneaked into the mine on
Dornsef Mountain. What is winked at in California may have
disastrous results in the coal mines of Pennsylvania. Especially when gnomes are involved.

Not that Tim Crockett knew about the gnomes. He was

just investigating conditions among the lower classes, to use his own rather ill-chosen words. He was one of a group of southern Californians who had decided that labor needed them. They were wrong. They needed labor—at least eight hours of it a day.

Crockett, like his colleagues, considered the laborer a combination of a gorilla and The Man with the Hoe, probably numbering the Kallikaks among his ancestors. He spoke fierily of downtrodden minorities, wrote incendiary articles for the group's organ, *Earth,* and deftly maneuvered himself out of entering his father's law office as a clerk. He had, he said, a mission. Unfortunately, he got little sympathy from either the workers or their oppressors.

A psychologist could have analyzed Crockett easily enough. He was a tall, thin, intense-looking young man, with rather beady little eyes, and a nice taste in neckties. All he needed was a vigorous kick in the pants.

But definitely not administered by a gnome!

He was junketing through the country, on his father's money, investigating labor conditions, to the profound annoyance of such laborers as he encountered. It was with this idea in mind that he surreptitiously got into the Ajax coal mine— or, at least, one shaft of it—after disguising himself as a miner and rubbing his face well with black dust. Going down in the lift, he looked singularly untidy in the midst of a group of well-scrubbed faces. Miners look dirty only after a day's work.

Dornsef Mountain is honeycombed, but not with the shafts of the Ajax Company. The gnomes have ways of blocking their tunnels when humans dig too close. The whole place was a complete confusion to Crockett. He let himself drift along with the others, till they began to work. A filled car rumbled past on its tracks. Crockett hesitated, and then sidled over to a husky specimen who seemed to have the marks of a great sorrow stamped on his face.

"Look," he said, "I want to talk to you."

"Inglis?" asked the other inquiringly. "Viskey. Chin. Vine. Hell."

Having thus demonstrated his somewhat incomplete command of English, he bellowed hoarsely with laughter and returned to work, ignoring the baffled Crockett, who turned away to find another victim. But this section of the mine seemed deserted. Another loaded car rumbled past, and Crockett decided to see where it came from. He found out, after banging his head painfully and falling flat at least five times.

It came from a hole in the wall. Crockett entered it, and simultaneously heard a hoarse cry from behind him. The unknown requested Crockett to come back.

"So I can break your slab-sided neck," he promised, adding a stream of sizzling profanity. "Come outa there!"

Crockett cast one glance back, saw a gorillalike shadow lurching after him, and instantly decided that his stratagem had been discovered. The owners of the Ajax mine had sent a strong-arm man to murder him—or, at least, to beat him to a senseless pulp. Terror lent wings to Crockett's flying feet. He rushed on, frantically searching for a side tunnel in which he might lose himself. The bellowing from behind reechoed against the walls. Abruptly Crockett caught a significant sentence clearly.

"—before that dynamite goes off!"

It was at that exact moment that the dynamite went off.

Crockett, however, did not know it. He discovered, quite briefly, that he was flying. Then he was halted, with painful suddenness, by the roof. After that he knew nothing at all, till he recovered to find a head regarding him steadfastly.

It was not a comforting sort of head—not one at which you would instinctively clutch for companionship. It was, in fact, a singularly odd, if not actually revolting, head. Crockett was too much engrossed with staring at it to realize that he was actually seeing in the dark.

How long had he been unconscious? For some obscure reason Crockett felt that it had been quite a while. The explosion had—what?

Buried him here behind a fallen roof of rock? Crockett would have felt little better had he known that he was in a used-up shaft, valueless now, which had been abandoned long since. The miners, blasting to open a new shaft, had realized that the old one would be collapsed, but that didn't matter.

Except to Tim Crockett.

He blinked, and when he reopened his eyes, the head had vanished. This was a relief. Crockett immediately decided the unpleasant thing had been a delusion. Indeed, it was difficult to remember what it had looked like. There was only a vague impression of a turnip-shaped outline, large, luminous eyes, and an incredibly broad slit of a mouth.

Crockett sat up, groaning. Where was this curious silvery radiance coming from? It was like daylight on a foggy afternoon, coming from nowhere in particular, and throwing no shadows. "Radium," thought Crockett, who knew very little of mineralogy.

He was in a shaft that stretched ahead into dimness till it made a sharp turn perhaps fifty feet away. Behind him—behind him the roof had fallen. Instantly Crockett began to experience difficulty in breathing. He flung himself upon the rubbly mound, tossing rocks frantically here and there, gasping and making hoarse, inarticulate noises.

He became aware, presently, of his hands. His movements slowed till he remained perfectly motionless, in a half-crouching posture, glaring at the large, knobbly, and surprising objects that grew from his wrists. Could he, during his period of unconsciousness, have acquired mittens? Even as the thought came to him, Crockett realized that no mittens ever knitted resembled in the slightest degree what he had a right to believe to be his hands. They twitched slightly.

Possibly they were caked with mud—no. It wasn't that. His hands had—altered. They were huge, gnarled, brown objects, like knotted oak roots. Sparse black hairs sprouted on their backs. The nails were definitely in need of a manicure—preferably with a chisel.

Crockett looked down at himself. He made soft cheeping noises, indicative of disbelief. He had squat bow legs, thick and strong, and no more than two feet long—less, if anything. Uncertain with disbelief, Crockett explored his body. It had changed—certainly not for the better.

He was slightly more than four feet high, and about three feet wide, with a barrel chest, enormous splay feet, stubby thick legs, and no neck whatsoever. He was wearing red sandals, blue shorts, and a red tunic which left his lean but sinewy arms bare. His head—

Turnip-shaped. The mouth—*Yipe!* Crockett had inadvertently put his fist clear into it. He withdrew the offending hand instantly, stared around in a dazed fashion, and collapsed on the ground. It couldn't be happening. It was quite impossible. Hallucinations. He was dying of asphyxiation, and delusions were preceding his death.

Crockett shut his eyes, again convinced that his lungs were laboring for breath. "I'm dying," he said. "I c-can't breathe."

A contemptuous voice said, "I hope you don't think you're breathing *air!*"

"I'm n-not—" Crockett didn't finish the sentence. His eyes popped again. He was hearing things.

He heard it again. "You're a singularly lousy specimen of gnome," the voice said. "But under Nid's law we can't pick and choose. Still, you won't be put to digging hard metals, I can see that. Anthracite's about your speed. What're you staring at? You're *very* much uglier than I am."

Crockett, endeavoring to lick his dry lips, was horrified to discover the end of his moist tongue dragging limply over his eyes. He whipped it back, with a loud smacking noise, and managed to sit up. Then he remained perfectly motionless, staring.

The head had reappeared. This time there was a body under it.

"I'm Gru Magru," said the head chattily. "You'll be given a gnomic name, of course, unless your own is guttural enough. What is it?"

"Crockett," the man responded, in a stunned, automatic manner.

"Hey?"

"Crockett."

"Stop making noises like a frog and—oh, I see. Grockett. Fair enough. Now get up and follow me or I'll kick the pants off you."

But Crockett did not immediately rise. He was watching Gru Magru—obviously a gnome. Short, squat, and stunted, the being's figure resembled a bulging little barrel, topped by an inverted turnip. The hair grew up thickly to a peak—the root, as it were. In the turnip face was a loose, immense slit of a mouth, a button of a nose, and two very large eyes.

"Get *up!*" Gru Magru said.

This time Crockett obeyed, but the effort exhausted him completely. If he moved again, he thought, he would go mad. It would be just as well. Gnomes—

Gru Magru planted a large splay foot where it would do the most good, and Crockett described an arc which ended at a jagged boulder fallen from the roof. "Get up," the gnome said, with gratuitous bad temper, "or I'll kick you again. It's bad enough to have an outlying prospect patrol, where I might run into a man any time, without—*Up!* Or—"

Crockett got up. Gru Magru took his arm and impelled him into the depths of the tunnel.

"Well, you're a gnome now," he said. "It's the Nid law. Sometimes I wonder if it's worth the trouble. But I suppose it is—since gnomes can't propagate, and the average population has to be kept up somehow."

"I want to die," Crockett said wildly.

Gru Magru laughed. "Gnomes *can't* die. They're immortal, till the Day. Judgment Day, I mean."

"You're not logical," Crockett pointed out, as though by disproving one factor he could automatically disprove the whole fantastic business. "You're either flesh and blood and have to die eventually, or you're not, and then you're not real."

"Oh, we're flesh and blood, right enough," Gru Magru said. "But we're not mortal. There's a distinction. Not that I've anything against some mortals," he hastened to explain. "Bats, now—and owls—they're fine. But men!" He shuddered. "No gnome can stand the sight of a man."

Crockett clutched at a straw. "I'm a man."

"You were, you mean," Gru said. "Not a very good specimen, either, for my ore. But you're a gnome now. It's the Nid law."

"You keep talking about the Nid law," Crockett complained.

"Of course you don't understand," said Gru Magru, in a patronizing fashion. "It's this way. Back in ancient times, it was decreed that if any humans got lost in underearth, a tithe of them would be transformed into gnomes. The first gnome emperor, Podrang the Third, arranged that. He saw that fairies could kidnap human children and keep them, and spoke to the authorities about it. Said it was unfair. So when miners and such-like are lost underneath, a tithe of them are transformed into gnomes and join us. That's what happened to you. See?"

"No," Crockett said weakly. "Look. You said Podrang was the first gnome emperor. Why was he called Podrang the Third?"

"No time for questions," Gru Magru snapped. "Hurry!"

He was almost running now, dragging the wretched Crockett after him. The new gnome had not yet mastered his rather unusual limbs, and, due to the extreme wideness of his sandals, he was continually stepping on his own feet. Once he trod heavily on his right hand, but after that learned to keep his arms bent and close to his sides. The walls, illuminated with that queer silvery radiance, spun past dizzily.

"W-what's that light?" Crockett managed to gasp. "Where's it coming from?"

"Light?" Gru Magru inquired. "It isn't light."

"Well, it isn't dark—"

"Of course it's dark," the gnome snapped. "How could we see if it wasn't dark?"

There was no possible answer to this, except, Crockett thought wildly, a frantic shriek. And he needed all his breath for running. They were in a labyrinth now, turning and twisting and doubling through innumerable tunnels, and Crockett knew he could never retrace his steps. He regretted having left the scene of the cave-in. But how could he have helped doing so?

"Hurry!" Gru Magru urged. "Hurry!"

"Why?" Crockett got out breathlessly.

"There's a fight going on!" the gnome said.

Just then they rounded a corner and almost blundered into the fight. A seething mass of gnomes filled the tunnel, battling with frantic fury. Red and blue pants and tunics moved in swift patchwork frenzy; turnip heads popped up and down vigorously. It was apparently a free-for-all.

"See!" Gru gloated. "A fight! I could smell it six tunnels away. Oh, a beauty!" He ducked as a malicious-looking little gnome sprang out of the huddle to seize a rock and hurl it with vicious accuracy. The missile missed its mark, and Gru, neglecting his captive, immediately hurled himself upon the little gnome, bore him down on the cave floor, and began to beat his head against it. Both parties shrieked at the tops of their voices, which were lost in the deafening din that resounded through the tunnel.

"Oh—my," Crockett said weakly. He stood staring, which was a mistake. A very large gnome emerged from the pile, seized Crockett by the feet, and threw him away. The terrified inadvertent projectile sailed through the tunnel to crash heavily into something which said, *"Whoo-oof!"* There was a tangle of malformed arms and legs.

Crockett arose to find that he had downed a vicious-looking gnome with flaming red hair and four large diamond buttons on his tunic. This repulsive creature lay motionless, out for the count. Crockett took stock of his injuries—there were none. His new body was hardy, anyway.

"You saved me!" said a new voice. It belonged to a—lady gnome. Crockett decided that if there was anything uglier than a gnome, it was the female of the species. The creature stood crouching just behind him, clutching a large rock in one capable hand.

Crockett ducked.

"I won't hurt you," the other howled above the din that filled the passage. "You saved me! Mugza was trying to pull my ears off—oh! He's waking up!"

The red-haired gnome was indeed recovering consciousness. His first act was to draw up his feet and, without rising, kick Crockett clear across the tunnel. The feminine gnome immediately sat on Mugza's chest and pounded his head with the rock till he subsided.

Then she arose. "You're not hurt? Good! I'm Brockle Buhn. . . . Oh, look! He'll have his head off in a minute!"

Crockett turned to see that his erstwhile guide, Gru Magru, was gnomefully tugging at the head of an unidentified opponent, attempting, apparently, to twist it clear off. "What's it all about?" Crockett howled. "Uh—Brockle Buhn! *Brockle Buhn!*"

She turned unwillingly. "What?"

"The fight! What started it?"

"I did," she explained. "I said, 'Let's have a fight.' "

"Oh, that was all?"

"Then we started." Brockle Buhn nodded. "What's your name?"

"Crockett."

"You're new here, aren't you? Oh—I know. You were a human being!" Suddenly a new light appeared in her bulging eyes. "Grockett, maybe you can tell me something. What's a kiss?"

"A—kiss?" Crockett repeated, in a baffled manner.

"Yes. I was listening inside a knoll once, and heard two human beings talking—male and female, by their voices. I didn't dare look at them, of course, but the man asked the woman for a kiss."

"Oh," Crockett said, rather blankly. "He asked for a kiss, eh?"

"And then there was a smacking noise and the woman said it was wonderful. I've wondered ever since. Because if any gnome asked me for a kiss, I wouldn't know what he meant."

"Gnomes don't kiss?" Crockett asked in a perfunctory way.

"Gnomes dig," said Brockle Buhn. "And we eat. I like to eat. Is a kiss like mud soup?"

"Well, not exactly." Somehow Crockett managed to explain the mechanics of osculation.

The gnome remained silent, pondering deeply. At last she said, with the air of one bestowing mud soup upon a hungry applicant, "I'll give you a kiss."

Crockett had a nightmare picture of his whole head being engulfed in that enormous maw. He backed away. "N-no," he got out. "I—I'd rather not."

"Then let's fight," said Brockle Buhn, without rancor, and

swung a knotted fist which smacked painfully athwart Crockett's ear. "Oh, no," she said regretfully, turning away. "The fight's over. It wasn't very long, was it?"

Crockett, rubbing his mangled ear, saw that in every direction gnomes were picking themselves up and hurrying off about their business. They seemed to have forgotten all about the recent conflict. The tunnel was once more silent, save for the pad-padding of gnomes' feet on the rock. Gru Magru came over, grinning happily.

"Hello, Brockle Buhn," he greeted. "A good fight. Who's this?" He looked down at the prostrate body of Mugza, the red-haired gnome.

"Mugza," said Brockle Buhn. "He's still out. Let's kick him."

They proceeded to do it with vast enthusiasm, while Crockett watched and decided never to allow himself to be knocked unconscious. It definitely wasn't safe. At last, however, Gru Magru tired of the sport and took Crockett by the arm again. "Come along," he said, and they sauntered along the tunnel, leaving Brockle Buhn jumping up and down on the senseless Mugza's stomach.

"You don't seem to mind hitting people when they're knocked out," Crockett hazarded.

"It's *much* more fun," Gru said happily. "That way you can tell just where you want to hit 'em. Come along. You'll have to be inducted. Another day, another gnome. Keeps the population stable," he explained, and fell to humming a little song.

"Look," Crockett said. "I just thought of something. You say human beings are turned into gnomes to keep the population stable. But if gnomes don't die, doesn't that mean that there are more gnomes now than ever? The population keeps rising, doesn't it?"

"Be still," Gru Magru commanded. "I'm singing."

It was a singularly tuneless song. Crockett, his thoughts veering madly, wondered if the gnomes had a national anthem. Probably "Rock Me to Sleep." Oh, well.

"We're going to see the Emperor," Gru said at last. "He always sees the new gnomes. You'd better make a good impression, or he'll put you to placer-mining lava."

"Uh—" Crockett glanced down at his grimy tunic. "Hadn't I better clean up a bit? That fight made me a mess."

"It wasn't the fight," Gru said insultingly. "What's wrong with you, anyway? I don't see anything amiss."

"My clothes—they're dirty."

"Don't worry about that," said the other. "It's good filthy dirt, isn't it? Here!" He halted, and, stooping, seized a handful of dust, which he rubbed into Crockett's face and hair. "That'll fix you up."

"I—*pffht!* . . . Thanks . . . *pffh!*" said the newest gnome. "I hope I'm dreaming. Because if I'm not—" He didn't finish. Crockett was feeling most unwell.

They went through a labyrinth, far under Dornsef Mountain, and emerged at last in a bare, huge chamber with a throne of rock at one end of it. A small gnome was sitting on the throne paring his toenails. "Bottom of the day to you," Gru said. "Where's the Emperor?"

"Taking a bath," said the other. "I hope he drowns. Mud, mud, mud—morning, noon, and night. First it's too hot. Then it's too cold. Then it's too thick. I work my fingers to the bone mixing his mud baths, and all I get is a kick," the small gnome continued plaintively. "There's such a thing as being *too* dirty. Three mud baths a day—that's carrying it too far. And never a thought for me! Oh, no. I'm a mud puppy, that's what I am. He called me that today. Said there were lumps in the mud. Well, why not? That damned loam we've been getting is enough to turn a worm's stomach. You'll find His Majesty in there," the little gnome finished, jerking his foot toward an archway in the wall.

Crockett was dragged into the next room, where, in a sunken bath filled with steaming, brown mud, a very fat gnome sat, only his eyes discernible through the oozy coating that covered him. He was filling his hands with mud and letting it drip over his head, chuckling in a senile sort of way as he did so.

"Mud," he remarked pleasantly to Gru Magru, in a voice like a lion's bellow. "Nothing like it. Good rich mud. Ah!"

Gru was bumping his head on the floor, his large, capable hand around Crockett's neck forcing the other to follow suit.

"Oh, get up," said the Emperor. "What's this? What's this gnome been up to? Out with it."

"He's new," Gru explained. "I found him topside. The Nid law, you know."

"Yes, of course. Let's have a look at you. Ugh! I'm Podrang the Second, Emperor of the Gnomes. What have you to say to that?"

All Crockett could think of was: "How—how can you be

Podrang the Second? I thought Podrang the Third was the first emperor."

"A chatterbox," said Podrang II, disappearing beneath the surface of the mud and spouting as he rose again. "Take care of him, Gru. Easy work at first. Digging anthracite. Mind you don't eat any while you're on the job," he cautioned the dazed Crockett. "After you've been here a century, you're allowed one mud bath a day. Nothing like 'em," he added, bringing up a gluey handful to smear over his face.

Abruptly he stiffened. His lion's bellow rang out.

"Drook! *Drook!*"

The little gnome Crockett had seen in the throne room scurried in, ringing his hands. "Your Majesty! Isn't the mud warm enough?"

"You crawling blob!" roared Podrang II. "You slobbering offspring of six thousand individual offensive stenches! You mica-eyed, incompetent, draggle-eared, writhing blot on the good name of gnomes! You geological mistake! You—you—"

Drook took advantage of his master's temporary inarticulacy. "It's the best mud, Your Majesty! I refined it myself. Oh, Your Majesty, what's wrong?"

"There's a worm in it!" His Majesty bellowed, and launched into a stream of profanity so horrendous that it practically made the mud boil. Clutching his singed ears, Crockett allowed Gru Magru to drag him away.

"I'd like to get the old boy in a fight," Gru remarked, when they were safely in the depths of a tunnel, "but he'd use magic, of course. That's the way he is. Best emperor we've ever had. Not a scrap of fair play in his bloated body."

"Oh," Crockett said blankly. "Well, what next?"

"You heard Podrang, didn't you? You dig anthracite. And if you eat any, I'll kick your teeth in."

Brooding over the apparent bad tempers of gnomes, Crockett allowed himself to be conducted to a gallery where dozens of gnomes, both male and female, were using picks and mattocks with furious vigor. "This is it," Gru said. "Now! You dig anthracite. You work twenty hours, and then sleep six."

"Then what?"

"Then you start digging again," Gru explained. "You have a brief rest once every ten hours. You mustn't stop digging in between, unless it's for a fight. Now, here's the way you locate coal. Just think of it."

"Eh?"

"How do you think I found you?" Gru asked impatiently. "Gnomes have—certain senses. There's a legend that fairy folk can locate water by using a forked stick. Well, we're attracted to metals. Think of anthracite," he finished, and Crockett obeyed. Instantly he found himself turning to the wall of the tunnel nearest him.

"See how it works?" Gru grinned. "It's a natural evolution, I suppose. Functional. We have to know where the underneath deposits are, so the authorities gave us this sense when we were created. Think of ore—or any deposit in the ground—and you'll be attracted to it. Just as there's a repulsion in all gnomes against daylight."

"Eh?" Crockett started slightly. "What was that?"

"Negative and positive. We need ores, so we're attracted to them. Daylight is harmful to us, so if we think we're getting too close to the surface, we think of light, and it repels us. Try it!"

Crockett obeyed. Something seemed to be pressing down the top of his head.

"Straight up," Gru nodded. "But it's a long way. I saw daylight once. And—a man, too." He stared at the other. "I forgot to explain. Gnomes can't stand the sight of human beings. They—well, there's a limit to how much ugliness a gnome can look at. Now you're one of us, you'll feel the same way. Keep away from daylight, and never look at a man. It's as much as your sanity is worth."

There was a thought stirring in Crockett's mind. He could, then, find his way out of this maze of tunnels, simply by employing his new sense to lead him to daylight. After that— well, at least he would be above ground.

Gru Magru shoved Crockett into a place between two busy gnomes and thrust a pick into his hands. "There. Get to work."

"Thanks for—" Crockett began, when Gru suddenly kicked him and then took his departure, humming happily to himself. Another gnome came up, saw Crockett standing motionless, and told him to get busy, accompanying the command with a blow on his already tender ear. Perforce Crockett seized the pick and began to chop anthracite out of the wall.

"Grockett!" said a familiar voice. "It's you! I thought they'd send you here."

It was Brockle Buhn, the feminine gnome Crockett had already encountered. She was swinging a pick with the others, but dropped it now to grin at her companion.

"You won't be here long," she consoled. "Ten years or so. Unless you run into trouble, and then you'll be put at really hard work."

Crockett's arms were already aching. "*Hard* work! My arms are going to fall off in a minute."

He leaned on his pick. "Is this your regular job?"

"Yes—but I'm seldom here. Usually I'm being punished. I'm a trouble-maker, I am. I eat anthracite."

She demonstrated, and Crockett shuddered at the audible crunching sound. Just then the overseer came up. Brockle Buhn swallowed hastily.

"What's this?" he snarled. "Why aren't you at work?"

"We were just going to fight," Brockle Buhn explained.

"Oh—just the two of you? Or can I join in?"

"Free for all," the unladylike gnome offered, and struck the unsuspecting Crockett over the head with her pick. He went out like a light.

Awakening some time later, he investigated bruised ribs and decided Brockle Buhn must have kicked him after he'd lost consciousness. What a gnome! Crockett sat up, finding himself in the same tunnel, dozens of gnomes busily digging anthracite.

The overseer came toward him. "Awake, eh? Get to work!"

Dazedly Crockett obeyed. Brockle Buhn flashed him a delighted grin. "You missed it. I got an ear—see?" She exhibited it. Crockett hastily lifted an exploring hand. It wasn't his.

Dig . . . dig . . . dig . . . the hours dragged past. Crockett had never worked so hard in his life. But, he noticed, not a gnome complained. Twenty hours of toil, with one brief rest period—he'd slept through that. Dig . . . dig . . . dig . . .

Without ceasing her work, Brockle Buhn said, "I think you'll make a good gnome, Grockett. You're toughening up already. Nobody'd ever believe you were once a man."

"Oh—no?"

"No. What were you, a miner?"

"I was—" Crockett paused suddenly. A curious light came into his eyes.

"I was a labor organizer," he finished.

"What's that?"

"Ever heard of a union?" Crockett asked, his gaze intent.

"Is it an ore?" Brockle Buhn shook her head. "No, I've never heard of it. What's a union?"

Crockett explained. No genuine labor organizer would have accepted that explanation. It was, to say the least, biased.

Brockle Buhn seemed puzzled. "I don't see what you mean, exactly, but I suppose it's all right."

"Try another tack," Crockett said. "Don't you ever get tired of working twenty hours a day?"

"Sure. Who wouldn't?"

"Then why do it?"

"We always have," Brockle Buhn said indulgently. "We can't stop."

"Suppose you did?"

"I'd be punished—beaten with stalactites, or something."

"Suppose you all did," Crockett insisted. "Every damn gnome. Suppose you had a sit-down strike."

"You're crazy," Brockle Buhn said. "Such a thing's never happened. It—it's *human*."

"Kisses never happened underground, either," said Crockett. "No, I don't want one! And I don't want to fight, either. Good heavens, let me get the set-up here. Most of the gnomes work to support the privileged classes."

"No. We just work."

"But why?"

"We always have. And the Emperor wants us to."

"Has the Emperor ever worked?" Crockett demanded, with an air of triumph. "No! He just takes mud baths! Why shouldn't every gnome have the same privilege? Why——"

He talked on, at great length, as he worked. Brockle Buhn listened with increasing interest. And eventually she swallowed the bait—hook, line, and sinker.

An hour later she was nodding agreeably. "I'll pass the word along. Tonight. In the Roaring Cave. Right after work."

"Wait a minute," Crockett objected. "How many gnomes can we get?"

"Well—not very many. Thirty?"

"We'll have to organize first. We'll need a definite plan."

Brockle Buhn went off at a tangent. "Let's fight."

"No! Will you listen? We need a—a council. Who's the worst trouble-maker here?"

"Mugza, I think," she said. "The red-haired gnome you knocked out when he hit me."

Crockett frowned slightly. Would Mugza hold a grudge? Probably not, he decided. Or, rather, he'd be no more ill tem-

pered than other gnomes. Mugza might attempt to throttle
Crockett on sight, but he'd no doubt do the same to any
other gnome. Besides, as Brockle Buhn went on to explain,
Mugza was the gnomic equivalent of a duke. His support
would be valuable.

"And Gru Magru," she suggested. "He loves new things,
especially if they make trouble."

"Yeah." These were not the two Crockett would have
chosen, but at least he could think of no other candidates. "If
we could get somebody who's close to the Emperor . . .
What about Drook—the guy who gives Podrang his mud
baths?"

"Why not? I'll fix it." Brockle Buhn lost interest and surreptitiously began to eat anthracite. Since the overseer was
watching, this resulted in a violent quarrel, from which
Crockett emerged with a black eye. Whispering profanity under his breath, he went back to digging.

But he had time for a few more words with Brockle Buhn.
She'd arrange it. That night there would be a secret meeting
of the conspirators.

Crockett had been looking forward to exhausted slumber,
but this chance was too good to miss. He had no wish to continue his unpleasant job digging anthracite. His body ached
fearfully. Besides, if he could induce the gnomes to strike, he
might be able to put the squeeze on Podrang II. Gru Magru
had said the Emperor was a magician. Couldn't he, then,
transform Crockett back into a man?

"He's never done that," Brockle Buhn said, and Crockett
realized he had spoken his thought aloud.

"Couldn't he, though—if he wanted?"

Brockle Buhn merely shuddered, but Crockett had a little
gleam of hope. To be human again!

Dig . . . dig . . . dig . . . dig . . . with monotonous,
deadening regularity. Crockett sank into a stupor. Unless he
got the gnomes to strike, he was faced with an eternity of
arduous toil. He was scarcely conscious of knocking off, of
feeling Brockle Buhn's gnarled hand under his arm, of being
led through passages to a tiny cubicle, which was his new
home. The gnome left him there, and he crawled into a stony
bunk and went to sleep.

Presently a casual kick aroused him. Blinking, Crockett sat
up, instinctively dodging the blow Gru Magru was aiming at
his head. He had four guests—Gru, Brockle Buhn, Drook,
and the red-haired Mugza.

"Sorry I woke up too soon," Crockett said bitterly. "If I hadn't, you could have got in another kick."

"There's lots of time," Gru said. "Now, what's this all about? I wanted to sleep, but Brockle Buhn here said there was going to be a fight. A *big* one, huh?"

"Eat first," Brockle Buhn said firmly. "I'll fix mud soup for everybody." She bustled away, and presently was busy in a corner, preparing refreshments. The other gnomes squatted on their haunches, and Crockett sat on the edge of his bunk, still dazed with sleep.

But he managed to explain his idea of the union. It was received with interest—chiefly, he felt, because it involved the possibility of a tremendous scrap.

"You mean every Dornsef gnome jumps the Emperor?" Gru asked.

"No, no! Peaceful arbitration. We just refuse to work. All of us."

"*I* can't," Drook said. "Podrang's got to have his mud baths, the bloated old slug. He'd send me to the fumaroles till I was toasted."

"Who'd take you there?" Crockett asked.

"Oh—the guards, I suppose."

"But they'd be on strike, too. *Nobody'd* obey Podrang, till he gave in."

"Then he'd enchant me," Drook said.

"He can't enchant us all," Crockett countered.

"But he could enchant *me*," Drook said with great firmness. "Besides, he *could* put a spell on every gnome in Dornsef. Turn us into stalactites or something."

"Then what? He wouldn't have any gnomes at all. Half a loaf is better than none. We'll just use logic on him. Wouldn't he rather have a little less work done than none at all?"

"Not him," Gru put in. "He'd rather enchant us. Oh, he's a bad one, he is," the gnome finished approvingly.

But Crockett couldn't quite believe this. It was too alien to his understanding of psychology—human psychology, of course. He turned to Mugza, who was glowering furiously.

"What do you think about it?"

"I want to fight," the other said rancorously. "I want to kick somebody."

"Wouldn't you rather have mud baths three times a day?"

Mugza grunted. "Sure. But the Emperor won't let me."

"Why not?"

"Because I want 'em."

"You can't be contented," Crockett said desperately. "There's more to life than—than digging."

"Sure. There's fighting. Podrang lets us fight whenever we want."

Crockett had a sudden inspiration. "But that's just it. He's going to stop all fighting! He's going to pass a new law forbidding fighting except to himself."

It was an effective shot in the dark. Every gnome jumped.

"Stop—*fighting!*" That was Gru, angry and disbelieving. "Why, we've always fought."

"Well, you'll have to stop," Crockett insisted.

"Won't!"

"Exactly! Why should you? Every gnome's entitled to life, liberty, and the pursuit of—of pugilism."

"Let's go and beat up Podrang," Mugza offered, accepting a steaming bowl of mud soup from Brockle Buhn.

"No, that's not the way—no, thanks, Brockle Buhn—not the way at all. A strike's the thing. We'll peaceably force Podrang to give us what we want."

He turned to Drook. "Just what can Podrang do about it if we all sit down and refuse to work?"

The little gnome considered. "He'd swear. And kick me."

"Yeah—and then what?"

"Then he'd go off and enchant everybody, tunnel by tunnel."

"Uh-huh." Crockett nodded. "A good point. Solidarity is what we need. If Podrang finds a few gnomes together, he can scare the hell out of them. But if we're all together—that's it! When the strike's called, we'll all meet in the biggest cave in the joint."

"That's the Council Chamber," Gru said. "Next to Podrang's throne room."

"O.K. We'll meet there. How many gnomes will join us?"

"All of 'em," Mugza grunted, throwing his soup bowl at Drook's head. "The Emperor can't stop us fighting."

"And what weapons can Podrang use, Drook?"

"He might use the Cockatrice Eggs," the other said doubtfully.

"What are those?"

"They're not really eggs," Gru broke in. "They're **magic** jewels for wholesale enchantments. Different spells in each one. The green ones, I think, are for turning people into earthworms. Podrang just breaks one, and the spell spreads out for twenty feet or so. The red ones are—let's see. Transforming gnomes into human beings—though that's a bit *too* tough. No . . . yes. The blue ones—"

"Into *human beings!*" Crockett's eyes widened. "Where are the eggs kept?"

"Let's fight," Mugza offered, and hurled himself bodily on Drook, who squeaked frantically and beat his attacker over the head with his stone soup bowl, which broke. Brockle Buhn added to the excitement by kicking both battlers impartially, till felled by Gru Magru. Within a few moments the room resounded with the excited screams of gnomic battle. Inevitably Crockett was sucked in. . . .

Of all the perverted, incredible forms of life that had ever existed, gnomes were about the oddest. It was impossible to understand their philosophy. Their minds worked along different paths from human intelligences. Self-preservation and survival of the race—these two vital human instincts were lacking in gnomes. They neither died nor propagated. They just worked and fought. Bad-tempered little monsters, Crockett thought irritably. Yet they had existed for—ages. Since the beginning, maybe. Their social organism was the result of evolution far older than man's. It might be well suited to gnomes. Crockett might be throwing the unnecessary monkey wrench in the machinery.

So what? He wasn't going to spend eternity digging anthracite, even though, in retrospect, he remembered feeling a curious thrill of obscure pleasure as he worked. Digging might be fun for gnomes. Certainly it was their *raison d'être*. In time Crockett himself might lose his human affiliations, and be metamorphosed completely into a gnome. What had happened to other humans who had undergone such an—alteration as he had done? All gnomes looked alike. But maybe Gru Magru had once been human—or Drook—or Brockle Buhn.

They were gnomes now, at any rate, thinking and existing completely as gnomes. And in time he himself would be exactly like them. Already he had acquired the strange tropism that attracted him to metals and repelled him from daylight. But he didn't *like* to dig!

He tried to recall the little he knew about gnomes—miners, metalsmiths, living underground. There was something about the Picts—dwarfish men who hid underground when invaders came to England, centuries ago. That seemed to tie in vaguely with the gnomes' dread of human beings. But the gnomes themselves were certainly not descended from Picts.

Very likely the two separate races and species had become
identified through occupying the same habitat.

Well, that was no help. What about the Emperor? He
wasn't, apparently, a gnome with a high I.Q., but he *was* a
magician. Those jewels—Cockatrice Eggs—were significant.
If he could get hold of the ones that transformed gnomes into
men . . .

But obviously he couldn't, at present. Better wait. Till the
strike had been called. The strike . . .

Crockett went to sleep.

He was roused, painfully, by Brockle Buhn, who seemed to
have adopted him. Very likely it was her curiosity about the
matter of a kiss. From time to time she offered to give
Crockett one, but he steadfastly refused. In lieu of it, she supplied him with breakfast. At least, he thought grimly, he'd get
plenty of iron in his system, even though the rusty chips
rather resembled corn flakes. As a special inducement
Brockle Buhn sprinkled coal dust over the mess.

Well, no doubt his digestive system had also altered.
Crockett wished he could get an X-ray picture of his insides.
Then he decided it would be much too disturbing. Better not
to know. But he could not help wondering. Gears in his stomach? Small millstones? What would happen if he inadvertently swallowed some emery dust? Maybe he could sabotage
the Emperor that way.

Perceiving that his thoughts were beginning to veer wildly,
Crockett gulped the last of his meal and followed Brockle
Buhn to the anthracite tunnel.

"How about the strike? How's it coming?"

"Fine, Grockett." She smiled, and Crockett winced at the
sight. "Tonight all the gnomes will meet in the Roaring Cave.
Just after work."

There was no time for more conversation. The overseer appeared, and the gnomes snatched up their picks. Dig . . . dig
. . . dig . . . It kept up at the same pace. Crockett sweated
and toiled. It wouldn't be for long. His mind slipped a cog, so
that he relapsed into a waking slumber, his muscles responding automatically to the need. Dig, dig, dig. Sometimes a
fight. Once a rest period. Then dig again.

Five centuries later the day ended. It was time to sleep.

But there was something much more important. The union
meeting in the Roaring Cave. Brockle Buhn conducted
Crockett there, a huge cavern hung with glittering green
stalactites. Gnomes came pouring into it. Gnomes and more

gnomes. The turnip heads were everywhere. A dozen fights started. Gru Magru, Mugza, and Drook found places near Crockett. During a lull Brockle Buhn urged him to a platform of rock jutting from the floor.

"Now," she whispered. "They all know about it. Tell them what you want."

Crockett was looking out over the bobbing heads, the red and blue garments, all lit by that eerie silver glow. "Fellow gnomes," he began weakly.

"Fellow gnomes!" The words roared out, magnified by the acoustics of the cavern. That bull bellow gave Crockett courage. He plunged on.

"Why should you work twenty hours a day? Why should you be forbidden to eat the anthracite you dig, while Podrang squats in his bath and laughs at you? Fellow gnomes, the Emperor is only one; you are many! He can't make you work. How would you like mud soup three times a day? The Emperor can't fight you all. If you refuse to work—all of you—he'll have to give in! He'll have to!"

"Tell 'em about the non-fighting edict," Gru Magru called.

Crockett obeyed. That got 'em. Fighting was dear to every gnomic heart. And Crockett kept on talking.

"Podrang will try to back down, you know. He'll pretend he never intended to forbid fighting. That'll show he's afraid of you! We hold the whip hand! We'll strike—and the Emperor can't do a damn thing about it. When he runs out of mud for his baths, he'll capitulate soon enough."

"He'll enchant us all," Drook muttered sadly.

"He won't dare! What good would that do? He knows which side his—uh—which side his mud is buttered on. Podrang is unfair to gnomes! That's our watchword!"

It ended, of course, in a brawl. But Crockett was satisfied. The gnomes would not go to work tomorrow. They would, instead, meet in the Council Chamber, adjoining Podrang's throne room—and sit down.

That night he slept well.

In the morning Crockett went, with Brockle Buhn, to the Council Chamber, a cavern gigantic enough to hold the thousands of gnomes who thronged it. In the silver light their red and blue garments had a curiously elfin quality. Or, perhaps, naturally enough, Crockett thought, were gnomes, strictly speaking, elves?

Drook came up. "I didn't draw Podrang's mud bath," he confided hoarsely. "Oh, but he'll be furious. Listen to him."

And, indeed, a distant crackling of profanity was coming through an archway in one wall of the cavern.

Mugza and Gru Magru joined them. "He'll be along directly," the latter said. "What a fight there'll be!"

"Let's fight now," Mugza suggested. "I want to kick somebody. Hard."

"There's a gnome who's asleep," Crockett said. "If you sneak up on him, you can land a good one right in his face."

Mugza, drooling slightly, departed on his errand, and simultaneously Podrang II, Emperor of the Dornsef Gnomes, stumped into the cavern. It was the first time Crockett had seen the ruler without a coating of mud, and he could not help gulping at the sight. Podrang was *very* ugly. He combined in himself the most repulsive qualities of every gnome Crockett had previously seen. The result was perfectly indescribable.

"Ah," said Podrang, halting and swaying on his short bow legs. "I have guests. Drook! Where in the name of the nine steaming hells is my bath?" But Drook had ducked from sight.

The Emperor nodded. "I see. Well, I won't lose my temper. *I won't lose my temper! I WON'T—*"

He paused as a stalactite was dislodged from the roof and crashed down. In the momentary silence, Crockett stepped forward, cringing slightly.

"W-we're on strike," he announced. "It's a sit-down strike. We won't work till—"

"*Yaaah!*" screamed the infuriated Emperor. "You won't work, eh? Why, you boggle-eyed, flap-tongued, drag-bellied offspring of unmentionable algae! You seething little leprous blotch of bat-nibbled fungus! You cringing parasite on the underside of a dwarfish and ignoble worm! *Yaaah!*"

"Fight!" the irrepressible Mugza yelled, and flung himself on Podrang, only to be felled by a well-placed foul blow.

Crockett's throat felt dry. He raised his voice, trying to keep it steady.

"Your Majesty! If you'll just wait a minute—"

"You mushroom-nosed spawn of degenerate black bats," the enraged Emperor shrieked at the top of his voice. "I'll enchant you all! I'll turn you into naiads! Strike, will you! Stop me from having my mud bath, will you? By Kronos, Nid, Ymir, and Loki, you'll have cause to regret this! *Yaah!*" he finished, inarticulate with fury.

"Quick!" Crockett whispered to Gru and Brockle Buhn.

"Get between him and the door, so he can't get hold of the Cockatrice Eggs."

"They're not in the throne room," Gru Magru explained unhelpfully. "Podrang just grabs them out of the air."

"Oh!" the harassed Crockett groaned. At that strategic moment Brockle Buhn's worst instincts overcame her. With a loud shriek of delight she knocked Crockett down, kicked him twice, and sprang for the Emperor.

She got in one good blow before Podrang hammered her atop the head with one gnarled fist, and instantly her turnip-shaped skull seemed to prolapse into her torso. The Emperor, bright purple with fury, reached out—and a yellow crystal appeared in his hand.

It was one of the Cockatrice Eggs.

Bellowing like a *musth* elephant, Podrang hurled it. A circle of twenty feet was instantly cleared among the massed gnomes. But it wasn't vacant. Dozens of bats rose and fluttered about, adding to the confusion.

Confusion became chaos. With yells of delighted fury, the gnomes rolled forward toward their ruler. "Fight!" the cry thundered out, reverberating from the roof. *"Fight!"*

Podrang snatched another crystal from nothingness—a green one, this time. Thirty-seven gnomes were instantly transformed into earthworms, and were trampled. The Emperor went down under an avalanche of attackers, who abruptly disappeared, turned into mice by another of the Cockatrice Eggs.

Crockett saw one of the crystals sailing toward him, and ran like hell. He found a hiding place behind a stalagmite, and from there watched the carnage. It was definitely a sight worth seeing, though it could not be recommended to a nervous man.

The Cockatrice Eggs exploded in an incessant stream. Whenever that happened, the spell spread out for twenty feet or more before losing its efficacy. Those caught on the fringes of the circle were only partially transformed. Crockett saw one gnome with a mole's head. Another was a worm from the waist down. Another was—ulp! Some of the spell-patterns were not, apparently, drawn even from known mythology.

The fury of noise that filled the cavern brought stalactites crashing down incessantly from the roof. Every so often Podrang's battered head would reappear, only to go down again as more gnomes sprang to the attack—to be enchanted. Mice moles, bats, and other things filled the Council Chamber. Crockett shut his eyes and prayed.

He opened them in time to see Podrang snatch a red crystal out of the air, pause, and then deposit it gently behind him. A purple Cockatrice Egg came next. This crashed against the floor, and thirty gnomes turned into tree toads.

Apparently only Podrang was immune to his own magic. The thousands who had filled the cavern were rapidly thinning, for the Cockatrice Eggs seemed to come from an inexhaustible source of supply. How long would it be before Crockett's own turn came? He couldn't hide here forever.

His gaze riveted to the red crystal Podrang had so carefully put down. He was remembering something—the Cockatrice Egg that would transform gnomes into human beings. Of course! Podrang wouldn't use *that*, since the very sight of men was so distressing to gnomes. If Crockett could get his hands on that red crystal . . .

He tried it, sneaking through the confusion, sticking close to the wall of the cavern, till he neared Podrang. The Emperor was swept away by another onrush of gnomes, who abruptly changed into dormice, and Crockett got the red jewel. It felt abnormally cold.

He almost broke it at his feet before a thought stopped and chilled him. He was far under Dornsef Mountain, in a labyrinth of caverns. No human being could find his way out. But a gnome could, with the aid of his strange tropism to daylight.

A bat flew against Crockett's face. He was almost certain it squeaked, "What a fight!" in a parody of Brockle Buhn's voice, but he couldn't be sure. He cast one glance over the cavern before turning to flee.

It was a complete and utter chaos. Bats, moles, worms, ducks, eels, and a dozen other species crawled, flew, ran, bit, shrieked, snarled, grunted, whooped, and croaked all over the place. From all directions the remaining gnomes—only about a thousand now—were converging on a surging mound of gnomes that marked where the Emperor was. As Crockett stared the mound dissolved, and a number of gecko lizards ran to safety.

"Strike, will you!" Podrang bellowed. "*I'll show you!*"

Crockett turned and fled. The throne room was deserted, and he ducked into the first tunnel. There, he concentrated on thinking of daylight. His left ear felt compressed. He sped on till he saw a side passage on the left, slanting up, and turned into it at top speed. The muffled noise of combat died behind him.

He clutched the red Cockatrice Egg tightly. What had gone wrong? Podrang should have stopped to parley. Only—only he hadn't. A singularly bad-tempered and shortsighted gnome. He probably wouldn't stop till he'd depopulated his entire kingdom. At the thought Crockett hurried along faster.

The tropism guided him. Sometimes he took the wrong tunnel, but always, whenever he thought of daylight, he would *feel* the nearest daylight pressing against him. His short, bowed legs were surprisingly hardy.

Then he heard someone running after him.

He didn't turn. The sizzling blast of profanity that curled his ears told him the identity of the pursuer. Podrang had no doubt cleared the Council Chamber, to the last gnome, and was now intending to tear Crockett apart pinch by pinch. That was only one of the things he promised.

Crockett ran. He shot along that tunnel like a bullet. The tropism guided him, but he was terrified lest he reach a dead end. The clamor from behind grew louder. If Crockett hadn't known better, he would have imagined that an army of gnomes pursued him.

Faster! Faster! But now Podrang was in sight. His roars shook the very walls. Crockett sprinted, rounded a corner, and saw a wall of flaming light—a circle of it, in the distance. It was daylight, as it appeared to gnomic eyes.

He could not reach it in time. Podrang was too close. A few more seconds, and those gnarled, terrible hands would close on Crockett's throat. Then Crockett remembered the Cockatrice Egg. If he transformed himself into a man now, Podrang would not dare touch him. And he was almost at the tunnel's mouth.

He stopped, whirling, and lifted the jewel. Simultaneously the Emperor, seeing his intention, reached out with both hands, and snatched six or seven of the crystals out of the air. He threw them directly at Crockett, a fusillade of rainbow colors.

But Crockett had already slammed the red gem down on the rock at his feet. There was an ear-splitting crash. Jewels seemed to burst all around Crockett—but the red one had been broken first.

The roof fell in.

A short while later, Crockett dragged himself painfully from the debris. A glance showed him that the way to the outer world was still open. And—thank heaven!—daylight looked normal again, not that flaming blaze of eye-searing white.

He looked toward the depths of the tunnel, and froze. Podrang was emerging, with some difficulty, from a mound of rubble. His low curses had lost none of their fire.

Crockett turned to run, stumbled over a rock, and fell flat. As he sprang up, he saw that Podrang had seen him.

The gnome stood transfixed for a moment. Then he yelled, spun on his heel, and fled into the darkness. He was gone. The sound of his rapid footfalls died.

Crockett swallowed with difficulty. *Gnomes are afraid of men—whew!* That had been a close squeak. But now . . .

He was more relieved than he had thought. Subconsciously he must have been wondering whether the spell would work, since Podrang had flung six or seven Cockatrice Eggs at him. But he had smashed the red one first. Even the strange, silvery gnome-light was gone. The depths of the cave were utterly black—and silent.

Crockett headed for the entrance. He pulled himself out, luxuriating in the warmth of the afternoon sun. He was near the foot of Dornsef Mountain, in a patch of brambles. A hundred feet away a farmer was plowing one terrace of a field.

Crockett stumbled toward him. As he approached, the man turned.

He stood transfixed for a moment. Then he yelled, spun on his heel, and fled.

His shrieks drifted back up the mountain as Crockett, remembering the Cockatrice Eggs, forced himself to look down at his own body.

Then he screamed, too. But the sound was not one that could ever have emerged from a human throat.

Still, that was natural enough—under the circumstances.

BY HIS BOOTSTRAPS

Astounding Science Fiction
October

by Robert A. Heinlein
(as "Anson MacDonald")

Heinlein was so prolific that John Campbell thought it necessary to use a pseudonym for him, since it might appear strange to have two stories by the same author in a single issue of the magazine. Actually, his following was so extensive by 1941 that it probably would not have mattered.

The time travel story was a staple in science fiction by the early forties, but here Heinlein gave it a wonderful twist—and wrote what many believe to be the ultimate story of its kind.

(Once again, Bob Heinlein scores. I agree with Marty that it is probably the best time-travel story in the sub-novel length ever written. I wish to say, though, that I think that John Campbell was far too ready to push for pseudonyms. I guess he felt it was just impossible to have two stories by the same author—by name—in the same issue, but he should have tried. Some of the *best* Heinlein stories came out under the MacDonald name and why should any reader not have known that? Not only was this story one of them, but "Solution Unsatisfactory" which appeared in the May 1941 *Astounding* along with "Blowups Happen" was another.—Well, he dominated 1941 and we can't help that.—I.A.)

SNULBUG

Unknown
December

by Anthony Boucher (William Anthony Parker White, 1911-1968)

Anthony Boucher was a sophisticated, witty man who led several lives. Best known as the founding coeditor of The Magazine of Fantasy and Science Fiction *(1949) he was also a talented mystery author, whose novel* Rocket to the Morgue *(1942) used the world of science fiction—fans and writers—as its setting. In addition, as "H. H. Holmes" and as Boucher, he was one of the most influential book reviewers of both mysteries and science fiction from the end of World War II until his death, most notably for the* New York Herald Tribune *and the* New York Times.

As a writer of science fiction and fantasy, he enjoyed a substantial reputation in spite of the fact that he never published a novel. His best stories can be found in the collections Far and Away *(1955) and* The Complete Werewolf *(1969). Especially outstanding are "Barrier" (*Astounding, *September, 1942), "Nine-Finger Jack" (*Esquire, *May, 1951) and "Q.U.R." (*Astounding, *March, 1943).*

"Snulbug" is a delightful fantasy typical of Unknown *in its too-short existence, and it was Tony Boucher's first published work of fantastic fiction.*

(I didn't meet Tony often. He was West Coast and I was East Coast and I didn't travel. We became friends at one stroke, however, as the result of the first letter I ever received from him.

In a story I wrote when I was just about thirty, I referred to the "paler (sexual) passions of the late thirties." That elicited a gentle reproof from Tony almost at once.

"You have a very pleasant surprise ahead of you, Dr. Asi-

mov," he said, and signed it "Anthony Boucher (1911–)."
He was, of course, just turning forty at the time.

We corresponded with reasonable regularity thereafter and
it is only fair to say that I did have the pleasant surprise he
spoke of and have continued to have it as the years continue
to roll by.—I.A.)

"That's a hell of a spell you're using," said the demon, "if
I'm the best you can call up."

He wasn't much, Bill Hitchens had to admit. He looked
lost in the center of that pentacle. His basic design was im-
pressive enough—snakes for hair, curling tusks, a sharptipped
tail, all the works—but he was something under an inch tall.

Bill had chanted the words and lit the powder with the
highest hopes. Even after the feeble flickering flash and the
damp fizzling *zzzt* which had replaced the expected thunder
and lightning, he had still had hopes. He had stared up at the
space above the pentacle waiting to be awe-struck until he
had heard that plaintive little voice from the floor wailing,
"Here I am."

"Nobody's wasted time and power on a misfit like me for
years," the demon went on. "Where'd you get the spell?"

"Just a little something I whipped up," said Bill modestly.

The demon grunted and muttered something about people
that thought they were magicians.

"But I'm not a magician," Bill explained. "I'm a biochemist."

The demon shuddered. "I land the damnedest cases," he
mourned. "Working for a psychiatrist wasn't bad enough, I
should draw a biochemist. Whatever that is."

Bill couldn't check his curiosity. "And what did you do for
a psychiatrist?"

"He showed me to people who were followed by little men
and told them I'd chase the little men away." The demon
pantomimed shooting motions.

"And did they go away?"

"Sure. Only then the people decided they'd sooner have
little men than me. It didn't work so good. Nothing ever
does," he added woefully. "Yours won't either."

Bill sat down and filled his pipe. Calling up demons wasn't
so terrifying after all. Something quiet and homey about it.
"Oh, yes it will," he said. "This is foolproof."

"That's what they all think. People—" The demon wistfully eyed the match as Bill lit his pipe. "But we might as well get it over with. What do you want?"

"I want a laboratory for my embolism experiments. If this method works, it's going to mean that a doctor can spot an embolus in the blood stream long before it's dangerous and remove it safely. My ex-boss, that screwball old occultist Reuben Choatsby, said it wasn't practical—meaning there wasn't a fortune in it for him—and fired me. Everybody else thinks I'm whacky too, and I can't get any backing. So I need ten thousand dollars."

"There!" the demon sighed with satisfaction. "I told you it wouldn't work. That's out for me. They can't start fetching money on demand till three grades higher than me. I told you."

"But you don't," Bill insisted, "appreciate all my fiendish subtlety. Look— Say, what is your name?"

The demon hesitated. "You haven't got another of those things?"

"What things?"

"Matches."

"Sure."

"Light me one, please?"

Bill tossed the burning match into the center of the pentacle. The demon scrambled eagerly out of the now cold ashes of the powder and dived into the flame, rubbing himself with the brisk vigor of a man under a needle-shower. "There!" he gasped joyously. "That's more like it."

"And now what's your name?"

The demon's face fell again. "My name? You really want to know?"

"I've got to call you something."

"Oh, no you don't. I'm going home. No money games for me."

"But I haven't explained yet what you are to do. What's your name?"

"Snulbug." The demon's voice dropped almost too low to be heard.

"Snulbug?" Bill laughed.

"Uh-huh. I've got a cavity in one tusk, my snakes are falling out, I haven't got enough troubles, I should be named Snulbug."

"All right. Now listen, Snulbug, can you travel into the future?"

"A little. I don't like it much, though. It makes you itch in the memory."

"Look, my fine snake-haired friend. It isn't a question of what you like. How would you like to be left there in that pentacle with nobody to throw matches at you?" Snulbug shuddered. "I thought so. Now, you can travel into the future?"

"I said a little."

"And," Bill leaned forward and puffed hard at his corncob as he asked the vital question, "can you bring back material objects?" If the answer was no, all the fine febrile fertility of his spell-making was useless. And if that was useless, heaven alone knew how the Hitchens Embolus Diagnosis would ever succeed in ringing down the halls of history, and incidentally saving a few thousand lives annually.

Snulbug seemed more interested in the warm clouds of pipe smoke than in the question. "Sure," he said. "Within reason I can—" He broke off and stared up piteously. "You don't mean—You can't be going to pull that old gag again?"

"Look, baby. You do what I tell you and leave the worrying to me. You can bring back material objects?"

"Sure. But I warn you—"

Bill cut him off short. "Then as soon as I release you from that pentacle, you're to bring me tomorrow's newspaper."

Snulbug sat down on the burned match and tapped his forehead sorrowfully with his tail tip. "I knew it," he wailed. "I knew it. Three times already this happens to me. I've got limited powers, I'm a runt, I've got a funny name, so I should run foolish errands."

"Foolish errands?" Bill rose and began to pace about the bare attic. "Sir, if I may call you that, I resent such an imputation. I've spent weeks on this idea. Think of the limitless power in knowing the future. Think of what could be done with it: swaying the course of empire, dominating mankind. All I want is to take this stream of unlimited power, turn it into the simple channel of humanitarian research, and get me $10,000; and you call that a foolish errand!"

"That Spaniard," Snulbug moaned. "He was a nice guy, even if his spell was lousy. Had a solid, comfortable brazier where an imp could keep warm. Fine fellow. And he had to ask to see tomorrow's newspaper. I'm warning you—"

"I know," said Bill hastily. "I've been over in my mind all the things that can go wrong. And that's why I'm laying three conditions on you before you get out of that pentacle. I'm not falling for the easy snares."

"All right." Snulbug sounded almost resigned. "Let's hear 'em. Not that they'll do any good."

"First: This newspaper must not contain a notice of my own death or of any other disaster that would frustrate what I can do with it."

"But shucks," Snulbug protested. "I can't guarantee that. If you're slated to die between now and tomorrow, what can I do about it? Not that I guess you're important enough to crash the paper."

"Courtesy, Snulbug. Courtesy to your master. But I tell you what: When you go into the future, you'll know then if I'm going to die? Right. Well, if I am, come back and tell me and we'll work out other plans. This errand will be off."

"People," Snulbug observed, "make such an effort to make trouble for themselves. Go on."

"Second: The newspaper must be of this city and in English. I can just imagine you and your little friends presenting some dope with the Omsk and Tomsk *Daily Vuskutsukt.*"

"We should take so much trouble," said Snulbug.

"And third: The newspaper must belong to this space-time continuum, to this spiral of the serial universe, to this Wheel of If. However you want to put it. It must be a newspaper of the tomorrow that I myself shall experience, not of some other, to me hypothetical, tomorrow."

"Throw me another match," said Snulbug.

"Those three conditions should cover it, I think. There's not a loophole there, and the Hitchens Laboratory is guaranteed."

Snulbug grunted. "You'll find out."

Bill took a sharp blade and duly cut a line of the pentacle with cold steel. But Snulbug simply dived in and out of the flame of his second match, twitching his tail happily, and seemed not to give a rap that the way to freedom was now open.

"Come on!" Bill snapped impatiently. "Or I'll take the match away."

Snulbug got as far as the opening and hesitated. "Twenty-four hours is a long way."

"You can make it."

"I don't know. Look." He shook his head, and a microscopic dead snake fell to the floor. "I'm not at my best. I'm shot to pieces lately, I am. Tap my tail."

"Do what?"

"Go on. Tap it with your fingernail right there where it joins on."

Bill grinned and obeyed. "Nothing happens."

"Sure nothing happens. My reflexes are all haywire. I don't

know as I can make twenty-four hours." He brooded, and his snakes curled up into a concentrated clump. "Look. All you want is tomorrow's newspaper, huh? Just tomorrow's, not the edition that'll be out exactly twenty-four hours from now?"

"It's noon now," Bill reflected. "Sure, I guess tomorrow morning's paper'll do."

"OK. What's the date today?"

"August 21."

"Fine. I'll bring you a paper for August 22. Only I'm warning you: It won't do any good. But here goes nothing. Good-bye now. Hello again. Here you are." There was a string in Snulbug's horny hand, and on the end of the string was a newspaper.

"But hey!" Bill protested. "You haven't been gone."

"People," said Snulbug feelingly, "are dopes. Why should it take any time out of the present to go into the future? I leave this point, I come back to this point. I spent two hours hunting for this damned paper, but that doesn't mean two hours of your time here. People—" he snorted.

Bill scratched his head. "I guess it's all right. Let's see the paper. And I know: You're warning me." He turned quickly to the obituaries to check. No Hitchens. "And I wasn't dead in the time you were in?"

"No," Snulbug admitted. "Not *dead*," he added, with the most pessimistic implications possible.

"What was I, then? Was I—"

"I had salamander blood," Snulbug complained. "They thought I was an undine like my mother and they put me in the cold-water incubator when any dope knows salamandery is a dominant. So I'm a runt and good for nothing but to run errands, and now I should make prophecies! You read your paper and see how much good it does you."

Bill laid down his pipe and folded the paper back from the obituaries to the front page. He had not expected to find anything useful there—what advantage could he gain from knowing who won the next naval engagement or which cities were bombed?—but he was scientifically methodical. And this time method was rewarded. There it was, streaming across the front page in vast black blocks:

MAYOR ASSASSINATED

FIFTH COLUMN KILLS CRUSADER

Bill snapped his fingers. This was it. This was his chance. He jammed his pipe in his mouth, hastily pulled a coat on his shoulders, crammed the priceless paper into a pocket, and started out of the attic. Then he paused and looked around. He'd forgotten Snulbug. Shouldn't there be some sort of formal discharge?

The dismal demon was nowhere in sight. Not in the pentacle or out of it. Not a sign or a trace of him. Bill frowned. This was definitely not methodical. He struck a match and held it over the bowl of his pipe.

A warm sigh of pleasure came from inside the corncob.

Bill took the pipe from his mouth and stared at it. "So that's where you are!" he said musingly.

"I told you salamandry was a dominant," said Snulbug, peering out of the bowl. "I want to go along. I want to see just what kind of a fool you make of yourself." He withdrew his head into the glowing tobacco, muttering about newspapers, spells, and, with a wealth of unhappy scorn, people.

The crusading mayor of Granton was a national figure of splendid proportions. Without hysteria, red baiting, or strikebreaking, he had launched a quietly purposeful and well-directed program against subversive elements which had rapidly converted Granton into the safest and most American city in the country. He was also a persistent advocate of national, state, and municipal subsidy of the arts and sciences—the ideal man to wangle an endowment for the Hitchens Laboratory, if he were not so surrounded by overly skeptical assistants that Bill had never been able to lay the program before him.

This would do it. Rescue him from assassination in the very nick of time—in itself an act worth calling up demons to perform—and then when he asks, "And how, Mr. Hitchens, can I possibly repay you?" come forth with the whole great plan of research. It couldn't miss.

No sound came from the pipe bowl, but Bill clearly heard the words, "Couldn't it just?" ringing in his mind.

He braked his car to a fast stop in the red zone before the city hall, jumped out without even slamming the door, and dashed up the marble steps so rapidly, so purposefully, that pure momentum carried him up three flights and through four suites of offices before anybody had the courage to stop him and say, "What goes?"

The man with the courage was a huge bull-necked plainclothesman, whose bulk made Bill feel relatively about the size of Snulbug. "All right, there," this hulk rumbled. "All right. Where's the fire?"

"In an assassin's gun," said Bill. "And it had better stay there."

Bullneck had not expected a literal answer. He hesitated long enough for Bill to push him to the door marked MAYOR—PRIVATE. But though the husky's brain might move slowly, his muscles made up for the lag. Just as Bill started to shove the door open, a five-pronged mound of flesh lit on his neck and jerked.

Bill crawled from under a desk, ducked Bullneck's left, reached the door, executed a second backward flip, climbed down from the table, ducked a right, reached the door, sailed back in reverse, and lowered himself nimbly from the chandelier.

Bullneck took up a stand in front of the door, spread his legs in ready balance, and drew a service automatic from its holster. "You ain't going in there," he said, to make the situation perfectly clear.

Bill spat out a tooth, wiped the blood from his eyes, picked up the shattered remains of his pipe, and said, "Look. It's now 12:30. At 12:32 a redheaded hunchback is going to come out on that balcony across the street and aim through the open window into the mayor's office. At 12:33 His Honor is going to be slumped over his desk, dead. Unless you help me get him out of range."

"Yeah?" said Bullneck. "And who says so?"

"It says so here. Look. In the paper."

Bullneck guffawed. "How can a paper say what ain't even happened yet? You're nuts, brother, if you ain't something worse. Now go on. Scram. Go peddle your paper."

Bill's glance darted out the window. There was the balcony facing the mayor's office. And there coming out on it—

"Look!" he cried. "If you won't believe me, look out the window. See on that balcony? The redheaded hunchback? Just like I told you. Quick!"

Bullneck stared despite himself. He saw the hunchback peer across into the office. He saw the sudden glint of metal in the hunchback's hand. "Brother," he said to Bill, "I'll tend to you later."

The hunchback had his rifle halfway to his shoulder when Bullneck's automatic spat and Bill braked his car in the red zone, jumped out, and dashed through four suites of offices before anybody had the courage to stop him.

The man with the courage was a huge bull-necked plain-clothesman, who rumbled, "Where's the fire?"

"In an assassin's gun," said Bill, and took advantage of Bullneck's confusion to reach the door marked MAYOR—PRIVATE. But just as he started to push it open, a vast hand lit on his neck and jerked.

As Bill descended from the chandelier after his third try, Bullneck took up a stand in front of the door, with straddled legs and drawn gun. "You ain't going in," he said clarifyingly.

Bill spat out a tooth and outlined the situation. "—12:33," he ended. "His Honor is going to be slumped over the desk dead. Unless you help me get him out of range. See? It says so here. In the paper."

"How can it? Gawn. Go peddle your paper."

Bill's glance darted to the balcony. "Look, if you won't believe me. See the redheaded hunchback? Just like I told you. Quick! We've got to—"

Bullneck stared. He saw the sudden glint of metal in the hunchback's hand. "Brother," he said, "I'll tend to you later."

The hunchback had his rifle halfway to his shoulder when Bullneck's automatic spat and Bill braked his car in the red zone, jumped out, and dashed through four suites before anybody stopped him.

The man who did was a bull-necked plainclothesman, who rumbled—

"Don't you think," said Snulbug, "you've had about enough of this?"

Bill agreed mentally, and there he was sitting in his roadster in front of the city hall. His clothes were unrumpled, his eyes were bloodless, his teeth were all there, and his corncob was still intact. "And just what," he demanded of his pipe bowl, "has been going on?"

Snulbug popped his snaky head out. "Light this again, will you? It's getting cold. Thanks."

"What happened?" Bill insisted.

"People!" Snulbug moaned. "No sense. Don't you see? So long as the newspaper was in the future, it was only a possibility. If you'd had, say, a hunch that the mayor was in danger, maybe you could have saved him. But when I brought it into now, it became a fact. You can't possibly make it untrue."

"But how about man's free will? Can't I do whatever I want to do?"

"Sure. It was your precious free will that brought the paper into now. You can't undo your own will. And, anyway, your will's still free. You're free to go getting thrown around chandeliers as often as you want. You probably like it. You can do anything up to the point where it would change what's in that paper. Then you have to start in again and again and again until you make up your mind to be sensible."

"But that—" Bill fumbled for words, "that's just as bad as . . . as fate or predestination. If my soul wills to—"

"Newspapers aren't enough. Time theory isn't enough. So I should tell him about his soul! People—" and Snulbug withdrew into the bowl.

Bill looked up at the city hall regretfully and shrugged his resignation. Then he folded his paper to the sports page and studied it carefully.

Snulbug thrust his head out again as they stopped in the many-acred parking lot. "Where is it this time?" he wanted to know. "Not that it matters."

"The racetrack."

"Oh—" Snulbug groaned, "I might have known it. You're all alike. No sense in the whole caboodle. I suppose you found a long shot?"

"Darned tooting I did. Alhazred at twenty to one in the fourth. I've got $500, the only money I've got left on earth. Plunk on Alhazred's nose it goes, and there's our $10,000."

Snulbug grunted. "I hear his lousy spell, I watch him get caught on a merry-go-round, it isn't enough, I should see him lay a bet on a long shot."

"But there isn't a loophole in this. I'm not interfering with the future; I'm just taking advantage of it. Alhazred'll win this race whether I bet on him or not. Five pretty hundred-dollar parimutuel tickets, and behold: The Hitchens Laboratory!" Bill jumped spryly out of his car and strutted along joyously. Suddenly he paused and addressed his pipe: "Hey! Why do I feel so good?"

Snulbug sighed dismally. "Why should anybody?"

"No, but I mean: I took a hell of a shellacking from that plug-ugly in the office. And I haven't got a pain or an ache."

"Of course not. It never happened."

"But I felt it then."

"Sure. In a future that never was. You changed your mind, didn't you? You decided not to go up there?"

"O.K., but that was after I'd already been beaten up."

"Uh-uh," said Snulbug firmly. "It was before you hadn't been." And he withdrew again into the pipe.

There was a band somewhere in the distance and the raucous burble of an announcer's voice. Crowds clustered around the $2 windows, and the $5 weren't doing bad business. But the $100 window, where the five beautiful pasteboards lived that were to create an embolism laboratory, was almost deserted.

Bill buttonholed a stranger with a purple nose. "What's the next race?"

"Second, Mac."

Swell, Bill thought. Lots of time. And from now on—He hastened to the $100 window and shoved across the five bills that he had drawn from the bank that morning. "Alhazred, on the nose," he said.

The clerk frowned with surprise, but took the money and turned to get the tickets.

Bill buttonholed a stranger with a purple nose. "What's the next race?"

"Second, Mac."

Swell, Bill thought. And then he yelled, "Hey!"

A stranger with a purple nose paused and said, " 'Smatter, Mac?"

"Nothing," Bill groaned. "Just everything."

The stranger hesitated. "Ain't I seen you someplace before?"

"No," said Bill hurriedly. "You were going to, but you haven't. I changed my mind."

The stranger walked away shaking his head and muttering how the ponies could get a guy.

Not till Bill was back in his roadster did he take the corncob from his mouth and glare at it. "All right!" he barked. "What was wrong this time? Why did I get on a merry-go-round again? I didn't try to change the future!"

Snulbug popped his head out and yawned a tuskful yawn. "I warn him, I explain it, I warn him again, now he wants I should explain it all over."

"But what did I do?"

"What did he do? You changed the odds, you dope. That much folding money on a long shot at a parimutuel track, and the odds change. It wouldn't have paid off at twenty to one, the way it said in the paper."

"Nuts," Bill muttered. "And I suppose that applies to anything? If I study the stock market in this paper and try to invest my $500 according to tomorrow's market—"

"Same thing. The quotations wouldn't be quite the same if you started in playing. I warned you. You're stuck," said

Snulbug. "You're stymied. It's no use." He sounded almost cheerful.

"Isn't it?" Bill mused. "Now look, Snulbug. Me, I'm a great believer in Man. This universe doesn't hold a problem that Man can't eventually solve. And I'm no dumber than the average."

"That's saying a lot, that is," Snulbug sneered. "People—"

"I've got a responsibility now. It's more than just my $10,-000. I've got to redeem the honor of Man. You say this is the insoluble problem. I say there is no insoluble problem."

"I say you talk a lot."

Bill's mind was racing furiously. How can a man take advantage of the future without in any smallest way altering that future? There must be an answer somewhere, and a man who devised the Hitchens Embolus Diagnosis could certainly crack a little nut like this. Man cannot refuse a challenge.

Unthinking, he reached for his tobacco pouch and tapped out his pipe on the sole of his foot. There was a microscopic thud as Snulbug crashed onto the floor of the car.

Bill looked down half-smiling. The tiny demon's tail was lashing madly, and every separate snake stood on end. "This is too much!" Snulbug screamed. "Dumb gags aren't enough, insults aren't enough, I should get thrown around like a damned soul. This is the last straw. Give me my dismissal!"

Bill snapped his fingers gleefully. "Dismissal!" he cried. "I've got it, Snully. We're all set."

Snulbug looked up puzzled and slowly let his snakes droop more amicably. "It won't work," he said, with an omnisciently sad shake of his serpentine head.

It was the dashing act again that carried Bill through the Choatsby Laboratories, where he had been employed so recently, and on up to the very anteroom of old R. C.'s office.

But where you can do battle with a bull-necked guard, there is not a thing you can oppose against the brisk competence of a young lady who says, "I shall find out if Mr. Choatsby will see you." There was nothing to do but wait.

"And what's the brilliant idea this time?" Snulbug obviously feared the worst.

"R. C.'s nuts," said Bill. "He's an astrologer and a pyramidologist and a British Israelite—American Branch Reformed—and Heaven knows what else. He . . . why, he'll even believe in you."

"That's more than I do," said Snulbug. "It's a waste of energy."

"He'll buy this paper. He'll pay anything for it. There's nothing he loves more than futzing around with the occult. He'll never be able to resist a good solid slice of the future, with illusions of a fortune thrown in."

"You better hurry, then."

"Why such a rush? It's only 2:30 now. Lots of time. And while the girl's gone there's nothing for us to do but cool our heels."

"You might at least," said Snulbug, "warm the heel of your pipe."

The girl returned at last. "Mr. Choatsby will see you."

Reuben Choatsby overflowed the outsize chair behind his desk. His little face, like a baby's head balanced on a giant suet pudding, beamed as Bill entered. "Changed your mind, eh?" His words came in sudden soft blobs, like the abrupt glugs of pouring syrup. "Good. Need you in K-39. Lab's not the same since you left."

Bill groped for exactly the right words. "That's not it, R.C. I'm on my own now and I'm doing all right."

The baby face soured. "Damned cheek. Competitor of mine, eh? What you want now? Waste my time?"

"Not at all." With a pretty shaky assumption of confidence, Bill perched on the edge of the desk. "R. C.," he said, slowly and impressively, "what would you give for a glimpse into the future?"

Mr. Choatsby glugged vigorously. "Ribbing me? Get out of here! Have you thrown out—Hold on! You're the one—Used to read queer books. Had a grimoire here once." The baby face grew earnest. "What d'you mean?"

"Just what I said, R. C. What would you give for a glimpse into the future?"

Mr. Choatsby hesitated. "How? Time travel? Pyramid? You figured out the King's Chamber?"

"Much simpler than that. I have here"—he took it out of his pocket and folded it so that only the name and the date line were visible—"tomorrow's newspaper."

Mr. Choatsby grabbed. "Let me see."

"Uh-uh. Naughty. You'll see after we discuss terms. But there it is."

"Trick. Had some printer fake it. Don't believe it."

"All right. I never expected you, R. C., to descend to such unenlightened skepticism. But if that's all the faith you have—" Bill stuffed the paper back in his pocket and started for the door.

"Wait!" Mr. Choatsby lowered his voice. "How'd you do it? Sell your soul?"

"That wasn't necessary."

"How? Spells? Cantrips? Incantations? Prove it to me. Show me it's real. Then we'll talk terms."

Bill walked casually to the desk and emptied his pipe into the ash tray.

"I'm underdeveloped. I run errands. I'm named Snulbug. It isn't enough—now I should be a testimonial!"

Mr. Choatsby stared rapt at the furious little demon raging in his ash tray. He watched reverently as Bill held out the pipe for its inmate, filled it with tobacco, and lit it. He listened awe-struck as Snulbug moaned with delight at the flame.

"No more questions," he said. "What terms?"

"Fifteen thousand dollars." Bill was ready for bargaining.

"Don't put it too high," Snulbug warned. "You better hurry."

But Mr. Choatsby had pulled out his checkbook and was scribbling hastily. He blotted the check and handed it over. "It's a deal." He grabbed up the paper. "You're a fool, young man. Fifteen thousand! *Hmf!*" He had it open already at the financial page. "With what I make on the market tomorrow, never notice $15,000. Pennies."

"Hurry up," Snulbug urged.

"Good-bye, sir," Bill began politely, "and thank you for—" But Reuben Choatsby wasn't even listening.

"What's all this hurry?" Bill demanded as he reached the elevator.

"People!" Snulbug sighed. "Never you mind what's the hurry. You get to your bank and deposit that check."

So Bill, with Snulbug's incessant prodding, made a dash to the bank worthy of his descents on the city hall and on the Choatsby Laboratories. He just made it, by stopwatch fractions of a second. The door was already closing as he shoved his way through at three o'clock sharp.

He made his deposit, watched the teller's eyes bug out at the size of the check, and delayed long enough to enjoy the incomparable thrill of changing the account from William Hitchens to The Hitchens Research Laboratory.

Then he climbed once more into his car, where he could talk with his pipe in peace. "Now," he asked as he drove home, "what was the rush?"

"He'd stop payment."

"You mean when he found out about the merry-go-round? But I didn't promise him anything. I just sold him tomorrow's paper. I didn't guarantee he'd make a fortune of it."

"That's all right. But—"

"Sure, you warned me. But where's the hitch? R. C.'s a bandit, but he's honest. He wouldn't stop payment."

"Wouldn't he?"

The car was waiting for a stop signal. The newsboy in the intersection was yelling "Uxtruh!" Bill glanced casually at the headline, did a double take, and instantly thrust out a nickel and seized a paper.

He turned into a side street, stopped the car, and went through this paper. Front page: MAYOR ASSASSINATED. Sports page: Alhazred at twenty to one. Obituaries: The same list he'd read at noon. He turned back to the date line. August 22. Tomorrow.

"I warned you," Snulbug was explaining. "I told you I wasn't strong enough to go far into the future. I'm not a well demon, I'm not. And an itch in the memory is something fierce. I just went far enough ahead to get a paper with tomorrow's date on it. And any dope knows that a Tuesday paper comes out Monday afternoon."

For a moment Bill was dazed. His magic paper, his fifteen-thousand-dollar paper, was being hawked by newsies on every corner. Small wonder R. C. might have stopped payment! And then he saw the other side. He started to laugh. He couldn't stop.

"Look out!" Snulbug shrilled. "You'll drop my pipe. And what's so funny?"

Bill wiped tears from his eyes. "I was right. Don't you see, Snulbug? Man can't be licked. My magic was lousy. All it could call up was you. You brought me what was practically a fake, and I got caught on the merry-go-round of time trying to use it. You were right enough there; no good could come of that magic.

"But without the magic, just using human psychology, knowing a man's weaknesses, playing on them, I made a syrup-voiced old bandit endow the very research he'd tabooed, and do more good for humanity than he's done in all the rest of his life. I was right, Snulbug. You can't lick Man."

Snulbug's snakes writhed into knots of scorn. "People!" he snorted. "You'll find out." And he shook his head with dismal satisfaction.

HEREAFTER, INC.

Unknown
December

by Lester del Rey (1915-   )

Although generally thought of as a leading science fiction writer, Lester del Rey is equally at home with fantasy. He had a number of outstanding fantasies in Unknown *during the too-short life of that great magazine, including "The Pipes of Pan" (May, 1940), "Forsaking All Others" (August, 1939), "Anything" (October, 1939), "Doubled in Brass" (January, 1940) and the wonderful "The Coppersmith" (September, 1939). A fantasy novel of note is* Day of the Giants *(1959). In addition, he edited the outstanding magazine* Fantasy Fiction *during its short run in the early 1950s, and presently edits the fantasy line at Del Rey Books.*

"Hereafter, Inc." is a remarkable story, one of the very best fantasies that examines the possible nature of one man's Heaven (or is it one man's Hell?).

(Lester and I have been friends for forty years, which is not in the least surprising in his case for he is an old man, but I don't quite see how that could be possible for me.

When I first met him, he weighed about 85 pounds and it was the general feeling that the reason he could write such convincing fantasy was that he was a leprechaun.

He is now gray and bearded but he has lost none of his volubility, none of his feistiness, none of his know-it-all characteristics (which would be unbearable except that he *does* know it all). He is no longer a leprechaun, however. It is my private theory (for those of you who have read *Lord of the Rings*) that he is Gandalf.—I.A.)

Phineas Theophilus Potts, who would have been the last to admit and the first to believe he was a godly man, creaked over in bed and stuck out one scrawny arm wrathfully. The raucous jangling of the alarm was an unusually painful

339

cancer in his soul that morning. Then his waking mind took over and he checked his hand, bringing it down on the alarm button with precise, but gentle, firmness. Would he never learn to control these little angers? In this world one should bear all troubles with uncomplaining meekness, not rebel against them; otherwise— But it was too early in the morning to think of that.

He wriggled out of bed and gave his thoughts over to the ritual of remembering yesterday's sins, checking to make sure all had been covered and wiped out the night before. That's when he got his first shock; he couldn't remember anything about the day before—bad, very bad. Well, no doubt it was another trap of the forces conspiring to secure Potts' soul. Tch, tch. Terrible, but he could circumvent even that snare.

There was no mere mumbling by habit to his confession; word after word rolled off his tongue carefully with full knowledge and unctuous shame until he reached the concluding lines. "For the manifold sins which I have committed and for this greater sin which now afflicts me, forgive and guide me to sin no more, but preserve me in righteousness all the days of my life. Amen." Thus having avoided the pitfall and saved himself again from eternal combustion, he scrubbed hands with himself and began climbing into his scratchy underclothes and cheap black suit. Then he indulged in a breakfast of dry toast and buttermilk flavored with self-denial and was ready to fare forth into the world of temptation around him.

The telephone jangled against his nerves and he jumped, grabbing for it impatiently before he remembered; he addressed the mouthpiece contritely. "Phineas Potts speaking."

It was Mr. Sloane, his lusty animal voice barking out from the receiver. " 'Lo, Phin, they told me you're ready to come down to work today. Business is booming and we can use you. How about it?"

"Certainly, Mr. Sloane. I'm not one to shirk my duty." There was no reason for the call that Potts could see; he hadn't missed a day in twelve years. "You know—"

"Sure, okay. That's fine. Just wanted to warn you that we've moved. You'll see the name plate right across the street when you come out—swell place, too. Sure you can make it all right?"

"I shall be there in ten minutes, Mr. Sloane," Phineas assured him, and remembered in time to hang up without displaying distaste. Tch, poor Sloane, wallowing in sin and ignorant of the doom that awaited him. Why, the last time Phineas had chided his employer—mildly, too—Sloane had actually laughed at him! Dear. Well, no doubt he incurred grace by trying to save the poor lost soul, even though his efforts seemed futile. Of course, there was danger in consorting with such people, but no doubt his sacrifices would be duly recorded.

There was a new elevator boy, apparently, when he came out of his room. He sniffed pointedly at the smoke from the boy's cigarette; the boy twitched his lips, but did not throw it away.

"Okay, bub," he grunted as the doors clanked shut, grating across Phineas' nerves, "I don't like it no better'n you will, but here we are."

Bub! Phineas glared at the shoulders turned to him and shuddered. He'd see Mrs. Biddle about this later.

Suppressing his feelings with some effort, he headed across the lobby, scarcely noting it, and stepped out onto the street. Then he stopped. That was the second jolt. He swallowed twice, opened his eyes and lifted them for the first time in weeks, and looked again. It hadn't changed. Where there should have been a little twisted side street near the tenements, he saw instead a broad gleaming thoroughfare, busy with people and bright in warm golden sunshine. Opposite, the ugly stores were replaced with bright, new office buildings, and the elevated tracks were completely missing. He swung slowly about, clutching his umbrella for support as he faced the hotel; it was still a hotel—but not his—definitely not his. Nor was the lobby the same. He fumbled back into it, shaken and bewildered.

The girl at the desk smiled up at him out of dancing eyes, and she certainly wasn't the manager. Nor would prim Mrs. Biddle, who went to his church, have hired this brazen little thing; both her lips and fingernails were bright crimson, to begin with, and beyond that he preferred not to go.

The brazen little thing smiled again, as if glorying in her obvious idolatry. "Forget something, Mr. Potts?"

"I . . . uh . . . no. That is . . . you know who I am?"

She nodded brightly. "Yes indeed, Mr. Potts. You moved in yesterday. Room 408. Is everything satisfactory?"

Phineas half nodded, gulped, and stumbled out again. Moved in? He couldn't recall it. Why should he leave Mrs. Biddle's? And 408 was his old room number; the room was identical with the one he had lived in, even to the gray streak on the wallpaper that had bothered his eyes for years. Something was horribly wrong—first the lack of memory, then Sloane's peculiar call, now this. He was too upset even to realize that this was probably another temptation set before him.

Mechanically, Phineas spied Sloane's name plate on one of the new buildings, and crossed over into it. "Morning, Mr. Potts," said the elevator boy, and Phineas jumped. He'd never seen this person before, either. "Fourth floor, Mr. Potts. Mr. Sloane's office is just two doors down."

Phineas followed the directions automatically, found the door marked G. R. SLOANE—ARCHITECT, and pushed into a huge room filled with the almost unbearable clatter of typewriters and Comptometers, the buzz of voices, and the jarring thump of an addressing machine. But this morning the familiarity of the sound seemed like a haven out of the wilderness until he looked around. Not only had Sloane moved, but he'd apparently also expanded and changed most of his office force. Only old Callahan was left, and Callahan—Strange, he felt sure Callahan had retired or something the year before, Oh, well, that was the least of his puzzles.

Callahan seemed to sense his stare, for he jumped up and brought a hamlike fist down on Phineas' back, almost knocking out the ill-fitting false teeth. "Phin Potts, you old doommonger! Welcome back!" He thumped again and Potts coughed, trying to reach the spot and rub out the sting. Not only did Callahan have to be an atheist—an argumentative one—but he had to indulge in this gross horseplay. Why hadn't the man stayed properly retired?

"Mr. Sloane?" he managed to gurgle.

Sloane himself answered, his rugged face split in a grin. "Hi, Phin. Let him alone, Callahan. Another thump like that and I'll have to hire a new draftsman. Come on Phin, there's the devil's own amount of work piled up for you now that you're back from your little illness." He led him around a bunch of tables where bright-painted hussies were busily typing, down a hall, and into the drafting room, exchanging words with others that made Phineas wince. Really, his language seemed to grow worse each day.

"Mr. Sloane, would you please—"

"Mind not using such language," Sloane finished, and grinned. "Phin, I can't help it. I feel too good. Business is terrific and I've got the world by the tail. How do you feel?"

"Very well, thank you." Phinease fumbled and caught the thread of former conversation that had been bothering him. "You said something about—illness?"

"Think nothing of it. After working for me twelve years, I'm not going to dock your pay for a mere month's absence. Kind of a shame you had to be off just when I needed you, but such things will happen, so we'll just forget it, eh?" He brushed aside the other's muttered attempt at questioning and dug into the plans. "Here, better start on this—you'll notice some changes, but it's a lot like what we used to do; something like the Oswego we built in '37. Only thing that'll give you trouble is the new steel they put out now, but you can follow specifications on that."

Phineas picked up the specifications, ran them over, and blinked. This would never do; much as he loathed the work, he was an excellent draftsman, and he knew enough of general structural design to know this would never do. "But, two-inch I-beams here—"

" 'Sall right, Phin, structural strength is about twelve times what you're used to. Makes some really nice designing possible, too. Just follow the things like I said, and I'll go over it all later. Things changed a little while you were delirious. But I'm in a devil of a rush right now. See you." He stuck his body through the door, thrust his head back inside and cocked an eyebrow. "Lunch? Need somebody to show you around, I guess."

"As you wish, Mr. Sloane," agreed Phineas. "But would you please mind—"

"Not swearing. Sure, okay. And no religious arguments this time; if I'm damned, I like it." Then he was gone, leaving Phineas alone—he couldn't work with the distraction of others, and always had a room to himself.

So he'd been sick had he, even delirious? Well, that might explain things. Phineas had heard that such things sometimes produced a hiatus in the memory, and it was a better explanation than nothing. With some relief, he put it out of his mind, remembering only to confess how sinfully he'd lost his trust in divine guidance this morning, shook his head mournfully, and began work with dutiful resignation. Since it had obviously been ordained that he should make his simple living at drafting, draft he would, with no complaints, and there would be no fault to be found with him there.

Then the pen began to scratch. He cleaned and adjusted it, finding nothing wrong, but still it made little grating sounds on the paper, lifting up the raw edges of his nerves. Had Phineas believed in evolution, he'd have said the hair his ancestors had once grown was trying to stand on end, but he had no use for such heretical ideas. Well, he was not one to complain. He unclenched his teeth and sought forbearance and peace within.

Then, outside, the addressograph began to thump again, and he had to force himself not to ruin the lines as his body tried to flinch. Be patient, all these trials would be rewarded. Finally, he turned to the only anodyne he knew, contemplation of the fate of heretics and sinners. Of course, he was sorry for them roasting eternally and crying for water which they would never get—very sorry for the poor deluded creatures, as any righteous man should be. Yet still they had been given their chance and not made proper use of it, so it was only just. Picturing morbidly the hell of his most dour Puritan ancestors—something very real to him—he almost failed to notice the ache of his bunion where the cheap shoes pinched. But not quite.

Callahan was humming out in the office, and Phineas could just recognize the tune. Once the atheist had come in roaring drunk, and before they'd sent him home, he'd cornered Phineas and sung it through, unexpurgated. Now, in time with the humming, the words insisted on trickling through the suffering little man's mind, and try as he would, they refused to leave. Prayer did no good. Then he added Callahan to the tortured sinners, and that worked better.

"Pencils, shoestrings, razor blades?" The words behind him startled him, and he regained his balance on the stool with difficulty. Standing just inside the door was a one-legged hunchback with a handful of cheap articles. "Pencils?" he repeated. "Only a nickel. Help a poor cripple?" But the grin on his face belied the words.

"Indeed no, no pencils." Phineas shuddered as the fellow hobbled over to a window and rid himself of a chew of tobacco. "Why don't you try the charities? Furthermore, we don't allow beggars here."

"Ain't none," the fellow answered with ambiguous cheerfulness, stuffing in a new bite.

"Then have faith in the Lord and He will provide." Naturally, man had been destined to toil through the days of his life in this mortal sphere, and toil he must to achieve salvation. He had no intention of ruining this uncouth person's small chance to be saved by keeping him in idleness.

The beggar nodded and touched his cap. "One of them, eh? Too bad. Well, keep your chin up, maybe it'll be better later." Then he went off down the hall, whistling, leaving Phineas to puzzle over his words and give it up as a bad job.

Potts rubbed his bunion tenderly, then desisted, realizing that pain was only a test, and should be borne meekly. The pen still scratched, the addressing machine thumped, and a bee had buzzed in somehow and went zipping about. It was a large and active bee.

Phineas cowered down and made himself work, sweating a little as the bee lighted on his drafting board. Then, mercifully, it flew away and for a few minutes he couldn't hear it. When it began again, it was behind him. He started to turn his head, then decided against it; the bee might take the motion as an act of aggression, and declare war. His hands on the pen were moist and clammy, and his fingers ached from gripping it too tightly, but somehow, he forced himself to go on working.

The bee was evidently in no hurry to leave. It flashed by his nose, buzzing, making him jerk back and spatter a blob of ink into the plans, then went zooming around his head and settled on his bald spot. Phineas held his breath and the bee stood pat. Ten, twenty, thirty seconds. His breath went out suddenly with a rush. The insect gave a brief buzz, evidently deciding the noise was harmless, and began strolling down over his forehead and out onto his nose. It tickled; the inside of his nose tickled, sympathetically.

"No, no," Phineas whispered desperately. "N—*Achee*OO! EEOW!" He grabbed for his nose and jerked violently, bumping his shins against the desk and splashing more ink on the plans. "Damn, oh, da—"

It was unbelievable; it couldn't be true! His own mouth had betrayed him! With shocked and leaden fingers he released the pen and bowed his head, but no sense of saving grace would come. Too well he could remember that even the smallest sin deserves just damnation. Now he was really sweating, and the visions of eternal torment came trooping back; but this time he was in Callahan's place, and try as he would, he couldn't switch. He was doomed!

Callahan found him in that position a minute later, and his rough, mocking laugh cut into Phineas' wounded soul. "Sure, an angel as I live and breathe." He dumped some papers onto the desk and gave another backbreaking thump. "Got the first sheets done, Phin?"

Miserably, Phineas shook his head, glancing at the clock. They should have been ready an hour ago. Another sin was piled upon his burden, beyond all hope of redemption, and of all people, Callahan had caught him not working when he was already behind. But the old Irishman didn't seem to be gloating.

"There now, don't take it so hard, Phin. Nobody expects you to work like a horse when you've been sick. Mr. Sloane wants you to come out to lunch with him now."

"I—uh—" Words wouldn't come.

Callahan thumped him on the back again, this time lightly enough to rattle only two ribs. "Go along with you. What's left is beginner's stuff and I'll finish it while you're eating. I'm ahead and got nothing to do, anyhow. Go on." He practically picked the smaller man off the stool and shoved him through the door. "Sloane's waiting. Heck, I'll be glad to do it. Feel so good I can't find enough to keep me busy."

Sloane was flirting with one of the typists as Phineas plodded up, but he wound up that business with a wink and grabbed for his hat. " 'Smatter, Phin? You look all in. Bad bruise on your nose, too. Well, a good lunch'll fix up the first part, at least. Best damned food you ever ate, and right around the corner."

"Yes, Mr. Sloane, but would you . . . uh!" He couldn't ask that now. He himself was a sinner, given to violent language. Glumly he followed the other out and into the corner restaurant. Then, as he settled into the seat, he realized he couldn't eat; first among his penances should be giving up lunches.

"I . . . uh . . . don't feel very hungry, Mr. Sloane. I'll just have a cup of tea, I think." The odors of the food in the clean little restaurant that brought twinges to his stomach would only make his penance that much greater.

But Sloane was ordering for two. "Same as usual, honey, and you might as well bring a second for my friend here." He turned to Phineas. "Trouble with you, Phin, is that you don't eat enough. Wait'll you get a whiff of the ham they serve here—and the pie! Starting now, you're eating right if I have to stuff it down you. Ah!"

Service was prompt, and the plates began to appear before the little man's eyes. He could feel his mouth watering, and had to swallow to protest. Then the look in Sloane's eyes made him decide not to. Well, at least he could fast morning and night instead. He nodded to himself glumly, wishing his craven appetite wouldn't insist on deriving so much pleasure from the food.

"And so," Sloane's voice broke in on his consciousness again, "after this, you're either going to promise me you'll eat three good meals a day or I'll come around and stuff it down you. Hear?"

"Yes, Mr. Sloane, but—"

"Good. I'm taking that as a promise."

Phineas cringed. He hadn't meant it that way; it couldn't go through as a promise. "But—"

"No buts about it. Down there I figured you had as good a chance of being right as I did, so I didn't open my mouth on the subject. But up here, that's done with. No reason why you can't enjoy life now."

That was too much. "Life," said Phineas, laying down his knife and preparing for siege, "was meant to give us a chance to prepare for the life to come, not to be squandered in wanton pleasure. Surely it's better to suffer through a few brief years, resisting temptations, than to be forever damned to perdition. And would you sacrifice heaven for mere mundane cravings, transient and worthless?"

"Stow it, Phin. Doesn't seem to me I sacrificed much to get here." Then, at Phineas' bewildered look, "Don't tell me you don't realize where you are? They told me they were sending a boy with the message; well, I guess he just missed you. You're dead, Phin! *This* is Heaven! We don't talk much about it, but that's the way it is!"

"No!" The world was rolling in circles under Phineas' seat. He stared uncomprehendingly at Sloane, finding no slightest sign of mockery on the man's face. And there was the hole in the memory of sins, and the changes, and—Callahan! Why, Callahan had died and been buried the year before; and here he was, looking ten years younger, and hearty as ever. But it was all illusion; of course, it was all illusion. Callahan wouldn't be in heaven. "No, it can't be."

"But it is, Phin. Remember? I was down your way to get you for overtime work, and yelled at you just as you came out of your house. Then you started to cross, I yelled again—Come back now?"

There'd been a screeching of tires, Sloane running toward him suddenly waving frantically, and—blackout! "Then it hit? And this . . . is—"

"Uh-huh. Seems they picked me up with a shovel, but it took a month to finish you off." Sloane dug into the pie, rolling it on his tongue and grinning. "And this is Hereafter. A darned good one, too, even if nobody meets you at the gate to say 'Welcome to Heaven.'"

Phineas clutched at the straw. "They didn't tell you it was Heaven, then? Oh." That explained everything. Of course, he should have known. This wasn't heaven after all; it couldn't be. And though it differed from his conceptions, it most certainly could be the other place; there'd been that bee! Tch, it was just like Callahan and Sloane to enjoy perdition, midguided sinners, glorying in their unholiness.

Slowly the world righted itself, and Phineas Potts regained his normal state. To be sure, he'd used an ugly word, but what could be expected of him in this vile place? They'd never hold it against him under the circumstances. He lowered his eyes thankfully, paying no attention to Sloane's idle remarks about unfortunates. Now if he could just find the authorities of this place and get the mistake straightened out, all might yet be well. He had always done his best to be righteous. Perhaps a slight delay, but not long; and then—no Callahan, no Sloane, no drafting, or bees, or grating noises!

He drew himself up and looked across at Sloane, sadly, but justly doomed to this strange gehenna. "Mr. Sloane," he asked firmly, "is there some place here where I can find . . . uh . . . authorities to . . . umm—"

"You mean you want to register a complaint? Why sure, a big white building about six blocks down; Adjustment and Appointment office." Sloane studied him thoroughly. "Darned if you don't look like you had a raw deal about something, at that. Look, Phin, they made mistakes sometimes, of course, but if they've handed you the little end, we'll go right down there and get it put right."

Phineas shook his head quickly. The proper attitude, no doubt was to leave Sloane in ignorance of the truth as long as possible, and that meant he'd have to go alone. "Thank you, Mr. Sloane, but I'll go by myself, if you don't mind. And . . . uh . . . if I don't come back . . . uh—"

"Sure, take the whole afternoon off. Hey, wait, aren't you gonna finish lunch?"

But Phineas Potts was gone, his creaking legs carrying him out into the mellow noon sunlight and toward the towering white building that must be his destination. The fate of a man's soul is nothing to dally over, and he wasn't dallying. He tucked his umbrella close under his arm to avoid contact with the host of the damned, shuddering at the thought of mingling with them. Still, undoubtedly this torture would be added to the list of others, and his reward be made that much greater. Then he was at the Office of Administration, Appointments, and Adjustments.

There was another painted Jezebel at the desk marked IN-FORMATION, and he headed there, barely collecting his thoughts in time to avoid disgraceful excitement. She grinned at him and actually winked! "Mr. Potts, isn't it? Oh, I'm so sorry you left before our messenger arrived. But if there's something we can do now—"

"There is," he told her firmly, though not too unkindly; after all, her punishment was ample without his anger. "I wish to see an authority here. I have a complaint; a most grievous complaint."

"Oh, that's too bad, Mr. Potts. But if you'll see Mr. Alexander, down the hall, third door left, I'm sure he can adjust it."

He waited no longer, but hurried where she pointed. As he approached, the third door opened and a dignified-looking man in a gray business suit stepped to it. The man held out a hand instantly. "I'm Mr. Alexander. Come in, won't you? Katy said you had a complaint. Sit right over there, Mr. Potts. Ah, so. Now, if you'll tell me about it, I think we can straighten it all out."

Phineas told him—in detail. "And so," he concluded firmly—quite firmly, "I feel I've been done a grave injustice, Mr. Alexander. I'm positive my destination should have been the other place."

"The other place?" Alexander seemed surprised.

"Exactly so. Heaven, to be more precise."

Alexander nodded thoughtfully. "Quite so, Mr. Potts. Only I'm afraid there's been a little misunderstanding. You see . . . ah . . . this is Heaven. Still, I can see you don't believe me yet, so we've failed to place you properly. We really want to make people happy here, you know. So, if you'll just tell me what you find wrong, we'll do what we can to rectify it."

"Oh." Phineas considered. This might be a trick, of course, but still, if they could make him happy here, give him his due reward for the years filled with temptation resisted and noble suffering in meekness and humility, there seemed nothing wrong with it. Possibly, it came to him, there were varying degrees of blessedness, and even such creatures as Callahan and his ilk were granted the lower ones—though it didn't seem quite just. But certainly his level wasn't Callahan's.

"Very well," he decided. "First, I find myself living in that room with the gray streak on the wallpaper, sir, and for years I've loathed it; and the alarm and telephone; and—"

Alexander smiled. "One at a time please. Now, about the room. I really felt we'd done a masterly job on that, you know. Isn't it exactly like your room on the former level of life? Ah, I see it is. And didn't you choose and furnish that room yourself?"

"Yes, but—"

"Ah, then we were right. Naturally, Mr. Potts, we assumed that since it was of your own former creation, it was best suited to you. And besides, you need the alarm and telephone to keep you on time and in contact with your work, you know."

"But I loathe drafting!" Phineas glanced at this demon who was trying to trap him, expecting it to wilt to its true form. It didn't. Instead, the thing that was Mr. Alexander shook his head slowly and sighed.

"Now that is a pity; and we were so pleased to find we could even give you the same employer as before. Really, we felt you'd be happier under him than a stranger. However, if you don't like it, I suppose we could change. What other kind of work would you like?"

Now that was more like it, and perhaps he had even misjudged Alexander. Work was something Phineas hadn't expected, but—yes, that would be nice, if it could be arranged here. "I felt once I was *called*," he suggested.

"Minister, you mean? Now that's fine. Never get too many of them, Mr. Potts. Wonderful men, do wonderful work here. They really add enormously to the happiness of our Hereafter, you know. Let me see, what experience have you had?" He beamed at Potts, who thawed under it; then he turned to a bookshelf, selected a heavy volume and consulted it. Slowly the beam vanished, and worry took its place.

"Ah, yes, Phineas Theophilus Potts. Yes, entered training 1903. Hmmm. Dismissed after two years of study, due to a feeling he might . . . might not be quite temperamentally suited to the work and that he was somewhat too fana . . . ahem! . . . overly zealous in his criticism of others. Then transferred to his uncle's shop and took up drafting, which was thereafter his life's work. Umm. Really, that's too bad." Alexander turned back to Phineas. "Then, Mr. Potts, I take it you never had any actual experience at this sort of work?"

Phineas squirmed. "No, but—"

"Too bad." Alexander sighed. "Really, I'd like to make things more to your satisfaction, but after all, no experience—afraid it wouldn't do. Tell you what, we don't like to be hasty in our judgments; if you'll just picture exactly the life you want—no need to describe it, I'll get it if you merely think it—maybe we can adjust things. Try hard now."

With faint hope, Phineas tried. Alexander's voice droned

out at him. "A little harder. No, that's only a negative picture of what you'd like not to do. Ah . . . um, no. I thought for a minute you had something, but it's gone. I think you're trying to picture abstractions, Mr. Potts, and you know one can't do that; I get something very vague, but it makes no sense. There! That's better."

He seemed to listen for a few seconds longer, and Phineas was convinced now it was all sham; he'd given up trying. What was the use? Vague jumbled thoughts were all he had left, and now Alexander's voice broke in on them.

"Really, Mr. Potts, I'm afraid there's nothing we can do for you. I get a very clear picture now, but it's exactly the life we'd arranged for you, you see. Same room, same work. Apparently that's the only life you know. Of course, if you want to improve we have a great many very fine schools located throughout the city."

Phineas jerked upright, the control over his temper barely on. "You mean—you mean, I've got to go on like that?"

"Afraid so."

"But you distinctly said this was Heaven."

"It is."

"And I tell you," Phineas cried, forgetting all about controlling his temper, "that this is Hell!"

"Quite so, I never denied it. Now, Mr. Potts, I'd like to discuss this further, but others are waiting, so I'm afraid I'll have to ask you to leave."

Alexander looked up from his papers, and as he looked, Phineas found himself outside the door, shaken and sick. The door remained open as the girl called Katy came up, looked at him in surprise, and went in. Then it closed, but still he stood there, unable to move, leaning against the wooden frame for support.

There was a mutter of voices within, and his whirling thoughts seized on them for anchor. Katy's voice first. "— seems to take it terribly hard, Mr. Alexander. Isn't there something we can do?"

Then the low voice of Alexander. "Nothing, Katy. It's up to him now. I suggested the schools, but I'm afraid he's another unfortunate. Probably even now he's out there convincing himself that all this is merely illusion, made to try his soul and test his ability to remain unchanged. If that's the case, well, poor devil, there isn't much we can do, you know."

But Phineas wasn't listening then. He clutched the words he'd heard savagely to his bosom and went stiffly out and back toward the office of G. R. Sloane across from the little room, No. 408. Of course he should have known. All this was merely illusion, made to try his soul. Illusion and test, no more.

Let them try him, they would find him humble in his sufferings as always, not complaining, resisting firmly their temptations. Even though Sloane denied him the right to fast, still he would find some other way to do proper penance for his sins; though Callahan broke his back, though a thousand bees attacked him at once, still he would prevail.

"Forgive and guide me to sin no more, but preserve me in righteousness all the days of my life," he repeated, and turned into the building where there was more work and misery waiting for him. Sometime he'd be rewarded. Sometime.

Back in his head a small shred of doubt sniggered gleefully.